EMPERORS
ONCE
MORE

EMPERORS ONCE MORE

DUNCAN JEPSON

Quercus

First published in Great Britain in 2014 by

Quercus
55 Baker Street
7th Floor, South Block
London
W1U 8EW

A CIP catalogue record for this book is available
from the British Library

ISBN 978 1 78206 800 6 (HB)
ISBN 978 1 78206 801 3 (TPB)
ISBN 978 1 78206 802 0 (EBOOK)

10 9 8 7 6 5 4 3 2 1

Typeset by Ellipsis Digital Limited, Glasgow

Printed and bound in Great Britain by Clays Ltd, St Ives plc

The future must not pay for the past.

PROLOGUE

It was the only photograph of them he had.

The image was oval, sepia-tinted, set at the centre of a rectangular print, the outer details bleeding into the white of the photographic paper. The couple stood on a dirt plain lined with wide shallow furrows. In the distance to the right was the outline of a low stone building, its roof tiled perhaps in traditional blue ceramic at the eaves.

He had shown the photograph to his aunt, his father's elder sister, producing it over dinner at New Year in his final year at university in 1981, three years after his mother had died and left it to him. His aunt held it close to her face for a few seconds, seeming quietly engrossed, only to then toss it on to the table in front of him.

'These are your great-great-grandparents. I think that's his third wife ... she was the political one. The smart one.' She picked up some turnip cake and dropped it into her bowl together with a little fish in soy.

'What did he do?'

'Hee-hee!' His aunt was fat and round, and tucked herself into a chinless ball when she laughed. 'Your great-great-grandfather was a farmer, a guard, a robber ... until he became a fighter and a killer. He did nothing and everything.'

He was dissatisfied with her answer and opened his mouth to ask questions, but she directed her gaze above his head.

'*Xiaojie*! Waitress, waitress . . . one more bowl of white rice,' she demanded.

The girl standing behind his seat nodded.

'Did you think we were from Imperial stock?' his aunt demanded, then, seeing his crestfallen expression: 'We're big rice eaters. We belong in those northern fields, working the soil.' Her chin disappeared once more as she shook with laughter.

'So, how did we get here?' he asked, a little embarrassed that he didn't know more of his own family's history.

'Like many others did . . . with an army, as bandits or refugees. This was over eighty years ago. These people' – she flicked her head in the direction of the photograph – 'knew nothing. They'd spent too much of their lives fighting. They were tough and crazy, believed in the power of magic and all sorts of ancient rituals.' She laughed again. 'And they brought us to Guangzhou and Hong Kong because they'd heard of Wong Fei-hung's heroic fight against the colonials, and wanted to join him. Fools!'

'The journey must have been hard for them?'

'Who knows? It was probably very boring . . . apart from the hunger and the fighting.' His aunt looked down at her bowl again and eyed a fish fin. Popping it into her mouth, she started to suck the juices like a happy plump cat.

He sat without speaking. Her thumb had left a small brown smudge of soy on a bottom corner of the photograph. He rubbed it with his finger; though the smudge faded he could still see it. He looked up at his aunt, who continued eating the next fin unperturbed.

Ignoring her and his own food, he held the photo below the table and stared down at the man and woman.

That night in his room at his parents' old home near the squatters' town of Diamond Hill on Fung Tak Road in north-east Kowloon, an apartment as small and mean as the countless others surrounding it, he lay on his bed. Even under the heavy breeze of the electric fan, he was sweating, he dreamed of dark brown earth reduced to dust. Bad luck had penetrated China's heartland, brought by foreigners. With their strange religion and fearsome machines, powerful and impossible, they had defeated its people. Now the Chinese viewed themselves as weak and defenceless. They felt the piss run down their legs in front of mightier men and women from the other side of the world, which until then China had believed it ruled from the centre. Yet the foreign devils preached of deliverance and humility; quoted the compassion of their god as they left Chinese children fearful and hungry.

He dreamed of the arid sepia landscape of the photograph; of distant scrub-covered hills and hard lumpy soil on the plains, unblessed by rain for a year. He found himself standing next to the man and woman, his unknown ancestors. He could smell the stink of their unwashed bodies, the powerful acidity of sweat and mould in their clothes. He could see that the man's hands were rough and sinewy, forged into fists of iron from farming and fighting.

Both his ancestors were small in stature, but stood up straight and proud. She was the first to look at him directly, and to speak. He did not recognize the dialect. To him the words sounded like barking as she snapped at him, telling him something urgently. The barrage of harsh sounds propelled him backwards and down into the dirt. He felt the rough baked earth under his hands and knees as he landed, cutting through his clothes to the skin. Through the blaze of the sun he could make out her silhouette, hard and dark, like a wet hide laid out in snow.

The man stepped forward then. From down in the dust he saw thick calves and flat feet pace slowly round him, then one foot was raised to roll him over. He looked up again, his head pushed down into the dry brown dirt, underneath the coarse sole, and saw the moving shadow of the man's long queue, the long woven pigtail hanging to his waist from his shaved scalp, as he turned back to consult his wife. They shouted at each other, and then the pressure from the foot eased and he was released. Side by side, his ancestors walked away into the distance.

After the dream he spent many hours studying the photograph. The man was young, maybe in his late twenties, and wore his hair Manchurian-style, though he did not come from the far north. This man was from the north-east of China, now a place of little account. He'd belonged to a village built from mud taken from the endless banks of the Yellow River, a place long since returned to the once-fertile brown earth. Without rain the farmland had grown dry and hard, and starvation followed.

In that era, the long drawn-back queue and shaved upper scalp were a sign that the man had been charged to work for the Qing government in some way, and had been awarded the right to wear his hair like that. Perhaps he had even been there at the end, fighting against the foreign powers at Tianjin, breaking up railway track and defying the Western allies. His tight queue pulled back his skin, accentuating a hard bony forehead and the narrowness of his eyes. Fierce pupils commanded the attention of his young descendant. He wore a jacket and trousers of a rough dark material that hung loose from his shoulders and round his waist, and left bare his powerful forearms and chest.

There was a sash of a lighter-coloured material swathed in a band from the man's left shoulder to right hip, which his descendant mentally pictured as being bright red.

The woman stood slightly behind her husband's shoulder, her hair caught back and up, revealing the effects on her skin of years of exposure to the elements and harsh sunlight. Her mouth was part-open, an expression of bewilderment at the photographer's work, but her eyes were hard and bright. She held a staff in her hand, perhaps for walking or tending livestock, perhaps for fighting. Her shirt was traditional and black, clearly of finer quality than the simple clothes worn by her husband, and her head was wound with cloth, which in his mind's eye her descendant saw as deep red also.

He found images of similarly dressed individuals in the university library's collection of historical photographs, and identified the couple as coming from Shandong, high up China's coast dividing the southerly Yellow Sea and the Bohai Sea to the north. According to legend, Shandong was earth and soil, a place for nurturing and growth. It was the origin of the Chinese people.

Shandong was the birthplace of all that was good and worthy about the Chinese, the young man recognized; all that had now been forgotten and betrayed. *Jen* and *li*, goodness and order; only its inhabitants and their faithful descendants would know and understand this.

Throughout his years of legal training with a firm on Hong Kong Island he kept the photograph in his wallet for safety. Then, at the age of twenty-five, he was promoted at work and gained access to the new photocopying machine. At first he was wary of using his employer's expensive equipment and made only a single copy of his sacred image while working late at night. Then, when he was repeatedly asked to stay late in the evening – to prepare instructions to counsel, document bundles or just to complete administrative tasks – he began to make more. In time he was promoted to research and given special access to the copier, allowing him to make hundreds, until he could no longer remember how many he had taken. At home he cut out shapes and single images, arranging them on pages of a notebook around which he rewrote the private histories he'd read and researched. He traced a timeline through wars and revolutions, victorious bandits and fallen warlords. Yet he was drawn most of all to the stories of the millions of poor and dispossessed, who over the centuries repeatedly rose from the yellow earth of his homeland to make their voices heard and change China's course. Urged on by the images in the photograph, he privately researched, collected and recorded their history.

Now, over thirty years later, the original photograph of his ancestors lay on the desk in front of him. He stared down at it, tracing the outline of the man's face, and then closed his eyes.

He sat back in the old wooden office chair he had been given after his father had died, and rested his tired eyes. His father's employer had not wanted the taint of being associated with a traitor, and had given it to him and his mother as a 'commemorative gift'. The old man had sat in this chair for over ten years, supervising the production line and managing the factory teams, until the afternoon he tried to prevent them from demonstrating with their fellow workers. His widow had put the chair in his, their son's, bedroom. Though at first he had refused to accept it and sit in it, had not even been able to look at it, he could not discard it either. In this moment, forty-eight years after his father's death, it was as important to him as the photograph was.

He opened his eyes. He was completely surrounded by heavy iron shelves arranged to form branching passageways spreading from his desk at the centre. Rising two and a half metres from the floor and each filled with journals, folders, encyclopedias, books re-bound, books decrepit with age, diaries, DVDs, video cassettes, spent laptops, maps and dozens of document boxes – all the records he had amassed over his decades of research and writing, since first beginning with the photograph.

They had given him the responsibility of researching and documenting everything, and he had done it better than anyone had ever anticipated.

He lowered his head. The solitary light above him cast a yellow circle around the photograph sealed in its protective bag. In the surface of the plastic he could see a distorted image of his own face, a ghostly simulacrum superimposed over that of his ancestor. He looked closer and picked up the photograph in cotton-gloved fingers. At last he put it back into the small red-lacquered box where he stored it these days, closed the lid and locked it. He got up from the desk, pushing the chair back behind him, and as he did so looked up at the nine flat-screen televisions suspended from the ceiling above the labyrinthine shelves. They showed different news programmes, blogs and forums, all of them silent until he adjusted the audio feed to the earpieces he wore.

The cavernous space was over ten metres high, the ceiling painted a dark red, though flakes of paint had chipped off it, leaving small patches of white undercoat visible. In the narrow passages between the shelves there was room for only one person. His desk stood at the centre of the labyrinth; the entrances to eight passages surrounded it, two in front and two behind, two to his left and two his right. He stood up and placed his left hand flat between the short legs of the lacquered box and raised it to his chest, letting his right hang by his side, deliberately unused. He looked towards a passageway to his right. It went straight for eight metres, then split into two further passages; each of which ran for two metres. These two passages split into four further passages that continued for four metres. They in turn split into eight passages, each of which ran for eight metres. He walked to the entrance of the passageway and entered.

One of two.

Three of four.

Six of eight.

At the end of the last passage was a large iron floor safe. It had a simple lock and key with a heavy brass handle to help open the door. He put the lacquered box on top of the safe, turned the handle and opened the door, then placed the box on the top shelf inside. He pushed the door closed, twisted the handle round and down, and then inserted a key and locked the safe. He straightened up in front of the safe and bowed slightly in prayer.

Opening his eyes, he looked at the safe again, then retraced his footsteps to the desk at the centre. Once there, he stood for a moment following the news feed in silence, then reached down for his briefcase and placed it gently on top of the desk. He opened it to retrieve a paper bag which he held respectfully and then turned and walked down one of the two passages at his back. Again the passages split as he reached their end.

Two of two.

Four of four.

Eight of eight.

Here a shrine hung on the wall, veiled in a thin red light from an electric bulb that seemed to be struggling for life. A copy of the photo was displayed at the back of the red platform in a plain black-lacquered frame. Four oranges were stacked in a simple gold bowl before it, under a red roof trimmed with gilt; the whole shrine was as big as a tea chest. He picked up each piece of fruit and examined it for imperfections.

He adjusted his earpieces as he went about the task, connecting to the audio channels from the televisions, and heard an economic analyst from CNN confirm in plaintive tones the current situation.

'That's right, Susan, China's growth forecast has been revised down even further. Over the last six years, we have seen it fall from double digits to a very modest single-digit figure. Now at 3.8 per cent, it means China is no longer the economic powerhouse it was supposed to be. Like Japan, it burst on the scene and then has flagged. And just as Japan made US investment, the Chinese bought Europe. They pretty much saved it from bankruptcy. Now it needs to concentrate on saving itself and not the world.'

The anchorwoman's confident Chinese-American tones slid smoothly into the conversation. *'Europe needed a bailout, like Greece and Spain seven years before, and the Chinese said to Europe, get yourself together, hit the agreed economic targets, and we'll buy the bonds. But the Europeans have dithered and it now has been five days since the European Union countries defaulted. In four days we have the key meeting of the G8 in Hong Kong to sort this out, otherwise this situation is going to get much worse.'*

After looking closely at all four oranges, he took out a brown paper bag and placed three of them inside before resting it on the floor. He picked up the bag containing replacements and, using his left hand, positioned three new oranges on the gold dish, with the one unblemished fruit placed on top. Next he lit eight sticks of incense and, holding them in both hands, thumbs facing up, genuflected four times in front of the shrine. Each time the incense was brought close to his face and then down to an angle of forty-five degrees. He inserted the sticks into the pot to the left of the fruit. Finally he closed his eyes and stood in front of the shrine to pray.

Back at his desk, he picked up the remote control and channel-hopped.

He looked round at the screens, different faces telling the same story to the world, but in different versions to suit different eyes. Western channels still pursued the illusion of perfection . . . beautiful hair and glossy lips, well-dressed men and women explaining the mechanics of so much misery under meticulous lighting . . . while the Chinese channels were artless and blunt, piping down raw propaganda and incomprehensible streams of data.

He reached down to the fourth drawer of his desk and retrieved a thick notebook. Placing it square in front of him, he opened it and turned the pages. The characters were mostly small and neat except for certain specific strokes, which were lavish and wide. Small *dian*, the tiny flicks that Westerners always mistake for commas, were impressed hard and dark, each a deep black hole in the paper. He put on the glasses that hung around his neck; started to flick through the pages.

Photos of one person, at different ages, from child to man. His entire life story to date, written in characters spread over the pages, both in traditional columns and set across it Western banner-style. Delicate footnotes and bold pronouncements of intent for his future.

Senior Inspector Alex Soong.

Summer

Chien
Heaven
═══════

STRENGTH

Thursday
17 August 2017

It had been four and a half hours. Alex had sat in silence until at last it became too much for him. He had been warned before not to do it while on a stakeout because it was against standard operating procedures, but the silence was unbearable. He needed to put something on and he could see no sign of human activity in the street except from the other team members, and even then he had to know where to look. He phoned his regular partner, Michael De Suza.

'Any sign of Chow?' With his Eurasian fellow inspector, Alex could speak English.

'Nothing, everything's quiet here. I reckon he'll wait another thirty minutes,' De Suza responded.

'I'll update the others.' Alex switched channels on his mobile to address everyone standing by, and switched languages to Cantonese. 'All teams, it looks like we'll have to wait another thirty minutes or so.'

A loud, sharp voice came back at him. Senior Inspector Ying, a hard-faced man from the organized crime division, would be coordinating the units working to seal off the roads once Chow had driven by.

'You're wasting our time, Soong. Chow's not coming. We should abandon this and get back to real work.'

Ying was openly trying to undermine him. Alex suspected him of involvement with the triads – and therefore possibly with their target Chow, a key money-launderer and fraudster in southern China.

'Senior Inspector Ying.' Alex kept it formal and correct. 'We have a reliable source who told us Chow is coming here tonight. As you all know, this man was once one of the most notorious loan-sharks in the city, and since then has stolen millions in pension-fund frauds. Senior Inspector Ying, I think you'll agree that on the evidence we have obtained it's worth waiting to apprehend him, whether it's thirty minutes or thirty hours.' Then he added: 'Or perhaps you have further intelligence you have not shared with us?'

Silence.

A text came through from De Suza. *DUMB BASTARD. Leave him. U want to keep this job??* ☺

'What if he does come, and heads down that alley between the buildings you're watching?' Ying needled him. 'You send men down there after him, they're easy targets. You *have* thought about that, Soong?'

Alex kept his irritation in check. 'Of course. If that happens I will go down myself. I've got more tactical training and experience in this kind of approach, so it's right I should go.'

'Right or correct? Two different things. Well, okay, you lead us into battle, Soong,' Ying sneered.

'Is there anything else?' Alex asked.

Silence.

'Okay then, we'll review the situation in thirty minutes. Out.' Alex closed the communications channel and read another message from De Suza: *What a jerk.*

What? Him or me?

BOTH OF YOU.

Alex flicked through his iPod and found the 1954 Miles Davis All Stars' album *Walkin'*. He turned the volume very low, so some of the softer muted passages were lost, but it was still Miles, J. J. Johnson and a young Horace Silver. After his first long stakeout, Alex had intended to bring a different selection of music each time, but the first album he'd brought along had been *Walkin'* and it had become a habit.

Alex had already filled up two empty Evian bottles with piss and didn't have a spare. He looked at them, lying by his feet, and began to wonder if his source had told him the truth. The man had said that Chow would arrive at a disused office block in this empty corner of Kowloon Tong at around 11 p.m. He was now at least three hours late.

Looking around at the array of red and yellow worn and ripped *Rental* and *For Sale* posters plastered on the shopfronts, Alex saw that this area had always been set apart from the Hong Kong of sleek glass-and-steel high-rise towers around the harbour. This was a low-income place, its mazy architecture steadily evolving across seven or eight decades. There were three or four eye-catching storeys of curved lines from 1940s French-style buildings with balconies and rough art nouveau details; simplistic multi-storeyed brick blocks thinly skimmed with white plaster; and end-of-the-century cheap glass and concrete low-rise office towers of fifteen floors or less. People continued to live their limited existences in the cramped apartments but the offices were empty. Business these days was conducted in China. Hong Kong was now a disused bridge sitting next to the multi-lane superhighway directly connecting mainland China to the world.

Typhoon signal 8, the same as a full-force hurricane in the US, had been hoisted earlier at 9.10 p.m., and that had cleared the streets for the whole evening; a good time for Chow to venture out. The wind was now strong enough to pick at the corners of the bills and heave the neon signage back and forth. Alex watched as paper was blown down the street and then whirled into the air. It was 2.18 a.m. He sat and listened. There was only light rain at the moment but it would soon pour down hard.

It was just over thirteen minutes since he had last called De Suza, waiting two blocks down the street in a vacant shop across from the building under observation. Alex trusted him, knowing that if Chow appeared then his fellow inspector would call it in at once.

It didn't stop Alex from calling him though.

'See anything?'

'Nothing.'

'It's still early yet,' Alex said, trying to reassure himself as much as his friend.

'I suppose so, but wasn't it also *still early* two hours ago? You getting worried yet?'

'Smartass. He'll come. Just hope the rain—'

'Wait,' De Suza cut him off. 'A car has just pulled up . . . and someone who looks like Chow is getting out . . . wait on my mark . . . yes, it's him!'

'Okay. About time,' Alex said softly.

'He's walking round his car to a narrow alley between the buildings. He's gone down . . . it's too dark for me to see him. Quick, backup!' De Suza shouted.

Alex changed channels on his phone and ordered: 'Now!'

In the mirror he watched the doors of the van parked behind him quietly open. Five officers in bulletproof vests, crouching slightly, moved across the empty road and down two blocks to join De Suza by the entrance to the alley. Alex flicked off the sound and got out. The street was otherwise empty. As he crossed the road to join De Suza he glanced up at the empty buildings and broken signage stretching up into the darkness; moths fluttered round the bulbs in the streetlights directly overhead. The first big drops of rain started to fall.

He paused, looking at the men of the small operations group. There were three young officers and two older, more experienced ones, plus Mike De Suza, who stood at least fifteen to twenty centimetres taller than everyone else.

Alex briefed them. 'Okay, I'm going to take the lead.'

The team said nothing. Over their heads De Suza looked to Alex for confirmation, thick black eyebrows raised questioningly above wide pale-brown eyes. It wasn't standard procedure for a senior inspector to go in first. Alex nodded back at De Suza, a big-chested and big-hearted man who had what his wife Mary described as a 'strong' nose and fleshy lips she loved to kiss. Mong, the youngest member of the team, appeared more than a little anxious. Alex put a thumb to the side of his nose, flicked it lightly and cocked his head back a little, smiling. Bruce Lee's classic gesture of confidence, something every kid in Hong Kong recognized. Mong smiled and Alex gave De Suza the thumbs-up.

'I'll go down alone,' he said firmly. 'If it's clear, I'll signal you to follow.'

Alex stepped into total darkness. With local businesses gone and money very tight, communal lighting was now rare in alleyways and sidestreets. He walked slowly forward, placing his feet gently to prevent himself from kicking anything and alerting Chow. He stopped. In the distance, he could hear keys jangling. A door opened in a building on the right side of the alley, about twenty metres from where he was standing. Bright light lit the opposite wall.

Alex instinctively wanted to remain standing, but this gave away any chance of controlling the situation. Training and experience had long since taught him to ignore this gut reaction. In the second that light burst from the doorway his peripheral vision had picked out a large garbage bin. He jumped over to crouch behind it.

After ten seconds the door shut and darkness descended once more. The sudden flare of light had caused Alex's pupils to contract, and now without light he could see nothing. He could not even identify the bin in front of him, and remained still until he could at least make out vague outlines.

Alex looked round at De Suza and the unit, now mere silhouettes about twenty-five metres behind him, and breathed out heavily. He walked slowly, with his torch turned low, towards the door twenty metres ahead. It was made of heavy wood with a metal plate bolted to it. There was one lock, which the door ram would take care of.

He went back up the alley quietly to rejoin the waiting men.

'Fortunately the door opens inward. We can use the ram.'

'He'll know we're here then,' Mong said nervously.

'Yes, he will,' Alex replied, smiling at the young officer and giving him a friendly tap on the helmet. 'So Ah Chong here' – pointing to the grinning heavyset older officer opposite – 'will use the ram and I'll go in first to see where Chow is. You, Mong, will take up the rear.'

'First again?' De Suza commented.

'Yes, again. Please don't quote procedure at me.' Alex winked at Mong.

'He drives his wife crazy,' De Suza whispered softly, and the young officer smiled.

They moved down the alley in formation. At the door, Ah Chong readied himself with the ram, which would produce about three tonnes of force. Alex rested his hand on the end.

He looked at each man in turn and they nodded back. Alex removed his hand.

Ah Chong heaved the ram into the door. It gave way easily, swinging in hard and crashing violently to the floor as the hinges buckled. The suddenness and noise provided a few moments of confusion, in which Alex rushed into the room, crouching low to minimize his visibility. As he entered he saw an old large iron filing cabinet against the far wall on his left, and looking to his right, in the diametrically opposite corner, he saw that Chow had been seated at a desk facing the door.

Chow was disoriented and stood up out of his chair, shouting and waving his arms, but then he gathered himself, turned the desk over for protection and dropped behind it. Alex noticed the desktop had been empty except for a bottle of Red Label and a large glass filled halfway.

It was a dark fetid place, deeply marked chessboard plastic tiling across the floor, stained whitewashed walls with two dusty strip lights across the ceiling. Alex moved quickly to crouch down behind the heavy-looking filing cabinet – offering him protection from Chow's line-of-sight while still allowing Alex to look across through the broken doorway at the team outside. There was little else in the room apart from the desk and a television, muted but playing some zany Japanese game show, attached high up on the same wall as the doorway.

'Chow? Stop screaming, Chow! This is Senior Inspector Alex Soong of the Hong Kong Police Anti-Corruption Task Force,' he said in his heavily accented Cantonese from behind the filing cabinet.

'You sound like a fucking *Dai Lok* to me! Go back north!' Chow replied, getting down behind the desk.

'That's me, a fucking Big Six!' Alex joked, though he secretly hated the Cantonese slang for mainlanders. The literal translation for the local Cantonese dialect for 'big land', or 'mainland', simply sounded the same as 'big six'. 'I know you have a gun, put it down!'

'You're going back to Beijing in a body bag, *Dai Lok*!' Chow shouted defiantly.

Through the gaping doorway Alex heard a crack of thunder, followed by the sound of heavy rain.

Chow fired three shots. The first was wild, but his aim improved with the second and third and Alex heard them whistle past the cabinet. In the doorway Mong shouted. As Alex turned in response he saw the young man go down and then De Suza's large hand grabbed the kid's collar to haul him out of the line of fire.

Alex heard Chow moving behind the desk. Glancing round the edge of the filing cabinet, he saw Chow stand up, fire two wild shots in the general direction of the cabinet, and scurry towards a door between cabinet and desk. Alex pressed himself back against the wall, as one shot went wide and one pierced the cabinet. Chow was skinny, with hardly any hair, wearing a dark suit, threadbare in the seat and at the knee. In his bony fingers, Alex saw he held a cheap small-calibre handgun – a tiny Saturday Night Special, as the Americans used to call them. He heard the door slam shut and lock.

Alex moved round the filing cabinet and remained crouched. Then he stood up and signalled to the huddle of armour-clad officers in the alley outside that they should remain there. From behind the locked door he heard shouts and then screams. It sounded like a girl, probably no older than ten. He moved round the cabinet to the inner door that Chow had just escaped through, and flattened himself against the wall right next to its frame.

'Chow, what are you doing in there?' he shouted. 'There's nowhere to go. You can't get out!'

Just the screams of a child in reply.

Alarmed by the sound, his heart raced once more. He struck the door hard with the palm of one hand.

'Chow, let her go!'

'Go fuck yourself! I have the little girl and her father. I want you to get a helicopter and fly me to Macao . . . otherwise I'll kill one of them now!'

Alex signalled to Ah Chong, squatting in the doorway, that there were two hostages.

'Going to Macao won't help you, it's still China. There's no escape. You know that,' he replied confidently. He looked round again to Ah Chong and beckoned him inside.

'Sir, what do you need?' Ah Chong whispered.

Alex brought his face closer to the left side of the officer's helmet, away from his earpiece on the other side. 'How's Mong?' he asked.

'Inspector De Suza took him back to the street but I understand he's fine.'

'Good. Now please get me Inspector De Suza and give him your shotgun. We're going to open this door. Tell the medics and support teams to be ready.'

Alex breathed out. The officer quickly left the room. Alex looked back at the locked door and dropped to a crouching position.

'Chow? What sort of helicopter do you want?' he called.

'You a joker? One that flies, you dumb shit!' the fraudster laughed. 'Get it soon or someone will be hurt here.'

His reply had come quickly and clearly, indicating that Chow considered himself to be in control of the situation and his actions.

Alex looked up to see De Suza above him. He was holding a

shotgun in his right hand. He squatted down beside him. 'A little girl wasn't part of the plan,' the big cop whispered unhappily.

Alex could only frown back in frustration.

'Ready?'

De Suza nodded.

Alex brought his face close to the locked door.

'Come on, Chow, you don't want to add murder to the corruption charges, do you? Let the girl and her father go. None of us wants anyone hurt, do we?'

'Fuck you, mainlander!'

De Suza emptied the shotgun into the lock and blew the door open. Alex charged through the thin smoke filling the doorway into the next room, clearing his mind of everything but the target. Looking about him quickly as he moved, he saw that Chow had trapped himself and the other two behind another desk, an older man to his right and a little girl restrained by his left arm. There were two filing cabinets and a safe by the door now three metres behind Alex. The girl was small, maybe only seven years old, with her hair cut in a cute bob like so many other Chinese girls. She was a little chubby with round cheeks, her wide eyes framed by long delicate lashes. Fear had drained the blood from her skin, leaving it almost translucent. She stared blankly at Alex's gun.

He stood on the other side of the desk with his pistol pointed close to Chow's face. The fraudster pressed his own gun into the child's cheek. The desk itself was covered in papers and money.

'Sir, are you the father? Are you all right?' Alex shouted to a second man huddled in a chair next to Chow.

'Yes, yes!' he cried out.

Chow looked from one to the other.

'Please can you tell your daughter to close her eyes and keep them tight shut until I tell her to open them?' Alex requested.

'Hey, shut up!' Chow regained his composure and shouted at the man next to him. The little girl started to scream louder.

'Siu Fong, close your eyes,' the father said softly, staring directly into his daughter's face.

Chow swung the barrel of the gun from the girl to her father. 'Shut up! This is the last time I tell you . . .'

Alex ignored him. 'Siu Fong, do as your Ba says and close your eyes.'

'Shut up!' Chow shouted frantically. He eyeballed Alex. 'Get me the helicopter or I'll shoot one of them!'

'Look, take me instead,' he suggested calmly. 'I make a much better hostage. You don't want to harm a frightened little girl, do you?' The child was rigid with tension. Alex saw that Chow was becoming increasingly unstable, the pistol wavering in his hand, and feared the man might actually hurt her.

'Siu Fong, you are a very brave little girl like the famous swordswoman Lady Yiu in the ancient stories who defeated the angry old ape god. Do you know that story?' Alex said, slowly and quietly.

'I told you to SHUT UP!' Chow yelled. He pointed his gun at the father's stomach and shot him. Blood spurted from the wound and the father was hurled back hard in the chair, which hit the wall close behind him. He collapsed under the desk. The little girl opened her eyes and started to scream. She looked desperately at her father and struggled against Chow's restraining arm.

'Siu Fong . . . Siu Fong?' The girl's dazed-looking eyes slowly moved from her father to Alex. 'Close your eyes again,' he continued calmly, 'and don't open them until I say.'

'Siu Fong, do as the policeman says,' her father gasped. His right leg extended unseen under the desk while the other was folded up but loosely splayed to the side. Blood covered his front. His eyes were tightly shut, fear replaced by excruciating pain.

The child squeezed her eyes closed. Chow pressed the gun against her cheek, the hot barrel scorching her delicate skin. Alex watched it redden and swell. She screamed louder, tears squeezing out from between her screwed-up eyelids.

Alex could smell her skin burning. Anger flooded through him.

'You leave her alone, Chow, or I'm going to fucking hurt you. Do you understand? *Do you understand?*' he was screaming. The girl looked just like his sister Xue had when they'd last seen each other. She had been small too, with the same deep brown pupils in big round eyes. In this moment of reflection he collected himself. Nevertheless he continued to scream at Chow, to convince the other man he was out of control. 'Touch her again and you won't leave this room . . .' Alex's jaw clenched shut on the words but his sharp eyes continued to weigh the situation.

Chow grinned.

'You still want that helicopter?' Alex finished and intended to say nothing further. He just looked hard at Chow and breathed slowly. He could hear De Suza moving next door, readying himself to burst in. Alex watched Chow glance towards the door as they both heard the sounds of the outside room filling up with people.

'Siu Fong, you are a very brave girl. I know it hurts but it will soon be over. Please keep your eyes shut. Close them as tightly as you can. Ba will be fine. Your Ba is okay,' Alex said softly.

'*Dai Lok*, I've warned you over and over . . . she'll die! It'll be messy and on your soul.'

He may just do it, Alex thought. *He's grinning now, believes he has control of the situation, but he's still nervous.*

Alex leaned further across the desk and touched his gun to Chow's forehead.

'Your gun is cheap. You should have one of these.' He pressed the barrel into Chow's forehead a little harder and spoke above Siu Fong's soft crying. 'But it's only in the movies that both sides have big guns. The one you've got, the Americans used to call a Saturday Night Special because cheap part-time gangsters used them. They misfire. You've had a few clean shots but there might not be another.' He kept his eyes firmly on Chow and did not look at the little girl.

Chow said nothing, just turned the gun from Siu Fong and pointed it at Alex's head instead. 'Oh, but it'll do for killing you, officer,' he replied, still grinning.

The injured man was unconscious now and Alex could see out of the corner of his eye that blood was pooling on the floor around him. Alex stood still for a moment, his breathing becoming deep and slow. 'Siu Fong, shut your eyes tight. I don't want you to see this,' he said, without taking his eyes off Chow's.

'See what?' the man shouted. 'Heh, see *you* die?'

Alex held his gaze for half a breath longer and then, without moving his head, looked suddenly hard to the left, as if expecting someone to come in. Chow followed the cue by instinct, but before his brain could receive an image of the empty doorway and the realization that no one was there, Alex's bullet had punched between his eyes and Alex himself was halfway across the desk, catching Siu Fong as she fell from the dead man's arm.

He did not watch the body fall to the ground but grabbed the little girl and spun round, covering her eyes and face, shouting for De Suza and a medic.

On hearing the shot, De Suza had dived through the doorway and gone straight to Chow's body to confirm he was dead. One look assured him. In these seconds, Alex had passed his partner and taken the girl back into the first room.

De Suza checked the father, who was still breathing but losing a lot of blood. Allowing the medics to attend to the wounded man, he returned to the outer room to join Alex. More police officers started to arrive, to preserve and contain the scene while the Forensics officers gathered evidence.

De Suza stood back and watched Alex. In the middle of this chaos, covered in blood and body-matter himself, he was on his knees frantically wiping the blood from Siu Fong's face and hands.

'Siu Fong, Siu Fong, you're very brave. You keep your eyes closed until I say, just like your Ba told you.' Alex was almost frenzied in his cleaning. 'It'll soon be over.'

'I will keep my eyes closed. What happened to that man?' she asked.

'He's gone, he's just gone, Siu Fong.'

'Did he leave?'

'He's never coming back, so you need never think of him again. Understand? In a minute a kind lady will come and take you out of here.'

She gave a little nod in reply, her chin pressing into the puppy fat round her neck. 'Will you come too?' she whispered.

'I must see if everyone else is okay first. I'll come see you later.' He frantically cleaned as much matter as he could from the little girl's face, avoiding the burn. 'Don't open your eyes until I say.'

Blood from Chow's fatal wound had splattered across her dress, hands and arms. Alex looked up at De Suza, frowning. 'Quickly, take off your shirt and soak it in some rainwater!'

Realizing it would take too long to remove his protective vest, De Suza ripped part of the sleeve from his shirt and moved through the increasingly crowded room to find water outside. He returned almost at once, rain dripping from his dark Kevlar vest, and handed Alex the wet dark blue sleeve.

'The typhoon is really picking up,' he reported.

Alex took the cloth and gently wiped the girl clean. 'I'll keep my eyes tight shut but it hurts so much,' she murmured.

The little girl was entering shock and starting to tremble. Alex wrapped her in the blanket given him by a female officer, who then bundled her up and took her out down the alley. As they left the building, he called after them: 'Siu Fong, you can open your eyes now.'

De Suza watched all this then stepped forward and placed a hand on Alex's shoulder. When his friend looked up at him, he was momentarily shocked by the mess of blood and matter that covered his face. He also saw that Alex's eyes were wide and wild, his body still pumping adrenalin.

'We'd better get you cleaned up too,' he said, hauling Alex outside – deeper down the alley and into the darkness.

'What happened in there?' he demanded.

'Fuck!' Alex leaned against the wall then fell forward, propping himself up with his hands on his knees, hyperventilating slightly. 'That fucking guy shot the father then burned the little girl's face ... she'll be scarred for life by that worthless shit! Then there's the risk of infection from Chow's blood in her open wound ... You saw her,' he gasped. 'I just wanted to hurt him so badly ... but killing him was never the plan. I didn't know anything about a little girl being there. She was so small. She looked like one of my sisters.'

Alex thought of his sisters, twins, whom he'd last seen standing in the communal yard of his parents' government apartment block in Beijing nearly thirty years before. He had stood with his mother at the window three floors above them. His mother wept, the only time she ever did this in front of him, as they watched his father kneel in front of the little girls and close their thick jackets against the dusty northern wind. Lin, eldest by an hour, had a ponytail and stood as she always did, straight-backed and silent, while Xue, her face framed by a low fringe, swung her arms at her sides and pulled at her father's beard. The two girls looked up and Alex waved down.

The Party had made his parents follow the one-child-only rule, so his sisters were taken away and split up. His father knew that one had ended up in Hong Kong, but was otherwise supposed to forget about them. However, he made a promise to his wife to find them when he retired. He searched the vast State migration and adoption records and asked through official channels until he was told to stop. Finally he came to Hong Kong, and eventually trailed along the border towns. He was relentless and obsessed. When Alex was posted to Hong Kong, he told Alex he hoped he would go on searching.

Alex gave a growl of frustration and suddenly reared up at De Suza, but the big man easily pinned him back against the wall using his shirtless forearm. Alex quickly calmed down, putting his hands on top of his head and pressing them into his closely cropped hair until his breathing grew calmer.

'Easy now. Let's wait here a few minutes.' De Suza breathed out hard himself. 'Have you told Jun about the twins?'

'Not yet. Since we've moved from Beijing and my parents have gone, it's probably safe to tell her. It's something I must do.' Alex said with resignation. 'She won't be happy I haven't told her. I didn't want to her to think we had political problems and then her parents would stop her from marrying me. Things can get too complicated, everyone has so many damn skeletons hidden away. And then it seemed irrelevant, they're either lost or dead.'

They stood in silence.

'I saw Chow. He's done,' De Suza abruptly announced.

'Good. Fucking good! Why did he have to hurt her?'

'Okay, stop this.' The big man's eyes stared resolutely into Alex's face, contorted by anger and the intense helplessness of someone who understands they have neither succeeded nor failed, but can in any event no longer alter the outcome. 'You make a fuss, and someone up there' – he turned and nodded up the alley – 'will come down and start asking questions about your conduct.'

'I still don't understand how innocence came to mean so little to these people. It has no power at all over them. As if it doesn't exist,' Alex murmured.

De Suza rested one big hand on top of Alex's head sympathetically and pressed down a little in jest. 'A person like Chow has probably never known innocence and so has never felt its loss.' He let his hand fall to his side. 'And without it, there's no self-awareness, no control, his perspective is completely warped.' He looked down the alley, past the broken doorway, to the police at the other end. 'Let's get this case sorted out and then come home with me for something to eat? Mary said she would cook a big breakfast if it was still Typhoon 8 and the kids couldn't go to school.'

They both looked up into the early dawn, the dark silver clouds tarnished black by the weight of more heavy rain to come.

'Okay.'

'Let's get back into the light, and get you cleaned up.'

'Give me another minute. How's Mong?'

'He's fine. Better than your shoes. You're never going to get rid of Chow's blood and all the rat shit.'

'Fuck 'em . . . and fuck Chow too.' The anger had drained away from Alex's voice. He was beginning to get cold and suddenly felt very tired as the adrenalin emptied from his system. He stayed still for a few moments, then looked up at De Suza, whose big face bore its usual rock-steady smile. It drew everyone to the man, a perfect crescent of ivory held firmly in place by his strong jaw. His warmth and generosity almost belied his clear commitment to law enforcement.

'Feel okay now?' De Suza joked, with fake commiseration. 'You'd better be. Yet again you didn't manage to stick to operational procedure. There'll be an enquiry.'

Alex nodded wearily.

They walked quickly back down the alley towards the main street. As they passed the open doorway of Chow's office they saw a body bag being wheeled out, mingled rain and blood washing down the black plastic. Alex stared ahead and they walked the rest of the way in silence. Once on the street, they went towards the vans, cars and motorcycles that marked the police presence. Ying had done his job, sealing off the street as soon as they'd confirmed it was Chow they had spotted.

Chow had once been the city's key money-launderer, but had also misappropriated a substantial amount of pension funds, leaving thousands of innocent people's health care and subsistence in doubt. Stealing from the deep pools of pension funds had become a common crime in these depressed times. Like all governments, the Chinese administration was struggling under the burden of the elderly and the unemployed; any large-scale theft from hard-earned pensions was now punishable by a life sentence or worse, and Chow had stolen much and often.

Alex stood in the middle of the road, surrounded by police who were working the crime scene and talking to the few local residents still living in the surrounding buildings, who had now emerged from their apartments. Everything was drenched, evidence washed away by the second. Blue lights flashed outside the empty shopfronts. The street was probably busier than it had been for months. Alex tried to calm his breathing using traditional *taiji chuan* techniques and momentarily detached his thoughts from the intensity of the last hour, but struggled to free himself from troubling images of tear-filled brown eyes.

'How did we end up with a dead man missing the top of his head, a bookkeeper in severe trauma and a child with facial burns?' a soft voice enquired.

Alex spun round to find the Captain of his Police Department standing behind him.

'I expected to find a man in custody. Instead he's in a body bag.' The Captain paused to let other officers move tactfully out of earshot. '*Another* body bag. We need to charge these people . . . make a public example of them. This is not helping the situation, is it?' The question was left to drift across to Alex on the typhoon's gale.

The Captain wore a frown on his pockmarked face. Like many Cantonese men, he was not tall or muscular and so not particularly physically imposing, but Alex knew he was sinewy and hard. He stood at least ten centimetres shorter than Alex himself, who would have been tall for a local Hong Konger but was only of average height for a Beijing man. The Captain's power rested in his eyes, which barely moved but seemed to drink in every nuance of the activity around him. In an interview room, one glimpse of his forbidding expression was known to have made many hardened criminals falter and lose confidence, forced into stupid mistakes.

'I didn't want this but it was the only option,' Alex told him.

'Was it?' the Captain asked. 'No matter. You're a policeman, you can't just kill people with impunity. You'll have a debriefing with Internal Affairs at 8.45 a.m. to explain tonight's events. I suggest you get the situation cleaned up quickly. I will see you later.' He walked away in the direction of his car.

Alex returned to his previous position and watched De Suza approaching him.

'What did he want from you this time?'

'Wanted me to clean up this *situation*. Sorry, breakfast is out. Give my love to Mary though.'

'Okay, I'll see you later.' De Suza ambled away, then turned to say: 'By the way, the girl is fine and so is her father.'

Alex didn't respond. His left hand had formed a fist, which he repeatedly squeezed and relaxed while his right hand massaged his left shoulder. De Suza watched him stare blindly down the street, past the flashing lights, police tape, and into the empty buildings.

Alex stayed at the scene until the pathologist had departed with the body, the main evidence had been gathered, and the small crowd had dispersed. He went back to his car. The two bottles of piss still lay on the floor by the driver's seat. He picked them up and gently dropped them into the passenger-side footwell.

His car was a red 1968 Ford Mustang GT-390, a beautiful piece of machinery brought to Hong Kong by an expatriate who had then had to sell it when he lost his job. It was impractical and prone to breaking down and parts were difficult to find, but for all these deficiencies Alex still felt it was more of a car than any new model available in Hong Kong. Jun hated it. She wanted a new Mercedes or at least a BMW; she wanted a modern car, not an antique, she said. To Alex the car was a beautiful classic and he enjoyed everything about it. Even when it broke down, its failure was a part of their relationship.

The Hong Kong roads had yet to fill up – that would start at around 6 a.m. – so he casually wound his way through the tight streets of Kowloon to the Eastern Tunnel, which would take him to Causeway Bay at one end of Victoria harbour on Hong Kong Island. The tunnel was empty, free from the horrendous daily traffic and its grim pollution, so the drive was short and peaceful. He wound down the windows and just cruised along until, about half a mile out of the tunnel, on the island he took the flyover straight to Happy Valley, drove round the racetrack there and up the hill to his apartment block. Miles still accompanied him on the stereo.

Jun would still be sleeping, so Alex entered the apartment quietly. The front door opened into a small reception area in which Jun had placed a bookcase for coffee-table books and a huge bowl full of dusty matchbooks from the 1980s that her mother had collected and given them, and that some more credulous guests had mistaken for installation art. He then turned right into the much wider living area. The living-room area was almost 800 square feet, which like most Hong Kong apartments was almost half the usable floor space, with the dining table for ten immediately upon entering, then behind it a square frame of sofas round a wide coffee table, ending with the television in the corner on the far left and a corridor to the much smaller rooms – the bathroom, study and main bedroom – in the far right corner. Running down the right side was the kitchen and spare bedroom.

He meant to head straight for the bathroom, but stopped briefly when he saw a couple of empty wine bottles and glasses smudged with lipstick on the glass-topped coffee table. Jun often had her girlfriends visit for drinks after they had been out for dinner. Usually she kept the apartment tidy and clean – she was a great fan of the clutter-free interiors of modern Western design – but it looked as if tonight had been a late one.

Alex stood above the empty glasses and looked down into his own bloody reflection. Jun's father, a very wealthy businessman from Hubei, had tried in vain to persuade her to allow him to buy them lots of Chinese-designed furniture, made by a business in which he had invested. She had rejected it all, and Alex was thankful. But only in favour of expensive Italian and French hand-crafted pieces, which her father could have had copied in his factory but wouldn't because he refused to engage in those old replica-making practices that he felt demeaned the Chinese. Instead he had hired European designers and brought them to China to work and train the local craftsmen and designers. After a few years, the Europeans would return and they would go on to create something new and exciting of their own. Eventually he wanted to stand toe-to-toe with European-based designers – even if it took a thousand years. Alex admired his father-in-law for his principled approach, to learn not to copy, unlike many Chinese businesses before, but the apartment had needed furnishing more quickly than the company would mature, so imported furniture it was. Jun had bought contemporary European designs, everything in shades of brown, and so the living room was a murky monochrome.

An ochre leather sofa and chairs with wooden legs stained dark; a coffee table with a walnut top and russet-lacquered legs; a dark-wood dinner table with a burnt umber leather surface, and tweed-upholstered dining chairs in a toning shade. Alex smiled to see all the autumnal shades around the room; it was comforting in its designer-led conformity. At the time they'd moved in Jun's mother had stocked the kitchen with the usual family appliances such as a large rice cooker, a water boiler and dispenser, and an extra gas ring for cooking with a wok. All of these Jun had consigned to storage so as to maintain the apartment's 'perfectly clean design narrative', as she described it, leaving just her coffeemaker and Alex's iPod dock visible.

This place had never felt entirely warm or homely to Alex, but it had become their shared space and the obsessiveness with which Jun always returned everything to its proper place had become a familiar and a reliable part of his life. The move to Hong Kong had been difficult: he had buried himself in his work and she had simply let him – the only condition being that she did not want his job intruding on their home life.

Entering the bathroom and looking at himself in the mirror, Alex found that Chow's blood was smeared on the upper half of his face and in his hair. He looked hard into his own eyes. There was a cloudiness to the whites, and the blood vessels were a bloated red. Faint lines were visible underneath them. He rested his hands on the sink and leaned hard, closing his eyes to try to think of nothing. Darkness came for a moment, but his mind drifted, sliding quickly to an image of him shouting at Chow. He saw himself red-faced and screaming, muscles and tendons in his neck pulled taut, like iron rods pushing his head up. His jaw ground up and down as the words were forced out and the barrel of the gun thrust hard into Chow's face. To the little girl, her face empty except for fear as he stood in front of her, he was as frightening as Chow. When he opened his eyes and looked down he noticed that his Timberlands too were spattered with blood. He jerked around to see if he'd left footprints behind him, saw none, and breathed out in relief.

Sitting on the edge of the bath, he removed his T-shirt and took off his belt, which he put to one side. He pulled lightly at his laces to undo them, and as they separated tiny dark red flakes of dried blood caked into them fell on to the pristine bathmat. He looked at the red powder on the white towelling and slowly pulled off each trainer to minimize the amount of Chow's blood that would fall onto their show home and into Jun's perfect life. He put the Timberlands square in the centre of the mat: the mat itself, the trainers and his blood-spattered trousers would have to go.

Alex turned on the shower and sat down on the toilet lid.

Through the transparent shower curtain, he watched the water splash against the plastic sheeting. With his elbows on his knees, he let his forehead rest in his palms. He looked down at his thighs, at the long dark scar just above his left knee where William Zhou had cut him during knife-combat training seven years ago. It had been a sunny day and in the glaring light Alex had missed William's lunge and ended up with a huge gash in his leg. William had been shocked, Alex had waved away his apologies, and their deep friendship had stemmed from that incident.

These days Alex badly missed his old friend. It had nearly broken him to see William's body after he had committed suicide. He had shot himself in the head, underneath the jaw, in October 2011. There had been virtually nothing left of his once-smiling face. Alex had identified the body for William's parents, verifying his identity by the scar on his wrist – the scar he himself had given his friend in exchange for the one on his knee.

Alex stood for a long while underneath the falling water. In a city that was so dirty, a shower often felt like a baptism. A chance to reflect and be renewed. He dried himself and walked naked along the corridor, away from the living room, past the half-dozen absurdly contrived wedding photographs on the walls, past his study, to the bedroom. He turned the handle slowly and inched the door open. The bedroom was completely dark, as Jun preferred, but he left the door slightly ajar to light his way. He climbed in beside his wife, who was lying comfortably in the middle of the mattress.

She moved on to her side so he could spoon around her. Jun was nearly as tall as he was, her long legs and slender waist toned by her years of ballet dancing, though nowadays she preferred her yoga classes. He wrapped one arm around her and slid the other underneath her neck, between the pillow and her shoulder, slightly trapping and pulling on her long silky black hair.

'Hey, stop that,' she mumbled. 'Are you naked?' She raised her voice slightly in amusement. 'What do you want? It's so early. Oh, god,' she said with a hint of weariness, but still in fun.

'Nothing, just a cuddle and a little sleep,' he whispered.

He held her but could not sleep. After an hour, his mind still racing, he got up and quietly opened the wardrobe to take out a change of clothes. He stood and looked at his Diesel jeans and clean light Timberlands and then groaned as he remembered he had committed himself to attending a lengthy lunchtime ceremony at the university to collect a posthumous award for public service on behalf of his father and grandfather. He would have to dress smartly. To Alex, smart meant plain black brushed-cotton Levis and a button-down shirt from Brooks Brothers.

He shaved, dressed, then went back to the kitchen and turned on the coffee machine. He leaned against the countertop and let the coffee drip into the pot.

Alex looked at his reflection in the cupboard door above the coffee machine and thought of William and Mike, to whom he was as close as he might have been to brothers. He smiled. It was nearly six years since William had died, and Mike De Suza was the first person Alex had let himself grow close to since then.

He sat at the four-seater kitchen table with his cup of coffee and flicked through some envelopes Jun had left stacked neatly for him. They were just bills. He dropped them back on to the table, leaned back in his chair and rubbed his weary eyes.

About 8 a.m., Alex poured a cup of coffee for Jun and walked back into the bedroom. The half-light breaking through the doorway fell upon her face, which was that of a classic Chinese beauty: pale skin, a small nose, cheeks that were high but not too angular, and lips that were neither full nor thin. Her thick black hair fell naturally over her left eye, and in more playful moods Alex loved to watch her sweep it back from her face and then look askance at him, knowing he was watching.

He sat down on the edge of the bed next to her. 'What?' she murmured.

'I brought you some coffee.'

She was not interested and simply rolled back into sleep.

'Jun, I'm attending a ceremony for Ba and Grandfather this lunchtime. Will you please come?' he asked softly in Mandarin, fully expecting a tirade in response.

'What?' she groaned from deep within her pillow. 'Do I have to?'

It was like coaxing a child.

'Well,' he said, a little more forcefully, 'it would be polite. And I would like it if you came.'

'Why didn't you ask me earlier? Give me some warning?'

'Would you have wanted to go if I had?'

'Don't interrogate me! I'm not some criminal.' She sat up abruptly. 'Ring me later . . . I'm going back to sleep now.'

Alex put the coffee on her bedside table. He kissed her softly on the lips and brushed her left cheek lightly with his fingertips. She glared back at him. 'I don't want to go,' she said aggressively in English.

'I had a difficult night and the morning is only going to get worse. It would be good if you could come at lunchtime,' he said slowly, trying to defuse the tension. Now he could see her deep brown eyes looking down, trying to avoid his. 'It would be good if you could come to support me.'

She slapped his hand away. 'What happened to you this morning?' she asked in exasperation, reverting to Mandarin.

Alex hesitated.

'What?' she said impatiently. She levered herself up under the duvet. He watched her move her lower jaw to the right side and bite her lower lip, an expression she would adopt when she knew she was about to hear something she would rather not.

'A criminal we were watching took a little girl hostage and burned her face.' He placed his hands on Jun's duvet-covered knees.

'*Ai*. That's horrible. Don't tell me any more.' She bent forward and put her hands to her own face. 'Oh, why do you tell me these things? I really don't want to hear. I know China and Hong Kong are brutal places. I know I should say something supportive to you when I hear what you have to do, but I can't deal with these images of you in my head. They're ugly and horrible!'

They sat in silence. Alex turned to look at Jun, who in turn stared down at the bed covers.

'I know police work is what you want to do, but I don't understand *how* you can do it,' she continued.

'Because I don't have any choice,' he told her.

She whipped her right hand out from under the duvet and slapped him hard on the cheek. 'No choice? I'm sick of this! Why can't you work for my father like he has suggested countless times? He will you pay three times as much as you earn now.' She stared at him angrily, demanding a positive response this time.

He rubbed his face with his palm. 'That's not what I meant. This is what I do, and I like doing it.'

'You like killing people?' she said sarcastically, though he could see tears forming in her eyes. 'What if we actually had a child? I don't know if we are unlucky or lucky not having any children.'

Alex looked at her. With his parents gone and sisters lost to him, she was his family and he knew that she, as an only child, like most other Chinese, had wanted to start a family; though she rarely mentioned it now.

'You know what I mean. I'm a policeman and a very good one. It's what I do.'

'And *I'm* going back to sleep. Ring me later.' She shuffled down the bed and rolled on to her side. He heard her sniffling but said nothing more to her.

He got up, and as he reached the door she spoke.

'I can't listen to those stories anymore. It was enough in Beijing, especially when William died.'

'I understand. I won't mention them again.'

'Thank you,' she said warmly. 'I'm sorry I hit you.' Her voice was tired and her words were drawn. 'There are some bills on the table that need to be paid today.'

He stood at the partly open door.

'Yes, I have them.'

Alex closed the door behind him, leaving Jun in total darkness. He looked again at the wedding photos lining the walls. Jun was smiling hard while he appeared to be wincing. He walked down the corridor back into the living room and looked round at all the brown furniture. He felt suddenly detached from the things in his own home; only his study seemed to be an extension of him. He had the interview with Internal Affairs at 8.45 and it was already 8.20. He took the garbage bag of bloodstained clothes, tied it up ready to go – but as he reached for the door handle, Galore, their British Blue cat, appeared and wound herself round his legs. Alex dropped the bag and bent down to stroke her.

When Jun had told her parents she was dating a detective her mother had immediately equated this with James Bond and had watched every movie. When they'd bought the cat his mother-in-law insisted they call her Galore, after Pussy Galore. Alex had tried to explain that the name was a joke, but his mother-in-law could not be persuaded otherwise and told him it was *he* who did not understand. The name had stuck.

Galore purred and meowed.

'Okay, hungry, heh?' He scratched her head and she reared up against his palm, purring loudly, wanting more.

Alex went back into the kitchen and Galore followed. He found her bowl and poured some dry cat food into it. He patted her again and talked to her, then grabbed the bag he had dropped by the front door and left the apartment.

Jun listened to Alex leave the bedroom and talk to Galore while he fed her. She lay still and listened to Alex bend down and give Galore a pat, then heard the cascade of cat biscuits shaken out of the box hit the plastic bowl.

She turned on her side and closed her eyes. She felt guilty for not wanting to listen to him describe his working life, deliberately not asking him about it, and she also knew that he tried to avoid bringing it into their home, but she was his wife and he should be able to talk to her when something bad happened. She had been warned that there would be such difficult times, but had not understood that they would be relentless to the point of suffocation. Every evening she could read on his face how the day had gone. She knew she should ask him about it but was often too fearful of the truth.

Her father had taken her aside only two days before their wedding in Beijing, in a brief moment when the two of them were alone – he had taken the afternoon off work to do some shopping with her and then later have the banquet tasting. They had arranged to meet her mother outside the main entrance to the brand-new Grand Hyatt Hotel at the corner of Tiananmen Square, and were waiting for her car to pull up, as she'd insisted they all go in together.

'Are you sure you want to do this?' he had started bluntly. 'Alex is a strong-minded and purposeful young man. Could be anything he wants to be. But there's no future in joining the police. It pays nothing and it's very dangerous. This is not the life I dreamed of for you.'

She could feel him looking at her but could not raise her eyes.

'If you want me to cancel the wedding then I'll support you,' he continued. 'Even if we lose all the money we spent on renting the ballroom here.' He nodded to the hotel behind him.

'No, I want to be his wife, the mother of his children,' she had told her father.

She breathed out and heard the cat scratching at the bedroom door. She leaned over to the other side of the bed and stretched out to pull open the door for the animal to slide her head and body through and then insinuate herself on to the bed.

Galore curled up on Jun's stomach and made herself comfortable there. Within minutes they were both asleep.

It was nearly 8.45 a.m. when Alex seated himself behind the metal table bolted to the floor in Interview Room 7. The desk and room were empty save for a microphone positioned directly in front of him. He waited. The room was small and windowless and the weak fluorescent strip lights barely lit the corners of the ceiling. It was the interview room used specifically by Internal Affairs.

The door finally opened at 9.25 a.m. and a tall thin man entered; Alex estimated he was probably in his early fifties. The man sat down, produced another microphone and a tape recorder from his pocket, and began to speak.

'Did you wait long?' he said as he squared his file in front of him and uncapped his pen, which he placed on top. 'Well, time for you to gather your thoughts. And your story, heh? I hope you didn't get dressed up for me.' His tone was sarcastic. Alex looked at his interviewer expressionlessly.

'Well, let's begin. This is the interview of Senior Inspector Alex Soong by Internal Affairs Officer Leonard Mak further to the killing, and possible murder, of Chow Yung Kwok by Senior Inspector Soong at around three forty-three, seventeenth August Twenty Seventeen.' He looked up at Alex. 'Soong, please will you recount the events that led up to the shooting of Mr Chow?'

Mak leaned forward, rocking on his elbows. Alex noticed that his glasses had several oily smudges on the lenses. He had large bags under his narrow eyes, and his skin was pale and waxy. It appeared that the interview would be in Cantonese. Alex's grasp of the dialect was functional but poor compared with his native Beijing Mandarin or his English, but he would manage as he had done with Chow.

He spoke softly and calmly. 'I had learned that Chow was to meet his accountant early in the morning if the typhoon signal was raised to 8, which it had been. A team . . .'

Mak cut him off.

'How had you learned this?'

'Through a contact.'

'Who?'

'A source.'

'Name?' Mak demanded

'I don't think so,' Alex said wryly.

'It is not a good idea to withhold information from me.'

'I'm afraid that any identification of my source would prejudice both this case and others.'

'I could get an order requiring you to disclose,' Mak warned.

Alex shrugged. 'Up to you,' he continued, and went on to detail how he had conducted the operation until, on his orders, De Suza had shot off the lock on the inner door.

'After firing several shots Chow went into the second room and locked the door. I approached it and told him to come out. He replied he wanted a helicopter to Macao as he had hostages he was willing to shoot.'

'It was at that point, at the mention of the hostages, you impulsively shot the lock out?' the interviewer interrupted again.

'It wasn't impulsive,' Alex shot back bluntly.

'So you don't think it was a foolish move?'

'No. He wasn't expecting it, and once done, the door swung open freely. I saw Chow standing in the corner of the room behind a desk covered in papers and cash. He was carrying a little girl of about seven years old in his left arm and a cheap snubnose in his right hand. The girl's father sat behind the desk to Chow's right.'

'This man is the accountant, a key witness to the fraud case you are investigating? And perhaps many other cases?' Mak asked.

'He is a witness, yes, but it was Chow we really wanted. I warned him he should release the other two immediately. At this point he had the gun to the child's head. Chow replied that he wasn't going to give up his hostages and so I suggested he swap me for her.'

'Do you believe that was smart? Allowing yourself, a senior inspector, to be taken hostage?' Mak asked condescendingly.

'Yes. It would have saved the child right then.'

Mak switched off the recorder.

'Are you a God-fearing man, Senior Inspector Soong?' he asked.

The room was getting warm and the IA officer took off his jacket, revealing large patches of sweat under his armpits.

'Yes.'

'Why is that? You are a Communist, from a family line of high-ranking Party academics. For all your Western manners and your pretty wife, you are really a hard-grinding cog in the State machine. I understand you can be one of the hardest cogs, when you choose to be. Does she know that? Does your wife know what you're really like?'

'Yes.'

'Really?'

'Yes.' Alex paused momentarily. 'Of course she does. She knows what I do and what I've done.'

'You act as if you answer to no one. Free from the laws of heaven and earth. I think your marriage, like much of your personal life, is for convenience only, something you arranged only to fool us. Your father was discovered dead in a car accident outside the border town of Ruili, near Burma, and you wanted the incident and your own father investigated posthumously. Is nothing sacred to you?' He cleared his throat, and then continued. 'Traditional Chinese filial piety, family respect, obviously can't matter much to you if you were willing to have your own father's name dragged into the dirt by having him the subject of an investigation.'

'I am going to assume that your mentioning my father's case was a mistake,' Alex said quietly. 'I don't know much about any god but I've seen enough to know that mankind is not the measure of all things. The life of an innocent child is worth more than the life of a thirty-three-year-old cog. The machine is large, it will keep running. I requested an investigation into my father's death because I could. I could not request an investigation into any other aspect of the incident. Does this have anything to do with Chow?'

'I'll decide what is to be included in this interview.'

He switched the recorder on again, and they went through the sequence of events in the stand-off, Chow's wounding of the accountant and threat to kill the child.

'And then you shot him in the head. One shot,' Mak said. 'If you had missed, you could have killed her. Unfortunately for us, and fortunately for you, there are no witnesses to this. The little girl had her eyes shut and the father was unconscious. All I have learned is what you told your team,' he finished in a doubtful tone.

'There was just the desk between Chow and myself, a very short distance. He was nervous and unsure of himself.'

'And you weren't nervous? It sounds to me like you were reckless.'

'No. I was nervous but in control of myself.'

'So there was no other option but to shoot him?'

'Yes. I gave Chow every option to stop and surrender his weapon. Ultimately I had no choice but to shoot him. Remember, he had just shot the father.'

There was a silence as Mak scribbled some notes.

'And how do you feel now?' he asked sarcastically.

'Tired but otherwise fine,' Alex replied curtly. Mak smiled and nodded. Alex kept calm. 'Sometimes there are very difficult situations when protecting one life means possibly having to take another. It is the worst decision for a policeman to face.'

The interviewer stopped smiling.

'I will be speaking to your Captain later today. He will tell you whether you will be suspended for further investigation. You may go – for now.'

It was 10.45 a.m. Alex took the three flights of stairs down the three floors from the interview room to street level to catch a taxi. He had only forty minutes to get to Hong Kong University, where he was scheduled to receive the award.

The main police station was based at the convergence of Central and Wan Chai – the two main districts of Hong Kong Island's harbour front, and the site of the worst traffic and congestion. Alex stood at the taxi stand and used the time to consider what he would say when he accepted the award. Usually he stuck to stories about his grandfather rather than his father: they were such different men that it was difficult for Alex to identify anything they'd had in common. One was a fighter and an artist who had helped to usher in the Communist revolution of 1949, the other a technocrat and academic, architect of the economic revolution of the 1980s. Alex decided to keep it simple and just talk of the greatness of revolution and the hard work of the people.

The taxi turned on to the short highway of Hennessy Road that had once provided a clear view of the harbour but was now walled in by a huge landscraper built on a newly reclaimed site. This mile-long marble-fronted shopping mall, complete with rooftop gardens and precincts, its building started two years before the financial crash, had fallen behind schedule and been finished as the crash deepened. It had been designed to be the pride of Hong Kong but now contained only a few open shops. Many of the vacant premises, which were mostly boarded up, were used by the homeless; the precincts and gardens had fallen into disrepair.

The taxi continued through the still-crowded narrow streets of Central district, which was walled by towering modern glass skyscrapers, reaching up seventy to eighty floors, and big luxury shopping malls like Landmark and Prince's Building, relics of the better times.

The city had been in slow decline since its zenith in early 2013 but, above Central, Hong Kong still had its super-wealthy living on the luxury Peak area, and in Mid-Levels – the belt of affluent housing running round the mountain just below the Peak. The inhabitants there were simply able to ride out the stagnation as their peers the world over had done. Every day the expensive cars would still purr down the main road, Garden Road from these mountain areas, passing Citibank Tower and Li Ka-shing's huge glassy Cheung Kong Center, to their underground parking space in Central. Many foreigners had been sent home, but it was still necessary to retain the services of a good number, as the tycoons and super-rich from the mainland still relied on them for certain essential management and technical skills.

After their argument, Alex knew Jun would not come to the university, but he decided to call her, hoping she might surprise him by agreeing. On his first attempt her phone was engaged and on the second it just rang to voicemail.

'Jun, please can you tell me whether you'll be coming for lunch at the university?' Alex tried not to sound too tired and frustrated. 'It would be nice if you did.'

He hung up and leaned back in the taxi seat. He closed his eyes for a second but his phone rang and jolted him back to attention.

'Hi, I can't come.' Jun's voice was flat and unapologetic. Alex recalled how playful it used to be when they spoke on the phone at the start of their relationship. Now there were fewer and fewer moments when Jun sounded loving and carefree.

'Is everything all right?' He knew she simply did not want to join him.

'Yes, I'm fine. I just don't feel like coming,' she said, without feeling the need to apologize. 'I told you this morning, it's a waste of time. The food is always bad, the people are boring . . . Just send them my love and I'll see you tonight.'

'I don't think they're interested in your love,' he replied sharply.

'Then fine, tell them nothing. See you later.' She hung up.

The taxi pulled into the university campus. He walked quickly from the taxi rank to the university's main entrance, which was plain and unassuming compared with the huge Soviet-style university buildings in mainland China. The campus held a mixture of buildings built first by the British and then by a variety of local donors.

He walked up some narrow stairs to an old stone and red-brick colonial building that served as the original university hall but that had been retained, complete with its smooth round pillar columns and heavy stone balustrades, to serve as a porch and atrium to the modern facility.

A man who was most likely Professor Lin, Dean of the History Faculty, was standing under the stone archway that framed the entrance. He was rubbing his hands together and clearly waiting for someone who was already late. He was so distracted that he only saw Alex when he was standing directly in front of him.

'Hello! Hello, Inspector, thank you so much . . . thank you so much for coming. But we are a little late and we should go,' he babbled in Mandarin.

'I'm sorry. Also my wife cannot make it. Apologies, but she sends her love,' Alex said with a degree of sarcasm.

'Oh, that is nice. Now we must go,' the Professor muttered urgently. 'Please follow me.'

He led Alex into the building and they turned left around a colonnade with a pleasant square in the centre. 'Yes, we must go quickly. I really admired your grandfather. A great man. Yes, a good man. Please follow me,' he continued.

They walked until they reached a formal gathering of people sipping wine or tea. Professor Lin immediately guided Alex to a small stage that the university had set up. He could see down the slope to a Starbucks below. Students were disappearing into the coffee shop. They clutched a Chinese textbook in one hand and a latte in the other. For a child growing up in the early and mid-Nineties, a cup of coffee was always considered for Westerners' consumption alone, and was available only in certain restaurants, McDonald's or hotels.

Lin got up on the stage next to him and squinted at the microphone. The small crowd before them was made up mostly of press and faculty members.

'Senior Inspector Soong Alex, we are most grateful to you for taking the time from your daily duties with the Hong Kong Police Force to join us today. It is a shame your wife could not be here also,' the Professor announced in Mandarin.

In reply, Alex gave a half-smile and a respectful slow nod, a move he had watched his father execute many times in the same circumstances. It was a gesture he had copied partly because he felt a closeness to his father whenever he repeated it, but also because it was deferential without being obsequious.

'Last year marked sixty-eight years since a group of passionate but poorly equipped revolutionaries established a new China. One of their number was Soong Zhan, Soong Alex's grandfather, a man who continued to serve the country and its people in a variety of government posts for the rest of his life.

'He was a man who never considered the cost of service. His son, Soong Xian Li, Soong Alex's father, helped lead the country as a senior industrial and finance adviser, loyally serving the people with equal generosity and dedication. Alex has continued their work. After graduating in engineering from NYU, he entered the police force, concentrating on corruption in the mainland government.'

Hong Kong people had always seen themselves as Hong Kongers first, not Chinese, and it was only since the global meltdown that they had begun to search for unity with the mainland. Alex sensed that Professor Lin was wrapping up his introduction.

'He has, as I'm sure you know, worked on some very high-profile cases, some leading to the execution of prominent officials . . .'

Until this point, the crowd had been fairly quiet, if starting to grow distracted as the speech wore on. The word 'execution' recaptured their attention.

As Alex got up on stage and positioned himself in front of his microphone, he noticed in the background several people who did not fit the usual description of attendees at these gatherings. Most obvious were four people in T-shirts and jeans worn with black Chinese slippers, but there was also a tall dignified older man wearing sunglasses and a dark, expensive-looking suit. His hair was thick and long at the back, dropping beneath the collar and curling up below his ears. The glasses were thin-framed, round and made of tortoiseshell, and he stood with arms folded, straight-backed and alone, slightly away from the rest of the crowd, singling himself out for attention. He was tall, perhaps 1.85 metres, with a broad and powerful physique. The people in T-shirts started chanting against inequalities in pay and welfare.

'Now let us have none of this. We need to show proper respect . . .' Lin pleaded.

Alex stepped in. 'Professor, if I may?'

Lin gladly conceded. Alex started speaking, loud and direct, throwing his voice to the back of the crowd as a policeman learns to do.

'Professor, it is an honour to be invited here today and to receive this award. My grandfather and father loved their country and wanted it to develop a strong voice in the international community. Even though the rest of the world is struggling and some Chinese are living in hardship, what they and their comrades built has held firm and ultimately brought Europe back from the brink of disaster. We have supported people in many parts of the world. Is that not greatness? We are respected because we have played our part.

'Thank you very much for this award,' he finished. 'My grandfather and father would be very proud.'

There was applause and Alex shook the Professor's hand. The few press photographers moved in closer and took photos, enough to satisfy the university's PR efforts.

They were interrupted by the arrival of a young woman.

'Professor Lin, thank you very much for inviting me, it was most kind of you.'

The Professor turned to look at the new arrival, and blushed. The woman was not glamorous but she was pretty, with an elfin face that was instantly striking. Her hair was pulled back into a rough ponytail from which strands escaped around her delicate ears and high forehead. She did not have particularly full lips but they formed a perfect little bow, and for a moment, Alex was captivated.

'So you are the son of the man every Chinese historian credits with burning all the books?'

'I'm sorry?' he said.

'Your father was the great *reformer* who started the book-burning during the Cultural Revolution, right?'

'No. He certainly did some things he later admitted he would undo, given the chance, but he didn't start the book-burning.' Alex was starting to feel a mixture of annoyance at this woman's attitude and embarrassment at this very public conversation about his father, but he still could not stop himself from meeting her lively, enquiring gaze.

'I'm only joking,' she teased. 'But you weren't sure, were you? That is what's so terrifying about our country's history. You collect an award for your father's and grandfather's work, but so many records are lost, so many ideas and events confused in such a long history, that you can never be entirely sure what work they did. Perhaps no Chinese is certain who they really are. We have all lost or concealed our true identities, don't you agree? Who exactly are the Chinese people?'

Professor Lin intervened. 'Professor Yi, you must not tease our honoured guest. Inspector Soong, Professor Yi comes from Harvard University, and specializes in Chinese history and anthropology at the turn of the twentieth century: the end of the imperial regime, the foreign invasion . . . all those chaotic events. Shall we walk to lunch together?'

'Actually, Professor Lin, I just came to tell you I cannot make lunch,' she said politely, then switched to English. 'Inspector Soong, it was a pleasure to meet you. Perhaps we can have a coffee one day and talk about those missing books your family owes us all?' She smiled. 'Actually I met your father. I interviewed him several times for a paper I worked on as a student. Most impressive – a very sharp mind. And he seemed very proud of you.'

Alex was surprised and Yi noticed this.

'You didn't know? Well, he only said a couple of things about you. One was that you were brighter than him and his father, as you knew the difference between right and wrong and were not afraid of the consequences of following your own vision. Is that true?' She paused again. 'I'm teasing again. Sorry.' She laughed at her own temerity.

'Well, as you say, he was very sharp. He must have been right.' Alex immediately wished he could retract the last comment, which made him sound boastful, but Yi was already departing.

The two men were left staring after her. She was wearing a simple black halterneck dress that finished halfway up her thighs, and on her feet a new pair of blue-striped Adidas Superstar 2 shell tops. Alex looked at the shoes and laughed to himself. He half wished he might meet her again.

Professor Lin introduced the Chancellor of the university, who led them through a back veranda off the garden terrace into the university's old staff dining room. Colonial in style, it had oak-panelled walls and a stucco ceiling. There were four long oak refectory tables with settings for ten around each. Alex noticed that the man in the suit and sunglasses was still with them, and was seating himself at a table occupied by journalists. Alex had learned from experience that such events took less time if the guest of honour took the lead, so he addressed the gathering briefly before sitting down.

'Professor Lin, thank you very much for today's ceremony. My grandfather and father would have been most honoured by this recognition of the work they undertook.'

'Inspector Soong, you are very modest. Your family's work is famous, as is your own,' Professor Lin responded. 'I would like to say more, but in this politically sensitive environment no speech or award can afford to appear too nationalist in tone. We Chinese, as the new superpower, now have to be very careful what we say.' The diners laughed in agreement. 'But there is nothing wrong with loving your country and serving it,' the Professor said boldly.

'Indeed! We should be proud,' shouted the man in the sunglasses and suit. 'We're no longer dogs! Yet we have eaten their debt like the opium we were fed by the British one hundred and fifty years ago.'

Amid murmurs of agreement Alex sat down and took a sip of water. His mobile vibrated. He pulled it from his inside pocket.

'I'm sorry but I must look at this.'

Citibank Tower immediately, he read. A message from De Suza.

Alex stood up. 'Apologies but I have to go. Police business.'

'Duty must come first, heh, Inspector Soong? We must all do what is necessary,' the man in the suit called out to him.

'Inspector Soong? Inspector Soong?' The same man's voice caught Alex again before he made it to the door. 'Please just answer me one question I have from your short but illuminating speech.'

Alex stopped and turned to face him. 'Yes?'

'Earlier you said that what has been built, the new China, has held firm. Helped the world, saving Europe. Do you think that is true? We are a country that has taken on so much debt, European debt and American debt, to help keep these countries with huge deficits alive. We have eaten it like the opium we were fed a hundred and fifty years ago to pay for Britain's huge deficits.' He paused and looked hard at Alex. 'Is that respect? Haven't we just been the fools again? Can you honestly say we stand firm?'

'I really must go, but I believe we do stand firm. We must play our role as a global power and I believe it's our duty. Anyway I'm a policeman and will leave the review of Chinese history to others who are much more qualified, such as Professor Lin.' Alex had continued to stand by the door and looked at Professor Lin for his intervention, who thankfully obliged.

'Yes, let me take that question,' the Professor intervened.

Alex's phone began to ring and he moved swiftly out of the door.

'What's going on?'

'It's pretty grim. Two Methodist ministers were shot on their way to get a coffee in Citibank Tower. Where are you?'

'Just leaving the university. I should be there in about fifteen minutes.'

'Okay, meet us at the entrance to the Tower.'

The taxi skirted along Robinson Road – one of a number of roads running across the city at various levels up the main mountain on the northern coast of Hong Kong Island. The city had spread from a central point where the British had first landed and built their docks. The berths had long gone and that initial landing site, eventually named simply Central, was now the location of the administrative, government and finance district. Two main roads, one down, Garden Road, and one up, Cotton Tree Drive, formed a spine that connected Central to the Peak residential area on the mountain above. Roads fanned out from these two main carriageways and extended three miles either side through the city across the northern coast.

The university campus was in the western part of Mid-Levels. Alex headed towards the Governor's House, Central district's highest point. The quaint white fort, now home to the Chief Executive since the handover twenty years ago, sat immediately above the other government buildings and law courts. Once strategically positioned to overlook the whole harbour and across to Kowloon, now they were forever nestled behind giant office towers stretching to the seafront and tall apartment blocks extending up to the Peak.

Alex knew there would be chaos at the scene, since his colleagues would have closed Garden Road to traffic. From the description De Suza provided, he guessed the victims had been caught on the pedestrian walkway that straddled the road and connected the law courts, the government buildings and St John's Cathedral to Citibank Tower and the Bank of China – two huge columns of office space on a patch of land between the two main roads.

Arriving at the scene, he explained who he was to the officers at the cordon and walked down the empty main road and underneath the walkway. As he did so he saw people surging out of the various huge office blocks. They would be on mobile devices already, sending waves of comments and photos via Bloomberg, Facebook, Twitter. For the moment the road was traffic-free. Alex looked up it to Mid-Levels and the thousands of apartments above. He scrutinized the zone beneath the bridge and saw nothing unusual. Finally he scanned his eyes in a 180-degree arc, taking in the buildings towering above him. Alex walked over to the entrance to Citibank Tower. When he reached it he realized a few journalists from the lunch had followed him and were melting into the media circus already encamped behind the tape marking off the Citibank side of the crime scene.

De Suza appeared at the top of the escalators leading to the podium level of the Tower and to the walkway.

'They're up here!' he shouted in English.

Alex worked his way through the crowd and took the escalator.

The first stretch of the walkway continued for about ten metres, which took it about a third of the way across the road below, before jinking leftward for twenty metres more, arriving then at the entrance to a small rock garden beyond which they could see the lawn surrounding the Cathedral and its straggle of low-level office buildings.

The two men lay in the middle of the second stretch, both of them dressed in clerical black with white collars. Blood had pooled around the bodies before following the camber of the bridge to the drains at the sides. There was brain matter splashed on the glass wall of the walkway about a metre from the nearest man.

Alex stood looking over at them while De Suza walked on, looking over the side of the walkway to the empty four-lane highway below.

'This is insane,' Alex said quietly. 'A fucking mess.'

'Yes, someone out there is incredibly angry about something. Better get on with it. We won't be able to keep Garden Road closed for long. Hope you had a good lunch?'

'Never got to it – just as well. *Gweilo* meal.' Alex didn't look up as he concentrated on the victims.

'Probably chicken,' De Suza quipped.

'Probably.' Alex raised an eyebrow. 'So what have we got?'

'First, see this?' De Suza pointed left to a bullet embedded in the tiled floor. 'Must be a six-hundred-calibre round. We don't see these often, if ever. Sniper slugs. High-velocity, probably fired from military hardware. This is way beyond the usual tools of the trade in this city.'

Alex looked down at the large metal round, then up at his partner.

'Let's walk through this before Forensics arrive,' he suggested.

'There's not much else to go on at the moment, but I have

spoken briefly to an administrator at the Cathedral and she said that for about the last month, most days at about one-thirty, these two have walked across here after lunch to Pacific Coffee, in the basement of Citibank Tower. Basically the same walk at the same time every day.

'As we already said,' he pointed to the round embedded in the concrete, 'this is a high-velocity round from a weapon with a range of up to two miles. Which widens the search area considerably.'

'But from an enclosed area like this there *are* no two miles,' Alex said thoughtfully, glancing round in front of them as he spoke. 'That would put the shooter in the harbour, or perhaps just the other side of it in Tsim Sha Tsui. We're surrounded by high-rise buildings here. US Embassy, law courts, Cheung Kong Center, Citibank Tower, Bank of China, the previous office of the Independent Commission Against Corruption, Bank of America Tower, Hutchison building.'

Alex bent closer to the bodies. 'If, as it seems, the two men walked side-by-side across the bridge from the Cathedral to the Citibank Tower, the one walking on the harbour side was hit first, in the side of the head. And here, the brain matter from the other side of his skull where the bullet exited has been thrown against his colleague's shoulder and back, so he was still standing. The bullet came from the direction of the sea, on their left as they crossed, and hit him square in the temple, cheek or ear area, so the shooter was somewhere between here and the harbour front.'

Alex moved to examine the next body. De Suza scribbled in his notebook.

'His colleague seems to have received the next shot full in the face. Perhaps he reacted and looked round at his friend, and as he did so the second shot caught him. If that's how it was then again it indicates the shooter was over there.' Alex nodded again in the direction of the road down to the harbour's edge.

'Since the economy crashed, there are so many empty offices and hotel suites available, plus all the stairwells and car parks – though most of those are too enclosed for a sniper to operate from. I suspect there are hundreds of possible firing positions but probably only a few really viable spaces to take those shots.'

He stood up and moved back to join De Suza. 'Okay, what can you tell me about these gentlemen?'

'Just two Chinese Methodist ministers. Both appointed here recently,' De Suza reported. 'I'm awaiting further details.'

They looked at the crowd below, which had grown considerably since Alex had started conducting a preliminary review. People were not yet overflowing into the road but were already lining the driveways and car parks of the nearby buildings.

'Did these two come to Hong Kong from the same place? Were they known to each other before?' Alex enquired.

'I have no further details, but we'll find out. And what about all those spectators?' De Suza nodded in the direction of the road below. 'We can't treat them all as suspects, but some could be witnesses. An office guy flips out and vents it on the Church, maybe?'

Alex shrugged. 'It's always a possibility. People here have been steadily losing jobs. It could be that someone just decided to find someone to take the blame. If we consider the onlookers below to be possible witnesses, somebody is going to have the miserable task of interviewing all those people.'

'Let's hope it's not us,' De Suza responded. 'We're not even officially appointed to this case. I just happened to be at the ATM at the base of the Tower when I heard the shots.'

Just then Alex's phone rang.

'Sir? . . . Yes, that's right . . . I've been here for fifteen minutes and Inspector De Suza for thirty . . .'

As he talked the Forensics team entered the walkway from the Cathedral end. He watched them approach, hefting their bags of equipment.

'Forensics have just arrived . . . Look, there are thousands, possibly tens of thousands, of people already here. Can we get the patrol officers to start taking names and details? It looks like a sniper operation. Perhaps we can approach some of the buildings, talk to security there. See if anyone saw anything.'

De Suza watched him nod to the unheard reply and then Alex looked up and raised his eyebrows in confirmation. De Suza put his thumb up and hurried back towards Citibank Tower and the escalators. Alex stood over the bodies, watching the technicians set up.

'How long will it take you to create a first-impression report on this?' he asked.

'Probably six or seven hours. We'll let you know when we're done,' the lead man replied.

Still on the phone, Alex continued to speak. 'They say seven hours for a first report. Look, there's another thing . . .' He moved away from the bodies and Forensics team and walked down towards the Citibank Tower. 'I'm no architect but most, if not all, the big buildings round here have a glass skin. You can't open the windows. So a sniper has to have acted from the top of one. That, or else from one of the few low-rise buildings at the far end of the road . . .'

He listened for a moment.

'All right. The officers on the ground will be asking witnesses to come forward . . . Yes, sir, we're on it.'

From above he watched people register what was happening and start to head back into the buildings so as to avoid giving a statement. Looking up at the glassy towers surrounding him, he could see the faint outline of office workers gathered by many of the thick darkened windows.

De Suza rejoined him.

'Man, the Hong Kong press are a pain!' he was grumbling.

'All those spectators at the windows . . . the killer could be any one of them.' Alex pointed his finger across the horizon.

'Who would want to kill two Chinese Methodists . . . Falun Gong?' De Suza half-joked. 'They're always hanging round outside the law courts next to the Cathedral. Maybe they've had enough of being ignored by people here.'

'I doubt it. Falun Gong are finished as a threat, if they ever were. Maybe these ministers were involved in something political.' Alex breathed in and looked up to the sky. It was still dark from the morning typhoon. 'Two ministers shot at range in Central on this walkway is so specific. Someone went to a great deal of trouble.'

'It's hardly the work of some angry banker with a gun club membership,' De Suza said wryly. 'Do you think they were gay and someone was blackmailing them and it went wrong?' he suggested half-jokingly. 'Maybe they met in seminary and finally arranged to work in the same city and church?'

'Even if they were, high-velocity weapons to kill two gay ministers is extreme. This seems more like an execution.'

They walked back up the walkway and rejoined the small Forensics team. The senior investigator, known as Pike, stood at the Cathedral end, near the entrance to the gardens.

'Anything new?' De Suza asked hopefully.

Pike, a small balding man with a prominent belly, was finishing speaking to one of his team, one hand scrabbling violently in his pockets as he spoke while the other held a notepad. He was in his early sixties but disliked the role of patriarch and preferred to be on the ground, working with his team. He continued searching his pockets in vain and, to end his torment, De Suza offered him a pen, which he took. He put up his thumb in thanks then raised an index finger to signal he'd be with them in a minute.

De Suza glanced impatiently in the direction of the Cathedral.

'Behind you!' he suddenly shouted.

Alex turned round to find an elderly Chinese woman standing right in front of him and reaching for the lapels of his jacket. Her face was twisted with fury. She launched herself at him and he took a step back to steady his footing. He quickly regained his balance and manoeuvred himself between her and the bodies.

'How could you have let this happen? These were good men. *Aiya! Ai!*' She was crying hard and using her grip on his jacket to pull herself up into Alex's face.

De Suza took up position behind his friend so that her view of the bodies was completely blocked. He steered them both away from the crime scene and towards the Cathedral.

'Madam, let's talk in the garden behind you,' Alex suggested politely, continuing to fix his eyes on hers. 'Just behind you.' He gently detached her hands from his jacket and turned her round. She followed his lead and they moved through the rock garden and on to the lawn by the Cathedral.

She was dressed very plainly, her hair put up in a neat bun. She continued into the Cathedral and sat down in the nearest pew. Alex and De Suza sat in the one in front and turned as best they could to face her.

'Madam, we are doing what we can,' Alex told her. 'The investigation has just begun. You must be patient. Please can you tell me how you knew these men?'

Her head dropped and she gripped her hands together in her lap. Alex reached over and pressed his own hand over them. He could feel that her skin was rough and her fingers hard and bony. These were hard-working hands. The woman started to weep. Alex looked up at De Suza and gestured for him to pass her his handkerchief. De Suza patted himself down and pulled out a freshly ironed square. He offered it to the old woman and she wiped her eyes.

'They were good men,' she repeated. 'I helped them with the Christian counselling group they ran. We worked with the poor, the lonely, addicts, and people who just wanted to talk. *Ai*, it's not right! How could God let this happen?'

'I understand they were newcomers here?' De Suza asked.

She looked at him and nodded. 'Yes, they only started last month. We had a vacancy for a while, which Reverend Fung filled, and then suddenly another minister passed away in his sleep and Reverend Lu filled that position. I worked with their predecessors and had just started helping them.'

Alex knew he would remain a central figure in this woman's recollection of this terrible day, and chose to be sympathetic and respectful to her, not merely official.

'Auntie, I am very sorry for your loss.' He paused to see her reaction but she looked to him, waiting for his lead. She did not seem to have another objective. 'Please take your time. We'll sit here with you a little longer. I presume it's okay for us to be here, or should we ask permission from the Dean?'

Alex looked up into the elegantly vaulted ceiling and then turned to the altar.

'You're not a Christian, are you, young man?' the lady asked Alex.

'No, Auntie, I'm of no religion at all.'

'And you?' She looked at De Suza.

'I was raised as a Catholic, ma'am.'

'I am from mainland China. My parents were Christians, as were my grandparents. In fact, they suffered greatly for their beliefs at the hands of ignorant Boxers and Manchurians.'

'It's an overlooked time in our history,' De Suza agreed.

'That's because it's difficult for us to acknowledge these things.'

She tapped her foot a little to emphasize her point, and gripped the back of their pew tightly.

'Ma'am, can you tell us any more about the two gentlemen?' De Suza asked in Mandarin.

'Not much. Both of them were married. Reverend Lu and his English wife are staying in temporary accommodation at the university on Conduit Road. I know they had worked in Africa for a while and were looking for something less complicated, so he took the post here. He was a quiet man but very kind. Reverend Fung had worked in Australia and studied in England. I think he was at Cambridge. Funny, he was born here but moved to England when he was very young. He's like a *gweilo* but he's Chinese really. Very smart and clear-headed, though. He and his wife have an apartment across the island in Stanley. His wife's Australian. I have all the numbers you'll need in my office. I'll fetch them in a minute. Both ladies are so nice . . .' Her eyes clouded over for a second and then refocused on Alex. 'Both men are native Hong Kongers, but I don't think either has any family left here, though I could be wrong.'

They escorted her outside and watched her return to her office in the admin block to fetch the phone numbers. They could see that the traffic had started to flow again. A hundred years ago, the Cathedral would have seemed like a huge building on its island of grass. Now, it was dwarfed by the giants of finance surrounding it, overshadowing it into virtual insignificance. Yet someone had bothered to notice this place, and the work and routines of its dedicated occupants.

The old woman rejoined them in front of the Cathedral doors.

'We would like to move their bodies as soon as we can.'

At the word 'bodies', the old lady turned involuntarily to look towards the scene of the killings. Alex reached out and took her hand. She looked back at him.

'Thank you very much for all the information,' he said, shaking the piece of paper she had given him, 'it is all helpful to us.'

'Thank you for sitting with me, officers. You were very kind.' She looked up at De Suza. 'I'll wash your handkerchief and send it back.'

'Here's my card,' De Suza told her. 'If you think of anything else about Reverend Lu and Reverend Fung that you think may be significant, please let me know.'

The crowds of office workers had started to disperse, no doubt because of the growing possibility of being interviewed by the police, but there was still a watchful horde of press and TV crews, plus the usual number of popular news bloggers and threaders.

Alex breathed in as they approached the mob and let his burly partner lead. De Suza ploughed through, clearing the way. Alex's mobile rang.

'Where the hell are you?' The Captain usually spoke in very local Hong Kong Cantonese, with all its subtleties and idioms that Alex, along with the rest of China, could barely understand. Alex, as he usually did, replied in English.

'I'm still at Citibank Tower.'

'I thought you were coming straight back?'

'I didn't say so, sir. You must have misunderstood me.'

'Don't argue! You're always arguing, Soong. Any new developments at the crime scene?'

'I'm in a crowd of journalists, can I call you back?'

'What? No! I might not hear from you for hours. Get out of the crowd now,' the Captain barked.

Alex moved into the area that had been taped off by the police. He saw De Suza head for a transport van and then glance back at him. Alex shrugged and pointed to the phone. De Suza laughed, holding his fingers to his head like a gun, then waved and got into the van.

'Sir, we have just been speaking with a lady who worked with both the victims at St John's Cathedral,' Alex reported. 'She gave us quite a lot of information and, while it still needs verifying, what came across strongly was that the two men were not connected in any but the obvious way. Both of them were Hong Kong Chinese originally, though one was largely raised in England. The other had recently returned here too after spending years in Africa. Both of them were married to *gweipors*, one Australian and one English. There doesn't look to be any obvious or immediate reason why they were killed in such a violent manner.'

'So we've barely made any progress, is that it? Anything else?' The Captain was still refusing to switch to English.

Alex puffed out his cheeks and sighed. De Suza and the van were driving off. Media were still arriving and the van crawled through the oncoming crowd to reach the filter lane from the Citibank Tower complex into Garden Road. Alex watched De Suza put his hand on the driver's shoulder and give it a friendly shake. Alex smiled to see his friend's display of warmth. He'd lifted the gloom of this city for Alex and Jun when they first arrived, making it feel like the home they had up until then failed to find on their own.

'Soong?' the Captain queried. 'Are you daydreaming?'

'Just going over the situation in my mind. Obviously we do need to examine the victims' lives more closely . . . and I've asked De Suza to follow that up. But it looks like they were executed by an exceptional marksman. Someone who was highly trained and had access to professional weapons. It could be religious in motivation, but I don't think so.'

'Anything else?'

'Yes, though this is just a suggestion. They were killed by shots to the face, and only two of them, one each . . . The shooter risked missing them completely by choosing head shots over body shots. It could be the sign of a strong personal element to the case.'

'Interesting. But, you know, this type of enquiry isn't why you were brought here from Beijing. Properly speaking I should take you off it immediately. But keep it for now. Report in person later.' The Captain hung up.

Alex put his phone in his pocket and surveyed the area. The media would keep arriving until word got out that the bodies had been removed. He watched them stand around talking to each other, sharing opinions and gossip. As they became bored of waiting for a police briefing they would speak about anything else, generating news from whatever was at hand. It was a job, and the truth alone was not enough to pay the bills. He descended the steps and approached the tape. As he did so people saw him coming and gathered to meet him.

'Hey, *Dai Lok*, what news have you got?' one scruffy individual yelled from the back.

'What's going on? Two ministers dead? Is this a holy war?' another voice called.

A short sweaty man in a yellow press vest and carrying a broadcast-quality camera stood in front of Alex and blocked his path.

'What about the killing of Chow this morning? What's your role now in Hong Kong? Here just to persecute us?' the reporter demanded aggressively. Alex looked down at the man, who was suddenly forced much closer by the press of the crowd behind. 'We want to know! This morning you shot and killed a fraudster, then received an award at lunch . . . and now you are here. Does adventure follow you or you it?'

Beads of sweat were running down the hard-talking man's forehead. He adjusted the camera strap and wiped his clammy forehead with one sleeve. A tall female TV reporter loomed into view behind the man's shoulder. While Alex concentrated on her the sweaty man looked round, following his line of sight.

'And a lady's man too, I see. Should we add that to the list?'

Laughter broke out around them. The Hong Kong press were amiable enough when it suited them.

'There was a tasty female academic at the *gweilo* lunch today,' someone added.

The short guy started up again. 'Come on, Soong. Give us a statement. Relax, Big Six. Now tell us, are you here to treat us like dogs?' the reporter smiled cheekily, though he was muscular enough to say what he liked.

This was a reference to Professor Kong Qingdong, the outspoken academic who a few years ago had said that Hong Kong people behaved like the dogs of the British imperialists. Alex thought it an unhelpful thing to say – and it reminded him of another comment he had heard earlier in the day. He looked around him, saw phones, digital cameras, recorders and tablets held up to record his response, and chuckled genially with the reporter.

'All right, all right. I do have a busy life, which I thank my father and grandfather for. And I'm very grateful for my job, which I have been given by the people of Hong Kong. But I'm not here – what did you write on your blog, Ah Cheuk?' He looked at the bearded man with long hairs sprouting from a mole on his cheek, standing four rows behind. The guy flicked his head in acknowledgement. '"Is Soong here to walk the dogs?" No, I'm not.' Alex looked the man in the eye. 'I'm here to do what I do best: help catch criminals. We will keep you updated on any further developments.'

The crowd of hacks laughed cynically.

'Come on! What sort of answer is that?' a photographer shouted from the back.

'*Aiya*, that's very polite! You pay us a lot of respect,' someone said from the middle of the pack.

'Tell us about your wife then. Why does she buy so much brown furniture?' called a voice.

They all looked round to see a girl dressed in cute Harajuku pink punk clothes.

'I posted a copy of an interview with your wife from *Prestige* society magazine and it showed some photos of her sitting in your living room. My fans and I have been following you as one of Hong Kong's coolest couples,' she explained earnestly. 'But why does Jun buy so much designer furniture in shades of brown? What's that about?'

Alex grinned and everyone else laughed. 'Finally . . . someone with a *proper* question. And you are?' he called back.

'Jenni Plum, blogger on fashion and all things cool.'

'Well, thank you. I'm glad to hear from someone who understands the value of proper research. My answer is that I've no idea, but when I get home tonight I will not rest until I have found out. Jenni Plum, I will make it my priority to find out and report back to you. For now I must be on my way.'

The mood had lightened and the reporters shuffled back for Alex to exit. He saw the police van return from taking De Suza to the station, but before he could reach it a tall female television reporter and her crew intercepted him. Teetering on her Jimmy Choos and in her late twenties, she was clutching a US network-branded microphone, which she thrust in Alex's face.

'Inspector, we understand two Methodist ministers have been shot and killed. Why do you think someone would do this?' She had a Californian accent and Alex found her Americanized Mandarin pronunciation quite alluring; each word had a sexy little curl to it. Her hair was styled and sprayed so much that it was probably windproof, but humidity from the typhoon had softened it out of shape so that it looked like a large black storm cloud hanging on her forehead.

'We're not ready to talk to the media on this matter. The Captain will be making a press announcement in due course,' he responded automatically.

'What does *that* mean? Can you tell us, are you personally responsible for investigating this crime?'

'Sorry, I've said all I can. You will get another statement in due course.'

Alex gently pushed his way past the interviewer and went to the driver's door of the van. 'Please can you take me back to the station?' he asked the driver.

'Oh, Senior Inspector Soong, yes, of course, but I'm waiting for a couple of other people too. Do you want to get in and just wait it out?'

Alex glanced up at the back of the van, which was empty. 'Sounds good. I could do with some peace.'

The uniformed officer unlocked the door and Alex climbed up into the passenger seats behind him. They sat in silence. Alex shuffled over to the window on the left-hand side and propped up one elbow.

The sky was darker now, with more rain coming. The city needed another downpour to wash away the daily drift of gritty pollution generated by the coal-dust power plant near Lamma Island, a few miles from the formerly fragrant harbour. The radio babbled as central communications kept people updated, issued orders and sought information. Alex's breath formed a thick cloud of condensation on the air-conditioned glass.

'Sir?'

'Yes.' He'd tried to respond warmly to the young officer but there was a trace of curtness to his voice.

'Oh, I'll let you rest.'

'No, sorry, what is it?'

'How is Mong from this morning?'

'Do you know him?'

'Yes, he's my friend from Kweilin Street.'

'Sham Shui Po?'

'Yes.'

Alex said more sympathetically: 'Earlier this morning I heard from Inspector De Suza that Mong's going to be fine. He was wounded in the shoulder, but it was only a small-bore round. He'll be in recovery for a short while. He showed bravery, though.'

'He was a cheeky kid at school.'

'Well, he's grown up well.'

'Do you like working with us?' the young officer asked. He was a skinny, gangling kid with eager eyes in a sharp-boned face.

Alex knew what he was really saying but decided to pretend otherwise.

'You mean, you and Mong?' he said.

The young officer turned round to face him fully.

'No, I mean Hong Kong people.'

'Yes, I like it here very much. But it's challenging,' Alex said with a touch of bemusement. 'This is a tight and traditionally minded community. It's hard to feel included here because everything is so particular to the place: the language, the entertainment, the food, the energy. You take it for granted because you were born here. As an outsider, it's difficult for me to get a handle on everything all at once. Hong Kong is a place with its own natural identity. It's not like Singapore, say, or even how China likes to see itself . . . somewhere that's been carefully planned. The work of man rather than God.' Alex laughed. He leaned forward, closer to the young man. 'But I like it here very much. The question though, even after four years, and it's the same for every mainlander, is does it like me?'

The driver smiled and nodded to himself. Alex rested one hand on the young man's shoulder.

'What's your name, officer?'

'Officer Ding, sir.'

'Nice to meet you.'

Alex's phone started to vibrate.

'Excuse me.'

Ding nodded.

'Hi, sweetheart, how was your lunch?' Alex said, a little sarcastically.

'It was fine, thank you,' Jun responded curtly. 'Did you know you are all over YouTube declaring that you'll investigate immediately why I buy so much brown furniture?'

'Well, it's of national importance,' he tried to joke.

'It's not funny!'

Alex didn't respond. He leaned against the window again and watched his own reflection grimace back at him. 'So buy something in a different colour,' he muttered.

'I would if we had the money. Shall I ask my father? Again?' she replied pointedly.

He traced his finger in the condensation on the glass. The vehicle's door opened, other officers got in, and the van set off toward the station.

'Do you want to do that?' he asked her.

'Don't play the investigator with me.' Jun stopped speaking for a moment but didn't hang up. 'All right, I'm overreacting,' she resumed apologetically. 'But have you looked at Ms Plum's blog?'

'Not yet.'

'Quite fun actually. I might contact her for style tips.' Her tone was much warmer now.

'That's my girl.' He smiled to hear her sounding more friendly. 'Look, sorry, got to go. 'Bye.'

The van snaked down into the edge of Wan Chai and then crept back into Central, drove for half a kilometre along the flyover and turned off towards the station. Alex collected his thoughts.

Anyone considering shooting two ministers crossing a pedestrian bridge in a busy area during the day would have two approaches. The first like Yang Wen, who allegedly killed tycoon Harry 'Cigar' Lam in Luk Yu Tea House in 2002, nearly fifteen years ago. Yang was supposed to have shot Lam at point-blank range during a busy breakfast, then simply walked out of the door into the chaos of a clear morning in Central. Supremely confident or just without any moral sense, that was one approach. But the bullets here were the wrong calibre, this was the work of a sniper. It was cold in execution but calculated and meticulous rather than gutsy. Care and planning were required rather than speed. And if it was a sniper then the shooter had to have somewhere quiet to operate from, private, with the assurance that it would remain so and that he could leave without raising interest from anyone. There must be few such places in Central with a sightline to the footbridge. The heat coming from the city and buildings would also have made the shots tricky, so it would require an expert marksman. But why only take two shots? What was so particular about these two ministers?

The van drove over the speed bump and Alex realized he was at the station.

For most of his first year as a qualified lawyer, he had been asked to continue his work on researching property ownership rights and titles. He had first been given the task during his training. While the other articled clerks wanted to meet clients and sit in on meetings, the unappealing piles of documents – strewn with hidden errors and inconsistencies concerning rights of way, boundaries and rights to develop – had allowed him to excel. It was tedious, antisocial work, requiring a level of attention to detail that was excessive even for lawyers, but it had also allowed him to specialize in an area of law that would prove to be highly lucrative, and it let him spend most of his time alone.

The partners recognized his nature and, already relying on him as a clerk, gave him his own office, so that he could provide uninterrupted service. It was specially positioned at the end of the corridor by the service lift so that box files could be brought to him more easily. The corner office, with its two windows, pleased him. Alone in his office, he felt above his peers, who were still required to share an office or, worse, a desk. He had even been given a wide table to assist in the nature of his work, and the remaining wall space was converted to shelving laden with box files, loose papers and bursting ring binders.

He soon understood how lucrative his work was for the firm. Any error in a document's drafting that he discovered led to dispute and perhaps litigation – all of which could be charged for – and satisfied clients meant further transactions. The chaotic headlong land grab in Hong Kong for a hundred years or more had created arrangements based more on personal relationships than the law, but with the new financing possibilities of the Eighties all these shortcomings had to be identified and corrected before further transactions could be carried out. To his surprise he found he was the right person in the right place at the right time.

The flow of work never stopped and his job was assured, but although he also knew that in order to earn more he needed to acquire and deal with his own clients, the prospect of managing his own relationships unsettled him. The call eventually came from Ah Noun, a lawyer of Chiu Chow descent and second-generation partner in the firm. His Cantonese was so heavily accented, it made him sound almost goofy and childish. The internal phone rang just before 11.30 a.m.

'Put your papers away for a moment and go to Jardine House to see my client Chi Lam. He has a new deal he wants to discuss.' Ah Noun paused. 'Look, don't get anxious, just listen and take instructions. Don't speak too much. Lam's a blunt talker and you don't want to get him started. Ask him to describe the deal to you, take notes and tell him I'll speak to him later in the week. I've got to go help my wife out with something.' Which covered more than one possibility. 'I'd be grateful for your help. Come and see me after lunch.'

The line went dead but he held on to the phone, a slight sweat breaking out over his palms as he cradled the receiver. He stared at the boxes of documents surrounding him. This was the chance he had wanted and dreaded.

He stood studying himself in the mirror on the back of the door. In the last few years he had filled out, becoming tall and muscular, yet he still felt small. His mind could not reconcile itself with his physicality; he could not feel his own presence. He put on his jacket and walked slowly down the corridor. There were a dozen offices to either side of him. Other lawyers looked up from their desks as he passed, visibly surprised that he was going to a client meeting on his own.

It was on the ninth floor of Jardine House, one of the first office towers in Hong Kong, just a few hundred yards from the Star ferry to Kowloon side. Lam was there to greet him, offering a plump hand, which he took cautiously. Lam, at least ten centimetres shorter, looked up at him and smiled.

'So Ah Noun sent *you* out here to listen to me? Well, good. Let's go sit in my office and talk about this development project and I'll introduce you to my partners.'

He followed Lam down a wood-panelled corridor and into a big office containing a large desk and a conference table at which three men were already sitting. The building was famous for its round windows and these gave the room an oddly nautical aspect. They all stood up and one man extended a hand.

'When you said he was a big lawyer around town, I didn't fully understand,' he laughed, looking at the new arrival. 'I'm Chun.'

He shook hands with them all and they exchanged business cards. Chun read the newcomer's name and then looked knowingly at Lam. They both smiled then quickly moved into a description of the deal, which turned out to be the clearing of old warehousing and factories to build new condominiums.

With the notes taken, he remained sitting and listened to the four partners talk generally about property developments around the booming city. Eventually their conversation moved to a discussion of other property tycoons who were making poor local people homeless in order to create expensive, commercially managed housing blocks, which were then leased back to the government for public housing.

'It's an outrage that some people are willing to do anything to make a dollar. Even screw their own communities,' Chun declared.

Lam nodded to encourage him to speak further.

'I lived in the community in Diamond Hill, back when it was still a squatter village. Lane after lane of *tong lau*. Those simple housing blocks with no elevators were the centre of people's existence, the community. Huge blocks destroy, not create, a neighbourhood. These developers are screwing their own people.'

Chun smiled. He looked like an intellectual, with little round glasses worn perched on a long elegant nose below a high forehead. He looked away from Lam.

'So, young man, what do you think?' he asked the visitor.

The question silenced the table.

'I agree that community is very important. People have to stand up for each other. I was brought up in Diamond Hill myself.'

Chun chuckled.

'We know. You're the son of that traitor who refused to let Chinese workers demonstrate against the tycoons and the British – and was killed for it.'

He looked at Chun. His jaw locked. He stared at each of the men around the table.

Lam interjected quickly but was not aiming to defuse the situation.

'Now, now, let's not make hasty assumptions. His son here may have very different views.'

It was already too late.

'All my life people have said this to me. My father did what he did . . . but, yes, you're right, I'm not him and I have a different view. That doesn't make my father a traitor!' he shouted angrily.

He stood up, followed to his feet by a man who had stayed quiet for the entire meeting. He spoke firmly and commanded the silence of the others.

'Calm down.' Then he turned to Lam and Chun. 'Stop this.'

The young man gathered up his briefcase.

'I will leave. Thank you.' He avoided making eye contact, feeling his skin burn and prickle under his office shirt and jacket.

'No, no, sit down. These men were just joking . . .'

He ignored their calls for him to return and walked quickly towards the exit. Behind him he could hear Chun and Lam laughing.

He rushed for the elevator. He felt overwhelmed by anger, but there was still an undercurrent of the same fear and humiliation he'd felt as a child . . . in the market, the streets, the school yard. As he waited for the elevator, the man who had spoken up for him came to stand beside him.

'You won't remember me,' he said.

'Sir . . .' He fumbled his words. '. . . I don't want to remember.' He pressed the button again.

'I met you at the hospital.'

He looked up at the man, now in his early forties, and recognized the face.

'Mr Tung? Look, I just want to leave.'

'Okay, but you have my card. Please give me a call. There are things we should talk about.'

The elevator arrived and he stepped in alone.

He returned to the office. Clutching his briefcase to his chest, he walked quickly down the corridor to his own office. Curious faces stared up at him as he passed; Lam must have called ahead. He failed to insert his office key properly and in his impatience dropped his bag. He needed to be in the office, to be alone. He got the door open and kicked his briefcase into the room, slamming the door hard. His phone rang. After twenty seconds he picked up the receiver.

'I understand there was an incident?' Ah Noun said with an amused snort. 'Don't worry . . .'

He put the phone down and ran out of his office, into the service lift and out on to the street.

He walked to the ferry, past Jardine House again, and home.

He crashed through the doorway and saw her sitting on the sofa. She looked up at him, her wide eyes welcoming. Alice was beautiful.

'What's wrong?' she asked urgently.

'Nothing,' he snapped. 'Why should anything be wrong?'

'You look hurt and fearful.' She could use only the simplest language with him.

He moved round the table towards her. She reached up to touch him but he grabbed her wrist and twisted it. She cried out.

'There's nothing wrong with me! It's *you* . . . you humiliate me.' He pulled her to her feet. 'I want you to leave!' he shouted.

He yanked her towards the door and had dragged her halfway through it when their three-year-old son appeared. He looked at the child: a half-caste boy, fair-skinned and wide-eyed. 'Go back to your room!' he ordered. The little boy stepped back, scared.

His mother looked frightened too, held by her elbows and unable to move. 'Go inside,' she said to the child.

He let go of her elbows and pushed her back into the small apartment. Then he picked up the child and shook him.

'Get back to your room!' he screamed into the little face, which was frozen in shock. 'And don't you cry. You'd better not cry.' He landed the boy hard on the floor so that he sat down painfully. Tears streamed down his face but the child had already learned to remain silent.

He turned back to his wife.

'No, please leave him!' she begged.

'No. It's you who will leave . . . you half-caste! You bring me nothing but bad luck. You aren't *whole*.' He pulled her by the hair through the open door. He shook her head and felt the hair rip from her scalp. They stood on the landing, two flights of steep stairs stretching below. There was only fury inside him. He let go of her and pushed. She fell head first on to the first steps below, then her body weight spun her over, dragging her down another ten, perhaps fifteen, steps. Her head cracked hard against the wall, her neck taking the full weight of her tumbling body. The snapping sound rang out but he did not register it. He watched her limp body tumble over and over until it rested in a heap at the bottom.

It had been necessary from the beginning and he had always known it. The bad luck was now gone and as proof, the police readily believed the young lawyer's explanation that her death was an accident, a sad misadventure of a young mother in a hurry to help her child.

He looked round to find his son standing at the open door, staring up at him, but he could not bring himself to look at the boy.

Summer

Chien
Heaven

Chen
Thunder

INITIATION

At 4.27 p.m. Alex entered from the underground loading bay and took the stairs up to the Captain's office on the third floor. They were so rarely used that it was a good place for him to retreat to when he wanted to think.

He had researched the Captain prior to joining the team, speaking to a few people in the People's Liberation Army stationed in Hong Kong and a couple of other local policemen the Captain had worked with previously. He was surprised to find nothing exemplary about his new boss; no awards for brilliance, though there were the usual citations for years of service to the community and acknowledgements of his dedication. The Captain was thoroughly local, and Alex had guessed before meeting him that he was probably no more interested and receptive to the modern mainland Chinese than he had been to the British. After living in Hong Kong half a year or more, Alex realized that most Hong Kong people had kept themselves almost entirely separate from the British. It had always been one country, two systems: the British system of administration and the Chinese system of making money.

The Captain's attitude was the practical one of all those who had lived under colonial rule: each to his own – which could be terribly unfair on the majority and of great advantage to a lucky few.

Upon Alex's first meeting with the brusque, uncharismatic Captain of his department he had been surprised by his superior's passion for classical Chinese history and culture, his pride in his small collection of Qing Dynasty painted scrolls and his enthusiasm for Chinese opera and classical music, the last of which Alex disliked intensely.

As he reached the second floor, he started preparing himself for the Captain's questions, as well as for a reprimand for his confrontational attitude towards Mak this morning.

Alex flicked his security card over the lock and pulled open the door to the third floor. He approached the secretary's desk.

'Mae, I think he is expecting me.'

'Oh, yes, he is indeed.'

'Thank you, Mae.'

'Pleasure. Go right in,' she said with a giggle. 'But knock first.'

Alex knocked on the office door, heard the usual grunt and went in.

'Soong, anything further since we spoke?' The Captain continued signing some papers, which he did by holding a ruler on the page below the line where his signature should be added. He also used the ruler to read, moving it down the page line by line as he went. He was a meticulous man, without inspiration or imagination, but he worked extremely hard and doggedly and was intolerant of people disposed to unnecessary short cuts, who were ill-prepared or else relied solely on intuition.

Alex closed the door but did not bother to take a seat, remaining standing behind the two chairs in front of the desk, which afforded him a good view of the Captain's receding hairline.

'Nothing to report yet but we've begun to look into the background of the victims, following up on the hundreds of people at the scene, and will soon start sweeping the area in the hope of finding the shooter's location.'

The Captain finally looked up.

'No wild ideas or conclusions?' He allowed himself to enjoy his little joke. 'Actually I like the personal motive idea. I think you should spend some time on that, it's got possibilities. Please sit down.'

'I'd rather remain standing, sir.'

'Why do you always have to argue?' The Captain did not look up but kept busily signing papers from the stack to his left. 'As you know, you were brought here to give us the benefit of your experience in fighting corruption and organized crime, so these apparently motiveless shootings are beyond your remit,' he said with a tone of finality.

'I understand, you've made this clear a number of times. But as you've also said, I've been invaluable in a number of different areas outside of my specific purpose here.' Alex paused to look for a response that was never coming. 'These murders show many of the hallmarks of an execution, and that might well point to organized crime or corruption of some sort. I can help.'

The Captain continued to sign.

'You do love your work, don't you? As I told you before, I think during our first-ever conversation, you're different from us. We belong to this community and, while there's work to be done here, there's also a balance to maintain. In the West, they use the law to turn chaos into order, while for the Chinese the law produces harmony from chaos. It's very different. Here in Hong Kong we still follow the old ways, and who's to say most people on the mainland don't secretly want the same?'

He looked up momentarily, but the signing did not stop. 'I

know you'll ignore this, but I warn you not to go poking around anywhere sensitive before you have talked to me.'

Alex knew the Captain had not finished, so did not bother to start replying – there was still the conclusion of the Internal Affairs interview to be pronounced.

His superior looked up and winked at him. 'We cannot have Methodist ministers executed, it is very bad for the community. Remember, there are many Chinese Christians. People often overlook the fact that Christianity is growing here in Hong Kong. So stay on this case for now and do your best to get to the bottom of it as quickly as you can.'

Alex made no comment but remained standing.

'Oh, yes,' the Captain continued after a weighty pause. 'Internal Affairs have cleared you but they have asked me to watch you closely. I told them it wasn't necessary. Yes, you killed that man and maybe you overreacted, but you have worked hard and maybe, like many of us, you are wound up a little too tight at the moment. Chow deserved it, he's no loss, but putting the girl at risk was reckless of you. I have to ask this . . . Do you require counselling? In fact, no, get some counselling.'

An image of Mak flashed into Alex's mind then and he snapped: 'I didn't shoot Chow to make myself feel better. I did it because he would have murdered the girl. He had already shot her father.'

The Captain slid his ruler to one side and put the pen down. He looked up properly at Alex for the first time. His eyes were hard and his pale yellow skin tight as he frowned and jutted out his lower jaw in contained irritation.

'Let's not continue this conversation. It cannot help you. If you've problems at home or with the job then work them out in the gym or on the range. Do the usual things, like the rest of us. Go see the shrink if necessary, fuck a whore if that is what you need. Up to you. Remember to get the counselling. And no media,' the Captain finished. 'Except, of course, when you announce the conclusion to your urgent investigation into your wife's brown furniture.'

Alex stood at the door without turning round.

'Mae showed it to me this afternoon. What the fuck were you thinking?'

Alex closed the door behind him. He approached Mae, who was in her early sixties and very neat and well organized, always dressed in smart trousers and white blouse. Her skin was still very smooth and her eyes were sharp and alert, but it was her control of the third floor that earned her universal respect. It was *her* floor and this was never questioned, not by the officers and not by the incumbent of the Captain's office, three of whom she had served. She smiled as Alex approached.

'Did you really have to show him YouTube?' Alex faked a whine.

'Well, you looked so sweet . . . Jenni Plum had you round her little finger. Your expression when you looked up at her!'

'What?'

'She captured it all on her phone. She starts speaking, you look up and see her – and then there's that smile. It's such a warm and confident smile. Not too many teeth on display . . . just enough. *Aiya*, so handsome!'

'What are you talking about?' he asked, dreading the answer.

She showed him on her tablet.

'That's not good,' Alex said softly under his breath.

'You should think of your wife,' Mae scolded him. 'You can't behave like this in public. Even if it's innocent.'

'I'll try.' He shook his head and made for the door again. He walked down a flight of stairs to the second floor and the general office area. Here it was noisy and chaotic. Wide desks were piled with loose papers that desperately needed converting to electronic copies. The high ceilings absorbed much of the noise but made the space feel empty at times. He didn't have much that was personal, but there was enough paperwork to fill his and another five desks, and on top of it a note from De Suza.

'In Room 3 with the old lady from the Cathedral again.'

Alex went through from the main office area into a wide corridor with nine interview rooms on each side. He stopped at the second on the left, Interview Room 3, and peered through the window. The old lady sat clutching a cup of tea. De Suza sat next to her at the end of the table, rather than opposite her. Alex knocked and entered.

'Excuse me, Auntie,' looking at the old lady who was now much calmer and sipping some tea, 'I just need to speak to Deputy Inspector De Suza.'

'By all means,' she replied sweetly.

De Suza stood up, collected his notebook, and the two men went outside to talk in the corridor. Alex started.

'How is she? What's she doing here?'

'Better. She came to tell us about some of the people who have contacted the ministers recently. They've only just arrived so haven't had time to get to know a lot of people here. But she's made a list of those she remembers. Oh, and Reverend Lu, the one from the UK, did come here for a few weeks in 2008. He spoke at Hong Kong University on the history of Christianity in China. But apart from that one trip, he hadn't been back here in years. The old lady says that when a few crazies came to confess their sins, which is not part of the Methodist faith, Reverend Fung would still speak to them. I also asked her about his emails, but that's not something she has access to.'

'Let's go in to her now so I can say hello. And when you've

finished, please can you take her home or wherever she wants to go? Don't give it to one of the others.'

'Sure. She's had a rough day.' De Suza paused, looking at him. 'You look tired too.'

Alex smiled and pointed a finger back to the meeting room.

The old lady looked up at them, her face more settled and calm than it had been earlier in the afternoon. 'Young man, you look tired. You need to get some sleep,' she told Alex.

'That's what I told him,' De Suza grinned.

'I just wanted to thank you for coming down,' Alex replied.

'I suddenly remembered a man came to see Reverend Lu a week or so ago and it reminded me that I should tell you about other comings and goings, so I made a list, but there's not much to it.'

'Well, it's very helpful. Do you know who the man was?'

'No, I didn't meet him, just heard he had an unexpected visitor. Maybe a friend from abroad, people are always coming by . . .' Then she broke off and addressed Alex again. 'Young man, look at you! You really must get some sleep.'

'Go get some rest, something to eat. We'll finish this,' De Suza told him.

Alex had liked Mike De Suza within minutes of meeting him. He saw him as part of the new China, like Alex himself. He also immediately liked his wife, Mary, who was the arms-flung-about-you-and-food-on-the-table-in-minutes sort.

'All right, you're both so bossy,' he joked.

Alex took the stairs up to the fifth floor where the canteen was. It was 6 p.m. and he had not eaten all day; even the university's chicken lunch would seem good to him now. The canteen was basic but their noodles, fried egg, spam and won ton dish was pretty decent. As he went into the canteen, the server looked at him and Alex nodded back.

'Usual?' the man called out. He had one of the most recognizable faces in the world. A Chinese version of Mr Burns from *The Simpsons*. De Suza had joked that if he ever committed a crime then he wouldn't get far, which was why he never served a poor meal. Alex nodded to him in reply, and sat down at a table by the window.

The canteen was empty and it was after only ten minutes that Ah Chok brought over the noodles and cup of coffeetea, yinyang, a specifically Hong Kong mixture that Alex had learned to like at De Suza's insistence. The last of Alex's noodles went down just as Ying appeared with the young officer who had driven Alex back to the station earlier. He was tall and sinewy when not sitting behind the wheel of a van.

'Rookie, you see this man here?' Ying went and sat on the edge of Alex's table. He looked over at the young man and pointed down to Alex. 'This is Inspector Soong of the great Soong family. You should learn from him because he is the star of this station. He was on YouTube only this afternoon talking to a little plum about his wife. He's a celebrity.'

The young man looked lost. He smiled diffidently at Alex, who focused his attention on Ying.

'Worried that people don't mention your wife, Ying? I've seen her and, believe me, I'm sure people talk. In fact, I think the zoology department at Hong Kong University are discussing her right now.' Alex glanced at the young officer. 'Actually Ding and I have already met. He was kind enough to drive me back. You getting off soon?' he addressed the young officer.

'Shortly, sir. Senior Inspector Ying said he'd show me the senior dining room.'

'Well, it's not much, Ding, but I reckon you'll be here one day, so let's hope they have better facilities to offer you then. Good luck to you.' Alex finished with a wink but felt he had embarrassed himself by reacting so rudely to Ying's remarks.

'Please can I finish my meal in peace?' he said more politely to his fellow senior inspector.

'As you wish, Soong.' Ying left the table, before Alex then walked to the cash till to get the TV remote. He switched on the television and flipped to the news. There was a live report from close by this afternoon's crime scene, where there were still quite a few lingering onlookers. Alex watched the coverage to see if there was anything of interest, doing his best to ignore Ying, seated with the young officer at another table.

De Suza appeared and gave Ying a cursory nod as he came over to Alex.

'You were supposed to come here to take a break. You look annoyed and just as tired.'

'See you later, celebrity,' Ying shouted over to them, and nodded to the rookie that it was time to leave.

De Suza picked up Alex's drink to take a sip.

'Ying had a lot to say. I took the bait. Like a fool,' Alex sighed.

'Well, you can't be too foolish because you're drinking yinyang, the only sensible drink for a Hong Kong policeman.' De Suza put the empty mug in the noodle bowl. 'Reverend Fung's wife has just arrived and she brought his sister. They're in Interview Room 5. By the way, the bodies have just been delivered to the morgue and the pathologists will start in the next hour. I'm going back to finish speaking to the old lady.'

'I didn't think Reverend Fung had any relatives here,' Alex said as he got up to go, picking up his empty bowl and leaving it on the counter as they walked out. 'Wasn't that what the old lady said to us?'

'Apparently they are estranged. Makes you wonder about the old lady's accuracy though.'

Inside the interview room, the sister was holding her baby boy, a plump toddler with a sprout of brown hair. It was a brighter and friendlier space than Interview Room 3: it had colours, cushions and a playpen for toddlers, and also some baby formula, baby-bottle warmer and sanitizer. Fung's sister was wearing a dark green V-neck jumper over a white T-shirt and her hair was pulled back in a rough ponytail. Her eyes were bloodshot and the little boy, probably no more than two years old, squirmed in her arms.

Alex turned his attention to Fung's wife, a small slim woman with a longish face and prominent but elegant chin. A few pale freckles dotted the skin below her sharp blue eyes. She was wearing a yellow floral dress that accentuated her narrow waist. She remained still, unlike her sister-in-law, who paced the room.

'Mrs Fung, my name is Senior Inspector Alex Soong. I am very sorry for your loss. Inspector De Suza and I are leading the investigation into the murder of your husband.'

'Can I see him? I would like to see him,' she asked, moving forward and pressing Alex's arm in entreaty.

'I think it's better that you wait until the pathologist has finished his investigation,' he told her.

Mrs Fung looked away. She let go and Alex pulled out a seat for her.

'Please do sit down.'

She obeyed. After briefly looking into the distance and then at Alex, she dropped her head into her hands and cried.

'I would very much like to ask you both some simple questions, would that be okay?'

They nodded. The sister held her baby tightly and rocked him gently to calm him.

'However, I need to do this separately.'

'What?' the sister snapped at him.

Mrs Fung offered: 'It's okay, I'll go wait somewhere and you can speak to Dorothy here.'

She left the room and was met by a female officer in the corridor who took her to a waiting area.

'Dorothy, I will try to make this quick,' Alex began. 'You and your brother rarely saw each other. Correct?'

'We didn't get on, it's true.' She immediately started to get restless. 'Look, what's this got to do with anything?' She paused. 'We just never saw eye-to-eye. He was intellectual and I was a free spirit. I liked to travel and just kept myself going with part-time work.'

'Did you know of anyone who might have disliked your brother?'

Silence. Alex stopped speaking and just looked at the woman, giving her time to collect herself. She stared into the distance while her son wriggled a little over her shoulder.

'I am very sorry for these questions but I must ask them. Can you think of any reason why someone might wish to harm your brother?'

'I had hoped to get to know him again.' The woman paused and steadied herself. 'There's no reason anyone would kill my brother. He was a very bright man who liked a simple life among uncomplicated people. I hadn't seen him properly in a long time. Steph . . . I mean Mrs Fung . . . is the person you need to speak to. They were inseparable.'

Alex reached round for a box of tissues from the other end of the table and placed it in front of her. She sat still with a tissue held to her eyes and the baby at her cheek.

'Thank you,' she said.

'I don't have anything further to ask you. I will ask an officer to drive you home, if you'd like, and we will contact you again when you can see your brother.'

'Yes, I'd like the ride home.'

Alex got up, opened the door and waved at an officer passing by.

'Officer Ng?'

The female officer stopped and turned back to face Alex, barely able to disguise her exasperation at being prevented from continuing on her way.

'Yes, sir?'

'You look tired.'

'Sir?' she responded sharply.

'I'd like you to take this lady home,' Alex said politely, recognizing that the officer was about to head home herself.

'But I . . .'

'I understand, and you'll be on OT. We're all in for a long and difficult night so we'll need everyone on duty.'

The officer nodded reluctantly and Alex opened the door wider to admit her. As he did the phone in the corner of the room rang abruptly. He looked up quickly at Mrs Fung.

'Thank you. I'll leave you with this officer. Sorry, I must take this.'

It was now 5.45 p.m. and Lok, a newly registered and hopeful real estate agent, had already stood waiting fifteen minutes for his client to arrive at a large secluded warehousing development in the north-east of Kowloon. Ken, his business colleague, had dropped him off, and Lok hoped the client would show up, as Ken wouldn't be back for another forty-five minutes and he was far away from regular bus and taxi routes. Lok did not like working into the early evening as he preferred to be at home with his baby son. The little boy would have his dinner at 6 p.m. and then his mother would put him down. Lok liked to watch him fall asleep; the child would quickly close his eyes and be away to a place that was unreachable until he returned, hungry, a few hours later. His birth had not been planned and it was an extra mouth to feed, but even with the tight financial situation, he and his wife felt the birth of a boy was definitely a sign their luck was changing since the property crash. Instead of being worried and frustrated, this positive omen motivated Lok to chase every lead.

The property he was showing tonight was a large warehouse a mile or so to the north-east of what was once Po Kong Village and its ring road, a now ghostly area of Kowloon. The warehouse development was relatively new, planned in 2008, delayed in 2010, and then foolishly begun again in 2011 and completed last year.

Warehouse 44 was one of sixty built on the industrial wasteland in five neat lines with narrow numbered roads between them. The area was private land, and as very few of the warehouses were leased as yet the landlord wasted no money on lighting the area, removing half of the light bulbs. Lok had had to request them to switch on the power to the two feeble lights, outside and inside the warehouse entrance, and even then he was only allowed ninety minutes' light. It had been an adventurous development in the boom times and was now one of a huge number of dreary empty monuments to the greed of the Chinese property market.

The client had phoned Lok's boss at their office in Kowloon Tong – a mere five miles from the site but a miserable hour's drive – and specifically requested Warehouse 44. Lok's boss was never going to attempt the evening traffic, certainly not to meet an awkward *gweilo*, so he was given the task. He was told who to call to have the power switched on – a random name, someone sitting in an office on Hong Kong Island who did it by remote – and was informed that the client would be a tall man with a beard and glasses, speaking English. He wanted the warehouse for a new toy and party favour import/export business. Lok's English was poor, but this was a potential deal, and his boss said the man had sounded serious on the phone, so Lok was committed to trying his best at least for twenty minutes or so. If it didn't lead to anything positive he would make some excuse to end the appointment, which hopefully the *gweilo* would believe.

Lok stood waiting at the entrance to Lane Four on which ran warehouses 37 to 48. The client suddenly appeared, striding calmly up the main road, which connected each of the six lanes. The air was hot and thick with humidity. Through the haze he approached like a giant striding down from the wilderness. He was much bigger than Lok had been warned, with broad shoulders and chest above a solid waist and hips. The man's face was hard to make out, partly hidden in the shadow cast by the wide brim of his battered English-looking felt hat, but also because his head was bent slightly forward, his chin pushed down against his chest, so that he was looking more at the ground than ahead of him. By the limited light of the estate he looked huge, and Lok felt small and intimidated.

'I'm sorry I'm so late,' the man called as he drew near.

Being shorter, Lok tried to look up into the stranger's face. He wore round tinted glasses covered with spray from the rain. Lok saw his own face reflected in them. A beard blurred the outline of his other features apart from the long nose. Aware that he was staring, Lok looked back at the road.

'We go to Warehouse Forty-Four as you requested. Each warehouse is large, six thousand, five hundred square metres, that is seventy-thousand square feet. This last used by successful local exporter. So very good luck here . . . but number forty-four not so good, but never mind you,' Lok said hesitantly. There was no way he was going to explain to the foreigner that the Chinese word for the number four was considered very unlucky, as it sounded like the word for death. Ignorance seemed best to get the deal done.

'There is two months' free rent if you sign now,' he continued.

The man stopped walking. Lok stopped with him.

'But you will lock me into a contract for fourteen months, right? It's a long time in these lean times.' The man didn't turn to the agent, just stood facing forward into the rain. 'Is this correct?'

'Yes, that is what we would hope to do. It seems a good deal to me.'

'But what happens if I can't afford fourteen months?'

'Then you speak to my boss. Shall we walk as it gets late?' Lok moved a step or two forward but the man did not move.

'I don't like Chinese stealing from Chinese. What if I have employees? Should I stop paying them to pay this foolish greedy landlord?'

He turned fast and stood closer to Lok. The smaller man dropped back.

'Tell me, would you steal from your own family?' The big man raised one hand, its outline black against the single light behind. He bunched his fist hard but brought it not towards Lok, but to touch his own lips in a gesture of concern. Lok flinched away from him.

'Sorry, I get angry. I just think it's wrong. Don't you agree?' The client's voice was muffled. He moved his fist a little away from his face. 'For one man to steal from his brother, isn't it wrong?'

Lok looked up, seeing his own reflection again in the spray-covered lenses. The man still did not move and Lok felt he was waiting for an answer. He stepped back, looking straight up at the client, half unsure and half relieved to hear what he was saying. He remembered losing jobs while others paid themselves a little more, being told to work hours that kept him from his family, and being denied opportunities unfairly due to his lack of connections.

'You mean loyalty to brothers and goodness in intent? That it's wrong to be unfair . . . like Confucius said? If you mean that, then I agree.'

'Yes. That's it. That's *it*.'

'I agree with you. But what can we do?' Lok wiped the rain from his face and looked up at the big man earnestly. 'I'm nothing. I can do nothing but swallow it all – even when my family are sick.'

'But you should be stronger than that! Together we can do a lot. More than you think. You too can play a role.' The other man let his arms swing by his sides again. 'Shall we continue?'

Lok quickly caught up with him and they walked along the empty road between warehouses crammed tight along each side of the road. Between the circles of weak light cast by the intermittent lamps lay patches of dark. Lok peered into the blackness and felt uneasy about what he could not see. He hurried still faster. The tall *gweilo* did not seem to mind and easily kept up with his pace. The only sounds other than their footsteps came from the rats scavenging amongst the broken wooden pallets and paper discarded between the warehouses.

'The economy is nothing here. How are things in your hometown? I bet better than here?' Lok asked.

'My home is here, always here,' the client replied softly, almost under his breath.

'What did you say?'

The English-speaker did not reply.

'Did you know that today someone killed two priests in Central district?' Lok made conversation as their destination was still a minute or so away.

'Yes, I heard,' replied the English-speaker. 'The world has become a truly terrible place.'

'This area very safe. It is very good place to rent – cheap and safe.'

They resumed walking in silence.

They stopped at Warehouse number 44. Lok removed the padlock and opened a small door, no higher than himself, forcing the English-speaker to bend low to enter. Once inside, Lok felt through the darkness on his left for the switch on the wall. He flicked it up as instructed and a weak interior light just above the doorway came on. It lit barely more than twenty metres in front of them, no better than the lamps outside, but just enough for Lok to see the closed doors of a standard twenty-foot metal shipping container at the edge of the weak light inside the warehouse. A vast blackness surrounded the container, making it look small.

Lok hesitated. He looked at the man now beside him, who stood with a half-smile on his lips. Lok was drawn to the doors of the container; they were closed, though they did not appear to be locked, the bar latch hanging loose, teasing him to look inside. He was also aware that this was not what he had been told to show the man.

'Sorry. Sorry. This container is wrong, should not be here. Tomorrow, we will move,' Lok said as he slowly approached it.

'But it looks as though it belongs here and nowhere else,' the man said from behind him.

Lok stopped in front of the container but did not reach for the handle. He looked at its deep red colour. The paint was not old, it was newly applied and thick, almost lacquered, in texture. He looked for brush strokes but the painting was beautifully finished. He had seen many doors in his line of work; this had been done by an artist, not a decorator. After a few seconds, he touched the cold metal handle. He pulled at the doors and had barely opened them fifty centimetres when a big black bird flew through the gap. Feathers fell against his face. A wing caressed his hair, glinting in the light behind Lok. The bird screeched angrily and beat its wings hard, as if relieved to feel the air underneath them. Talons scraped deep across Lok's face as it lurched into the air above his head.

The English-speaker, still several metres behind, was able to duck out of the way. The bird flew over him and into the warehouse wall. It dropped to the ground, dead or exhausted, landing on its chest, its claws briefly continuing to twitch and scratch at the concrete flooring. Lok had fallen awkwardly and was clutching his forehead; he felt warm blood swelling between his fingers.

'What was that?' Lok was shaking. He tried to stand but fell back to his knees. He had sprained his ankle and was unable to get up on his own. The English-speaker came up and stood over him, briefly watching him struggle to raise himself. After a few seconds the foreigner bent down, put his hands under Lok's armpits, and lifted him up.

'That thing looked like a raven. It seems to have been so scared it flew straight into the wall. I think it's dead. How are you feeling? The cut seems bad.' The English-speaker spoke quietly and calmly, as if unwilling to disturb the silence in the darkness behind the metal doors.

Lok was unsteady on his feet, but once he had regained control he pulled out a pack of tissues and held one to his head. He pulled it away and looked momentarily at the bloodstain before he replaced the tissue. Now he wanted to know, he must know, what was behind the doors. With his free hand he took the handle again and opened the door wider to peer inside.

Lok bent over instantly and vomited. Straightening himself, he wiped his mouth and looked hard into the dim interior. The stench was overwhelming. He could see the outlines of four bodies sprawled across the floor. One body lay close to the doors, and in the limited light he could just see that it had deep bite marks and cuts in its flesh. He could also see a number of dead black birds littered about the container. Some had their necks broken and lay trampled and bent into the corners where they had been thrown. Others had simply lain down and died of hunger. A few had had bites taken out of them, dried blood on the mouths of the corpses evidence of this final desperate act.

'*Aihh*. Come here. Come here,' Lok called out weakly. 'There are bodies.'

The English-speaker came into the container and looked around. He did not vomit or retch but simply stood behind Lok, observing the scene.

'What a sight. Yes, quite amazing.' They stood in silence for a while. 'Don't you think it is amazing that people could do this to each other?' The man took two steps towards the nearest body. 'Look at what this one has done . . . so hungry he bit into this bird while it in turn pecked at his cheek and clawed him.' He turned to look at Lok. 'And this one, with the clenched hands . . . I think she was praying.'

'What?' Lok was confused. 'We should call the police.'

'No,' the English-speaker said quietly, 'it is not time yet.' He switched from English to Cantonese. 'They will come to find you soon. I'm sorry but this is your role. Someone will come for you, in time.'

Lok turned his head in surprise at hearing the English-speaker switch to perfect Cantonese, the tones natural and correct. Then the foreigner's right arm reached around Lok's neck and pulled his small frame close. Lok felt his back squeezed against the man's large chest. He was lifted up, the pressure on his throat not enough to strangle him but enough to terrify him.

The man placed his left hand firmly on Lok's forehead, holding him tighter, and then his right hand slowly drew a razor blade deep across his neck and throat. The blood gushed from Lok's neck, his arteries completely severed. It took only a short time before he went limp in his assailant's arms, but the foreigner continued to hold the slight body upright until the final rasps of air in the lungs had emptied out. Then he let Lok drop to the floor.

The man brought out a camera and took a picture of the interior of the container. The flash momentarily outlined the corpses of the four dead humans and two dozen or so dead ravens, and the glistening deep red still flowing from Lok's gaping neck. He drew in a deep breath and held it in, as if to savour the experience. He continued to take photos, but touched nothing.

It was another twenty minutes before Lok's colleague Ken arrived to collect him. Lok should have been at the end of Road Four waiting, but there was still plenty of time, nearly forty minutes, before the power would be switched off. Ken drove slowly up the road, careful not to miss his friend squatting on the kerb's edge waiting for him. He saw nothing until he noticed the light cast from within the warehouse. He decided to wait in the car, thinking Lok must be selling it hard. Perhaps he even had a deal, which would be a blessing for both their families. Ken had parked a little before the entrance to 44, on the opposite side of the road. The rain started to come down harder. The typhoon had threatened to envelop the city all day, but all there had been so far were intermittent showers. Now rain pelted the windscreen and Ken sat in the car watching water form a solid sheet across the glass until the wipers swept back to clear it momentarily.

He watched the lit doorway for any signs that Lok was finishing and continued sitting there for a further ten minutes, largely from his reluctance to get soaked outside. Then, out of boredom, he decided to drive to the door, jump out and quickly join Lok.

They had only been working together a few months, as Ken

had previously been in mobile phone sales. That industry had run dry, with people now buying them cheaply online. Though Lok was finding business difficult, he'd suggested Ken should join him at the agency so they could work together as a team. The two old schoolfriends would be able to help each other, pool resources and share business contacts while generally saving money.

He drove across the narrow road and parked as close to the small warehouse entrance door as he could, almost blocking the entrance and leaving him little space to open the driver's door. He squeezed himself out and slipped through the entrance into the warehouse. The interior light revealed a raven lying on the floor in front of him. It seemed to be dead and Ken pushed it with his foot. It twitched a final time and he shouted out and stepped back in surprise. He studied the dead bird, and became aware that his nostrils were picking up a sharp putrid smell.

The door to the container stood half open. Ken cautiously pulled it wider still. As the door swung back he retched and then vomited. He looked at the vomit spread over the concrete and his left shoe, looked at the terrifying shapes inside the container. Nearest lay Lok's body, neck gaping. Ken screamed. He called his friend's name but there was no response. He stood looking into Lok's lifeless eyes, which stared emptily back at him, and the violent redness from the open throat.

He staggered back then turned and ran to the car. Panicked, he pulled the door open, repeatedly slamming it hard against the warehouse entrance and wall as he tried to struggle back into the driver's seat. It kept bouncing back into his body. Ken's heart was beating fast and his lungs ached. He pushed himself through the gap, and as he did so the door's edge jabbed his ribs and he screamed in pain. He looked around and saw nothing but the warehouses' faint lights and the darkness yawning in front of and behind his car. At last he had rammed himself into the car seat and pulled the door closed. He realized he could still see the edge of the container from his seat. He watched it for a few seconds. Nothing moved. He peered through the driving rain. Still nothing moved.

He looked again in the direction of his dead friend, then scrabbled to find his phone and call the police. He was passed to an Inspector Michael De Suza. Ken cried and at times could barely catch his breath as he hyperventilated. He could not find words to describe what he'd seen, his voice weak and reluctant. Each sound competed to be heard against the drumming of the rain hitting the thin aluminium shell of the car. He felt he was losing his mind.

'Ken, Ken . . . please take a breath. Describe for me exactly what you saw,' De Suza coaxed him.

'I have seen my friend Lok, with his throat cut like a pig,' Ken shouted. 'I have seen those pictures . . . that is what they do to pigs when they butcher them!'

He shivered. Sweat dripped from his right temple from the heat of the phone pressed against his ear, and tears formed in his eyes.

'Ken, tell me where you are.'

He looked around and realized he was still alone on a dark road miles from anywhere. He felt trapped in his small car with the silent darkness pressing on the windows. He was a city dweller. This place was empty but for corpses, one of them that of his best friend.

'I am in the new warehouse area north-east of old Po Kong Village and ring road. Warehouse forty-four, Road Four.' Ken sobbed, then blurted: 'He's dead . . . I'm going to drive away.'

'No, no! Stay there. We will be with you soon.' De Suza raised his voice a little to compel Ken to listen to him, just enough to be firm. 'Stay in the car and lock the doors. Now keep your breathing slow, and if you can find a bag to breathe in, it will calm you. Please do not hang up! Stay on the phone with me.'

Still holding the phone and connected to Ken, De Suza picked up another and dialled Interview Room 5. Alex answered.

'You need to get out to Hung Hom. There's been another murder.'

'Details?'

'Not much at this point, except I've got a scared kid at the other end of the line. He's out in a vacant warehousing development. Says his friend has been butchered there.'

'Someone had better finish the interview with Reverend Fung's wife then. We're about done. And you need to find out what you can about this warehouse place. Any security man, cameras, owner's name?'

'Okay. Now I've got to get back to the kid, he's in serious stress. You'd better get out there fast!'

De Suza took his hand off the other receiver and brought it to his mouth.

'Ken . . . Ken, it's me. Inspector De Suza. I needed to speak to the officer who is coming to you. Senior Inspector Alex Soong is on his way. Sit tight.'

De Suza switched phones and heard Alex's voice.

'Ask that young officer who was with Ying in the canteen, his name's Ding. He drove us back from Citibank Tower earlier, he seemed reliable. Get him to drive the old lady home and then take the sister and her child. You interview the wife, she should be fine to wait. I'll tell her now.' Another thought struck Alex. 'And get them looking harder for the sniper's location.'

'All right, get going.'

Even with the lights flashing and the sirens blaring, the going was slow, as the traffic on Gloucester Road, the main road following the coastline, was being lashed by heavy rain – level 3 now after the typhoon level 8 of the previous night. Alex switched off the sirens; they were clearly serving more to irritate his fellow drivers than to motivate anyone to make way. There was simply nowhere for them to go.

The road, only a few miles long but in places four or five lanes wide, was walled, like every other inner-city road in Hong Kong, by tall buildings, some modern, but most of them shabby or crumbling towers of concrete and glass containing hundreds of tiny living and working spaces. They loomed into the sky, cutting out the sunlight even on bright days, but their crushing presence during rain exerted a gloom that made the drivers defensive and selfish.

For fifteen stop-start minutes he drove on: through the tunnel under the harbour, past the public housing blocks and out of the city into a more industrial area of old factories and disused loading spaces and gantries. A turning off the main commercial drag took him into some flatter land earmarked for development, and then to the warehouses. The area felt forlorn and isolated. He reported to De Suza.

'I've just arrived. Any background?'

'I've not found out much. There's no camera system apart from at the gate, but no one's looked at that in a while and the power is due to go off in twenty minutes.'

'What?'

'It's on some sort of energy-saving timer, but we're trying to find the man who controls it. I'll keep you informed.'

'I'll check things out here . . . give you a call in a few minutes about support.'

'Okay. The kid's name is Ken and his dead friend is Lok. Take Road Four on the estate to Warehouse Forty-Four.'

'Who chose those particular numbers?'

'Some twisted freak.'

Alex had found the road. He switched off his headlights and drove slowly towards the warehouse. When he saw the small blue Nissan hatchback wedged in close to the entrance under the dim security light, he parked a little further down on the other side of the road so as to remain in the dark. He got out quietly and walked towards the parked car.

As he drew closer Alex could see somebody sitting in the driver's seat. After stopping twenty metres away to unclip his pistol, a Sig Sauer P250 with a seventeen-round magazine, he continued to walk slowly towards the car. Its brake lights were on and he could hear the engine turning over. From ten metres away he saw that the driver's door was badly dented.

He approached the passenger side, stopping short of square on to it. A man sat slumped in the driver's seat, hands motionless on the steering wheel. He heard a faint movement on the ground ahead. Rats and snakes, he told himself.

Ken was very young, with a light unshaven down still on his cheeks. Alex also saw a stud in his left ear which he must have pulled or caught on something. There was blood congealed on it and drips had fallen on to his neck and down the collar of his grubby shirt. His hair was short and spiky, as most urban Chinese kids wore it. It looked slick with sweat. His eyes appeared to be only partially open. Alex reached forward and tapped the glass with his left hand, holding his gun at the ready in the other, just below window level.

'Are you Ken Chan?' he shouted in Cantonese.

'Yes . . . yes, I am,' the kid stuttered, eyes wide and staring now. Blood vessels had burst in them and he had rubbed them so raw that they were swollen. Looking blankly at Alex from underneath his inflated lids, he moved to unlock the driver's door with shaking hands but could not manage it.

'Are you okay? Are you hurt?' Alex spoke slowly, putting his gun away as he did.

Ken shook his head. 'I'm not hurt. I can't move. What happened to Lok?' He trailed off.

'I'm going to smash the window to unlock the door. Sit back.'

Ken returned to a slumped position in his seat and placed his hands between his thighs. He dropped his head and closed his eyes. Alex took out his expandable steel baton, flicked it open and smashed the window.

'Ken, I want you to stay here. Do you understand? Just stay here. More police will arrive soon. Don't worry.'

The kid nodded.

'I'm cold,' he said through trembling lips.

The adrenalin had left Ken's system and he was tired and spent. He shivered incessantly as Alex watched him. Fear.

'Your ear is cut. Anywhere else hurt?' Ken shook his head in reply. 'Just stay here.'

Alex ran back to his car and snatched a blanket from the trunk. He also grabbed his Remington 870 12-gauge shotgun and holstered his pistol. He returned to the hatchback and got into the seat next to Ken.

'Sorry about your window. I'm going to wrap this blanket round you . . . I think you're going into shock. You should keep warm. Does your car have heating?'

'Yes, it's a Japanese car,' the kid whispered.

'Okay, I'll turn it up and you keep warm under there. I'll be back in a couple of minutes.'

Alex squeezed between the side of Ken's car and the entrance to the warehouse. He thought that there were perhaps five or six minutes of power left before the timer De Suza had mentioned killed the lights. He stood inside the warehouse, ten metres away from the open doors of the container. The weak light from behind him reached as far as the container's entrance, leaving the rest of the warehouse behind in pitch blackness.

There was just enough light for him to see the body lying on the threshold in a dark stain of blood. Alex glanced down by his feet and saw a dead raven, its body almost skeletal. Its eyes had already dried out and disappeared before its last blind flight, propelled by pain.

He switched on his torch and walked forward. Casting its thin beam ahead of him, he stepped around Lok's body and entered the container to find four more bodies, three Chinese and one *gweilo*, badly pecked and clawed. Two were missing an eye and all had multiple deep cuts across the cheeks and, where he could see them, their hands. The skin was pale and translucent; death had come a while back. The torch beam lit the floor in tiny yellow circles. Bird after bird. Feathers and excrement smeared across the metal base as the people had slipped and fallen, running to get away in the darkness. Some ravens had a wing ripped off, others had bloody chunks bitten from their necks and bodies. He noticed that the *gweilo* was missing a right hand. The blood on the stump was clotted so it must have been cut after the victim died. That victim wore a cross, which caught the light and reflected its outline on to the wall opposite. A foul stench filled Alex's nostrils and pulled at his guts and throat. He stepped outside and retched while fumbling blindly with his phone and at last inserting the earpiece. He set it to hands-free.

'De Suza . . . get assistance here straight away . . . it's a multiple homicide. One of the most horrible things I've ever seen. I can't describe it. I need a full homicide team and lights . . . tell them to bring lots of lights and generators. I'm going to walk deeper into the warehouse to check it's clear . . .'

Alex slung the 12-gauge over his shoulder and unclipped his Sig. Holding the torch in his left hand, he gripped the pistol firmly in the other. He took the right-hand side and slowly started to walk round the outside of the container with his back pressed against its outer wall.

As soon as he left the circle of light cast from the doorway he was plunged into a dark void, just the torchlight left to illuminate the cavernous space of the warehouse in front of him. He shone it at head height from one side to another and realized how deep the floor space was. The beam lacked the power to reach far, which left much of his surroundings hidden. He walked the length of the container and reached the first corner. Its metal edge dug into his back and nothing but the dark lay in front of him.

He stood at the first corner for thirty seconds or so, casting his torch beam around the immediate area and feeling a primal fear of the enveloping darkness and the horrors that might emerge from it. He turned the corner, still with his back pressed hard up against the far wall of the container. His steps felt illogically small and careful, as if one false move might send him plummeting, although he stood on solid ground.

He continued to walk, leaving the container behind him, sweeping the torch left and right. He paced on into the darkness for thirty metres. The feeble beam caught various pallets loaded with boxes left by the previous owner. He approached one stack slowly and looked at the print on the side: luxury pillows and duvets. He stepped away from the packing box, back into open space, and swept the torch around.

The doorway to the warehouse and the container were now some distance behind him, perhaps as much as fifty metres. Deep into the far end of the warehouse in front of him he could hear a dripping sound and air whistling into the building, maybe the sign of another door. He could also make out shapes of other pallets and machinery, which led to a packing slide, the shiny metal rollers catching the light. He saw the warehouse was of simple construction: metal walls and a basic flat portal frame with light Z purlins on the roof. No windows. Just a huge shell.

A shot went off. It felt close. The sound echoed around the warehouse. Alex switched off his torch.

'Senior Inspector Alex Soong?' The words boomed from the far end of the interior. His name echoed a little against the bare concrete floor, but more so in his own ears.

Another shot.

'Inspector Soong, I can still see you. The light from your earpiece is still visible.'

Alex fumbled with his earpiece. 'I'm turning this off. I'll keep the mobile in my pocket . . . maybe will pick up something,' he whispered into the microphone.

'Fine,' the Captain responded, having joined the line.

The lights to his earpiece and mobile disappeared.

'That's smarter,' the voice let him know.

Alex tightened his grip on his pistol. His heart raced as he sprayed the torch beam across the space only to see its light fade into the darkness in front of him. That voice . . . it had sounded somehow familiar.

'There's no way from here but forward.' A pause and then again: 'No way but forward.' The words had been spoken in Mandarin. It was an expression Alex's old friend liked to use.

'William?' Alex peered into the depths of the warehouse in front of him then down at the ground. It was so dark he could not even see his feet. 'William?' No, it was impossible.

'I'm afraid he's dead,' the voice informed him. 'You must remember. You identified the body.'

Alex walked to his right. If he kept one foot in front of the other and maintained a straight line he should make it to the wall. He felt his sleeve silently brush against the stacked boxes.

'Alex, where are you going?' the voice called out.

He continued walking until he reached the wall. He looked behind him and saw the faint light over the entrance. There would be no light soon. The voice continued in Mandarin.

'I can still see you, I came with night vision. But look,' laughter in the voice now, 'I'm leaving shortly. Your backup will be here soon, but I did want to talk to you finally.'

Silence.

'You must be tired,' the voice commiserated.

Alex regained his composure.

'What do you want from me?'

'Just to talk to you. For you to listen. Alex, it's time we changed everything, asserted ourselves again, become again the great Middle Kingdom that once ruled Asia for thousands of years. We Chinese are no longer second-class global citizens. This time it's our world – yet at present we are still beholden to them.'

The voice spoke very classical Mandarin, lyrical, with full accents on the tones and a beautiful cadence and structure.

Alex slowly backed off, away from the voice and towards the entrance.

'Beholden to whom?'

'The West, of course.'

There was a loud click as the electricity was switched off and the miserable interior light was extinguished.

'First opium, then religion, then political ideology, and now debt. First US debt and now European . . . must we consume every Western poison?'

'How is killing these innocent people an answer?'

'Respect is long overdue. We're told to progress, grow and make money, so we Chinese can save the West from itself, buy their goods and ease their debt. But then we're reprimanded like children for being vulgar, greedy and untrustworthy. After all they did, it's pure hypocrisy!'

'But why kill these people?'

'Every narrative needs to motivate its main characters, to carry it through to the end. Before others take it up and tell a new story.'

'And this is *your* story? It's insane.'

'Only these first chapters are mine, beginning with the killing of traitors. Then, as I say, others will take it from here. I was hoping you would be one of them.'

Alex was confused for a moment. He did not understand what was meant.

'Me?' he shouted angrily. 'I would have nothing to do with something like this. Were you waiting here for me?'

There was silence for ten or fifteen seconds but it seemed an age.

'You might yet be persuaded.'

The voice seemed very close this time.

He hurried backwards, perhaps ten metres, away from the

direction of the voice and closer to the entrance, his gun and torch still held in front of him. He looked over his shoulder quickly to find the entrance but he felt himself panic and without focusing he couldn't see it.

Then he heard in the distance, deep in the back of the warehouse, a door open and wind rush in briefly before a slamming sound. His torch beam simply could not reach there.

Alex stood still and listened for any further movement. Nothing. He breathed. Then he turned and slowly scanned for the entrance to the warehouse, eventually seeing through the darkness to its edges framed by the pale red light from the rear brake lights of Ken's car immediately outside. He walked quickly towards it and was relieved to step out into the road. He walked round the back of the Nissan and sat down in the passenger seat next to the motionless figure of the driver. Alex closed the car door and stared straight ahead like Ken. The road in front was empty. All that could be seen was the rain coming down and the darkness beyond. The only sounds now were of Ken's sniffing and heavy breathing. Ken turned to Alex, his eyes still swollen from crying, his hair flat against his skin and dishevelled from sweating. 'Did you see anyone in there?'

'No . . .' Alex hesitated to reply, trying to get a measure of how to respond. The kid's nightmares would be bad enough without the knowledge he had been sitting here alone with the likely killer of his friend still inside. 'No one. We're alone.'

Ken turned back.

'I'm sorry you lost your friend,' Alex said in Cantonese. 'I understand that you were both in business together?'

Ken started to cry again. 'How can one human being do that to another?'

'It's a very terrible thing. Just tell me how you came here and what you saw, then when my colleagues arrive, you can quickly write a statement and we'll take you home.'

'Lok had an appointment. We were told it was with a *gweilo*. He'd described himself as a big, tall man. He had said he was starting a toy business and would need to use a warehouse.' Then Ken turned to Alex and started shouting. 'We knew something was wrong! Who can start a toy business in these bad times? But, you know, stupid *gweilos* . . . so we thought we would go ahead. Meet him and rent something, a good start to our partnership.' He looked at Alex with tears rolling down his cheeks. 'Now Lok is dead. His throat cut like a pig.'

He held on to the steering wheel and shook it violently.

'How could we be so stupid? We thought we were being so clever! We took his poison and ate it gratefully. The *gweilo* fooled us and he killed Lok.'

'Why did you say poison?'

'What?'

'You just said: "We took his poison."'

'We did. We were happy and greedy, and ate what he gave us.' Ken started to cry again, the tears rolling down cheeks. He let go of the steering wheel, exhausted by his outburst, and slipped down in his seat.

Alex said nothing more until the police cars and vans arrived. As officers descended from their vehicles and approached the car, he put up his hand to delay them.

'We will try our best to find Lok's killer.' He rested his hand on Ken's shoulder and gave it a slow pat before pulling the blanket closer round him. 'Now I want you to stay here. I'm going to get out and speak to the other officers and then I'll come back with more blankets for you and some tea. Or, if you are ready to get out, you can sit in one of our vans. Up to you.'

'I'll stay here a bit longer,' Ken whispered.

Alex got out and found De Suza.

'We heard some of what happened but lost a lot when you switched off your earpiece,' De Suza explained.

Officers clustered around, awaiting instructions.

'We need light and lots of it,' Alex announced.

'We brought generators and lights. There was no luck getting the power on again.'

Alex addressed the team of twenty gathered round him.

'We need to move this car then set up lights inside the warehouse within a metre of the wall so as not to contaminate any evidence. I myself, Ken, Lok and his murderer have been between the door and the container. The man who spoke to me inside there may be the same individual as the one who killed Lok, but we should not assume that at this moment.' He pointed to three officers. 'Please get Ken some more blankets and a cup of tea and try to move him from the car. You guys' – he pointed to five others – 'get the lights and generators ready. We will also need to take some lights and a generator down into the back of the warehouse.'

Pike arrived with a team of two, each carrying several body-bags.

'You again?' Alex said. 'Once you're in there, you won't be taking calls for a few days.'

'I brought all these,' Pike replied, shaking the black bags, 'but is it that bad?'

'Worse, I'm afraid. Give us fifteen to set up the lights.'

Alex spoke to the remaining officers.

'I believe the individual I spoke to left by an exit at the rear of the warehouse. Please split into two groups and go round either side.'

Then he spoke to De Suza alone.

'As you'll see for yourself, the situation inside is completely insane. Then that voice . . . for a moment, I thought I heard my friend William.'

'The one who took his own life?'

'Yes. He even used William's favourite phrase: There's nowhere to go but forward.' Alex breathed out heavily and rubbed his eyes.

'You should get indoors,' De Suza said, nodding towards the van. 'Dry off, warm yourself up. I can start things rolling in there.'

'Okay, thanks. I think I've got some dry things in my car. Before you go . . . any further news on the two victims from earlier?'

'We spoke to the parents briefly. There's nothing criminal or murky to report, though we'll need to check in Africa too in Reverend Lu's case. If they were up to something then it was kept secret from their families. There's no evidence that they knew each other before arriving in Hong Kong. Fung's wife doesn't remember him ever mentioning Lu until he met him at the Cathedral. I spoke to Mrs Lu by phone and we're seeing her tomorrow morning. It seems unlikely at this point that they were involved in anything shady.

'Reverend Lu's wife did say one interesting thing. She told me about their trip here a few years ago, when her husband came to lecture on the spread of Christianity in China. A number of people were very argumentative during the lecture apparently, and she remembers her husband being called a Judas, ridiculously enough. She says he received hate mail after the talk.'

'Does she still have any of it?'

'She's going to look.'

'There could be something in it, but it would need to have been a pretty serious argument for them to want to execute Lu several years later. And why someone else too, and in such a manner?'

The two men looked at each other and then at the warehouse. Alex broke the silence.

'It was scary in there.' He grimaced. 'I haven't seen anything like this before, it must've taken months of planning and thinking. I think they died of starvation or maybe thirst before their bodies started metabolizing themselves. And then he came here today, killed the boy to get us here and waited for whoever was going to show up.'

De Suza cut in.

'Waited for *you*. He addressed you by name, saying he wanted to speak to you, didn't he?'

Alex pressed his hands to his head. He wanted to shout and scream. Instead he just continued to let the rain hit his face. He blinked as it got in his eyes and mixed with the sweat and dirt and ran off his face.

'Alex. Come on, get yourself in the van, you need to dry out and get a hot drink inside you.'

Alex looked at his phone. It was still only 8.25 p.m.

Summer

Chien
Heaven

Li
Fire

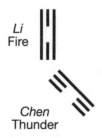

Chen
Thunder

ILLUMINATION

As De Suza walked towards the warehouse, Alex became aware of some new arrivals. The media were out again in full force and were now clustered behind police tape between where he currently stood and where he had parked his car.

He studied the pack, looking for Jenni Plum and hoping she was absent so that he could avoid further embarrassment. Scanning the crowd, he found her standing with the female news reporter who had tried to interview him in the early afternoon. As they saw him approach they called out to him.

'Senior Inspector Soong, please can you give us a few words? We understand you were first on the scene. What did you find?'

'I can't comment at this time,' Alex said flatly. 'I need to get through to my car. Excuse me.'

The reporter's cameraman pushed in closer.

'We understand that you've found several bodies in the warehouse, including that of a young man, realtor Chan Lok Shing. Can you confirm this?' the female reporter pressed him.

'Sorry? What did you say?' He was forced to shout to be heard above the noise of cameras and further questions. There was no hope of any real communication, it was pure feeding frenzy. Alex had had enough. 'Please come with me,' he said.

'An exclusive?' the reporter gasped.

'What? I'm not going to give you a statement. I'm going to arrest you,' he replied angrily.

She seemed completely unperturbed. 'Then please just answer my question first.' She brought the microphone up to his mouth and gave a quick thumbs-up to her cameraman.

'No names are being released, families are yet to be informed. There is nothing further to say at this point.'

'But you are currently leading this investigation, aren't you? Were you the first at the crime scene? Can you tell us what you saw? How many dead in the container?' She fired out the questions as soon as he finished speaking, impervious to his refusal.

It amazed Alex how quickly information could be bought, how much everyone seemed to know, all the time. He thought of the warehouse and the words spoken from the darkness, the voice that reminded him of William.

Suddenly he screamed at her at the top of his voice. 'How dare you do this? Where did you get this information? Where? You broadcast details that ruin lives and devastate families. Tell me where you heard this.'

He pushed forward through the crowd. The iPhones rose quickly into the air and cameras snapped at him, the many sharp little teeth of the beast.

Alex confronted the reporter. Her pupils had widened and even under her generously applied foundation he could see that her face had drained of colour. He lunged closer. Her accomplice, the cameraman, with a close-up of Alex's expression, suddenly dropped his camera from his shoulder and put his open hand against his chest to hold him off.

He had barely touched Alex before he had twisted the cameraman's left hand and arm over, forcing the man's body down and bringing him to his knees. The cameraman, held down on the wet road, screamed in pain. Alex did not look at him but kept his focus on the interviewer. She shouted more questions at him, while Plum and the hoard of iReporters continued to suck up more content.

'What are you doing? Let him go!'

Several officers had moved closer to Alex. One of them picked up the cameraman by the upper arm and brought him inside the police cordon. Another one came to Alex's side. It was Ding, the young officer who had driven him earlier.

'Sir, sir, you should walk away! Let me help you,' he said insistently, bumping against Alex to get him to turn away from the cameras.

'Yes . . . thanks. You're right. Get me to the van, Okay?'

Ding moved forward to stand in front of Alex, who dropped back a step. They both made for a van parked in front of the entrance to the warehouse. The reporter shouted after them: 'The Chinese people have a right to know about such events and how they are to be protected from them. We have a right to know . . .'

Her voice dwindled under a barrage of camera shutters as he and Ding walked away.

Ying appeared from nowhere, with a toothpick in his mouth like an oriental Sam Spade. He walked past Alex and did a double take, seeing him look so wet and twitchy.

'You got to learn to keep it together, Soong. You're freaking people out.'

He should have been taken down, fast and hard. Head hitting the ground and that smile wiped away. But it would only have made things worse. Alex continued walking towards the van.

Inside Alex found Ken wrapped in two blankets. They had cleaned his face, and the blood from his torn ear. His swollen eyes looked less raw, and he had fallen asleep. His sleep would be deep at first after the shock he'd suffered, but soon the nightmares would begin.

Alex thought of the voice in the darkness. It had been recorded by technical support, but at present he just wanted to relive it in his mind. He thought of each step on the concrete floor of the warehouse, unable to see his feet, the torch light unable to illuminate the unseen watcher's face. He had sounded so like William. No. His friend's face had been blown away, but the scar had still been there; it was William in that mortuary, William's body he saw cremated . . .

Ding reappeared and gave Alex a couple of blankets and a cup of hot Ovaltine. He drank it. He was also given a pair of police-issue sweatpants and a shirt to change into. He did not look forward to sleep but felt his eyelids betray him.

De Suza's large hand shook him awake.

'Hey, we're going to make a move.'

'How long has it been?' Alex asked.

'An hour or so. It's just before ten.' De Suza sat next to him. Alex saw that Ken had gone.

'Christ, it's a mess in there!' De Suza shook his head in disbelief and continued: 'Here's the plan. You need to chill. There's a lot of processing to be done here and we're taking care of that. We're trying to get the bodies out quickly though for a cursory examination before the debrief, which must happen tonight.' Alex looked away from his friend's concerned face to the floor of the van. 'Obviously you need to be there for the debrief, but we don't need you till then. So go back to the station with Ding now and I'll drive your car when we pack up here.'

Alex was grateful for the offer. 'I agree with the plan except for the last bit. I'll drive myself back and catch up with things at the station until debrief. I'm going to sit here for another ten minutes then I'll go.'

'Good. We've counted twenty-seven of the ravens!'

Alex remembered the skeletal bird, its eyes merely deep red scabs, and its beak and claws torn from scratching and pulling at the metal door trying to survive.

The main road back to Hung Hom was empty. It was unsettling to be on a quiet road in Hong Kong, like someone turning down the music suddenly, and he was relieved to get to the Eastern Corridor Tunnel, which he had queued to exit only three hours before. As he was about to switch on the radio, his phone rang.

'Soong, until now I have been pleased that you have not been like the other inspectors,' the Captain's voice said abruptly. 'A number of officers who have worked high-profile cases have sought to inflate their own importance in press interviews, in an attempt to become celebrities. Some even think they can be bigger than the force. But your performance just now was something altogether new. Apart from over one hundred and twenty-five thousand hits on YouTube, there's not a shred of merit to it!'

'Sir, I was very . . .' Alex tried to interrupt.

'You stepped out of line. Your defensive move on the cameraman can be explained away, but your continued engagement with the reporter . . . It is a part of *my* responsibilities.

'I do get it,' he continued. 'You've been through a lot today and it's not over until we catch these people, but you've got to learn to manage yourself better. You understand? Anticipate a situation and know exactly how you're going to react, like you do when you're in the field. Sort it out, Soong.'

'Sir.'

'Good.'

'Where are you now?'

'I am coming into the office and should be there about ten forty-five. I need to debrief everyone on this evening, speak to Forensics about the earlier two victims, and file my report on Chow.'

'Okay, that's good organization. See you at the debrief.' The Captain was about to hang up. 'Oh, yes, and your wife has been looking for you. She says she's not happy about your performance either.' He paused. 'I assume she's referring to YouTube as well.'

Alex hung up and took the risk of switching off his phone. He tossed it on the passenger seat and switched on the stereo. He let his thoughts surf the music for a while but inevitably they circled back to the murders, this afternoon's and tonight's.

He tried to imagine the ideal site from which to shoot the ministers. It would have to be of a height that would allow the shooter a clear view of the two men and little chance of being disturbed. The roofs of skyscrapers were simply too high; the victims would have been hidden by the canopy over the walkway. There were very few options, but even at the right height, anyone who could take such a shot would have had considerable training, and part of that would be in leaving no trace. So it made sense to suppose that it was the work of an organized professional rather than a sociopath.

Alex's car settled into the long queue for the toll to Hong Kong side, though he would eventually slip into a toll-free lane for the police available only on the Kowloon side. As the music played on, he relaxed a little more and felt looser.

Neither crime scene had shown any evidence of carelessness; both were staged with meticulous discipline and planning. The scene in the warehouse was difficult to assess in the darkness, but he knew from all the corruption and organized crime cases he'd worked that to make such arrangements was beyond the chaotic mindset of a street criminal or gang of thugs. To hire the container, capture and imprison four people and dozens of birds, then return and kill another man, required a high degree of stability and thinking. Such a complex project would have to have been well-resourced, conceived some time ago, and have strong enough motivation to see it through to the end.

Experience told him that with such a large number of vari-ables – the four people, the ravens, the container, the warehouse, the realtor – so many things to juggle, such a project either worked near-perfectly or failed completely. This seemed to have worked perfectly, but what was the objective? Had the killer stayed behind, waiting for Alex? Was it William? Ken was the only witness to the crime scene and he knew nothing. The number they'd had for the warehouse-viewer would probably be a burn phone and a useless lead.

As Alex emerged into Causeway Bay the traffic flowed freely and he could see that he would be at the station in a few minutes. He needed a little more time to think, so turned left and skirted through an area of narrower streets lined with small restaurants and bars.

Were the two cases connected? There was no common evidence or witness. They had taken place in very different locations, with different victims and methods. He had certainly happened to be present at both, but that had to be coincidence. Yet . . . the man at the warehouse had waited for him. He had said he had been waiting to meet Alex. At the first crime, Alex was merely the duty inspector on the case. But tonight . . . Ignoring the anomaly of his presence at both scenes, if no other connection was established then these two crimes would be treated entirely separately and run by different teams.

Yet in his gut Alex knew this wasn't right. The two crimes were connected. Running them separately would slow their investigation and only serve to allow those involved to escape or, worse, continue. The next question made his adrenalin surge again. What else was planned?

It was now 10.28 p.m. Alex sat behind the wheel and loosened up; he realized that he ached in every joint, bone and muscle. He switched his phone on and it instantly started to vibrate. Jun's name appeared on the illuminated screen. She could make his day or destroy it. He picked it off the charger to see which it would be.

'Alex, where are you?' she said impatiently, voice high and quick, betraying a deeper frustration than if merely enquiring as to his current whereabouts.

'I'm just in the car heading back to the station,' he said.

'Will you get dinner there? I've eaten with the girls.'

Little choice for him then. Good thing he'd eaten before the warehouse call.

'Yes, I suppose I can.' He felt and sounded deflated, and she heard it.

'If you'd told me when you were coming back, I could have left something for you. You just don't tell me and you know I have plans! We couldn't wait for you, we had reservations . . .'

He cut her off. 'You don't realize how insane it's been. There's so much shit going on . . .'

'Why do you have to be so angry and hurtful? We agreed this morning that we wouldn't discuss your work.'

She was right but he should not have agreed to it. He needed to speak about it. He felt that he wanted to scream, to describe to her the details of the atrocities and hurt he'd seen today. 'I'm sorry,' he said, reining himself in. 'It's been an extremely difficult day.'

'Well, come home and rest,' she said in a milder tone.

'It's not as simple as that.'

'It could be, if you took that job with my father.'

He shook his head and gritted his teeth. His lower lip twitched against the upper.

'We have talked about this too. This is what I do.'

'Well, don't get upset about it then. You chose to do it.'

The traffic lurched forward.

'I suppose I'm just asking you to care.'

'Care?' she shouted. '*I* called *you*. Since you're determined to play the victim with me, then what about your latest video? Are you mad? Acting like a thug just to impress some cute blogger.' She breathed out angrily through her nose. 'I'm going out to enjoy myself. I'll see you when I see you.'

As he opened the door, the red light from the shrine was the first thing to catch his eye before the overhead strips clicked on.

Two of four.

One of two.

He looked up at the televisions, which automatically switched on when the door was unlocked. They displayed the carefully selected mix of news channels, blog sites and forums at the outer reaches of the internet. He found the earpieces, inserted them.

'The breaking stories today are the vicious murders in Hong Kong. Two Methodist ministers were murdered execution-style on a public walkway near Citibank Tower, and it is understood that later in the evening there were further murders of at least one person held in a container in a warehouse development north-east of Po Kong Village, the site of the 1967 riots. We now go live to our correspondent . . .'

He switched to the audio of a different channel. A white man in a light blue shirt, standing with the Central police station at his back, spoke into a microphone.

'Susan, we have been watching the situation all day. We understand that Senior Inspector Alex Soong was actually involved in an incident with reporters following the stories, which has gone viral on social media sites during the last hour.'

The picture turned to Susan, sitting long-legged on the side of a desk, her beautiful hair looking as contrived as her concerned expression.

'Let's see if we can see that?' The clip appeared in an insert box on the bottom right of the screen. 'Good grief, he takes him down very quickly! Presumably *our* cameramen wouldn't go down quite so fast . . .'

The full piece was played again. He scanned the other channels; they all carried the story. He logged on to the site of the blogger who'd captured the footage. Her hit-count was now over nine hundred thousand. He flicked to Google and searched for the story. He switched from English to Chinese and there were already hundreds of entries arguing about Alex Soong's behaviour; forum users suggesting mainland policemen should not be allowed in Hong Kong, some saying a serial killer was on the loose, and others suggesting the murders were part of a Japanese retaliation against the Chinese government for its threat to take back the Diaoyu Islands by force.

He smiled then leaned down and picked up his briefcase from the floor and placed it on the desk. He opened it then gazed at the brown bag inside. He took it and placed it gently on the table. The sides of it had patches that were wet and dark, perhaps rotten, yet the edges of the paper were still crisp.

He picked it up and turned into the passage behind him.

Two of two.

Two of four.

Eight of eight.

He stood before the shrine. As the red light washed over the bag, the dark stains almost disappeared. The bag was placed on the floor and he took nine incense sticks from a stack to the left of the shrine and lit them. He looked at the oranges; it had only been a day and they were still unblemished, but he took them down and placed them on a gold plate on a table positioned below the shrine. He picked up the bag and held it out before the shrine. He looked at the photo, at his ancestors, but it was the woman he stared at. He fixed on her, the rough sepia image of a face he had had in mind for many years.

He opened the bag and removed a withered right hand, severed at the wrist. It was wet and decomposing, the skin over the bones yellow and loose. Muscles had tightened the fingers, drawing them into a claw. The nails were torn but underneath what was left there was dried blood. The third finger had a thin metal band round it. He placed the hand palm up on the gold plate. Stared at the image of the woman and smiled. He surveyed the shrine with its new offering, a thin smile of satisfaction on his face. It was finally time, after so much waiting and preparation. It was as it should be. He smiled and bowed three times to the ancient image in the frame.

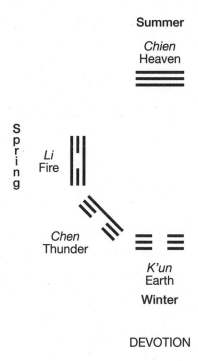

DEVOTION

When Alex got to the station, the media were already camped outside the gates. He had to stop at the security gate for clearance, giving them the chance to crowd the sides of his car. Harajuku siren Jenni Plum quickly appeared. Bending down, she peered in on the passenger side and snapped a few shots. She leaned against the closed passenger window, small breasts, rosy lips and long eyelashes pushed flat against the glass.

'Alex? Why didn't you take the job with your father-in-law?'

He stared straight ahead.

A familiar hairstyle appeared at the driver's side window.

'Senior Inspector, are you going to issue an apology to our cameraman? Will you take yourself off the case?'

He gritted his teeth.

The gate officer nodded to him as he walked past to the elevator. As he approached it, the doors opened. De Suza was already back.

'It's becoming a bit of a flash mob outside. Your performances have been popular,' he observed.

Alex looked irritated.

'Okay, I'll leave it alone, but the others are already talking about the shit they're going to give you.'

Alex frowned. 'Why are you all back so soon? I thought you'd be a few hours at least.'

'The Captain called everybody in for a full update. And I do mean everybody,' De Suza stressed, raising his eyebrows knowingly. 'Including Mak. IA's going to want to know where the media got the initial tip-off.'

Alex chose to ignore this. 'Dead ministers, a dead realtor, dead unknowns and dead birds. We really don't know much, do we? Where are they with reviewing the crime scenes?'

'The pedestrian bridge is finished but closed for the moment, so it's still available for further visits. They've been at the container a while but nothing so far. No hair, fingerprints, personal items, nothing from a person who was not a victim. But we're still in the middle of the processing, and then they'll look at the end of the warehouse where you think someone was hiding.'

'Think? Someone *was* there. So you have nothing,' Alex fumed. 'Nothing at all?' De Suza placed his hand on his partner's shoulder and gave it a reassuring shake. 'Not one thing.'

'We've got prints from the unknowns in the container and we're running them in the NEC AFIS system with the help of the Immigration Department. It's going to be a few hours before we hear any results. Then there's the birds. Who the hell gets hold of twenty-seven ravens?' De Suza was shaking his head. 'It's fucking weird, really fucking weird. And the *gweilo*, he was German. We're trying to find out more about him now.'

The elevator passed two floors and then stopped to take on two people. Alex moved to get out and pushed De Suza's arm to indicate he wanted him to follow. The lift door closed.

'Let's take the stairs.'

'Really?'

Once there, they stopped on a landing between floors and turned to face the narrow window.

'I'd rather talk here,' Alex explained.

De Suza looked at his partner's bloodshot eyes and pale skin. 'You need to sleep, man.'

'I know.' Alex rubbed his eyes with his hands then drew his palms slowly across his face as if hoping to wipe away the fatigue. The yellow and white fuzz of the surrounding city lights spread across the glass in front of him.

'How long have we got until the meeting?'

'About twenty minutes.'

'Okay, quickly then. The two Methodist ministers. I think the shooter was on the old ICAC building.'

'What?'

'I think it's the only place those shots could be taken from. It's a good height, it's got very limited traffic and few people are allowed up there.'

'Brilliant,' De Suza moaned. 'We go marching into the ICAC . . .'

'Now the containers,' Alex pushed on. 'Like the first, this scenario was extremely well planned. It was discovered today for a reason. The two events have a purpose even if we don't know what it is. These cases are most definitely connected.'

De Suza interrupted. 'You know that isn't going to go down well. People will be hoping to make their name on one of these cases, and I know what you're going to say next. You think you should be in charge of both.'

'Yes. The man in the warehouse said he had been waiting to meet me. I'm in this somewhere for these people. We should use that to draw them out. Sidelining me will just make them change their plans, and then whatever evidence we have will be wasted because they'll take another course. I'm involved in this somehow.'

'And your dead friend who committed suicide? William? I know you said you thought you heard him, but listening in the dark can play tricks on the mind.' De Suza looked at him. 'You've had a long day, buddy. Let's not mention him in the briefing, okay?'

'You're right, let's drop that. It was just hearing a familiar phrase that played tricks with my mind. What about any information on the other tenants and the owner of the warehouses?'

'We talked to the owners, who were not completely helpful because the more media this generates the less likely they are to be able to sell them. There are sixty warehouses of which only twelve are rented or sold. The ones immediately surrounding Warehouse 44 are vacant. Most of the space that's rented out has been leased to local companies for long-term inventory storage.'

'Anything of interest about those tenants?'

'Most are offshore companies based in the Cayman Islands, British Virgin Islands, etc. It's going to take time.' De Suza trailed off at the thought of the paperwork involved in tracking all the offshore companies.

'Where's the meeting being held?' Alex asked.

'Nine.'

'We'll take the lift the rest of the way.'

Back in the lift, Alex pressed the button for the ninth floor but suddenly said: 'I'm going to take the elevator down to reception. I need to see the duty officer. I'll see you in the meeting room.'

'What? Why? You've got nine minutes . . . don't be late, for fuck's sake,' De Suza called out after him as he took the next elevator down to the first floor. 'Remember it's on nine.'

Alex went straight down to the reception area for the general public. Out of the stairwell, he entered a corridor that led to the reception and processing areas. Late in the evening the place was often empty, and when he needed a break from the noise of the upper floors Alex would come down and walk about just to slow things down. The work in this area was chiefly concerned with registration issues, administration, and petty local complaints. Much of it was undertaken by junior officers or senior men who were either close to retirement or had been injured in the line of duty.

Alex liked listening to people talking of simpler and less violent problems and watching police help people without using guns or threats. He leaned against a wall and let his head drop. He breathed in the silence and remained still for a long twenty seconds.

Although it was nearly 11.15, there was a short queue of people there, most likely to report stolen cars or lost property, or else just drunken tourists looking for directions. Alex decided he would take just a minute or so more. He watched the people in the queue and the duty officer attending to them.

'Inspector Soong?'

He swung round.

'We met earlier – Professor Yi.' The slight figure in front of him smiled, and he saw the familiar dimple and immediately wanted to smile back, but stopped himself.

'What are you doing here? Come to file a report on some missing books?' he joked, briefly forgetting everything that had concerned him a few moments ago.

'Very funny. No, I've been using my brother's car and had a minor accident with a taxi. Driving on the other side of the road has been a bit tricky for me. So I need to report it for the insurance claim. Unfortunately, he's not in town to help me – if he had been he probably wouldn't have lent me the car. Standing here I've found out Hong Kong has much better, and more complicated, administration than when I grew up here, so I'm a bit lost.'

'I didn't realize you'd lived here.'

'Well, it was only for a few years. My parents adopted me from an orphanage here when I was small, and my brother, though he's my adopted brother. Then after a few years we all went to Boston.'

'So you speak Cantonese?' he asked cheekily.

'It's pretty basic but I speak Mandarin. My adoptive parents came down from China at the end of the Sixties.'

Alex smiled and looked at the few people in front of her in the queue. 'Let me get you the forms. It's late and it'll be quicker that way.'

'Why, that's extremely kind, officer,' she said, caricaturing the accent and graciousness of Scarlett O'Hara. Alex laughed out loud and relaxed for a second.

He went through the doors into the back office of the floor and to the administrative area of the duty officers' desk. An older officer Alex recognized was sitting there, sipping herbal tea.

'*Eh*, there is a friend of mine out there who has had a knock in her brother's car. She just needs to file the report. I'll take her the relevant forms, then can you help her with the rest?' he asked.

'Sure,' the officer replied.

Alex took the forms, but when he got to the door leading to the public area, he stopped momentarily and looked through the window at Yi. He watched her, standing patiently, slowly tapping her right foot. She stood very straight. Though she wore no make-up and just a pair of faded blue jeans and a fitted *Bathing Ape* T-shirt with the usual cartoon monkey's face on it, he quietly admitted to himself that she was actually rather striking.

He stopped looking at her and went back through the doors.

'Here are the forms.' He handed them to her. 'I have to go to a meeting now, so another officer will take the forms back from you in a few minutes.'

Yi stood in silence for a few seconds. She looked up at him and it made Alex feel very self-conscious.

'I'm glad to see you have pacifist beliefs. They are always very popular with the police,' he stammered out awkwardly, and stuck out his hand. 'Well, see you soon. Good luck, and I hope you get things sorted out with the car.'

She stuck out her hand too and took his. 'I'm sure we will. We have the luck of Guan Gong shining down on us.' She pointed up to the traditional Chinese godlike figure placed high on the wall in the entrance to the station for good luck, surrounded by the glow of a naked red light bulb. 'He was an old martial arts god, the god of war, and now he works for the police, I see.'

Alex looked up at the figure. 'Indeed. And after all that has happened today, we're going to need the old man's help.'

Her hand was soft and warm and he didn't want to let it go. She looked down at it and he followed her line of sight. They both let go.

'Look, thank you for the forms. I owe you a coffee at least some time, though I'm leaving tomorrow.'

'Oh, it was nothing,' he said, still rooted to the spot.

'It was very kind of you to help with the forms, after the day you've had.' She met his eyes directly again. 'I overheard a conversation between two officers while you went to get the forms. They said that you'd had a long day, and that you shot someone early this morning.' She seemed unsure of his reaction after she'd said this, clearly wondering whether she had crossed a line.

'Oh . . .' He was relieved by the simplicity of her confession. 'Yes, that's true. Part of the job sometimes. I haven't processed it yet . . . haven't had the time. Those guys should not be talking about it in public though.'

'I can't imagine doing that. In my work I have studied historical events, revolutions, wars, uprisings, that have involved hundreds of thousands of deaths, yet I cannot imagine the tragedy of having to take another human life. I appreciate the strength and bravery involved, but what a terrible thing to have to do.'

Her face was very close to his. He thought how easy this conversation had been, and appreciated the clarity of Yi's mind. He looked at the little mole just under her left eye and she saw him looking at it.

'According to traditional superstition, that mole under your eye means you cry a lot,' he commented.

She withdrew a step. 'Sorry, you don't want to talk about your work. I was intruding,' she said hurriedly.

'No. But I guess I'm not really used to talking about any of this except with my partner.'

He suddenly remembered the meeting.

'I'll let you get on with the form-filling. Looking at the length of them, you could be here all night.' He glanced at his watch. He was already five minutes late. 'I should go.'

He put out his hand.

'A proper and formal goodbye.'

She took it and they shook again.

'Thank you very much. And get some sleep, officer,' she commanded, cocking her head back and giving him a broad smile.

He let go. Just.

'Have a safe trip back. What time do you land?'

'Officer, you're lingering.'

She's flirting a little now, he thought to himself. I should go.

'I leave at twelve forty-five p.m. tomorrow and get home about twenty hours later, thanks to my cheap ticket to Boston routed through Vancouver.'

She did not continue talking but glanced down quickly at his wedding ring. His left thumb automatically touched it.

'Have a safe trip, I should be going,' he said resolutely.

*

Once through the doors, Alex watched Yi through the windows, as he had done ten minutes before. She was already scribbling away on the forms. Feeling in a more positive mood and momentarily forgetting his tiredness, he continued to watch her and then started to imagine going back through the doors to speak to her again. Perhaps a question on Chinese history. If he could only think of some burning question about ancient texts or practices, then he could sound vaguely credible. Or just simply go ask her to meet him for a coffee or bowl of noodles tomorrow morning before her flight. Maybe he could, maybe he should, it would be the courteous thing to do, return to check she had the forms completed correctly, though he hadn't shown much competence or knowledge of the form-filling process.

A large familiar hand grasped his shoulder.

'What are you doing here? It was time to go about eight minutes ago,' said De Suza's voice behind him. Then he stuck his head over Alex's right shoulder. 'What are you looking at anyway?' He edged Alex aside so he could get a better look. 'Very nice.' He looked down at his friend. 'Do you think I should ask her out?' he said in very rough Cantonese.

Alex blushed slightly and blurted out: 'But you're married.'

'Oh, I see, it's like that.' De Suza's broad face was no more than a few centimetres from Alex's. 'But so are you, buddy. Remember? Tall, attractive, long legs ... fangs. Sleeps in the dark all day. Remember her?'

'Hey, she may be the undead but she's my undead,' Alex retorted.

De Suza looked back through the window.

'Smart, is she?'

'Yes. Very.'

'Witty.'

'I think so.'

'She's cute.' The big man thought about it. 'I say we fight for her.'

'Point taken,' Alex replied wearily.

De Suza put his hands on Alex's shoulders and turned his friend around to face the lift. 'You have enough to think about at the moment.' He pressed the button.

Alex looked up at De Suza and laughed.

'You are going to get yourself into trouble,' De Suza teased.

'Fuck you,' Alex laughed in Mandarin.

De Suza laughed back and shook Alex's shoulder roughly.

Alex and De Suza reached the ninth floor and went straight to the meeting room, where the Captain was already at the front addressing a room full of uniformed and plainclothes officers. He was introducing the Forensics team who would debrief them on the findings from the crime scenes and the bodies of the murdered priests. The warehouse dead had so far received only a preliminary examination. Alex and De Suza slipped in and stood at the front by the entrance. Alex looked around the room and found Mak sitting comfortably three rows from him. Mak grinned, perhaps to intimidate. Alex merely nodded politely in reply and returned to staring at the projection screen ahead.

Pike led them through his analysis of this afternoon's crime scene. His verdict on the angle of the men's wounds was the same as Alex's.

'Both shots used high-velocity sniper rounds from the same gun, a QBU-88, normally referred to as a Type 88, a mainland-made weapon,' he announced.

Alex immediately thought that the shooter was probably Chinese, as few foreigners would ever use a Chinese-made weapon, they'd prefer a Western-crafted product. Such a weapon would also be hard for a foreigner to obtain in Hong Kong, without the right connections.

'Both victims died instantly.' The Forensics officer took a breath. 'So what else did we find? No fingerprints, but then the killer is very unlikely to have visited the site. There was also no hair, skin, sweat or other human evidence other than from the hundreds of thousands of people who have used the walkway every day. There is little we can tell you other than that both were single head shots. In our opinion, it was very personal.'

'We should check out the usual religious activists . . . the Muslims, Christian fundamentalists and Falun Gong,' someone shouted from the back.

'It seems unlikely to be them,' De Suza shouted. 'These groups are small in Hong Kong, and aren't interested in this kind of public spectacle. We've had no trouble from them. There aren't any fundamentalist Christian groups like those in the US, and Falun Gong have never achieved anything here.'

'There are few enough of them left anyway,' Alex put in. 'This does seem to be personal, between these two priests and their killer.' He paused for a moment then asked Pike: 'Any thoughts on trajectory and the location of the shooter?'

'Nothing yet.'

'De Suza – background on the victims, please?' requested the Captain.

'Negative so far. No gambling, triad involvement, hookers, no Big Six family in Shenzhen. However, one of the men did lecture at HKU a few years ago and received some hate mail for his trouble. His wife is looking for this and will bring it in if she still has it.'

Alex intervened. 'We need to find the location of the shooter and perhaps see if there is any word about someone buying a Type 88. Also check CCTV on the street for any activity, though it's long odds against finding something.'

'Looks like our prodigal sons have some good ideas. So what's next then?' the Captain asked, with barely a nod in their direction.

The picture of the two dead ministers on the screen in front of them was now replaced by a grisly shot of the interior of the container. A new member of the Forensics team introduced these findings.

'Forty-foot shipping container. All markings as to origin and any previous destination have been removed. There's nothing, not even adhesive marks. It was thoroughly cleaned and repainted before it arrived at the warehouse. Also, whoever was responsible for that rubbed the whole thing down to remove prints, leaving nothing on the outside and nothing so far on the inside. At this point we haven't checked the bottom. We found that the interior was also newly painted before the victims and birds were imprisoned.'

A more graphic picture of the four mutilated and starved bodies and twenty-seven dead ravens, plus the body of Lok, filled the screen, and everybody fell silent.

'Five dead in total, one female and four males, all in their twenties. Four Chinese and one German, who was carrying an ID card that states he is Oliver Derm from Münster. Four died of dehydration and infection, but by the time they died they were starved and had lost significant body weight as well. Three of the four had tried to eat the ravens. The bodies of seven birds had bite marks. These three victims had also started to contract various diseases from the flesh they'd ingested. The fifth died from severed internal and external carotid arteries, and bled out quickly.'

De Suza interrupted: 'What can you tell us about the Chinese victims' background? What were their teeth like, for example? Any signs of surgery?'

'Yes. Good question, sir.' De Suza smiled at the rookie pathologist's enthusiasm and politeness. 'The teeth were in poor condition, showing little early dental care. So they were probably from a poor background or else had unthinking parents. However, two of them had large fillings, which indicates that at some point their circumstances improved and they found themselves in a position to obtain dental treatment. The size of the fillings indicates decay had manifested for some period before they took or had the opportunity for dental care. One had received surgery, a hip replacement, possibly due to what looks like an accident. We're tracing the hip joint.

'One victim' – the Forensics officer used a laser-pointer to highlight the wretched individual – 'was without a hand, and two others were without eyes. The hand was taken post-mortem, possibly just before Senior Inspector Soong arrived. The eyes were removed by the birds pre-mortem.'

'Have we been able to identify any of them apart from the realtor?' the Captain asked.

'We've got the fingerprints running through the AFIS system with the Immigration Department, but nothing so far. There's nothing from missing persons either. We're trying the consulates here and the embassies in Beijing, but again nothing so far. Tissue samples show they were heavily drugged, which would have put them out for two or perhaps even three days. The ravens were also drugged, but in their case it was only a light sedative, which would not have lasted more than a day at the most.'

The Forensics officer faltered for a moment and cleared his throat.

'We have found that certain areas of each victim's body were coated with rotten meat paste. When the ravens came round, after probably being starved first, they smelled the paste and went straight for these areas on the victims' bodies. As the victims were much more heavily sedated, they would not have felt the initial pecks, and even when their flesh was removed they would not have been able to fight back effectively. We believe,' he went on, his voice wavering, 'that whoever organized this deliberately sought to mutilate the eyes, hands, feet and groin area of each victim.'

There was a stir throughout the room as the meaning sank in.

'It's fucking crazy,' someone said aloud to themself.

'How much harm can a raven do, for God's sake?' someone else murmured.

'A raven can kill a young goat or lamb. They are aggressive omnivores,' the officer replied boldly, clearly now having everyone's attention.

'How long did it take the victims to die?' De Suza asked.

'For three of them about six days, at least two of which they spent unconscious. It is an extremely painful way to die. Horrible, in fact.'

'And the fourth?'

'The German man survived a further two days, sustaining himself by eating flesh from the birds and from other victims.'

The room, filled with seasoned senior policemen and policewomen, fell silent. Some just stared at the picture of the inside of the container, black with congealed blood, with only Lok's recently murdered body surrounded by deep red.

'Chan Lok Shing was attacked from behind and had his throat slit with a thin-bladed razor-like implement. The cut was so deep it nearly removed his head. He bled out.'

The officer stepped down. The Captain took centre-stage again.

'What else do we know?' he enquired.

De Suza stood up. 'On the container case, only a small number of the sixty warehouses in the development are used. So far, we think it's just for storage. Basically the area is rarely visited. We're looking at the footage from the entrance camera but it only goes back twenty-four hours. We assume the individual who killed Lok Shing had blood on his clothes. There were stains heading out of the warehouse but they stop some way after it and there's nothing further. Possibly he bagged the clothes in the dark and then took them with him.'

'Okay, thanks, Inspector De Suza,' the Captain responded. 'Soong, those of us who heard the recording of the conversation you had in the warehouse were surprised to hear you calling out a name. Do you have reason to believe the perpetrator is known to you?'

Alex breathed in deeply.

'No, it was foolishness on my part. He used a phrase a friend of mine was fond of, that's all. It was pitch-black, my torch barely penetrated the darkness immediately in front of me and I was pumped full of adrenalin.'

'Fine. We should go over those recordings again in any case, strip them down, see if there's anything else going on in that warehouse that was picked up from your phone. The next step is to identify the victims, then establish why they were chosen. I want to catch these people before they kill again.'

Around the room there were muffled sounds of agreement.

'I agree with all that's been said,' Alex interjected loudly as people started to talk to each other, 'but we're failing to consider the motive behind these killings.' He paused and De Suza groaned quietly in anticipation. 'I think the two cases are connected.'

'Let's guess, Soong. You want to run them both,' Ying announced.

'I didn't say that. I just believe the cases are connected. And, yes, we should run them together.'

'So you are wanting a little more glory, heh? I would have thought after your performances on YouTube, you'd be satisfied for the moment. Isn't that enough attention for one day?' Ying continued, raising a few laughs. 'I was thinking about this earlier. I'm always seeing your wife in magazines, attending parties for the rich and famous, but never you. Well, maybe I will soon, heh?'

'That's enough Ying,' the Captain intervened. 'And, Soong, the cases will be run separately because they are currently completely distinct and independent incidents, separated by time, place and victim profiles. We have *no* reason for treating them any other way. No one has yet offered a tenable connection.' He looked hard at Alex. 'If you can establish a connection, I'll combine them and you'll be in charge.'

'Seriously? This golden boy thing has gone far enough,' Ying muttered audibly.

The Captain scowled at him. 'Soong? Anything more to say?' he enquired.

'I believe the connection is there and I will look for it,' Alex said.

The Captain turned on him then. 'No, you won't. You'll stick to your work and leave other people to theirs. You and De Suza, you're on the ministers. Ying and Chao, you're both on the container. Keep me updated regularly, please. Remember, everyone, the day after tomorrow is the key meeting of global economic and finance leaders to discuss the default by the Europeans. It's a priority. We are severely short-staffed for the next four days. Everyone, and I mean everyone, will have to cover, some of you taking on more than one set of official responsibilities.'

When he'd finished speaking, the Captain made his way through the crowded room. Alex approached him but his superior spoke first.

'I know, you think I'm making a mistake . . . though I'm not sure why. In fact, I've no idea at all what goes on in your head. If you've anything else to say, you'd better mention it now. Don't keep anything back. You've done some good work today but also caused a fair amount of embarrassment.' He came in closer so that only he and Alex could hear their further exchange. 'And I know you hate Ying and think he's crooked, but I believe you're wrong. He's a good detective, just from a different era.'

The Captain walked on and De Suza joined Alex as Ying sauntered past. Alex felt that the older man had wormed his way up through the system, primarily by knowing how to play it. He was no genius, but he was hard and callous, and knew enough people to get his way.

'You work your case and I'll work mine. All right, Soong?' Ying said. 'If you have a lead I expect you to share it, and I'll do likewise.' Ying spoke quickly and without much effort at subtlety: his Cantonese was from the heart of Mongkok, and he was rightly proud of it. He would only speak Mandarin reluctantly, and didn't care for the mainland or its people. Ying had mostly worked the triad and organized crime area, and Alex was fairly sure he had been reached by the gangs. In twelve years he had never managed to charge any high-level members. It seemed to Alex like an obvious arrangement. Too often Ying's cases would fall apart at the last minute. 'If you have a problem with me then just tell me,' he was saying.

'Fine, okay. You're going to get someone else killed!' Alex shouted at him, pointing a finger in his face.

The words, Ying couldn't care less about, but a finger pointed at him so directly and blatantly, in public . . . He straightened up and leaned hard into Alex's personal space. But he did nothing, as he could see over Alex's shoulder that the Captain was storming back towards them.

'Enough! What the fuck are you doing? People have *died*. I have to speak to the Chief Executive to give him an update, and we don't have much to keep him happy. He'll then have to tell Beijing. Just get on with your work, both of you. Remember, if you keep me happy then I can keep the Chief Executive happy. But if not, where the Chief Executive's shoe goes, mine will go twice as hard.'

Ying looked as though he was going to butt in. 'Ying, get going!' snapped the Captain.

The Captain stayed behind with Alex and De Suza. 'You're beginning to annoy me, Soong. Haven't I told you three times today to get on with your job? Yes, you're twenty times smarter than Ying, and possibly fifty times fitter, but you're behaving like you're half his age. You're tired and stressed. Get some sleep or do whatever you do to relax.' He started to walk away then came back and up close to Alex. 'I can't believe I am saying this to you again within less than five minutes!'

He poked an index finger into Alex's chest.

'Sort it out.' Then he turned to De Suza. 'Rein in your partner . . . with extreme prejudice if necessary.'

He marched off.

Alex nodded in the direction of the Forensics team, indicating that De Suza and he would stay behind and consult them further.

'Please can you just show those slides again?' he asked them.

'Sure.'

Alex turned to De Suza and suggested they sit at the back, to view them from a distance. 'I want a different perspective. If these killings are connected, then there must be some visible link between them. Something he is communicating, intentionally or subconsciously.'

They sat down, De Suza squeezing his large frame into the seat next to Alex.

The first slide was a wide shot of the interior of the container. Alex noted the three bodies on the right propped against the wall, the three males, with the female in the rear on the left. Lok's body was slumped on the floor centre-front. The woman had a large patch of hair ripped from her scalp, presumably by a bird after its claws had become entangled. The next slide closed on the severed right hand of the German in the rear of the container. In the dark the disfigurement was visible only because the stump at his wrist had been placed prominently in his lap. The body of the Chinese male nearest the container's doors had its left eye missing. Dark satin feathers and wings were spread around the container's floor and the large limp bodies of the birds lay scattered among the human remains.

'What do you remember thinking when you were standing there?' De Suza whispered to Alex. 'Close your eyes and think back.'

He looked at the image projected on the wall, got up and walked slowly towards it, and continued to walk with slow, regular steps until he was almost inside the image on the screen. He scrutinized each sickening detail of the image. Felt again the fear of being in that vast space, knowing that while he was in the fetid, blood-spattered container there was blackness beyond it, a vast unnatural dark. He looked at the pathetic remains. Pieces of flesh torn away, an earlobe plucked off, multiple puncture wounds from the birds' sharp beaks, and scratches and gouges in the skin left by razor-sharp claws. He looked at Lok, poor kid. Then up and across to the body slumped in the far left-hand corner of the shot, and then back to the three male bodies.

There it was.

Round the neck of the German with the missing hand. A cross suspended from a thin silver chain. Alex remembered how it had glinted in the beam of light from his torch. In the photograph the easily recognizable shape was reflected on to the opposite wall of the container. It seemed unreal. What place had any god in such a monstrous scene? The man had lived on in the pitch-black for several days; he'd heard everything . . . the screeching of the birds, their wings beating aimlessly in flight to nowhere, and perhaps the dying cries of the others . . . but he saw nothing. He was the last one. God protected him, or the Devil tormented him, for that long.

Alex continued to brood over the image.

'Pike,' he shouted, 'please show me all the close-ups. Slowly.'

While they reviewed each shot, Alex studied them all intently. He moved from left to right, traced lines on the projection following the contours of bodies, and noted changes in clothing and old scars and markings on their skin. He looked over every detail again and then returned to the huddled figure of the man. The cross, small though it was, seemed carefully positioned. It was tight around his neck on a choker-length chain, an unusual arrangement for a religious ornament, and the links that supported it looked as if they could easily be broken.

'Pike, were any of the others wearing any jewellery at all?'

Pike looked at the youngster who had given the presentation. 'Matthew, just check, any of them wearing jewellery?'

The kid reached into the plastic tub he had packed up and fished out four files. He thumbed through each.

'No, none of any kind apart from the cross.'

De Suza joined Alex.

'What've you got in mind?'

He sidestepped the question and directed another at the pathologist.

'What about Lok? Did he have any jewellery on him?'

Matthew fished out a fifth folder and flicked through.

'No.'

'Can you show me all the close-up photos again? One by one, slowly.' Alex looked at the ears, fingers, wrists and necks of the five victims. 'Again, please. And, Pike . . . Matthew . . . Did you guys look to see if there were obvious marks where jewellery had been removed?'

The Forensics team glanced at each other sidelong.

De Suza watched his friend, no longer tired but energized and alert, run his hand over the projected images of arms, cuts, clots of blood, hollow faces and shrivelled lips and eyes.

He turned round looking excited.

'Did you see any impressions, lines, discoloration on the skin ... marks left by jewellery that had been worn for a long time, such as wedding rings, bracelets, earrings?'

'No, we didn't. But it was just a preliminary review ...'

Alex walked up to Matthew, who was tall and gangly and wearing a white coat that was too short for him and probably not his own. 'Can we go down there and take a look now?'

Pike smiled at Alex's enthusiasm and addressed Matthew. 'Can you finish here, please? I will take the two detectives downstairs to look at the bodies.'

The head pathologist walked out of the meeting room and called to the two police officers behind him: 'It's twelve-forty. If we're going to look at the bodies then let's get on with it.'

They chased after him and caught up at the elevator lobby. The doors opened and the three of them descended. They had reached the fifth floor when Officer Ding got in.

'What are you still doing here?' De Suza asked.

'I was just finishing some paperwork, and then Senior Inspector Ying asked me to accompany him for a bowl of noodles.'

'Ah,' said De Suza. 'And how do you know S.I. Ying?'

'Oh, he's an old schoolfriend of my father's.'

'Is that how you became interested in joining the police?'

'No, my ... ah, here's my floor.'

They stopped at the first floor. Ding alighted and said goodnight.

'He seems a good kid,' De Suza commented to the other two.

'Yeah, I thought so earlier when I met him in the van,' Alex agreed. 'Hope he doesn't get in too deep with Ying.'

The elevator stopped.

The mortuary was dimly lit by several low-energy bulbs. Pike flicked on the full lighting, which bathed every inch of the room in bright white. This room was by far the cleanest part of the eleven-floor building. Alex admired the brightness of all the steel instruments and well-scrubbed surfaces.

'Pike, it's beautifully clean and neat down here. If my wife could see this, she'd be a big admirer.'

Pike smiled at him. 'Yes, but is it brown enough for her?'

'Very amusing,' Alex cut in.

'Right, the bodies . . . which are not in such a good state. Follow me.'

He took them into a cold room in which there were two six-body refrigerator units. He pulled the first door open and the cadaver out on its metal shelf.

'The rioting in 'Sixty-Seven was the last time we had more than six cadavers in the police station at one time, and I'd hoped I wouldn't be on duty when that happened again. Terrible events.'

They looked at all five bodies. Morticians had cleaned them up after the pathologists had done their initial work. In the half-light of the container, Alex had not been able to make out any human features, just shocking glimpses of blood and decomposing flesh. He looked down at the man who had been wearing the cross. He was quite young, perhaps only in his mid-twenties. His body was emaciated and dehydrated, the skin had lost all elasticity. Desecration, was all he could think, to treat another human being so.

He stood back so as not to obstruct Pike's view. 'This was the individual wearing the cross, correct?'

'Yes, that's right.'

'Please can you look now to see if there are any visible marks or signs that he had worn it for any length of time?'

Pike checked. 'There's nothing.'

'Okay.'

De Suza stood at the other side and scanned the ragged and abused body for any tell-tale signs. 'Nothing else I can see, Pike,' he confirmed.

'Let's check the others,' Alex requested.

They followed the same procedure. With each fresh body came a wave of sadness and fatigue that Alex found hard to contain. By 1.30 a.m. they had finished.

'Three rings missing, two bracelets and a pair of earrings,' Pike concluded.

'Pike, I'm sorry to ask, but can you check the stomachs of the birds?' Alex requested.

Pike continued while Alex and De Suza turned away for a few moments.

'Okay, if that proves there was no other jewellery in the container, then why leave only the cross on a German?' De Suza asked aloud to no one in particular.

'And was it even the victim's in the first place?' Alex responded.

'Gentlemen, it has been a long day for us, as it has for both of you,' Pike told them. 'Why not sleep now and leave us to work on the birds?'

'Thank you, doctor,' Alex replied and the two went down to the car park together.

They stood silently just a few steps outside the elevator.

'What's your thinking on this cross?' De Suza asked, putting his hands in his pockets and flexing his knees to stretch.

'I think it's a message for someone. Maybe us, maybe someone else. It's the only piece of jewellery at the scene and it's a cross. One that, forensically speaking, the wearer doesn't show much evidence of having worn before. We need to look closely tomorrow, but whatever sort of cross it is, it's a symbol of Christianity, and *that's* the common element between the two killings. Listen to this . . .' Alex looked around to check they were not being overheard. The car park was virtually empty at this hour. '"First opium, then religion, political ideology, and now debt. Must we consume every Western poison?"'

De Suza listened closely to the words Alex had heard in the warehouse.

'Say it again?' he asked.

Alex repeated the question.

'Who is *we*?' De Suza asked aloud.

'He means all Chinese. The opium traded by the British and devoured in China in the nineteenth century. Ideology is clear enough, must be Marxism, and debt refers to the trillion and more Euros China has swallowed to keep Europe afloat.'

'What do you know about problematic religions in China?'

'Actually, nothing. It's never been something I've wanted to get involved in. White-collar crime, corruption and murder, they've always been my areas. I've deliberately stayed out of everything religious or political. After my father and grandfather, I think the Chinese people have heard enough on these matters from our family.'

'So if you have had nothing to do with religious-based investigations and we focus solely on the unique fact of the second case, which is the personal contact with you, then the first and the second crimes seem entirely different and unrelated. Two separate and distinct cases.'

'But they *are* connected. There's something specific and detailed in their manner of execution, as well as their lack of any obvious motive. And it can't be pure coincidence they occurred on the same day.'

'Let's stop this,' said De Suza. 'We're not getting anywhere. You need sleep, and frankly so do I.' He turned to go. Alex stood and watched him take long strides towards the security gate. He shouted after his partner:

'Hey, thanks for today.'

'For what?'

'Just generally keeping me together.'

'Shut up! Get some rest,' De Suza laughed.

Alex made his way through the car park. It was silent except for his footsteps. He got into the car and turned on the engine. Just as he had slipped it in gear the Captain appeared at the driver's window. Alex lowered it.

'Pike called me and said you had asked him to look at the birds.'

'Yes, but it's nothing at the moment.'

'He wants my sign-off on the overtime so he can proceed with your request. So is it a something, as Pike said, and I should tell him to proceed, or a nothing as you've just said, so I can tell him to ignore it?'

The Captain looked down, placing his hands on the frame of the open window.

'Okay, it's a something.'

'But Soong, which case does this something relate to? Because the case with the birds isn't yours.'

'It's primarily to the second case but . . .' Alex admitted sheepishly.

The Captain did not hide his displeasure. 'For God's sake, can't you just do what you're told? Give me a clear reason why I should sign off.'

'I think they are connected.'

'We've been through this.' The Captain breathed out hard, rasping his lips, and then smirked in mock despair. 'Come on Soong, stop making this so difficult on yourself. What did we say?'

'I work on the first case.'

'Yes.'

Alex undid his seat belt and turned to face the open window properly.

'The results from the doctor's search are relevant to my case,' Alex stated clearly.

'Then I'll sign off. For the sake of both our jobs, make sure everything is straight.' The Captain walked round the car and looked at him through the windscreen. 'Stay away from Ying. Understand?' He scratched the back of his neck, waiting. 'Understand? Say it.'

'I understand.'

Alex closed the window and pulled out into the thin midnight traffic of Central.

He took the main road under the flyover unhurriedly, driving parallel with the curve of the racetrack in Happy Valley. It had been sad to watch the track, more than a hundred and fifty years old, fall into disrepair. Receipts there had dropped as people turned to more profitable, if illegal, ways of gambling. The Hong Kong Jockey Club, a founding pillar of the local community, then began to falter on its charitable commitments, most of its revenues being placed into the community. Alex had admired the grandstand, though he wasn't much interested in horses or gambling himself. But the racecourse had previously funded hospitals, care for the elderly, arts projects and support for disabled people, as well as being Hong Kong's largest employer. Its demise pushed many more towards government handouts which, like much of the rest of the world, Hong Kong could ill afford. The track had now been reduced to holding one public race a month, as well as hosting private races in which wealthy owners and breeders displayed bloodstock for their own amusement.

Alex rounded the track and drove up the hill towards his home. His block was a low-rise, only nine floors, with no lift. It was only two-thirds occupied, the lower floors largely left empty, as anyone who was looking to rent would instantly demand a more prestigious higher apartment, knowing that the landlord was desperate.

After leaving his car, Alex walked across the yard and nodded to the security guard who'd opened the gate for him. He entered through the double doors into the bottom of the stairwell. The stairs began on the right, fifteen concrete steps per flight, ascending in a spiral. They and the walls were worn and rough; a lick of paint, minimal lighting and some damp-proofing were the landlord's only concession to maintenance. Jun and a number of other female residents constantly complained, being frightened by the dark shadowed areas on the stairs as they climbed to their various apartments.

Alex was exhausted. Looking up at the stairs curling above him, he realized he had last walked up them eighteen hours ago after having shot Chow. He sat on the bottom step and closed his eyes, leaning his shoulder heavily against the wall on his right. He was tired and still twitchy from the repeated adrenalin rushes that had allowed him to continue working and functioning all day and half the night, and even though he desperately needed rest he was not keen to be home. If Jun was back from drinks with the girls, he hoped she would be sober and in a friendly mood. He wanted a long slow kiss from her, to stay close to her in bed until he had to return to the station in the morning. His feet dragged as he climbed slowly through the patches of shadow and light.

Pinned to the door of his apartment he saw a red envelope addressed to him. At first he went to rip it open carelessly, thinking it was a note from Jun, but then he noticed that the Chinese characters used on it were ancient. Not the older traditional form used in Hong Kong – as opposed to the modern simplified version used in China – but a kind much more ancient than either. The calligraphy was beautiful and carefully crafted. The ink was a deep black, mixed properly from an ink tablet, not a bottle. Alex looked hard at the envelope and took his pen from his inside jacket pocket, using it carefully to lift a corner and see if there was anything written on the reverse. There was nothing. Taking his handkerchief, he unpinned the envelope and, holding it by the edges, examined it more closely. He was about to use his other hand to open it when the few remaining stair lights went out.

'Shit!'

He gently slid the envelope into his jacket pocket and felt from the edge of the doorframe to his right across the wall for the switch. He flicked it up and down a couple of times with no result. He stood for a moment in the darkness, then heard a voice drift down the stairwell from a higher floor.

'Alex Soong, join us. Join us and honour your ancestors.'

'Who is that?' he said slowly. 'If you want to speak to me, come out and show yourself.'

'Alex Soong, join us,' it called out again, more softly this time, the volume barely above a breath.

Alex flicked the switch again in vain. He moved his hand to find the banister beside the stairs and rushed up a few steps, but almost immediately stumbled and fell to his knees. A sharp pain stabbed under his kneecap from the hard edge of the concrete. Then suddenly the lights flickered back to life and he picked himself up and raced on. He had been less than a minute in the darkness but his eyes were tired and sensitive and they hurt from the sudden brightness of the light. He looked up the stairwell at the six floors above him and in the dim light thought he saw somebody running ahead. He drew his Sig and chased up the remaining flights. At the top was a wooden door leading to the roof with a *Do Not Enter* sign. He stopped to one side of this and listened.

Nothing.

His lungs were hurting after his charge up the stairs and he did his best to contain his heavy breathing as he laboured to catch his breath. After twenty seconds or so, he'd still heard nothing, so he pushed the door open.

'Look, there's nowhere to go from here. So come out.'

He stepped through onto the open flat area of the roof of the left wing of the building. It was a broad space with two satellite dishes set seven or eight metres in front of him. A large black water tank loomed immediately next to the doorway, sitting on the roof above the central stairwell to the building, dividing the space between the two wings. Beyond the dishes and the tank there was nothing but a nine-floor drop to the ground on each side. No sign of anyone else.

He turned to check the roof of the right wing. There was a narrow gap between the doorframe and the water tank, which led to the opposite side. Here there was nothing but an empty expanse of roof and, in the middle, a broken plastic chair. He holstered his pistol.

Alex walked across the flat space and stood at the edge of the building, behind a low parapet wall. He looked down on to the car park below and then across into the neighbouring apartments. For a moment, he watched those very few people who were still awake sitting in front of their televisions and computers. He went over to the chair, placed in the middle of the space, probably for a security guard to sun himself and sleep in. But to Alex it felt as though someone else had been here.

He patted his right pocket to check that the envelope was still there.

'Fool! If you'd lost this, you'd have been a stupid careless bastard,' he reproved himself, and scanned once more through the dark of the rooftop, still hoping he would find some evidence that he had heard an actual voice, that he had been chasing a flesh-and-blood person instead of a dream. That he had heard William's voice; that his old friend, whom he still missed terribly, had not deserted him. There was nothing. He walked back to the top of the stairs.

The dim lighting remained on and he stood inside the open doorway looking for any evidence of the presence of another person during the last twenty minutes. Again he found nothing. Perhaps a small remote speaker could have been fixed to the ceiling, to cast a voice down the stairwell? But he found no sign of such a device.

He walked down, carefully and slowly, the half-light making his inspection incomplete. But with each flight he took, his confidence that he had actually heard or seen another person began to waiver.

Back on his floor, he stood under the feeble bulb and retraced his movements from first seeing the envelope. He turned the light off and, in darkness again, glanced up towards the higher floors. He had doubted his senses, but now – even with the tiredness – he was certain there had been a man's voice, speaking to him in Mandarin, subdued but still clear and precise. It had been the same voice he had heard earlier this evening, he was sure of that too, as he stood in the darkness, remembering. There had been a tightness to the pronunciation that he had not perceived in the warehouse, though that was hardly surprising given the circumstances.

He heard a faint shuffling and turned the light back on to glance at his neighbour's door, where the sound had come from. The dark brown paint was chipped and scratched, and the frame had received repeated knocks by something hard enough to create a significant dent halfway between the lock and the floor. Not surprised at his neighbour being up and about in the early hours of the morning, Alex knocked lightly on the door.

He and Jun had rarely seen Mrs Chan during the last year unless they had deliberately visited to check she was not in need of food or household goods. On first moving in, they had learned from the security guard to the block that she had lived in the building since it was constructed in 1958, and had long since assumed the job of ensuring that owner and tenants maintained her high standards of neatness and behaviour. She'd performed this role very diligently for many years, but age and loneliness had finally caught up with her, weakening her concentration and coherency. Now she often wouldn't be seen for weeks. Then suddenly there would be notes left on the doors of other apartments, some long since vacant, reprimanding the occupants for garbage bags not removed, unnecessary smells and laundry hung out wantonly . . . even though laundry was no longer hung and garbage bags were now collected by the caretaker.

Her husband had held a very good position in a *gweilo*-owned plastics factory in the Po Kong Village area on Kowloon side, a place later to become the epicentre of the terrible civil unrest in '67. He was a senior project manager, which afforded him the means to live on Hong Kong Island and buy a home in the newly built apartment block in Happy Valley. Mrs Chan had not wanted to work, as was the preference of most women born into her generation. Their views rested uncomfortably between the long-entrenched traditions of their parents, who had escaped to Hong Kong from lives of peasantry, poverty, war and extreme politics in early twentieth-century China, and the more ambitious and emancipated generation that grew up in the emerging Asian economies of the late Sixties. Caught in the confusion of that generation whose burden it was to make the transition from five thousand years of tradition to global modernity, not knowing whether to brave the leap forward with nothing but faith in

Western-style progress or to hold fast to the old ways, she decided to play it safe and do what she believed would give her the most face and respect.

So she became a lady of leisure, a *Tai Tai*, and the dowager of the building, taking afternoon tea in the old Hilton Hotel in Central, or venturing across the harbour on the Star Ferry, before the first tunnel was built in 1972, to the Peninsula Hotel in Tsim Sha Tsui. Then, suddenly, after she had spent nearly a decade in this leisurely existence, her doting husband died in the riots in 1967. These were the only bloody uprisings during British rule, but a clear sign of the simmering frustration and anger that many people felt at the growing inequalities in Hong Kong society, and further fuelled by sympathy and support from Communist factions on the mainland.

The riots started with general opposition to pay and benefits, then line workers and labourers began to understand that they too had a voice, and when it went unheard or was dismissed they looked north to the Cultural Revolution on the mainland for inspiration, and chaos ensued. Homemade bombs were produced, police brutality was not uncommon, and a television newsman was dragged from his car and burned alive. Alex had learned the details of these riots as part of his preparation to come to Hong Kong, comparatively insignificant as they were compared with the millions of lives lost during the mainland's self-inflicted revolutions, rebellions and other incidents.

Mrs Chan's husband had been a quiet man who enjoyed his work and life at home with his family. At the beginning of the riots, he was fatally injured when he tried to help a colleague at the plastic flower factory who was attempting to stop a gang of employees from destroying machinery and rioting. The colleague was stabbed in the stomach and died in hospital three days later.

During the struggle, Mr Chan suffered terrible head trauma and died. He was not listed as a fatality of the riot, merely as a victim of violent crime – one the British administration did little to prosecute.

Mrs Chan had lived alone ever since losing their only child to typhoid. The prospects of remarriage for a middle-aged widow were very limited. Unable to maintain her standard of living, she withdrew from her friends and former social circle. She struggled to maintain appearances, and lived frugally on the salary she received from working as personal assistant to a director of one of the great local trading companies. Eventually age and her increasing poverty had clouded her mind and left her muddled, prone to fantasy, and alone.

Once again, Alex knocked politely at the door. He was tired and hoped his conversation with his neighbour would be straightforward. Most of all, that she would not ask him in for a bowl of noodles. Silence. He knocked again.

'Mrs Chan, are you there?' He tried to speak gently, but also loudly enough to be heard through the thick front door. He could now hear movement inside the apartment, and then after a minute the rattling of a security chain. 'Mrs Chan, it's Inspector Soong.' He corrected himself quickly. 'It's Alex . . . from next door.'

The door opened slowly and Mrs Chan peered through the gap above the chain. Alex had not seen her in months. Her cheeks looked hollow, her lips thin and rough. She was glassy-eyed, and seemed to be afraid. Hearing someone knock, she had quickly applied some foundation, lipstick and mascara before she had come to the door, but the only effect it had was to make her appear odd and over-painted. A stale and mouldy smell of cheap Chinese food, garlic, ginger and coriander wafted from deep within the apartment behind her as she looked at Alex.

'Mrs Chan, how are you?' he asked patiently in his politest Cantonese.

'What is it you want?' She stumbled over her words.

'Just to check that you are okay. I think someone was here earlier.' She looked at him, and then over his shoulder at the narrow landing area, her eyes moving a little erratically. She was obviously still wary of her neighbour's intentions.

'Do you remember me?' he asked.

'Yes, yes,' she said, more assertively. 'You live over there.'

'That's right. Do you remember what I do?' he asked slowly.

'You're the mainlander, aren't you?' she shot back. 'You know, those mainlanders caused the riot . . .'

'Yes, I was brought up there, but I studied in the West . . . in America.'

'Well, that's no better. Foreigners telling us what to do. We should have our own say.'

Alex ignored these comments. 'How are you, Mrs Chan?' he continued politely.

'*Ai*, it is fine, I am surviving. It was the same for my parents, I am like them. Lucky to eat and sleep. I will tell you, there's no money and I have no one to care for me.' She stopped talking and studied him closely. 'I wish I had a son. Even a useless one is better than no son at all.' She sucked at her teeth momentarily. 'Your parents must be very proud and glad they have a son,' she said slowly.

'Unfortunately they died a few years ago.' Alex wanted to move away from this topic. 'I think I had a visitor about thirty minutes ago. Did you see anyone come to my door this evening?'

'There are always people coming and going. I never know who they are. People so busy doing nothing, and everything a mess.'

'Anyone come here this evening?' He felt he would eventually get there.

'People. There are always people.'

'Someone pinned a letter to my door and I wondered if you had seen anyone. I know you keep a watchful eye on our building.'

'Yes, I try to. Well, as best I can. But it is difficult, with so many people coming and going. People are in such a hurry to make money now. There is no more politeness, no courtesy. But they must look after themselves.' She sighed, and looked at the ground, shaking her head. Alex could see that she had lost a lot of hair recently. Perhaps she had not been able to pay for her hairpieces to be fixed, or perhaps she was malnourished – though quite possibly it was both.

She continued: 'When my husband Ah Mun was alive, we would go out and people would greet us. Now nobody does anything. I don't remember seeing anyone. I'm sorry, I can't help you.'

'That's okay, Auntie. That's okay. Would you like me to go and get you some rice, roast pork, choy sum, some fruit and vegetables from the midnight market?' Alex asked gently.

'*Haw*, you're so polite!' She paused, pulling the door against the chain a little harder, as if to be more welcoming. 'For a mainlander you're so polite.'

'I was brought up with traditional values.'

'Well, that's right. Your parents must be proud of you.' She smiled at him and nodded.

'I think they are.' Alex smiled warmly back. 'Would you like me to get you any food from the late-night market?'

'Thank you, but I have enough. I can manage.'

'And you're sure you saw no one?'

'Oh, yes, yes, a man came, just as I said. He was tall. Must have been a *gweilo*. I looked through my door and saw his chest close to my door, right underneath the light, but I was too afraid to speak to him.'

'Do you remember what he looked like?'

'He was too tall for a Chinese.' She raised her skinny arms high to signal he was taller than Alex. 'But I could not see his face.'

'That is very helpful. Can you remember what time it was?' he asked hopefully.

'No. No, indeed. I can't remember that at all. It was certainly a while ago,' she said apologetically.

'Well, Mrs Chan, please call me if I can get you anything. It's no bother at all.'

'Ah, your parents brought you up well. They must be proud. Your parents must be so thankful to have such a thoughtful son,' she repeated.

'Yes,' he said, and started to pull her door shut.

'Come again soon, young man,' she called as it closed.

'Now remember to lock the door,' he gently reminded her through the door, and after a little fumbling he heard the deadbolt turn and a latch fall into place.

He turned, crossed the landing and slipped his door key into the lock, turning it slowly till he heard the lock release. He pushed the door open very gently and held it ajar for a few seconds, listening for any movement inside. Silence. He drew his Sig, for the fourth time that day.

The apartment was dark when he entered. It was now 2.25 a.m. and he guessed Jun had not yet returned home. Often she had late-night drinks in Central with friends who were similarly immune from the pain of economic collapse. He stood just inside the front door. The apartment was still and quiet until Galore appeared and wound herself round his legs, demanding to be fed. He closed the front door quietly and remained standing for a few moments longer, though Galore clearly sensed no danger and pressed him harder for food.

He walked a few paces forward, slowly rounding the corner into the living room, picked his way through the brown furniture that had caused him so much grief during the day, and went down the corridor that led to the bathroom, the two bedrooms and his study. The corridor was dark but he noticed a light on in the guest bedroom, immediately to his right. He stood with his pistol in his hand.

'Jun, are you here?'

There was silence. He stood just outside the door to the room, reached over and slowly turned the handle. He pushed it ajar and waited a second or two before calling out again.

'Jun?'

'Yes? What do you want?' she asked curtly, irritated at being disturbed. Clearly she was not in any danger.

He holstered his pistol and stuck his head into the room. He saw that the double doors of the two huge built-in wardrobes on the opposite side were flung open. His wife was standing with her back to him, her mobile jammed between her right shoulder and cheek while she sorted through a wall of clothes, each garment dressed in its own transparent plastic cover. These hung above a foundation of shoe boxes, each with its own identifying photo attached.

'Lucy, I've got to go. Alex just came home.' Jun turned and looked at him. Her eyes conveyed the fact that she was seeking confirmation that he was unharmed, but also that she was not happy with the unnecessary danger he put himself in. 'Speak to you in twenty. I'm sure I'll find them,' she said quickly into the phone in her slightly transatlantic English, then hung up and dropped the phone on the spare bed.

'We were just talking about you being on the news today.' She'd switched to Mandarin. 'Look, I'm sorry I was so short-tempered with you after lunch and this evening. I didn't know all the shit that had happened. Are you all right?'

He smiled. 'I'm very tired, I think I need to get some sleep. Will you come with me?'

'That's sweet, my love, but I'm not really tired yet and I have to find these shoes for Lucy. She needs them for the weekend.' Jun turned back to the wardrobes. 'I'll forgive you for flirting with the blogger.'

'I wasn't flirting,' he said, joking with her.

'But what the hell were you doing later on? You don't want to take my father's job offer but . . .'

Alex sighed in an attempt to dissuade her from continuing. Ignoring him, she pressed her point further.

'You're in prime position to get another promotion and move to a more strategic role, off the streets, and then you go and do that! I don't understand you at all sometimes. Why did you do it?' she continued as she searched for the lost shoes. 'Here they are!' she shouted before he could reply.

She stood up, holding a Jimmy Choo Couture shoebox. Alex noted her long legs, slender in tight leggings worn with light brown suede Uggs. In her uninhibited joy at finding the shoes for her friend, the box held aloft in triumph, eyes joyful in success, he wanted to rush over to her, hold her, kiss her, fall with her on to the spare bed and sleep for a day, or a year.

She gently dropped the box on the mattress and turned to close the wardrobe doors. Then she picked up the shoes and airily brushed past him into the lounge. Her hair wafted close to his face; it smelled fresh and inviting.

'You could have switched the lights on,' she shouted from the living room as Alex stood and looked at the bland contents of their spare room. 'You haven't answered me!'

'You haven't really asked me anything.'

'I asked you why you did it.'

'Did what?' Alex knew where this conversation was heading but didn't want to make it easy for her. He remained leaning against the wall, looking at the bed and the crummy black-and-white photograph of a cat sitting in a leather armchair, a red ribbon tied round its neck providing the only touch of colour in the composition. It was one of the ugliest gifts they had received from her parents.

'The cameraman? Why beat on the cameraman?' Jun shouted from what sounded to Alex like the kitchen.

'Did anyone come and visit this afternoon or evening?' he shouted back.

'Don't change the subject. You should be promoting yourself more or you'll never get ahead. Why hit the camera guy? What had *he* done? Tash said she saw the video and that you just went psycho.'

'Look,' he said in a flatter voice, 'please stop mentioning those crazy bloggers and reporters.'

He took one final look around, to check everything was in good order, before he returned to the living room. Jun was seated in her brown leather armchair, legs folded underneath her and her slender neck extending long and straight from a camel turtleneck. She was lighting a cigarette with one hand while texting on her mobile with the other. As much as their relationship was frustrating and at times falling apart at its seams, Jun still captivated him. She lived in a way that he could not.

Alex felt like screaming at her: *I killed a man, I watched his head explode, and later I saw things that no one should see.* But he could not bring himself to say the words, to explain how tired, anxious and haunted by the day he felt, how he wanted to cry and shout all at once. But that was his world, not hers. Like many people, Jun had learned to turn a blind eye to inconvenient truths, preferring to concentrate only on those prominently featured on the web and television, YouTube and in magazines.

'I'll do it my own way,' he murmured. 'Will you please tell me if anyone came to the apartment today? Especially this evening.'

'Nobody came, okay?' she answered bluntly.

'A number of people died today, we all need to be careful,' he said impatiently.

'What has the death of two priests got to do with our visitors?'

'Nothing,' he replied cautiously.

'Were you expecting anyone? Well, then. Look, I'm going to call Lucy again . . .' She dialled and the line connected. Lucy's voice answered. 'Hey, I found those shoes for you,' Jun announced.

For a few minutes Alex watched Jun, curled up in the armchair chatting. She had been full of ambition when they'd first met in Beijing, she had graduated in Classical Chinese Art and History from the great Tsinghua University and he in engineering from NYU.

On every campus there is always that group of girls who collect together under the common banner of beauty and confidence and become inseparable . . . until they discover they all want the same thing and only one of them can get it. Jun was the leader of her gang, and Alex had not been that thing. True, he had a good family background, had never been purged, never sought the attention of the press, was not greedy or corrupt, was a first-class student and also a martial arts champion and skilful chess player. His family was well known in Beijing, but he was determined that after studying abroad he would go into law enforcement. This was generally considered an obscure ambition when there were pots of money to be made in business.

In the summer of 2000, he'd come back for a few weeks to visit his family, and in the afternoons would sit on the grass in the grounds of Beijing University campus, to read and work. During that time he would occasionally see Jun and her friends sitting having a picnic, sharing food and drinking tea. And then one afternoon, while he was reviewing the results to an experiment he'd finished at NYU before returning home to China for the holidays, Jun approached him. She stood over him. Looking up into the spotless white-yellow of a rare Beijing sun, revealed by a lucky fall in pollution levels that day, he saw the dark silhouette of long legs, a lithe body with a slender neck, and on top of that an almond-shaped face under a glossy ponytail. She was asking to borrow his calculator.

'We're arguing about something and we'd like to borrow it to finish the debate. Would that be okay?' she asked very sweetly.

The answer was already yes, but he couldn't help but continue what she'd started: 'Well, what's the problem? Perhaps you don't need the calculator?'

'What do you study?'

'Engineering.'

'Oh. Well, it's not really in that sort of field.'

'And you?'

'Classical Art and History. A double major.'

'History?' he said, rather incredulously.

'What? You don't think I could study history? What did you think I would study?'

He hesitated.

'You didn't even think I was a student, did you?' she answered for him.

'Oh, yes, but I thought you were . . .' He swallowed his words. 'Well, it doesn't matter what I thought. What's the problem?'

'Well, we want to go to New York and we've only got a certain amount of money so we're looking at all the different alternative routes.'

He picked up the calculator and offered it to her. Then said in English: 'See you there.'

'You study in America?'

He stood up and saw her face properly. Her eyes were soft and her skin like porcelain, but natural-looking and glowing. He could not help but take a step closer to her.

'I do.'

'What's it like?' She cocked her head and he watched her ponytail flick against the side of her head.

He smiled and then sucked through his teeth in a feeble attempt to sound wise and thoughtful, but excitement at meeting her at last and enthusiasm for his newly adopted home overcame his efforts to play it cool and impress her.

'It's brilliant and miserable all at once. It makes you laugh and sing and then makes you feel like you are choking and suffocating. You can turn a corner and see the saddest thing, like an old bag lady on the street, surrounded by shopping carts, and then turn another and be amazed to find the coolest thing in the world.'

'Such as what?'

He had nearly tripped himself up there.

'Er . . . such as a movie set in Central Park.'

'You've seen a movie set?'

'Yeah.' He was now exaggerating beyond what was wise, as he couldn't think of the name of the movie he'd seen being filmed. 'You see them all the time.'

'Which actors have you seen?'

'I was out getting a coffee, near Central Park, and I saw Christian Bale, shooting *American Psycho*.'

'Wow, I'd love to see that!' Jun hesitated then asked: 'That was a crazy film. You like that sort of thing?' She smiled as she spoke.

He looked to the sky for inspiration.

'No, it was really gruesome, but I like being scared stupid in the movie theatre.' He laughed.

She nodded and bit her lip, which she then released. He saw it swell with blood for a second and wanted to kiss it.

'I can tell you more, if you'd like to meet me for a coffee?' he said.

'Okay, but not too late.' She smiled cheekily at him.

'I don't have your number.'

'I'll leave it on here,' she pointed to the calculator's screen, 'when I give you it back.'

'But it's solar-powered.'

'Then you'd better stay in the sun where I can see you.'

She returned to her friends and he tried to return to his work, which was impossible while he was without his calculator.

After that they had coffees, lunches and dinners, and when she came to New York with her friends, he showed them the Statue of Liberty, Ellis Island, Mott Street and Park Avenue. But he and Jun went alone to the Empire State Building and held hands for the first time as they walked through Central Park.

She told him that she intended to teach after finishing her degree, then after a few years complete a master's degree. But China changed in those years. After a wait of five millennia the future had finally arrived. New York, Paris, London and LA came to Beijing, Shanghai and a few other great cities; China was awarded the Olympic Games in 2001, Tarantino filmed *Kill Bill* in 2002, *Vogue China* launched in 2005, and Western brand names rained down on every city and town. It wasn't the best of Western culture, but it was close. Jun had begun to train as a teacher, and had seriously intended to continue when she came to Hong Kong, but somehow had never got round to it.

He looked at her now, talking excitedly on the phone, chatting about shoes, wine and restaurants. She knew nothing of the lives lived far from shopping malls and smart bars. She had once cared deeply about bigger issues, but had grown desensitized over the years of self-indulgence.

He left her talking and went to the bathroom. After locking the door, he grabbed a pair of tweezers from the lower shelf of the bathroom cabinet above the basin and sat on the edge of the bath. Using the tweezers, he pulled out the red envelope from his jacket and held it up to the light above the cabinet. Thick red paper, folded in a very specific and intricate arrangement. Through it, he could see a dark roundish shape against the light. Alex had never seen anything like it before. It reminded him of the way the red packets are folded for the traditional Chinese wedding gifts: *guo da li*. But this folding was different in detail, much tighter and with a specific symmetry and pattern down front and back. It looked like a complex puzzle.

He decided to open it carefully and hopefully avoid tearing it. He examined it closely, seeing that the paper locked together in the middle and could only be opened out by holding each side and pulling and twisting it gently, to release the interlocking paper cuts. Slowly he opened the envelope. There was no letter inside, just writing in thin black ink, handwritten calligraphy, in the centre of the inside of the envelope. The characters were of some ancient form and certainly not simplified. He could roughly translate the line.

When they are wiped out, rain will fall and visitations will disappear.

It meant nothing to him. He whispered it again to himself a few times but it didn't remind him of anything. There was also what looked to be a small red paper lantern, very ordinary and containing no further message or symbols. He managed to reassemble the envelope, though any quick inspection would clearly show it had been opened already, and returned it to his jacket pocket. He flushed the toilet and ran the tap in the sink for a few seconds before unlocking the door and rejoining Jun, who was still sitting in the armchair talking on her mobile.

She looked up at him with no expression on her face.

'Why don't you use the landline? It's cheaper,' he suggested casually.

She stared hard at him in reply.

'Yes, come round now and bring Tash. It's late . . . or is it early? . . . but we can have a bottle of wine. This is too important not to discuss.'

Jun put the phone down. She could see that Alex was annoyed.

'What? Do they have to? I need sleep,' he told her.

She got up and gave him a kiss then turned towards the kitchen.

'Then get some. Tash's boyfriend proposed this evening. There's so much to discuss! But we'll be quiet, I promise.'

She soon returned from the kitchen. 'Now, I've made you this hot chocolate. Go into your study, drink this and listen to some music for fifteen minutes. Then go to bed, it's very late.' She said this most charmingly while still managing him out of her way.

'Thank you for this.' He held up the mug of chocolate. 'Okay, but seriously, don't be loud.' He watched her tidy up the already tidy room then get out glasses and a bottle of French red. Galore followed Alex as he turned down the corridor to his study.

The study was his private space. It contained his books and vinyl collection, and he would regularly fall asleep on the sofa while he was meant to be reading and listening. When that happened, and Alex realized it was a distinct possibility now, Jun would come in and spread a blanket over him. In the morning he would wish he could watch her do it, as he knew it would make him fall in love with her all over again.

He closed the door to the room, and as he did, heard the bell ring and Jun's two friends enter: kisses for everyone. He went to his collection, six shelves of vinyl jazz, and pulled out the 1950s disc *Hank Jones' The New York Rhythm Section*. Dog-tired, Alex wanted to hear the ballad 'Mona's Feeling Lonely', a composition by the great side-man bassist Milt Hinton, aka The Judge. It was sweet and lovely, a simple arrangement but profoundly effective, carrying Alex away for a few minutes.

It was now 2.50 a.m. He lay down on the sofa. Around the walls were album photos, covers and posters, and he looked up at his favourite and his first, which had been given to him by his father. It was a copy of a photo taken by Hinton of Louis Armstrong, his long-time friend, sleeping deeply and very comfortably in a hotel in Seattle in 1954. Alex had always imagined that Satchmo had just finished a big session that night, and after his hard work and a few drinks was out for the count. Alex wanted that sleep, dreams of music and rhythm, dancing brass and thumping wood . . . not screaming, and twisting muscle and skin, hollow eyes filling with blood, bones cracked and splintered. There was no Chinese substitute for the soothing silken rolling of Hinton's bass lines, no Chinese instrument told those stories or expressed those emotions. He needed this sound: emotional, heartfelt and, most important to Alex, human.

He closed his eyes and his head fell a little further into the pillow propped against the arm of the sofa, the desk at his feet and the chocolate, now mostly finished, resting on the floor next to him. He briefly opened his eyes, partly to check everything was well and to feel for his pistol under the sofa, but mostly to look at the old black-and-white photo of Armstrong hanging on the facing wall. His thoughts returned to the first of many conversations with his grandfather and father after he had graduated in 2002, when the three of them would sit and drink tea together in his parents' apartment and Grandfather would chain-smoke, sending cloudy yellow-brown fumes to hang just below the ceiling.

'You should have been first in your class Ah Guo,' his grandfather half joked, half chided, 'but I guess we will have to settle for third.' He laughed at Alex and got out of his armchair to refill his teacup. The man had lived off tea and cigarettes since he was fifteen, sixty-five years before. He placed one hand on Alex's closely shaven head and gave it a gentle pat.

'You're too easy on your grandson, Ba,' Alex's father had lectured them both. 'Our country has serious problems and we need everyone to work at full capacity, to be at their best. The best talents utilized to obtain the best performance.'

The three of them were in the living room of an old government-provided housing apartment in south Beijing, very close to Tian Tan, the beautiful Ming Dynasty-built Temple of Heaven. Alex's father had declined the opportunity to get involved in discounted deals for senior government officials to purchase private apartments and chose to remain in the block, which was at least consistent with the reason he had chosen to serve the government: to guide the future and guard the past.

Their block was one of six forming an old Soviet-style compound, but each apartment had been updated with good modern kitchen facilities, fitted wardrobes, double beds, air conditioning for the summer, heating for the cutting Beijing winters and a new coat of paint. No landscaping had been done, as the residents were all of an age when they had lived through enough change for one lifetime: Beijing was undergoing heavy structural changes again and they preferred to retain something familiar, no matter how dreary.

The apartment consisted of two bedrooms – one for his parents and the other shared by Alex and his grandfather – and a central living room, which had a dining table with six wooden chairs, three armchairs and a sofa. It was a supposedly temporary home his father had first been assigned in 1979 and which had become permanent as the family was rarely together, always travelling across the country on official duty. Alex's mother had been working in Harbin in northern China for the last six months, and so it had been just the three of them since he had returned from graduation two weeks before.

His father lit a cigarette and offered it to his grandfather. Soong Zhan had lost two fingers from his right hand during the fighting against the Kuomintang, the Chinese nationalists who eventually fled China and established Taiwan, and though he had learned to compensate with his left for many activities, it was easier for him if someone else lit his cigarettes.

His grandfather sat back down.

'So, Xiao Guo, what's next?' his grandfather asked Alex. 'The economy is the next focus. You could train to be of help there.'

'Yes, yes, you can be of most service to the country in this area. Do you have a plan, Alex?' his father put in.

Alex drew in his breath sharply and looked at the two attentive faces.

'I am thinking of joining the police with the aim of working with the newly formed Anti-Corruption Task Force. They are building up specialist teams. Though it's only a small initiative now, I think they will do important work for the country.'

'He is brighter than us, isn't he, Ah Xian?' Alex's grandfather said to his son. 'He sees our country's future.'

'Do you really think that corruption will increase to the point where we need a special task force? Do you have so little faith in the people?' His father was not as amused or impressed by the plan as his grandfather was.

'People are still human,' Alex calmly replied. 'As the economy improves, they will want more. They have had nothing to date, and already there are so many temptations. In ten years' time, will you be able to trust people to act purely in the interests of the country? In the 1950s, everything was taken from them . . . you know all this. Eventually people were forced to eat grass, worms, bark, they were so hungry. They ate shit, and lived and died for what?'

His father had gradually become very angry. 'Then you do not understand at all what we have built! You do not believe in the work of the people. Instead of being the preserve of a selfish imperial elite, this country is now for the people. The people will work for the nation, they will not betray it or each other.' He was shouting now. 'Didn't you understand anything we told you?'

'I heard you say these things, many times, but like your generation, mine will fight its own battles. Corruption will be ours,' Alex angrily replied, and then instantly regretted that he had raised his voice to his father.

His grandfather stepped in.

'I ate grass, as you say, Alex. We'd have to pick the shit out of each other's backsides with a stick because we were so constipated, and stand on each other's stomachs in order to move our bowels. Your father knows this. At a time when Westerners were dancing to the music you love, we had mutilated ourselves for a word . . . a phrase. For nothing at all. We just believed, like your father. In fact, more so.'

Alex was about to talk then, but his grandfather raised his hand and Alex held his tongue.

'But, remember, China didn't really exist before our era. It was just a huge land mass, a patchwork of beautiful and often empty lands that for many centuries had been fought over by emperors, princes, warlords and bandits. Its boundaries grew and shrank with the wind. Pieces were joined on and broken off, and the people working the land, peasants who knew nothing but farming for survival, would have to pay and pay for it time after time. They paid with their lives, their goods, their sons and daughters. Then the foreigners came and the peasants realized that the Imperial might was an illusion. It was not all-powerful, but only a weak voice that echoed faintly over the fields and across the deserts . . . a tempting whisper from centuries ago. So we went from being ruled by this weakness to being controlled by ghosts. The white man took everything. We ate his opium, his religion and his magical ideas called science.'

Alex's father had been nodding in agreement all the while.

'To build a nation, we needed to be one people, with one language. That didn't come easily when there were so many different groups,' his grandfather said. 'You know, we call ourselves Han Chinese but we are Cantonese, Shanghainese, Fujian, Anhui, Manchurian, and so on. Yes, when I look around, I know it's ugly, petty and at times very cruel here, but we are ruling ourselves for the first time. It's only the start of something that will not be finished in our lifetimes. The West has been developing fast since the Industrial Revolution, but it still has poverty, crime and corruption. Perhaps it's simply that in some respects its best is still much better than ours. But we're catching up fast.'

He looked momentarily uncomfortable at his own admission, and turned his head to stare out of the window briefly before glancing back at Alex. 'It's very disappointing to me to hear what you have just said. For us Chinese people to have fought for a hundred and fifty years, since the First Opium War, eventually to be defeated by each other . . .' He stood up, in some distress.

Alex was shocked by his father's reaction. His eyes were wide and watery above a mouth set in a stubborn line. Alex did not say anything further. His father pointed a trembling finger at him as if to say more but slowly lowered his hand to his side. He looked at his own father and shook his head. 'I will not believe the country will be threatened by its own people. Nothing could make me more sorrowful.'

He was about to leave the room when Soong Zhan responded: 'I'm old, I've had my fair share of fights. I've been on the winning side and the losing side. Sometimes on the same day.' He laughed to himself then told his son: 'You brought your son up well. He's right. The people have had nothing for thousands of years and now they want as much as they can swallow. There will be blatant and flagrant abuse.'

He chewed his false teeth and looked at Alex then. 'My worry is that the future will be far more violent and dangerous than anything we ourselves experienced. And I worry for my grandson. He is the only one I will ever have.'

Alex looked back at his grandfather and reached out to take his hand. His father sat down again and dropped his head back against the chair's headrest.

'I know,' Alex's father acknowledged in a low voice. Then he turned to Alex and leaned in closer with a smile. 'We're both very proud of what you've achieved, and your mother is too. Graduating from the US is a significant achievement.' He placed his hand on top of Alex's, squeezed it and gave him a wide smile. 'We've got you a present.'

He walked to the stout wooden sideboard where he dropped slowly down on his haunches and opened the left-hand door. He reached in and took out a parcel tied simply with rough twine.

'It's not much but it took us all sorts of phone calls and emails to get someone to send it to us.'

He handed Alex the brown-paper package, no bigger than a place mat.

'Thank you. What is it?'

Ah Xian smiled at his own father 'Children, heh?' He looked back at Alex. 'Open it and find out.'

He took the wrapping paper off, and there in his hands was the photo of Armstrong slumbering, his bed filling the entire photo, with only his head and that famous satchel mouth visible, the rest of him hidden under a pile of blankets and covers. Alex looked up at his father in surprise.

'Thank you. I didn't think you approved of my interest.'

'Well, I'm a little less hardline than I sometimes seem. Well done on graduating.'

During that summer Alex's relationship with Jun grew stronger, then he joined the police.

Two years later Alex was accepted into the national Anti-Corruption Task Force, as he had wanted. He had worked hard, studied, trained, and excelled in everything. On his first day he'd met William, the cocky big-hearted young man who challenged the class prodigy at every stage.

They stood on the parade ground in sweats, waiting for instruction, and William got down and did twenty quick one-handed press-ups. When he'd finished he got up, wiped himself down and smiled to himself . . . but he couldn't march a damn, and Alex would tease him that he was fit, quick and smart but no dancer. Between them, though, they cut up the awards, and on graduating both elected to work fighting white-collar crime.

Initially, the five four-man anti-corruption teams were based in Beijing and Chongqing, the two biggest cities. Their establishment was a response to the growing theft of public funds and extortion of the people, who needed permission from local bureaucrats to do anything from internal travel to giving birth. Alex joined a team in Beijing, William was moved to one in Chongqing for undercover work. Both the General Secretary Xi Jinping and Chinese Premier Li Keqiang had stated from the early days of their appointments and the launch of the *China Dream* that stamping out corruption was key to ensuring civil order. But the teams were still vulnerable to the need to show success to justify their existence and ensure further funds were provided to develop the programme.

At first a lot of time was spent on easy targets, the low-hanging fruit. And corruption was systemic, as there had rarely been a sustained commitment to the rule of law in China, only the deterrent of fear. The people had feared the gods, feared execution by the Emperor, and feared political reprisals. The rule of law was not stillborn but it needed incubation. In the meantime, the corrupt officials could also detect an easy mark, and soon members of the anti-corruption teams in Chongqing were persuaded to act in their own interest, leading to team members undermining each other as they took bribes from gangsters, businessmen, politicians and foreigners to focus their attentions elsewhere. Alex knew that William often let his heart rule his head and, undercover, he was eventually swallowed whole by a lifestyle and opportunities he couldn't resist.

Alex left for Hong Kong before the unit was finally shut down: three of the eight officers in Chongqing were quietly executed for corruption, and one, William, took his own life when he understood what he had forsaken. His body was brought back to Beijing and Alex identified his friend from a scar. Yet Alex needed to see his face too, to see once more the man he had not seen for two years, the friend he would miss. The pathologist advised against it but Alex pulled the sheet back slowly.

Where William's face had been – that cheeky grin and the hard, wild eyes – was a vacuum of dark red pieces of bone, skin and teeth.

He had been just a small boy and only wanted to see his father. He had managed to see him twice since the man had been admitted to hospital two days before, but it had been very difficult. The first time was on the night of the incident. He had lied his way through the police cordon. Huge Sikhs clutched wooden batons and had stood across the streets while the riots continued, but the area was still deemed unsafe. Slipping past the cordon, he headed down to the eerie silence of the narrow streets between the backs of the newly built and whitewashed low-rise apartment blocks. He had followed the streets from Fung Tak down into Po Kong Village and occasionally saw people in the distance scamper across the road, heading for the safety of their homes, afraid of the violence and reprisal of violent mobs and gangs. It had always been a dangerous area at any time.

At the end of the road he had turned left, into the back of the hospital gardens, and walked round by the path between the lawns and the main building until he arrived at the front of the old late-Victorian building, previously barracks for British soldiers. He had climbed the steps and looked into the dark, cool entrance, where he saw the sign for the Emergency ward. As he stood there two men had pushed past him; he heard them complaining about the hospital's treatment of people fighting for workers' rights. They ignored the eleven-year-old. He watched them walk away before he headed towards the ward where he waited outside the matron's station until she had understood he wasn't going away.

'Who are you looking for?' she called out from her room, refusing to move from her desk and paperwork.

'My Ba, Seng Kwan.'

'Ah, he's sleeping.'

'I'd just like to see him for a minute.'

'Can you come back in two hours, young man?'

'No.'

'It would be better.'

'Once I go home I won't be able to come out again.'

'I see. Well, come with me then and I'll take a look.'

She had sighed but then got up and put the cap on her pen, placed it on the papers and squared them against the desk. In fact she had an air of gentleness that had made him feel at ease when she sat down next to him on the seats in the corridor.

'What's your name?' she asked.

'Seng Pok.'

'Siu Pok, your father isn't very well. He's very ill. It may be a good idea to bring your ma here soon.'

He had nodded compliantly without understanding.

'I'll take you to see your father, but bring your mother as soon as you can,' the matron repeated.

She stood up and reached out to take his hand. He looked at it. Her fingers were so clean, her nails short and neat. He stood up and then let her lead him to his father's bed.

The ward contained eight beds on each side, with short cupboards and a desk set in the middle of the room, between four centrally located beds, at which another nurse sat. He and the matron stood a few metres from Ba's bed.

She bent down and whispered in his ear: 'Just wait here.'

She approached the junior nurse, who listened and then nodded once. The matron returned and took his hand again. They stood on the left side of the bed, over the bandaged torso of his father. He was tall, at one metre eighty, a big man, but his cheeks looked hollow and his skin waxy and pale.

'Your father was hurt very badly . . .' Stabbed hard with a long shiv made from waste strips of metal from a cutting press. '. . . and his right hand was crushed. We had to amputate it.'

It had been jammed into a casting press and held there so they could stab him.

He had looked at his father's arm inside the blanket, followed it down to the point where the hand should have been, and then walked round the bed to the left hand, which he took hold of and squeezed hard.

The matron watched him and saw his expression. She put her arm around him and bent down close to hear what he had to say.

'Will he get better?' he asked, in a voice that was cracked and fragile.

'He was very brave. Now he is very ill. But we'll see.'

He looked at his father's closed eyes, the rise and fall of his chest. This man, a dim and brittle impression of the one he loved, coughed but did not wake. He pressed his cheek to the limp fingers, squeezed them tight, but his father did not respond.

The matron left the boy in order to speak to the nurse at the desk. Some minutes later the nurse suggested he sit on a chair that she'd brought him, sliding it under him while he continued to hold on tight to his father's hand.

The patients in the other beds watched silently until he left an hour or so later.

Afterwards he could not remember the walk home, or even climbing the many flights of stairs to reach the apartment. He could recall he had opened the door to find himself alone and then gone straight to his room. He lay down, and buried his face in the pillow, closing his eyes, and in his imagination saw his father's chest rising and falling. The image faded and he slept.

When he awoke he heard his mother in the kitchen cooking supper.

'Where did you go? I had to shop on my own,' she said sharply.

He stood in the entrance to the kitchen and watched her clatter the spatula inside the wok.

'To see Ba. You should go.'

'No, I cannot. He caused such trouble for everyone, with his stupidity and stubbornness. He should have let them go, what business was it of his if they got their skulls cracked? Always wanting to talk and help. Interfering in people's lives. Now we look fools together with him.'

He stood in the last light of the day, which was framed by the main window of the apartment. She banged the utensils again. Then she glared at him and walked over quickly to deal with his disobedience. She bent down and pushed her chin in his face, with her hands projected either side of him, talking fast and loud.

'So where can he go now? *Aiya*, stupid man! He has no future, he's better off dead.'

He stepped back, out of range, as she waved her hands and arms.

'You are insolent.'

'But he was brave!' he had shouted at her.

'He's a coward and he is a traitor. That's what they say.'

She began to cry then and returned to the cooking. Tears hit the hot wok and turned to steam. 'I married a weak man.'

'The nurse told me he was brave.'

'The nurse? Shut up, you foolish boy. You'll get us into trouble. You'll bring trouble.'

'No, I won't.'

She reached down and slapped him hard on the legs, the movement given bruising force by the heavy jade bangle on her wrist. The sound of flesh on flesh left a deep silence in its wake, a brutal gash in movement and sound. It was the quiet that he had feared most in their relationship.

'You come and see him!' he shouted through the tears, rubbing his calf.

'Show me proper respect! We will go and you'll learn what a weak man your father really is.'

She had grabbed his hair and pulled him outside the door. She held his shoulder and propelled him forward down roads that, once away from the main tenement blocks, were largely empty. He found himself back on the street between the freshly painted apartments. They could hear the occasional distant shout from crowds rushing by on parallel streets to join in the demonstrations that had broken out around Hong Kong. They had walked fast to avoid trouble.

But at the hospital she halted, nervous of the bad luck such places attract, so he grabbed her wrist as she turned to go and pulled her with him towards the entrance and up to the first floor. She followed reluctantly then yanked her arm free. Taking a step back, she slapped him again. He saw the matron approach. His mother had already moved towards the stairs, eager to leave.

'Hello? Siu Pok?' the woman had called to him. She stood over him and rested one hand on his shoulder, giving it a pat. Then she looked at his mother, trying to remain unnoticed on the stairs. 'Mrs Seng, I need to talk to you now. Please come with me.'

He had not seen fear on his mother's face before. She looked lost and muddled.

'Yes . . . yes, of course.' She rushed back up the stairs and the matron led her to a bench up the corridor. He touched the blood on his cheek and breathed in the strong metallic smell.

He watched them sit down together. His mother in flared nylon trousers, tight at the waist, had brought her knees tight together. Her hands, at first nervously clasped in her lap, were suddenly pressed to her face. She cried. No one else could be seen in the corridor, but he heard the clanging of metal trays being stacked in a room somewhere close. His mother continued to cry.

He turned and ran down the stairs. Coming out into the dark of the early evening he saw demonstrators march past the hospital grounds about fifty metres away. He walked up to the railings and watched them pass by. He saw written on the banners lines that he had heard his father say to friends when they sat together at home. Banners swayed above him as the crowd moved on, chants were bellowed out, calls for the British to leave and for local people to rise up against foreign powers and the wealthy elite. The rhythm of the shouting drew him, and he shouted too as men and women walked on. He stepped forward to the edge of the crowd and pushed his way in, then he slipped and fell. A hand reached down under his arm and pulled him to his feet.

'Little brother, keep upright, it's too dangerous to lie down here,' a voice above laughed.

Steady on his feet now, he felt the friendly hand on his shoulder again and looked up to see a smiling young man.

'You're a bit young for this,' another voice joked with him.

He looked up and behind him as he walked. He felt the heat of the crowd on his bare arms as people jostled around him. The friendly young man wore a simple white shirt with dark grey cotton trousers and an S-shaped buckle on his belt. His face was wide with a broad nose and sleepy eyes hidden under thick full lids. His skin was smooth except for a few short bristles over his mouth and on his chin. His hair had not been combed and stuck out from above his ears.

'My father marched here sometimes,' he said. 'I heard him shout with you.'

'Well, where is he today?' another voice asked aggressively.

'He can't come today.'

'What's your Ba's name?' the same voice demanded. The speaker had a round shaven head and beady eyes that held the boy's attention so that he nearly stumbled to the road again.

'Seng Kwan . . .'

The gentler of the two, his saviour from moments earlier, grabbed his hand and quickly pulled him out of the crowd and to the side of the road.

'What are you doing?' he protested.

'Your Ba . . . Your Ba did the right thing. But this is an angry time and people are very confused. There's a lot of crazy talk about him. All stupid, don't listen to it. Never believe it. He tried to save them, he was no traitor.' The young man led him back the few metres they had walked from the hospital gates, and knelt down in front of him.

'My name is Tung. You remember that if you need help. I'm at the university.' He looked the boy over to see if he had hurt his knees in the fall and then straightened his shirt and gave his collar a friendly pull. 'I think your father was a good man. You remember that and try to ignore what other people say. Good luck in your life. Hopefully, everything will change for you.'

The young man stood up and gave him a pat on the shoulder, then ran off down the roadside. After thirty metres or so he had disappeared into the crowd again.

He had stood at the entrance to the hospital and watched the demonstration until it ended, by which time it was nearly 10.30 p.m. He returned home to find the apartment empty. The silence made it feel different. It felt vast, as if nothing could fill it. He stood on the rug in the living room, in the darkness. He looked down at his bare feet, digging his toes into the short nylon fibres. His ankles and calves bore the marks of being hit many times by the switch his mother used to discipline him. He went to his room and lay on the bed. At first he let his eyes fill with the yellow light from the sign outside, but slowly they had closed in a glowing haze.

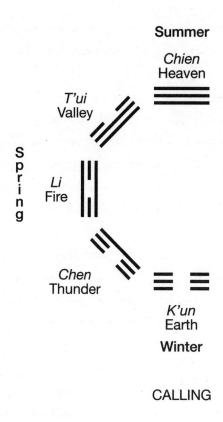

Friday
18 August 2017

Alex woke in the dark. There was a blanket over him. He reached under the sofa and felt for his pistol. It was as he had left it. He closed his eyes again. He remembered his grandfather's words from their conversation on the day they'd given him the photograph.

'The white man took everything. We ate his opium, his religion, and his magical ideas called science.'

These were the same sentiments expressed by the voice in the warehouse. His grandfather had also expressed a sense of deep-rooted inferiority, saying that Chinese people could have been so much better and have played a more prominent role in the world, instead of repeatedly being the victims of circumstances largely of their own making. It had motivated him, and his generation, to fight a revolution to overturn the old malign status quo that had existed for so long. Believing that they were leading their generation and future Chinese to a glorious new era, instead they went over the precipice and descended into near-self-obsessed madness, almost eviscerating the country, leaving tens of millions dead. It was not spoken of by his father's generation save for small gestures of admission and recognition, such as giving Alex the photo, signs of affirmation that his son's interest in things beyond China was acceptable.

Alex opened his eyes and pulled the blanket closer to his chin.

It smelled of Jun's soap. He got up, took his pistol and walked across the corridor and into the bedroom. It was pitch-black here and he could hear Jun snoring lightly. He slowly edged round the bed to her side and climbed in next to her. He reached for her hand, tucked his fingers between hers and slipped back to sleep.

It was three hours later that he woke again. It was 8.25 a.m. Jun turned over and looked at him. She brought out her hand from under the duvet and touched the lines on his forehead.

'Did you sleep okay? You're already a bit late for work.'

'Really? Shit, you should have woken me.'

'You were sleeping so peacefully.'

He smiled at her.

'That's nice but I have to get back.'

He got up hurriedly and went round to the door, then stopped and bent over to kiss her.

'Thank you for the blanket.'

He went to the bathroom and returned dressed ten minutes later to find Jun sleeping again. Back in his study he took the red envelope from his other jacket, then fed Galore and quickly left the apartment.

On the landing outside he stopped and looked up the stairwell, as he had the previous night. He looked at the staircase winding upwards to the roof, and recalled his chase up to nothing. He questioned his own state of mind at that time; knew he was just very tired and most certainly on edge. It was possible he'd seen a shadow and heard the wind. He stood for a while longer, looking again at his front door. There was a hole there where the pin had been, that much was true. He looked at the light fitting and bulb on the wall and glanced over at Mrs Chan's door. He followed the doorframe down to the floor and scanned it for anything discernible. Nothing.

Down the stairs to his car and into the morning traffic, he reminded himself that at the station he must appear to focus on the two ministers, no matter where his thinking might lead him.

As he approached the station he saw that the press and other media had enlarged their camp, adding a few more foreign crews. Cameras snapped and rolled as he arrived. His car was too distinct. He turned the Mustang into the car park. With its security cameras, heavy railings and guards, it was probably one of the safest places in Hong Kong, yet still Alex felt uneasy. He remained sitting inside it for a few minutes, though he knew he should have been racing for the lift and his desk. He felt the red envelope in his pocket. He had bagged it while he watched the cat eat. He patted his hand against it from outside his pocket and took a deep breath.

He sat considering his own impossible situation, whether he should disclose this potential evidence to the Captain and the rest of the team. In his gut he felt that his life was now not his own; someone had the power to intercede and change its course without him knowing.

And was it William who had contacted him?

He decided that until some hard evidence of his own relevance to the cases was discovered, he would not tell anyone, including De Suza. Best to keep him out of it, though the idea of hiding a secret from his good friend made him feel even more uneasy. But, Alex rationalized, better that no one else knew, rather than to put De Suza in the difficult position of being the only other to know. The note was personal but actually, he reasoned, there was no evidence at all that the message was connected to yesterday's events. It was just an envelope with a strange archaic quote written inside.

Alex got out of the car to find his friend approaching him.

'Hey, what are you doing here? You're so late. Did you get some sleep?'

'How did you know I'd got in?'

'Oh, I asked the duty security guard to let me know so I could catch you before you got upstairs.'

'Why? What's going on?'

'They're finalizing the plans for the visit of the international bigwigs tomorrow. Just running through the planning stages. Ying is working up some ideas on the warehouse.' They looked at each other. 'And the pathologist came back to us.'

'And?' Alex said sharply.

De Suza paused and looked at his partner.

'Did you get enough sleep last night?'

'I got some.'

'Pike said none of the ravens contained any jewellery. It looks as though it was all removed from the first four victims, but more interestingly he checked Lok's hand and his wedding ring was missing. His wife confirmed this.'

They stood by the lift and Alex pressed the call button.

'Was it of any value?'

'His wife said that his was just a metal band because they didn't have enough money. So, no.'

Alex moved forward and pressed the button a few times.

'That's unlike you,' De Suza observed.

'What is?'

'Pressing the button more than once. You hate people pressing the button when it has already been pressed,' De Suza said quietly, and moved to stand in front of Alex, between him and the lift. 'You all right?' he whispered.

Alex looked up at him defiantly.

'I am. I'm just . . .' He looked around him to check no one was around.

De Suza interrupted. 'Look, the voice . . . the man in the warehouse yesterday. It's just there's a personal element there and people are concerned about it. We don't understand why he seemed to know you,' he said bluntly.

'People?'

'There's talk.'

'What?'

'Well, lots of us heard it over your phone, even though the reception was poor, and so naturally people are asking how did that man know you would be there? And then you called William's name afterwards. This is a police station. People are asking themselves whether you're involved.'

Alex looked irritated. 'Do you think I am?'

'What? Seriously, don't be stupid. No, of course not. Look, let's get up there. Don't take it personally. We'll figure out what's happening.' De Suza put his hand on Alex's shoulder and gave it a friendly shake. 'Let's just agree we'll share everything. Keep each other in the loop.'

Alex nodded without looking at him.

The lift door opened and they went straight to the general office. On the open-plan floor it was as De Suza had described it. Four big teams were completing the mobilization of hundreds of units for the international economic conference the next day. They expected it to be hostile and tense on the streets, with a high possibility of angry protests and rioting.

The Captain approached.

'As you know, tomorrow is the first day of efforts to resolve the debt situation. The international delegations are all coming here and it's soaking up manpower and going to require many road closures around the Convention Centre and a lot of duty officers working the barriers. There's talk that the government are going to ask the foreigners for return of the compensation that was previously demanded of us unjustly. If this happens it will be a potentially explosive . . . Never mind that now. Soong, where are you with the ministers?'

'This morning we're going to try to identify the position of the shooter and speak to Lu's wife. She thought she still had the threatening letter from their last trip here, when he was accosted at one of his lectures.'

The Captain nodded and waved them away.

'Where does Mrs Lu live?' Alex asked De Suza.

'Out by the university, in the accommodation for visiting lecturers. It was supposed to be temporary until they found an apartment.'

De Suza called first and they left the office within minutes. It didn't take long before they arrived at the back entrance to the university, high above the campus where Alex had nearly eaten lunch the day before.

It was bright and hot. No weather for a jacket. Alex slipped his off and tossed it in the back seat. He closed the car door and looked down. They had parked at the top of the long driveway and service entrance to the university. The walk was steep but short, bending down to the left with the two-storey apartment block laid out in a single strip that bordered the driveway on the right, small balconies fronting each unit. From the top of the driveway they could see across the whole campus and down the mountain. They were right in the heart of Hong Kong, only ten minutes from the station, but it was quiet and Alex liked it.

They climbed the stairs of the block to the upper floor, where

Alex looked up at De Suza, who was shuffling from foot to foot and standing tight against the wall, his big frame almost obscuring the window by the door. He was starting to sweat, and looked unhappy in the gathering heat.

Lu's wife, Iris, came to the door and without hesitation beckoned them inside. She was a classic pear-shaped English lady, with silver hair and a pale complexion that was never going to be exposed to the sun. The flat was lit only by the sunbeams streaming in through the windows. The décor was simple, organized as temporary accommodation – functional, comfortable but unremarkable – and reminded Alex of his parents' apartment. There were many photographs of the couple, their children, congregations with Lu presiding, and various groups and community projects. It was an open square room with a desk behind the door, below the front window, and a sofa and armchair in the middle of the floor. To the right, two long simple bookshelves were already full.

'Ma'am, I'm very sorry for your loss.' Alex looked round and she followed his gaze. 'You both lived such a full life.'

'Yes, my husband was a scholar, but he also enjoyed the company of others – jamborees, weddings, christenings ... and, unhappily, funerals. I suppose I must think now about planning his.' She spoke English so clearly and precisely that it was a joy for him to hear it.

They had yet to sit down. 'Ma'am, if this is too soon, we can come back,' Alex offered.

'No, no. It's fine. Besides,' she looked at both men in turn, 'you have to catch the people who killed my husband. Please sit down. I have found something in his letters, but I also found his diaries from the time of our last trip here. Let me get them. Do you want a drink? Officer,' she turned to De Suza, 'you look like you could do with a glass of water.'

He smiled widely. 'That would be excellent, ma'am.'

'I'll be back.'

The two men sat and looked round the room. She was back within minutes with a tray containing three glasses of water and an old envelope, and a diary tucked under her arm.

'Okay, here you go.' She passed the glasses to each man. 'Now here is a letter from some foolish man. He writes to say my husband's talk was wrong and goes into a lengthy account of how foreigners owe the Chinese compensation for their past wrongdoings, and asks who are they to be so arrogant. Those are my words, but here it is.' She gave Alex the letter and he fished a plastic evidence bag out of his jacket and dropped it in. 'The second and maybe more important piece is this entry from my husband's diary of the time.'

Her fingers found the strip of paper that marked a particular entry. She opened it and cleared her throat in a manner that Alex guessed she must use when reading during a service.

'"March nineteenth 2006. It went well. What a relief! The room was packed and extra seating was required. I had heard how many people in Hong Kong (and China, dare I even mention this!!) were joining congregations, but I had no idea what enthusiasm and devotion there was among these new communities. It was very heart-warming and a pleasant surprise. The subject also drew interest from other individuals, and I was surprised less favourably by the number of people who still bear us malice for the work of early Christians in China and the growth of the Church in Asia. Still, two or three hecklers did not spoil the occasion. The lecture went well, though I did not tread as carefully as I should have done in relation to the rejection of old superstitions, such as ancestor worship, on becoming Christian. My own prejudices rose a little too high. Tolerance, man, tolerance.

Indeed it was a little insensitive of me, especially being Chinese myself. Tomorrow, meeting with the Chancellor and then to St John's.'"

She rested the diary on her lap, then looked up at them.

'I also want to read you the entry from a few days after this.' She cleared her throat again automatically. '"March twenty-third 2006. I have not told Iris, and I do not think I will, but I received another threatening letter today. This one came in a box with a thick piece of rope tied into a hangman's noose. There was a note saying: 'Even Judas knew what he had to do at the end.' It is pretty comical in a way, except that such care seems to have been taken over the creation of these props. I have decided that if I do not hear anything further then I will leave it, otherwise I will take it to the police. Do not want to worry Iris with this, she has been so patient coming on the trip.'"

She closed the diary and handed it to Alex, who took out another plastic evidence bag.

'Do you have the box with the rope?' De Suza asked immediately.

'I haven't found it, but this is only a temporary home, so most of our things are still in storage. I can ring the Church administrators who organized the storage, to allow you to look there.'

'We would appreciate that,' De Suza replied politely. 'Let's see if we can do it this afternoon. Will you come with us? We know how very tired you must be.'

'I am, but I'll do what I can to help. I'll arrange for you to visit the storage depot.'

Alex cleared his throat and they turned to him.

'In the first entry, your husband mentioned his own prejudices against superstition. Do you know what he meant by that?'

'Well, his family were not very educated, simple traditionally minded people. They couldn't understand why choosing

Christianity meant that he could not also follow their non-Christian beliefs.'

'Well, it's difficult,' De Suza interjected. 'A single god always seems a bit inflexible to me.'

Alex shot a look at his partner, unhappy with such a personal intervention. 'Ma'am,' he continued, 'your husband felt strongly about this subject?'

'Well, yes, but that's families, isn't it? His parents could not understand why he wouldn't participate in the grave sweeping, or keep a small temple in his house. On the one hand they would say: "They are such small things, why not do it?" And on the other, he would say: "If they are such small things, what is the problem with ignoring them?" They would say better to believe in everything and be safe, and he would reply it is better to believe in one thing and be clear as to who you are.'

De Suza nodded. 'I agree. It's difficult.'

Alex looked at him again and frowned a little.

'And what happened?'

'Well, it would just keep coming up when they visited us in the UK, US or wherever we were. Not big arguments, but I think my husband saw them as demeaning his whole way of life. He had chosen a path that was characterized by the importance of choosing one belief, not one that compromised, covering all bases. Intellectually he could understand, but emotionally it made him a little annoyed with his parents.'

Alex sat back and thought this through. De Suza took the opportunity to raise a couple of questions of his own.

'Did you feel that you should just help the situation along and join his parents for grave-sweeping and the other traditions? You know, to make the whole thing easier.'

She seemed slightly taken aback by his suggestion and cocked her head to one side in bemusement. Her lips pursed briefly in contemplation, then she said: 'Well, no, officer. You see, we choose a faith in order to believe in something ... Christianity, Islam, Buddhism. That is what guides one. It's not about believing in *everything* and hoping something sticks. For what purpose? One believes in something and proceeds from there. One's actions are guided by those beliefs, so cathedrals are built, communities established, and schools opened. Remember,' she said with heavy emphasis, 'believing in everything is to believe in nothing, and from that nothing will grow, whether one is from the East or the West. My husband's parents, like many Chinese of their generation and before, believed in ancestor worship, traditional gods, Confucianism, Imperial worship ... remember, the Emperor was considered a god ... superstition, animism, Buddhism and some Taoism. Everything and perhaps nothing.'

She spoke in a tone that was close to condescension.

'But do you think, as a *gweilo*, you are in any position to tell us what to believe?' De Suza shot back testily.

'You asked about my husband and *his* beliefs. The question of whether I or anyone else can comment on someone else's is a separate issue. But, no, I believe none of us has the right to require another to believe something.'

Alex gently grabbed De Suza's arm.

'I think we should go. I have a lead I'd like to follow. Ma'am, thank you for your time, and let us know about access to the storage depot so we can look for the letter and the noose.'

They all got up and the detectives were politely shown to the door. As it closed behind them, Alex turned on his partner.

'What's wrong with you? You're Eurasian, for God's sake.'

'What's that got to do with it? Besides I'm Chinese, the white part of me wasn't my fault,' De Suza continued as they walked along the balcony to the staircase. 'I can believe what I want. You heard her. I was taught to respect the old values.'

'Well, to be honest, I think you should have shown her more respect,' Alex said firmly, going down the steps. 'You're saying now you're only Christian because of Mary?'

De Suza stared down into his face without responding. Alex breathed out softly. 'I don't want to argue about this. I have a call to make. Are we going to do this together or not?'

De Suza pinched the bridge of his nose and rubbed his face. 'Look, sorry, this type of talk makes me angry. I just hate . . .' He was hesitant over the next words.

'Being told what to do?'

'Yes, especially by white people.'

'She's just lost her husband. You could have been a little more patient, like you are every other day.'

'But still, they can be so condescending.'

'Okay, we can get into this at another time.' Alex relaxed a little and stretched his neck. 'The religious aspect keeps on cropping up in this case. We should find out more about why that is.'

Alex walked down the steps from Iris Lu's house and De Suza followed. In the cool of the stairwell, Alex stopped to make a call and his partner sat down on the concrete steps.

'Hello, is that Professor Lin?'

'Yes.'

'This is Alex Soong. I just wanted to say thank you for yesterday and sorry again for leaving so abruptly. I'd be grateful if you could answer a quick question. I'm in the university, so can I come down?'

'Well, Alex, to save you the journey, what's the question? And I'll tell you whether or not I'm the person to help you,' the Professor replied promptly.

'It's about the relationship between Chinese cults and Christianity. Is there any recent history of violence or antagonism between them?'

'Interesting. May I ask what the context of this question is?'

'I'm not entirely certain myself, but it relates to a murder, so it's violence in the extreme.'

'Well, what I can tell you is that historically there has been little recent organized Chinese cult activity against Christian groups. Obviously there has been considerable political activity against Christians at times in China and other parts of Asia, but with the threat posed by militant Islamists, as well as the current economic difficulties, Christianity is not considered a priority these days. Historically, the Jesuits were pretty welcome at the Ming Imperial courts when they first came to China, bringing much knowledge with them. The two most widely recognized candidates for first into China were Michele Ruggieri and Matteo Ricci – Ricci was honoured by the Imperial Court as a great cartographer and mathematician. He actually became an adviser to the Ming Emperor Wanli in Sixteen Hundred and One, and was the first Westerner to be invited into the Imperial Court. You might say it was a good start. But the nadir in East/West relations came with the Boxers, and then of course the hardline Communists in the twentieth century.'

Lin laughed. 'Sorry I'm rambling. Look, I can't think of any cults, groups or activities that have pursued any real violence against Christians other than political factions. You know, one of the best people in the world to speak to you about Christianity, Chinese cults and China is Professor Yi, the young lady you met yesterday.'

Alex smiled to himself with unguarded satisfaction. 'I met her last night actually. She came to the police station to report an accident.'

'Oh, dear, is she okay?'

'Yes, she's fine. It was a minor knock, but she needed to report it for insurance purposes.'

'I'm glad she's okay. Do you want her number?'

'Yes, please. And by the way, Professor, before you go, can you tell me who the tall man was at lunch? The one who asked me those pointed questions.'

The Professor read out the number and continued: 'You know, we were talking about that yesterday afternoon. We have no idea. He just turned up and we were too wrongfooted to ask him. We did contact the food and beverage manager, who said the person in question just appeared at their door, politely asking them to set another place, and so they did. Then he left early before we realized none of us knew him. Strange man indeed. I do apologize for his attitude.'

'Well, it wasn't your fault, Professor. Speak to you soon, and thanks for her number.'

Alex hung up and looked at De Suza, busy messaging his wife on his iPhone.

'Mary says hello and tells you to get more sleep.' Alex smiled and De Suza continued: 'So Christianity could be a theme. But what about the location?'

'Well, there's one place . . .'

'Please don't say it,' De Suza groaned, looking up at him.

'It's the perfect spot. You know it.'

De Suza stood up and put his phone into his pocket. He walked past Alex and continued down the steps on to the now-baking concrete driveway.

'The old ICAC offices? The fucking ICAC!' he shouted to Alex, who was still standing behind him in the shade. 'The Captain will love it. He was a junior officer in 'Seventy-Four when the Commission investigated the corruption in the force after extraditing the Police Chief – they just ripped through it looking for others.'

'Cleaned it out though.'

'Yes, but that's not the point, is it?' De Suza replied sharply.

'Sorry, but the shots were fired from that direction and most likely from that height, so we're going to have to get the Captain to ask them to open up their old offices.'

'The place has been closed and locked down for ten years now. Rumours are that all the juicy stuff is still stored in there.'

'Well, they're going to have to open them up. It has the clearest line of sight to the walkway, and for obvious reasons it's very private. But look, we're just interested in the building . . . not the people or the Commission.'

'Think of something else, can't you?' De Suza pleaded as Alex emerged. 'Because however hard you work to dress it up, they're not going to like the implication. Not one bit.'

Back in the Mustang Alex wound the window down and switched on the air conditioning, a function not available in the original model but which the previous owner had sensibly fitted. He dialled the number Lin had just given him.

'Hello, is that Professor Yi?'

'Hi, yes.'

'This is Senior Inspector Soong. We met yesterday.'

'Ah, Alex, how nice of you to follow up on the car accident. I filled out the report and they said they would contact my brother about it.'

'Oh, yes, that's good news.' He paused, realizing that he had completely forgotten about the car. 'I was also ringing about another matter that I understand you might be able to help us with.'

'Oh, yes?' The pitch of her voice suddenly became a little higher and she sounded harassed. 'Look, I'm really sorry but I'm just going through Security and Immigration and I'm very late for my plane. I can call you back once I'm in Boston. I really enjoyed meeting you. 'Bye.'

The phone went dead.

He frowned and instantly rang back.

Nothing.

He dialled another number.

'Can you put me through to the duty immigration officer at Chek Lap Kok? ... Excuse me, sir, this is Senior Inspector Alex Soong of the Fraud and White-collar Crime Division. We have reason to believe that an individual going through the Immigration process at the moment is implicated in an investigation we're conducting. We are seeking to detain her for questioning. Please can you assist us and pull this person out of line and hold them until we get there? The name is Associate Professor Elizabeth Yi.' He paused to listen to the duty officer's complaint. 'Yes, I'm sorry for this short notice, we should have listed her.'

It would take a little more grovelling than that.

'I apologize. And thank you for your help.'

He hung up.

De Suza raised his eyebrows. 'She won't be happy, being hauled off her plane and taken into custody.'

'She was rushing through Immigration to board a flight back to the US. We'd have lost her for twenty-plus hours. I don't want to risk that if she can help us.'

'Seriously, do you really think she'll have any answers? Or are you just trying to see her again?'

'I'm hurt you would suggest that,' Alex joked. 'So far we've got nothing apart from the possibility that religion, specifically

Christianity, is relevant, but in a historical context rather than in a contemporary way. Professor Yi is meant to be the world expert on early Christianity in China, so her insights could be crucial in determining the motivations on both cases.'

De Suza still looked sceptical. 'You realize we're fast approaching a point of no return?'

Alex nodded.

De Suza continued: 'Once she's on side, I hope she can lend your vague theory some substance, otherwise there are going to be a whole lot of very pissed off people. Starting with the Professor herself, Immigration . . . not to mention the Captain.'

'I get the message,' Alex replied flatly. 'I still believe we're being led somewhere, and I think we've got to follow this lead.'

They drove away from the campus. A plump old woman, with a face made rough and lined by constant heat and strain, sat on a stool manning the Stop/Go sign, flipping it backwards and forwards to let the traffic through. Alex tapped his fingers against the steering wheel as they waited in line.

'There's a lot of anger out there,' Alex said all of a sudden. 'In order to get by, people are having to do things now that many thought they'd left behind for good.'

'I know what you're saying,' De Suza sighed. 'Mary wants me to consider moving to Australia. She can work there with her family and they can help with the kids. But what the hell would I do? I could retrain, but I'd start again from the bottom. Apart from that it's work as a waiter. I can't face that.'

Alex said nothing but smiled. De Suza took a little time to let his frustration with the situation settle. 'What's the next move?' he finally asked.

'I'll head to the airport to collect the Professor and let Immigration rip me a new one. I think you should follow up with the guys looking for the shooter's position and, if it does seem to be narrowing down to the old ICAC offices, call the Captain and get him to speak with the Commissioners there.'

'Thanks,' said De Suza sarcastically. 'Waiting tables in Australia is suddenly a lot more appealing.'

Back at the station De Suza took the elevator straight to the third floor. He stepped out and found the Captain standing there, a scrap of paper in his left hand and his right balled into a fist.

'Just you, heh?' he said.

'Yes, Soong has gone to . . .'

'The airport perhaps, to pick up a mystery suspect?' The Captain completed the sentence. 'I've just received a call from the head of Immigration, demanding to know why one of my officers requested the detention of a history professor from a prestigious American university. What exactly has Soong got in mind?'

'I understand you're angry but there was no time to call you. Actually, there is another thing you're not going to like . . .'

'First things first.'

'Soong believes there is a strong Christian theme behind the killings.'

'An act of religious terrorism?'

'No, not that.'

The Captain stepped back. He clenched his jaw for a moment and demanded: 'You'd better explain then.'

'Pike concluded that the victims in the container, even the realtor, appeared to have had jewellery removed from their bodies. All except for one cross, left around the neck of the male victim without the hand. There is good reason to believe this was planted and therefore is a message. Also, one of the Methodists had lectured here on the history of Christianity and Chinese society a few years ago, and had received threatening correspondence as a result. While these murders are horrific they lack the element of strong public outrage and fear that religious terrorism normally seeks to provoke. Basically we have reached the point where we want to find out more about the introduction of Christianity to China. Hence the Professor, who is an authority in the field.'

The Captain nodded.

'There's a cogent line of thinking there. And the second thing?'

'I need to check with the team working to locate the sniper site but . . .' De Suza hesitated, concerned the Captain might not react well to the next suggestion. 'We believe the gunman may have been on the roof of the old ICAC offices.'

The Captain exhaled sharply through his nose, then nodded.

'If this is your conclusion, make your move officially. I've no problem getting into it with them, they're a solid outfit, but we must be sure to get our facts right first . . . or there will be consequences.'

He threw the balled-up paper into the waste bin underneath the elevator call button and pressed it to go back to his office.

De Suza's desk phone rang. It was Alex.

'Have you seen the Captain?'

'Yes, he was pretty easy about contacting the ICAC. I think he's going to enjoy giving them a little poke, if everything is done properly.'

'Did Immigration cause any problems?'

'Yeah, but I explained our thinking and he seemed to think it was justified, but it's your problem when you get there. How far away are you?'

'I'm just getting on to the Stonecutters bridge. I'll call you later.'

Alex had made good time since leaving De Suza at the station in Central, and continued without trouble onto the Tsing Sha Highway that flew over old Stonecutters Island, before making for the Nam Wan Tunnel and from there to the huge Lantau Link suspension bridge to Lantau Island and then the airport. The final stretch of highway now led nowhere else except the lonely housing estates spotted around the runways and service buildings. It was a fast journey – the usual thirty minutes done in twenty.

He thought of Jun making him chocolate the night before, covering him with a blanket, and of their fingers twined together in the darkness. He knew these were the moments they most enjoyed sharing in their marriage. It was the separate individual experiences, enjoyed or suffered alone, that he wanted and needed to share with her as well.

He pulled into the departure drop-off point, leaving the car with its hazard lights on, then ran in and went straight to the Immigration Office. As he approached he could see through the partially obscured windows the Professor sitting opposite the duty officer, arms folded and lips thinned out in anger. She saw him approaching and appeared to speak sharply to the officer, who also looked infuriated. Alex showed his badge to the security guard outside.

'You!' The Professor sounded very annoyed, getting up from the table and striding towards him. 'What the hell are you doing? This man says I'm required in connection with a criminal investigation. It was only a minor accident . . . but apparently it needs further enquiries.'

The duty officer, a skinny man with sunken cheeks, nodded to Alex without getting up.

'I have already told your Captain this is unacceptable,' he flatly announced.

'I apologize for the situation, sir,' Alex said politely. 'I can take it from here.'

Without a word the officer got up. He picked up his file and walked directly towards Alex, who moved out of the way to let him pass. The man said nothing further and merely closed the door, leaving Alex and the Professor alone. He decided that he would continue the charade for now and then explain the real situation in the privacy of the car. He secretly admired her confrontational attitude. She looked confident in the knowledge that she had not committed a crime. She gripped the handle of her travel bag impatiently but otherwise stayed outwardly calm, not expressing her frustration openly.

'Professor, would you please follow me?' He opened the door. 'May I help you with your bag?'

She walked straight past him. 'Seriously?' she snapped sarcastically.

He led her to the drop-off zone and slid some of the junk from the car's interior into the trunk. He opened the door for her and she responded with a curt thank you. Within a few minutes they were heading back along the highway towards the tunnel and the bridge.

Alex drove for five minutes, trying to decide the best way to explain why she had been prevented from leaving. He glanced at her as he changed gears. She was wearing dark loose-legged culottes, tight at the waist, and a loose simple strappy white vest, with sunglasses perched on top of her forehead. Sitting in the bucket seat of his Mustang, she looked diminutive but still very feisty. He realized how much he enjoyed watching her.

'So you got the insurance report sorted out?' he began.

'Yes, Officer,' she responded with assumed meekness.

He knew he was not meant to be fooled by it and left the resulting silence undisturbed for a few minutes before he finally offered his explanation.

'Look, I'm sorry about this but I feared you'd simply get on the plane . . .'

'That was the plan,' she shot back dryly.

'Professor Lin described you to me as a world authority on Christianity and Chinese cults. I need your professional opinion to help me in a current enquiry.'

She moved in her seat, shifting her hips and recrossing her legs. He glanced over and took another quick look at her, but it was her air of resolve and strength of mind that captured his attention most this time.

'Did you mean that you in particular need it or that the Police Department needs it?'

'It is my line of thinking, but my superior officer knows of it. As does my partner. Please, let me explain a bit more, and then if you think I'm wasting your time I'll take you back to the airport.'

'Okay, take me back,' she demanded.

'Seriously?'

'No.' She laughed. 'Your persistence is intriguing. Tell me what you have so far.'

'You're a hard woman.'

'I'm a professional historian, Officer.'

'As you probably heard, two Methodist ministers were murdered here yesterday. They had recently arrived in Hong Kong, but did not know each other previously. It was the first time in a while that the Cathedral had had two overseas-educated Chinese ministers. Both men were shot in the head from long range – something that may indicate a personal element to the crime. We also know that, some years ago, one of the ministers gave a lecture at HKU on the subject of Christianity in China, and there were several threatening remarks made to him at the time. He was later sent a hangman's noose, together with a reference to Judas. These details aren't known to the public but are not confidential. What I am about to tell you *is* confidential and details have not yet been released.

'Yesterday evening, in a derelict warehouse development, we found a shipping container loaded with three Chinese individuals and a *gweilo*, a young German male, who had all been starved to death. They had been locked in the container together with twenty-seven ravens, which had inflicted considerable harm on them. One victim had had a hand removed after death, and we think that same victim had a cross deliberately placed around his neck. Furthermore, we found strong indications that all other jewellery had been removed. To support that theory there was a fifth, more recent victim who had accompanied someone to the warehouse and was murdered there last night. His wedding ring, the only jewellery he wore, was also removed. I believe the cross was planted as a message to us, and that the theme of Christianity is central to this case.'

As Alex recounted the facts, Yi shifted in her seat and turned towards him, concentrating on the details.

'You'd experienced all this before I saw you last night?' was all she commented when he'd finished.

Alex did not answer.

She seemed momentarily distressed by the images he had conjured in her imagination, and then she refocused.

'How can I help?'

'Is there anything in Chinese history that would incite someone to target Chinese Christians? And if so, can you fill me in on the background, please?'

He watched her sit back and slip off her shoes, old canvas Converse classics, then tuck one foot under herself. She wriggled a little to get more comfortable while her brow remained creased in thought.

'You know your sneakers,' he said, to break the silence.

'On an untenured associate professor's pay, you've *got* to know your sneakers.'

They entered Nam Wan Tunnel, and the greenish hue of the tunnel's interior lighting filled the car.

'What you just told me is terrible,' she began. 'I'll help if I can, of course. I'm not sure how relevant this is going to be, though.

'Other than by the State machinery itself, there's been little organized activity in recent history. You have to go back to the Boxer Rebellion to find a formal and relatively coherent plan by Chinese civilians to eliminate Christians. The prime movers in it were peasants from Shandong province, starved and thirsty, enduring a terrible drought that brought them out of their parched fields in the belief that a powerful magic brought by foreigners, i.e. the magic of Christ, was causing the drought. The Boxer movement disappeared as fast as it had arisen. As soon as the rains fell they simply returned home to the fields.'

She glanced at him enquiringly.

'I'm not sure if that's of any help to you. But the terrible murder of two Christians does have strange echoes of the past. At the beginning of the Rebellion, two foreign preachers were shot by the Boxers, and it was this that sparked the ensuing confrontation with foreign powers in China. There had been a number of Chinese Christians terrorized and murdered before then, but it was the killing of these two foreign preachers in particular that made the world take notice, and after some further provocation, caused war with China to break out.'

Over Stonecutters Island, Yi looked into the distance at the ICC building stretching up into the sky on the horizon ahead.

'You know, I'm pissed at you for making me miss my flight, but I do understand why you want to solve these terrible crimes,' she told him.

They bore left with the International Commerce Centre tower, ICC, visible in the distance and Victoria Harbour beyond.

'This is a beautiful place. A real testament to Asia's rise,' she mused. 'To my parents, Hong Kong was this golden city. It was safe from the Communist Party and a new beginning for them. It's where they adopted me. I don't remember much but I came here again a few years ago and was amazed, and it's even more impressive now.'

Alex looked over at her briefly to see her looking back, but he didn't interrupt her.

'People forget that if you look back to the Sixties, only fifty-five years ago, there were no high-rise buildings here, most of Asia was in abject poverty, and war and genocide, poverty and disease were rife throughout the region. Hong Kong's rise has been as miraculous as it looks.'

'Yes, but there's tension too.'

They sped through the tollgate and down into the gaping entrance of the expensive and therefore empty Western Tunnel. Yi thought of her own parents, hurt and starving in the madness of the Cultural Revolution at the end of the Sixties. Her father had been tortured so severely that he lost an eye and was never again the man her mother would later describe herself as meeting and falling in love with. They eventually escaped to Hong Kong to become academics, and then nearly fifteen years after settling down they had decided to start a family by adopting two unrelated children, first a boy aged twelve and then a year later a girl aged four, two of the many cast-offs from the same country that had treated the couple so poorly, but like so many, that they could not help but continue to love. Like many overseas Chinese, they had had great reservations when their adopted son declared that he wanted to return to Hong Kong to join the property boom before the handover in 1997. The family had lived happily and safely in Boston since leaving Hong Kong in 1987. Yet the elderly couple also understood the pull of China and one's home, and eventually let him go.

The Professor looked down at the iPod between them.

'There's nothing on this but jazz.'

'Yes.'

'Have you ever seen the film *Jazz on a Summer's Day?*'

'Of course, Newport Beach, 1958. Great film.'

He looked at the towers of Central closing in on them fast and realized that he had enjoyed this journey back, this conversation, perhaps more than he should.

'In 1958 my parents were still in China, and a few years after that film was made they were starving in the western province of Anhui. Yet on Newport Beach, it looks so gentle and peaceful, with people sipping long iced teas on a glorious day. That difference is a little humiliating. It leaves a bitter question: after five thousand years, how did we end up so far behind?'

Each step along the pale corridor and its tiled floors had felt light and insubstantial, a long silent glide towards the prenatal ward, propelled by the excitement and anxiety of imminent fatherhood. The phenolic smell of detergent and the washed cloth of surgical gowns, nurses' uniforms and bed linen had reminded him that this was no dream, but also recalled his previous visit to a hospital, when he'd accompanied his mother to visit his father.

Nearing the end of the corridor, he had approached the entrance to the maternity ward. He felt suddenly determined to be an attentive and thoughtful parent. He was twenty-six, four years older than his own father had been. Turning into the ward, he located her bed and was ready to be joyful and happy with his wife and newborn. But when he arrived at her bedside and looked down into the cot he was shocked by how Western the child looked. He was Eurasian, more than half-caste, but still not whole, a quarter white military bastard and three-quarters Chinese. He flinched as he stared into the baby's thick, strong Western features. He looked at his young wife and her loving expression as she cooed over her newborn. Her Western father was unknown to her, a soldier on the way to or from his home country, so he could not estimate how the little boy might look as he grew up. But he was already uncomfortable with his own reaction. He sat beside the young mother – she was barely twenty years old – and held her hand. Yet he had not been able to bring himself to look at her. What had they created?

'He looks very healthy,' she had said excitedly, peering into her baby's face with an expression of delight while he himself stared down at the neatly swaddled bundle that was his son.

'He looks very Western to me. Did you think he would look like that?' he asked.

'I never thought about it. I guess he takes after my father.'

'Yes, I guess so,' he answered dryly. 'I thought he would look more Chinese. I'm Chinese and you're half.'

'Maybe white features are stronger?'

He could not look at her. He felt that somehow she had fooled him, betrayed him even. She had known what would happen, and that he would not like it. She had known all along. He looked at the beds around them, watching out for the prying eyes, those judging him a fool. She had embarrassed him, perhaps deliberately. He got up and stared down at her. She was beautiful, with lovely hazel eyes whose warm innocent calm had made him bend and yield to her. Now those eyes seemed glassy and dull, slow to respond. It had not been innocence but ignorance, he decided. He peered into the cot, at the dark brown hair and large body, head and limbs: not Chinese proportions. As the baby grew, he hated her more for the deception she had practised. He was already a big man for a Chinese, but this creature might well outgrow even its own father. It had lumpy features, a large round head, looked ungainly when it started to walk. This would not be his child.

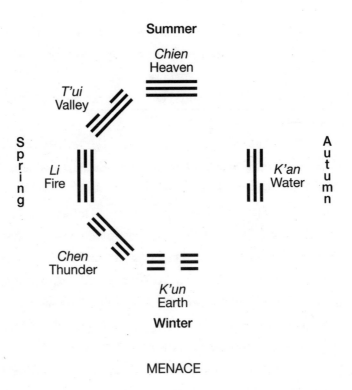

MENACE

Alex turned into Arsenal Street and saw the group of media camped outside the entrance to the station car park.

'It might be better if you hid yourself,' he suggested to Yi.

'Why?'

'The press are everywhere.'

She shrugged.

'Suit yourself.' He shrugged back half-mockingly.

The press crowded round the car as it stopped briefly before the security barrier. Photographers and cameramen avidly filmed Yi, and Alex saw Jenni Plum busy with her iPhone. He pulled into the car park, leaving the mob behind, then switched the engine off and looked at Yi. As formidable as she could be when she had her back up, there was an air of calm about her that was charming and comforting to be around.

'I'm very sorry for today,' he told her. 'I realize I caused you a lot of inconvenience, but I think that somehow you hold the key to these cases. Thank you for bearing with me.'

She started to look for her shoes in the footwell. 'I was pretty mad when they pulled me out of the line, but from what you have told me there does seem to be some sort of connection with my special subject.' She stared through the windscreen at the white-painted concrete wall in front of her, focusing on nothing in particular. 'I don't believe the motivation is against Christianity as such, because while it's increasingly popular in China, so are many other problems of greater concern. It's always attracted the attention of the authorities, but there are very few recorded instances of recent civilian action against it. It's generally a government issue – and these murders are not.' She turned to him and he watched her ponytail swing above her back and bare shoulders. 'I'll sort things out in the US and give you three days, how's that?'

'That's great, thank you.'

They got out, leaving her luggage in his car, and walked to the elevator.

'What were those two bottles in the bottom of the footwell?' she asked.

Alex blushed. 'Let's keep moving,' he mumbled.

They went straight up to the third floor. De Suza was on the phone. He glanced over his shoulder and winked at Alex as he arrived and nodded a casual hello to Professor Yi. Off the phone, he spun round in his chair to face them.

'Hi,' he said. 'I'm Mike De Suza. So he convinced you to stay in Hong Kong?'

'Elizabeth Yi,' she said. 'And kidnapped would be more like it.'

'Hold on, you can't use that kind of word in this building,' Alex broke in. 'Mike, what's the latest on the shooter's location?'

De Suza hesitated and Yi took the hint.

'Why don't I wait somewhere until you need me?'

'We have to go upstairs soon to a meeting room on ninth,' De Suza told Alex. 'Ying has found something apparently. We've not found a thing on the location. It's time to make that call to the ICAC.'

'Okay, let's get up to the meeting and hear Ying first.' He turned to Professor Yi. 'I'll ask an officer to take you to an interview room where you can wait.'

Alex looked around and saw Ding at the other end of the room.

'Officer Ding, can you come here, please?' he shouted across the desks, and the young officer came over. Alex told him where to take the Professor and then the two detectives headed up to the meeting room, using the stairs rather than the elevator.

'Do you know what Ying has?' Alex asked De Suza once they were in the relative privacy of the stairwell.

'No idea. The rumour is that he has solved the case already and is planning to head up a team later this afternoon to arrest those responsible. But no details have been released.'

'Sounds like bullshit to me.'

'I agree.'

'Someone goes to all the trouble of obtaining the container, the victims, the realtor and the fucking birds. They time everything precisely and leave not a shred of evidence. Yet Ying has it solved in less than twenty-four hours? It's total bullshit.'

Alex was walking quickly, hurrying to get to the meeting and hear what Ying had to say.

De Suza put a hand on his shoulder to slow him down. 'Look, whatever happens, don't go off on Ying or the Captain. He can't have solved this already, but don't confront him until you have thought things through properly.'

Alex looked indignant. 'I *always* think things through.'

De Suza smiled. '*You* know what I mean. *I* know you wanted to lead both these cases, so I'm just saying, let the red mist pass, that's all.'

Alex rolled his eyes and nodded in agreement.

They arrived at the meeting room to find the Captain, Ying and his team sitting in the first few rows.

'Finally, you got here,' Ying said sarcastically. He stood up, waving his hand for the two new arrivals to take seats quickly. He then looked at the Captain, who indicated with a little wave of his open palm that Ying should begin speaking.

'During last night's pathology report we discussed the three unknown Chinese victims' teeth. I had the dental pathologist look at them and he believed that those three were young but their teeth were in a state of decay very similar to that found in many mainlanders in their twenties who have been without effective dental care.'

Ying called out to one of his team, who was holding the remote for the projector. The gruesome crime-scene picture of the container and the emaciated victims was brought up on the screen.

'The container reminded me of the way illegal immigrants are transported, as I'm sure it did many of you. This is a scenario a snakehead could easily arrange. These are most likely illegals who willingly got into that container, believing it was a chance for a better life.'

De Suza interrupted: 'But why the ravens? And why leave this thing there?'

'I believe it's a message to someone. The message is conveyed in the doing of it . . . the power and unrestrained freedom to commit this act. We've just been left to clear it up. It's a theatrical show, intended to make a point to someone.'

'What about the voice speaking directly to Alex?' De Suza challenged.

'It's the same thing . . . a taunt. Making a big "fuck you" to us, to his rivals, plus showing his own people exactly what can be done, if you have the balls.'

Alex broke in here. 'So you have someone specific in mind?'

Ying nodded for the slide to change and turned to look square at Alex.

'That's right.' On screen came a picture of an older man with fine grey hair smoothed back very neatly. A mole under his lower lip sprouted a long ugly hair, left uncut for luck. 'It's Lo.'

Alex and De Suza groaned. As far as anyone knew Lo had come down from the north during the 1950s and made his name with a successful and legitimate warehousing and delivery business, a few restaurants and karaoke bars across the city and some cheap but successful film productions. He was notorious as a trafficker in people and drugs, but over the years the police had become known for always keeping one eye closed to his activities.

'Come on,' De Suza laughed, 'he's the biggest human trafficker around. Why would he do this? Why would he ever *need* to do this?'

'Slavery and trafficking are on the rise. Over fourteen million people in Asia a year, that's two million up from three years ago. We think Lo's been under pressure and is doing what we'd expect him to do, which is strike first. Prove to the competition who's on top.'

Alex and De Suza looked sceptical. 'What about the other evidence? Such as the cross . . .' Alex started to add, but De Suza tapped his arm and he stopped speaking.

'What other evidence?' Ying said suspiciously.

De Suza quickly fielded the question. 'My partner was going to ask about the hand that was taken.'

Ying leaped on this remark. 'All part of the same show!' He slammed one hand down dramatically on the table in front of him. 'Hand!' He pointed to his right eye. 'Eye.' He pulled at one earlobe. 'Ear. Birds . . . could be cats, dogs, it's all just for shock value. You're reading too much into it, when instead it couldn't be simpler. You guys always analyse too much.' Ying leaned back and looked up at the ceiling in feigned frustration. 'Policework is fundamentally simple: the bad guys do the bad things.'

He returned to looking at his colleagues and then specifically the Captain. 'I want to arrest Lo now. Do I have the go-ahead?'

The Captain stayed still and did not respond for a while, staring at the picture of Lo on the screen. 'Bring him in, question him . . . but keep it tight and sensible.'

Ying gave him the thumbs-up and looked at his team. He led them out, staring down at the two seated detectives with a smile as he did so.

'Inspector Ying,' the Captain called out before Ying could reach the door, 'the media are already all over yesterday's events. Try to keep this low key?'

The Captain and De Suza stood up while Alex remained seated.

'Neither of you is convinced, I take it?' the Captain asked.

De Suza looked at Alex, who spoke up.

'It doesn't seem accessible enough to be what Ying's saying it is. In 2012, for instance, the Mexican drug gangs made horrific but powerful statements of intent to their competitors by killing and mutilating hundreds of people. In just one instance forty-nine members of one gang were found dismembered in plastic bags. But gang wars usually stay within gangs, and here we have blameless preachers and total unknowns.'

The Captain walked towards the screen and studied Lo's photograph. 'For what it's worth, I think you're right, but this cannot be approached on gut feelings alone. While we wait for them to bring Lo in, what have you got?'

De Suza took the question. 'We've checked the buildings in the area surrounding the first crime scene. They are mostly just too tall and sheeted in glass skins. The windows don't open and the roofs are far too high to get a shot off from: the shooter would have had no visual, as the ministers would have been under the canopy of the walkway at the time. Which leaves just one location: a corner of the roof of the old Independent Commission Against Corruption building, *friends* of government officials, tycoons and the police.'

The Captain looked down at the floor.

'Okay, so we're agreed on this. Before I ring the Commissioner of the ICAC, I want to know every last detail of why you think it's the site. Oh, and I see you got the mystery woman?'

Alex looked confused.

'She was photographed by that blogger girl the moment you entered the car park. It was posted immediately – *Mystery Woman in Detective's Life*,' the Captain said with more than a little amusement.

'Shit!'

De Suza chuckled and replied to the Captain: 'At present, until we have more information, she's not sure how she can help. But she's sticking around for the next few days.'

Alex slid one hand into his jacket pocket. He felt guilty for not disclosing the existence of the envelope to the others, particularly De Suza, but if he did he knew he would be suspended, particularly with Mak's recent interest in him. He reasoned again that it really meant very little, but felt more and more anxious about it.

'Okay, I'll ring the Commissioner, and you two go over to the ICAC – but be courteous! Where is the Professor now?' the Captain finished.

'We have her in an interview room on the second floor.'

'I'd like to meet her.'

They left the room together and took the lift down to the second floor in silence. The Captain stood against the window of the interview room and looked at Professor Yi before going in to meet her.

'Quite pretty,' he confirmed.

He and De Suza entered the room, but Alex's phone rang and he stayed out in the corridor.

'Mystery woman?' Jun's voice exclaimed.

'She's a consultant,' he hurriedly explained.

'In what ... criminology?' Fortunately Jun seemed to be in a mood to tease him.

'Chinese history,' he replied earnestly.

'What else?' Jun laughed. 'Okay, be careful. Chinese women are very alluring and tricky.' He sensed her smiling at the other end of the line. 'You should know this by now.'

'I do.'

'Hey!' She feigned indignation.

They both laughed.

'I'd better go,' he said.

'Okay, love you. Stay safe.'

Inside the room the Captain had just introduced himself to Professor Yi. 'Ma'am, I am sorry for the inconvenience and unorthodox manner of our approach. It was ...'

She cut him off. 'A bit dramatic, but I understand. I've called the few people who needed to know I would not be arriving and it's fine for a couple of days. If I can help, I certainly will.'

'That's extremely accommodating.' He extended his hand to Yi. 'Thank you for your help. Whatever you need ... these two will make sure you have it.'

'Shall I check back into the hotel?' Yi asked De Suza once the Captain had left.

'We'll do that for you under a false name. We're going to be gone for an hour or so. We'll come back to find you at about three-thirty. Anything you need, just call these numbers.' Alex wrote his and De Suza's mobile numbers on the pad in front of her.

They left Yi digging around in her luggage for her phone charger and went straight to the car park. As they got in the car, De Suza received a text from the Captain.

A go on the ICAC. Contact Wong Shek. He'll take you to the roof.

Alex pulled out fast and arrived at the security gate at some speed, startling the press and media. Before they could ready their cameras, the gate had been raised and the Mustang was on the road. The old ICAC office was only a few blocks' walk, but about ten minutes' drive through the tortuous one-way traffic system that had evolved in Hong Kong.

'Okay, I think we just go straight to the roof. No discussion or speculation with the people there.'

'I agree,' said De Suza. 'These guys are the Internal Affairs of everyone's affairs, and if they're pissed with us then they'll just get in our way.'

They looped round and parked at the top of the car park over which the three floors of the ICAC used to be located. A central lift took them into the building right above it and they found a man already waiting at the doors.

'So you guys think someone might have used this building to shoot those two priests,' the man started in.

'Wong Shek?'

'That's right. This all seems incredible to me.'

'Yes, we realize that. We just want to strike this off the list of possible locations,' Alex said politely.

'Okay, a few rules before we go anywhere. This is still a live site with lots of files and evidence stored here. No looking unless I say so.'

Alex and De Suza exchanged their police identity cards for ICAC passes and were required to hand over their mobile phones and firearms. Wong took them to a door that led into a wide corridor marked only by rows of numbered but otherwise featureless doors on both sides. Each had a further security lock of its own. The corridor extended for thirty metres then turned sharp right.

'Keep going to the end.' Wong pushed them along.

'You guys basically just left and locked the door?' Alex asked pointedly.

'No, this location is still visited by maintenance and for various meetings,' Wong Shek corrected him.

They took the right and continued. Every ten metres there was another black door with a number and a security key pad. Halfway along the corridor were the elevators. They waited. No one else appeared. The building around them could have been empty, though there was no way of knowing. They went straight to the top floor. Here there was a similar layout, but with a few doors left open, through which they caught glimpses of some serious hardware and technology, all of which still seemed live and operational.

At the end of the corridor was a small coffee bar, and on the left a metal door with the word 'Utilities' on it. Wong stopped in front of it. He opened his iPad and looked at them. 'I have a list here detailing the recent use of this door.' He scrolled down it. 'The last person used it two days ago. One of our technicians, Chen Jiang Meng, went in there during the morning.'

'Then where did he go?'

'Let me check.' He scrolled through some other lists. 'It appears he went on holiday after lunch.'

'That's very convenient,' De Suza commented.

'Let's get the door open,' Alex said calmly.

'We're just waiting for the key.'

'Why would he go in there?' De Suza queried.

'He's a mid-level tech solutions guy, so might have gone in to look at the core, which still provides a service.'

'So this leads to the roof?'

'There's a ladder that leads into a small enclosed space on the roof, then out on to the roof area.'

'Windows to the enclosed space?'

'Slats.'

'So inside is hidden from anyone?'

'Yes.'

'Just like it is on Google maps?'

'What?'

'Go check it out. Okay, we'll go up there and see if there are any signs of someone using it as a location.'

They heard someone coming up behind them and turned to see a man in white overalls and black work boots approaching. He pulled out a key card, walked past the three men and swiped it down the lock.

'Thanks very much,' De Suza called out, and the man took a step back to pull the heavy metal door open. He stepped inside first, the others crowding in behind.

'Whoah! What the hell?' the new arrival shouted.

'Shit,' De Suza called out. They stared down at the body of a middle-aged man with his shoulders and head slumped awkwardly between two thick cable ducts running up the grey concrete wall opposite. The space was barely three metres square, mostly cabling and routers attached to the wall and a ladder leading upwards. He was lean and had a closely shaven head. His eyes bulged as he stared sightlessly across the bare floor. His tongue was enlarged and he had bitten through the tip; blood had collected and clotted round his lower lip like clownish lipstick. He was wearing white overalls and on the floor was a white paper hairnet. In the corner rested a long white 88 sniper's rifle.

Wong was on his phone straight away and then off again in seconds. He turned to the two visitors. 'Gentlemen, I need you out of this room.' He raised his hands in front of them to shepherd them out of the small grey concrete cube. They stood their ground.

'Wait a second,' De Suza, who was much bigger than Wong, remonstrated politely. 'We need to gain access to this scene now.'

'Yes,' Wong responded, pushing up against him, 'in time. But for the moment we've certain protocols.'

'You mentioned you run services from here. What are you doing?' De Suza interjected.

'They are nothing to do with your case.'

'I think we'll determine that. This man is connected to an ongoing investigation,' De Suza started. 'We need and should have access.'

While his partner stalled Alex took the opportunity to observe as much of the scene as possible.

Type 88 rifle.

'And we want to work in the spirit of cooperation but . . .'

Small red paper envelope held between the index finger and thumb of his right hand.

'. . . we need to establish what he was doing and whether we have been compromised.'

'Sir, we know what he was doing. He was on the roof shooting people.'

No jewellery. Eyes narrow-set. Scar above the left. Thin, gaunt face with long sharp chin. Muscular hands, strong shoulders with solid forearms. Maybe one metre seventy tall.

'We don't know that for sure.'

Long rectangular object in his right-hand pocket. Maybe an anemometer?

'Well, he wasn't checking the WiFi router.'

Looking up . . . ladder to the roof, small metal hatch at the top with security lock.

Alex grabbed De Suza's arm to lead him out.

'Let's go.

'Sir,' he addressed Wong, 'will you call us? When we can come and collect the body.'

'We'll call you,' Wong shouted after them.

In the corridor, they could see several men in dark suits running towards them.

They were marched down the corridor to the elevator and then out to the lift lobby again, where they took back their mobile phones and firearms and were led to the exit elevator. The doors opened to the car park and they hurried towards the Mustang.

'What did you get?' De Suza asked.

'I think the first thing was that he was one of theirs. Second, he was well prepared. Third, he committed suicide, and finally he had a tag of red paper in his hand.'

'Any idea what that means?'

'Not at the moment, Alex lied guiltily.'

Alex's phone beeped, indicating that he had a voicemail. He listened. It was the Captain. 'Soong, get back here. Ying has brought Lo in but he isn't saying anything useful and it seems he doesn't know anything. I want you to speak to him.'

At the station they took the lift down to basement level 3, to the holding area and interview rooms for dangerous suspects. The doors opened on to a caged area, with a security check before they could enter a bright white-painted corridor off which lay several simple white windowless interview rooms, each with a screwed-down table, chairs, and a retaining bolt in the floor for the interviewee's chains and cuffs. Each interview room had a viewing room next to it with a command desk filled with monitors, camera-control units and audio equipment. They found the Captain and a technician watching Ying interview Lo and went quietly to sit behind him. He took his headphones off and spoke without turning away from the monitor in front of him.

'What the hell happened?'

'Can we speak freely?'

'Simon here can't hear a thing with headphones on,' indicating the studious technician, who paid them no attention.

'We got up there and found a man, who appeared to be the sniper, dead in the utility well leading to the roof. It looked like he had killed himself and had been there at least twenty-four hours.'

'Name?'

'Chen Jiang Meng, mid-level tech specialist as far as they know.

They're looking into it now and most probably driving themselves crazy. He must also have had sniper training from somebody. From the looks of it he made the shots and then killed himself straight away.'

De Suza entered the conversation. 'He had a little red envelope or piece of paper clutched in his hand. The gun was leaning up against a corner of the room.'

'Red envelope? Like a packet for New Year?'

'No,' Alex replied, 'something smaller. It had characters on it that I couldn't make out. De Suza, did you see them?'

'No, I was keeping Wong busy.'

'They shut us out after that and said they would contact us as soon as they were ready.'

'But he was one of theirs?'

'Yes, sir,' De Suza told him.

The Captain looked thoughtful and the two detectives sat back.

'How's Ying doing?' The Captain nudged Simon, the large young man with cropped hair and light issue jumper who was sitting beside him. He looked up and took his headphones off.

'Sir?'

'Put it on the speakers.' The kid channelled the feed through the speakers.

Through the glass they watched Lo, a tanned sixty-seven-year-old, his face liberally sprinkled with large moles and small dark patches of pigment and topped by thinning grey hair neatly combed back. These signs of age belied the sharpness of his mind. He brushed the top of his hand underneath his chin and turned his head to look at Ying, who was standing behind him leaning against the wall.

'Inspector, you're repeating yourself. I'll have this conversation with you, without a lawyer present, because I like to help the police with their enquiries. But a gang war between snakeheads? Sir, I don't even know what a snakehead is.'

'We know you know. Everyone knows you know. There are kids in the street who know you know.'

'Kids! I would never harm kids.' Lo started to get up. 'Now I think you need to show me out. And ask my driver to come and pick me up.'

The Captain spoke into the microphone on the desk. 'Ying, you've been in there an hour or so. I think you should come out and let Soong try or you're going to lose him.'

Simon turned round to Alex and offered him an earpiece. He took it and walked out. Ying stared into the camera to express his annoyance at being pulled from the interview, and walked past Lo towards the door.

'What . . . you're leaving?' Lo laughed. 'That's all you have?' He stood up and held his hands palms up by his sides, in fake offence and disbelief. 'Don't leave, Inspector Ying,' he implored sarcastically, then sat down again as the inspector closed the door behind him.

Outside Alex gave his fellow officer a nod. Ying flicked a new toothpick from side to side with his tongue and stared at Alex as he walked by.

'Afternoon, Mr Lo,' he said, entering the room. 'I'm Senior Inspector Soong.'

'Sure.' Lo smiled at him dismissively. 'You can all come to speak to me if you want. Happy to see you if you're next on my appointment calendar.'

Alex pulled out the seat opposite Lo and tucked himself in close, resting his elbows on the tabletop. He brought his face nearer to Lo, who instinctively leaned back a little.

'You know that there have been a number of murders recently.'

'Do I? Not me, sir,' Lo replied calmly.

'Just now, with Inspector Ying, you said you wouldn't harm kids. But we know you've used them in the past.'

'You don't know anything.'

'We have a container with several dead, all in their twenties. Not many people have such ready access to containers and transport as you?'

'I wouldn't know. I'm in the rubber seal, car parts and transportation businesses.'

'Yesterday morning I shot Chow in the head. He'd run books for all sorts of people ... laundering money, illegal transfers. I was looking at those books. I think I saw your name.'

'My name? No,' said Lo, a little too hastily. 'There are a lot of Los in Hong Kong. Whole telephone directories crammed with them.'

'I think I know your name when I see it. But if it's not your name then whose is it? Should we start interviewing some of your people? Maybe they can tell us which Lo it is. Maybe they can help us with all the names in the telephone directory you mentioned. As you said, there are plenty to get through. You wouldn't mind if we rounded up some of your guys to help us, would you?'

'Officer, if you've got nothing formal to charge me with then I think I should be going. I like to see my granddaughter in the evenings and it's getting late.' Lo was nervous now.

'You have a nice family,' Alex persisted. 'Ever buy them presents? It wouldn't be good to buy them presents with money from someone like Uncle Chow. It would be almost like receiving stolen goods. You know how the law works, it's very complicated these days.'

'Are you threatening my family?'

'Not me,' Alex responded innocently. 'But we have to follow

every lead, and there are a lot of names in those books. They all received laundered money or goods bought with laundered money.'

Lo hesitated.

'What is it you want to know?'

'How did a container with dead bodies and lots of dead birds in it end up in a vacant warehouse north-east of Po Kong Village?'

Lo looked down at the table and saw the lights above reflected in the shiny hard surface.

'I deliver containers. What happens after a container is delivered is up to the owner. It's got nothing to do with me what's in them, or what happens once they're off a truck.'

'Don't be so naïve. We've already got people dusting for prints.'

Lo just grinned and stared down at the table, moving his elbows from resting on to down by his sides. 'You won't find mine there, or the prints of anyone who works for me.'

'Okay.' Alex looked at the window. 'We'll do it your way. We'll start by questioning all your people and all your family until we're sure none of them are mentioned in those books. And then we'll look at all your friends and business associates. Chow's books have a lot of names. We also have his accountant, who is fine and I'm sure will help us. We'll connect it with your family. All the way down the line until I get to your unborn great-granddaughter.'

Lo smacked his lips and sat back. He closed his eyes for a short while.

'Fuck you. Leave them alone. He wanted a container and three young people: two men and a woman, but all Christians.' Lo shook his head defiantly.

'What about the *gweilo*?'

'What *gweilo*?' Lo looked confused.

'The German!' Alex shouted at the old man.

Lo paused, looked briefly across at the glass, and returned to

Alex. 'Three Chinese. That was all he asked for.' He looked anxious but then smiled and composed himself.

'Who did?' Alex barked at him. 'What's the point to all this?'

Lo stood up from his seat and Alex met the hard black of his pupils.

'The German was from Münster?'

'Yes, why?'

'So the plan has moved on. Look, my role is done, I simply moved the container and found three people. You'll understand soon and then it'll all make sense. He's already spoken to you twice, hasn't he?' Lo looked at him knowingly. 'I was just transport, it's all I've ever been. To be clear, my family had nothing to do with this, but I helped him for them. China's situation must now be made to work to our advantage. And besides, as you say, you have Chow's files.' He smiled, resigned to his fate.

Confused, Alex glanced back into the two-way window. Lo had sat down again, pushing his chair away from the table. He brought his right hand up to his mouth. Between his fingers he held a small red packet, which he bit into and started chewing fast. Simon shouted into his earpiece and Alex turned to see Lo, still chewing, with a smile of triumph on his face. Alex leaped across the table at him, only for the older man to push his chair backwards and out of reach. The chair tipped over suddenly and Lo landed hard on his back. When Alex reached him Lo was already convulsing, his breathing arrested. The others rushed in from next door and stood over Alex, watching the old man shake and spasm then fall still.

Alex looked at the Captain. 'That was the same kind of red packet we saw with the shooter this afternoon. We need to get the pathologist to extract what's left of it.'

The Captain ignored this. 'Everybody get out except for myself and Soong. Ying, go and get the pathologist and Forensics. De Suza, next door.' The Captain turned to the desk and pulled the remaining chair out. 'Soong, sit.'

'What?'

Ying left and De Suza made for the door. Ying exited but De Suza remained in the room. The Captain looked at him.

'De Suza, you trying to tell me something?'

'Just that Alex has been messing us around with this for the last twenty-four hours, and as his partner and friend I want to hear it.'

'Fair enough,' the Captain agreed.

Alex sat down hard in the chair. He spread out his fingers and placed his palms face down on the tabletop. The Captain paced across the room, leaving Lo's body, the upturned chair and table between them.

'What the fuck is going on, Soong? Some of that was directed at you. On a very personal level.'

The Captain stopped pacing and looked down at the snakehead's twisted body. In death it looked feeble and wasted, the expensive tailoring and cloth of his suit no longer concealing his bony limbs. The Captain raised his head to stare at Alex.

'We couldn't hear that conversation in the warehouse properly. Something was happening there but I gave you the benefit of the doubt. And now here we are. Lo, a snakehead, a trafficker, just spoke to you directly. What is it that you are involved in? I want full disclosure here and now.'

Alex felt inside his pocket and pulled out the red envelope in the plastic evidence bag. He placed it on the table. De Suza watched silently.

'You have one too?' the Captain said.

'No, this isn't the same. I received it last night. It was pinned to my door.'

'Did you speak about this to anyone?'

'No.'

'Not even your partner?'

De Suza grunted. Alex saw his friend's face turn taut with anger and disappointment. The big man stared at Alex reproachfully.

'I'm sorry,' Alex said to him.

'Never mind that. Explain to me exactly how you found this,' the Captain barked.

'It was pinned to my front door when I got home last night. Then, as I picked it off, I thought I heard a voice coming from the floors above. I looked up and thought I saw movement. I raced up there but found nothing, nothing at all.'

'What did the voice say?'

'I couldn't tell. I really think I must have imagined it, because when I got to the roof there was no one. It was completely empty. But here is the envelope.'

'What's in it?'

'Just some writing. And a small red lantern.'

'What?'

'There's nothing here that means anything to me. It's strange. I Googled it, but nothing.'

'This is why you've been pushing for the Professor to help, isn't it?'

'Yes.'

De Suza broke in. 'Why didn't you tell me about it?'

'After the warehouse, this was too confusing.' Alex looked at his friend, pleading for his understanding. 'Someone seems to know things about my life that even I don't know. They seem to think I'm part of something when I'm not. I feel completely blind and under someone else's control.' He looked at his fingers, splayed out flat against the table. He studied the backs of his hands, followed the little cuts and scars left on his skin by bruising encounters with wrongdoers in the days when life had been simple. 'I've never felt so out of control,' he admitted. 'Never. My life has always been my own, but now I can sense how powerful these people are. They are so organized and well prepared.'

The other two watched him closely.

'You sound as if you're in awe of them,' De Suza said.

'No,' he replied sharply. 'But look what they have done. We think of the finance geeks in white-collar crime as sophisticated compared with scum like Lo, but to carry out what we have seen requires highly detailed advance planning. A man in ICAC to recruit ... a snakehead charged with obtaining the victims ... who else is implicated?'

De Suza came over and rested his hand on Alex's shoulder. 'The Forensics team is waiting outside.'

The Captain directed him to open the door. 'Come in. It's all yours,' he called. 'Whatever you do, we want whatever is left of the red packet in his mouth.'

Pike looked at him, bemused.

'Okay, sure. But how did you guys manage to let him kill himself in here?'

'He was only here for an informal interview. He pulled this thing from out of nowhere and there it is,' De Suza replied bluntly. 'It was impossible to stop him. It's all caught on tape and audio.'

'Was that part of his plan?' Pike asked.

'We have no idea what his plan was or is,' the Captain said as he walked past Pike and his team. 'Just get us that red packet and whatever else you can find. De Suza and Soong, take that red envelope to the Forensics lab and then let your Professor see it. Clearly it's some sort of superstitious relic.'

The three of them left the interview room and the Captain

went to rejoin Simon in the observation room next door. Alex and De Suza negotiated the security cage and waited for the elevator.

'I'm sorry,' Alex said, concentrating on the shiny surface of the doors, which reflected the two men, standing side by side but not together.

'You lied. In this business, partners share everything. Hiding things from me like that is unacceptable,' De Suza told him, his voice trembling with anger.

'I felt like someone was messing with my head. I didn't want to talk about it.'

De Suza said nothing. At the second floor, they went straight to the interview room where they had left Yi, only to be told that she had gone to the canteen with Detective Ying. Alex kicked out at a chair in frustration.

De Suza grabbed him by the collar, pushed the door shut with his foot and held him against the wall. 'What the hell is wrong with you?'

'Fuck, I don't know! Guess. It's twenty-six hours since the ministers were shot and we've still got more questions than answers. More bodies as well. And in all this, Ying is trying to screw me!'

'Screw you? Are you blind? Ying is doing what Ying always does . . . looking out for himself.'

De Suza had Alex off his toes by now. 'I'm going to let you down before you try to get out of this hold, but get your head in the right place, okay?'

He let go of Alex, who shook himself then righted the chair. De Suza picked up the phone and called Officer Ding. 'Can you go upstairs to the canteen and fetch Professor Yi? She's the lady with Inspector Ying. Bring her down to Interview Room Three. Thanks.'

Alex sat down and pulled out the plastic bag containing the red envelope.

'I'll show her this quickly then Forensics can come and collect it,' he said.

De Suza's nostrils flared. That wasn't the order in which they'd been told to do things.

The two men sat in silence during the five minutes it took Ding to appear with Yi. He politely opened the door for her, and she came into the room smiling.

'What's happened?' she said, when she noticed their expressions. 'Should I come back later?'

De Suza went and sat at the end of the table. 'No, no, we're good.'

'Yes, we are,' Alex agreed.

'Did you have some food?' De Suza continued.

'Yes. Inspector Ying came to introduce himself then took me upstairs for some congee. He talked a lot about you two. You're quite the team. He seemed to admire you guys . . . I think.'

She smiled airily at them both and Alex managed to pin a smile on his face in return, but it was not convincing, and watching him struggle made Yi uneasy.

'Shall I sit down?' she said.

'Yes, please. And then can you tell us what you make of this?' Alex slid the plastic bag in front of her. 'Inside there's some old writing that says something like "When they are wiped out, rain will fall and visitations will disappear,"' he explained. 'Sorry, but you can't touch it until Forensics have had a look.'

'That's very interesting. I want to see those characters as soon as possible,' she said excitedly.

'I found it pinned to my front door late last night.'

'So this is your full Chinese name?' she commented, reading the calligraphy on the front of the envelope. 'Your name is very strong . . . a common Shandong name, in fact. But the phrase you just mentioned. Can you repeat it again?'

'"When they are wiped out, rain will fall and visitations will disappear,"' he said, with no sense of its meaning.

Yi spoke like an excited pupil finally allowed to give the right answer. 'This was a chant, a prayer and a saying of the Righteous Harmony Society, otherwise known as the Yihetuan Movement.'

'Who?' De Suza shot back at her.

'They were the peasant men and women who became known as the Boxers, as in the Boxer Rebellion of Nineteen Hundred. I spoke about this to Alex on our way back from the airport.'

De Suza looked across at him. 'Nice of you to share that too.'

Yi looked at them both.

'Please continue,' De Suza said politely.

'As I said, the Boxers would chant this because they believed that the foreigners had caused the great drought that afflicted the northern part of China during Nineteen Hundred and Nineteen Hundred and One. They were simple people who practised ancestor worship. They prayed to their ancestors and to the local gods for rain. Casting around for the cause of the drought, they saw the foreigners and their god as being responsible.'

She gently ran her finger across the plastic bag covering the surface of the envelope. 'In a way, this thing is living history.'

She looked down at it with a gleam in her eyes. 'The uprising was not very organized, more opportunistic. People retaliated where they could against foreign interference, which they believed threatened their continued existence. They came out of the fields to murder Chinese Christians at first, then to burn churches and to murder foreigners. Ultimately, when the rains came again, they disappeared back into the countryside as quickly as they'd appeared. They believed they had won and their fight was over.'

She breathed in a little harder. 'But before then they were used by the Imperial Qing armed forces in attacks on the foreign powers, all the participants in the Great Game in fact . . . the Russians, Japanese, Americans, British, French and the newly established German empire. A familiar list . . . they'll all be here again tomorrow for the debt conference.'

She bit her lip in thought.

'The Boxers were brave but proved to be unreliable soldiers. In fact, not proper soldiers at all. They did not show any signs of being interested in politics or in alignment to the Qing Imperial throne; they were not primarily driven by such motivations. Those who witnessed events generally recorded the same thing: that when the rains eventually came the Boxers pretty much vanished back into the grassy plains and deep Shandong soil, to resume their farming.'

'But what about the envelopes?' Alex asked.

'The Boxers believed strongly in magic and superstition, conducting slow complex rituals before an offensive, which left them very open to attack themselves. They armed themselves with a red sash, plus spells and incantations, and believed, though it was proved otherwise on many occasions, that they were impervious to bullets. They mutilated their victims, cutting off hands, feet and ears, and gouging out eyes. They were devout in their superstition, completely unshakable in the face of pain or death. And in case that way of thinking seems far removed from life today, remember that you guys here have a little altar in your reception area, a nod to the old gods . . . that triads also worship. Many believe the Boxers were simply the foot soldiers for organized gangs formed centuries ago, such as the White Lotus Gang. Their superstition and ritual passed down, embellished and coloured by time. Ritual is still fundamental to the Asian way of life, from the red envelopes at Chinese New Year to initiation ceremonies for the Triads.'

'Professor, maybe you've been buried in your books for too long,' De Suza commented. 'To people in Asia it's not ritual, it's just life.'

'Well, that's true.' She picked up the plastic bag. 'I would very much like to see inside the envelope, study the writing . . .'

'Sorry, you'll have to wait, as I said,' Alex told her. 'Oh, as well as the writing, there is also a small red paper lantern. At least, I think that's what it is.'

'Really?' Yi grew excited again. 'Then this whole thing is a kind of Boxer artefact revisited. Remember, the actual Boxers were peasants who generally could not write. So this thing' – she picked it up – 'has been made up by someone who has blended two parts of Boxer lore to create something new for their own purpose.'

'Two?' Alex queried.

'It's quite simple. The Boxers would leave red tags for people, to warn them to get out, and "red lanterns" was the term commonly applied to Boxer women, who were believed to hold immense power. Red balloons were sometimes used, though made from paper back then, as a summons to gather people together. A balloon was a recognized call to arms. This is a call for you, Alex, to join them in the fight.'

'Against whom?' he asked immediately.

'Sorry, in this case I don't know. But if the narrative continues to parallel actual events as it has done so far, then ultimately it will be against foreigners . . . against non-Chinese.'

Alex's phone rang and he answered.

'Yes, sir, that's good news,' he concluded.

'That was the Captain. Iris Lu has confirmed we can go to the storage facility and collect the hate mail that her husband received and the ICAC have released the body to us . . . it's just coming in to Pike now. I'll go to the storage place, you go look at the body with Pike – and take the envelope with you before the Professor pockets it.'

Yi slid it over to De Suza.

'What shall I do?' she asked Alex.

'Come with me – but don't touch *anything* unless it's been bagged.'

In the Mustang, Yi tucked one foot under herself and they pulled out into the media frenzy at the gate. There was a rapping on the windows with microphones and cameras. The press had broken out of their cordon.

'What can you say about local businessman and transport tycoon Lo Tak Wan?'

'Is it true he's dead?'

'His driver said that he hasn't come out of the station and was badly hurt during questioning . . .'

Alex saw eager faces crowding in. He drove straight into the road, nearly colliding with oncoming traffic. Cameras and Phones caught his surprised expression. Once free of the pack he dialled the Captain. 'Sorry, can you just flick this on to hands-free?' he asked Yi urgently, and tossed her his phone.

She put the device in the saddle and Mae's voice came through the speakers.

'Yes?' she answered coolly.

'It's Alex here. Please can you put me through to him?'

The line clicked.

'Yup?' the Captain responded.

'There were media people banging on my windows as we left,

saying they'd heard Lo was dead. I thought you should know. His driver was mentioned.'

'Okay, fine. I'll deal with it.'

He hung up. The phone rang back at once.

'Captain?' Alex replied.

'No.'

They had passed through Central and were speeding towards the entrance to the Western Tunnel. Alex froze. He knew this voice in Mandarin. Low and assured, each word spoken slowly and purposefully.

'Who is this?' He looked at Yi and pressed his fingers to his lips to indicate she should not speak.

'We're reaching out to you again, Alex Soong. There are supporters and family who want you to believe and to join.'

The voice carried an indulgent, paternal tone this time.

'Join what?' Alex snapped.

A sound reached the microphone at the other end of the line; perhaps the swallowing breath of an older man, perhaps a grunt of exasperation.

'To follow first and then to lead,' came the reply. The voice stressed the last word.

'You'll have to give me some more details. Who are you and what do you want from me?'

Silence for a beat. They raced through the artificial light of the tunnel, picking up speed as Alex waited for the reply.

'We want to you to know that you have always been right. Deep down in that blackness, you have always been right. With your father and grandfather, constantly arguing about the future, you were right to listen to your grandfather. We have all had enough of the poison they feed us. We're choking from it, blind with pain. We must reject it.' He breathed in deeply. 'You have felt it too.

Every day you feel it . . . vomiting until our guts bleed and our teeth rot.'

The car barrelled out of the tunnel exit and went fast towards the tollgate. Alex shot through the gate at twice the speed limit. A red light flashed.

'You don't know anything about my family,' he protested, hearing the slight tremor in his own voice, a fragility detectable only in his own chest and throat. But the other man's voice stayed even and strong. Unshakable.

'Yes, we do. We've been watching you for years. You know it is impossible to be of two places. One can only come from one. A person can only have one home or no home at all. Your family had honour. It's time for you to preserve it and do what you know is right.'

'Don't talk about my family!'

The voice continued, imperturbable. 'You can kick, spit and punch, but you are only fighting yourself. You have ingested so much poison that you can't live without it. Give it . . .'

Yi reached over and cut the connection. The line went dead. Silence. He whipped his head round to face her.

'Why did . . .'

She put her right palm to his cheek and pushed his face forward again.

'Look at the road!'

Alex touched the brakes slightly to avoid a car trying to overtake on the inside.

'Please, just pull over before you kill us!' she shouted at him.

He took the next slip road into a park for lorries dropping off containers at the port, and skidded to a halt. He leaned back and breathed out hard through his nostrils, pressing his palms over his eyes.

'I'm sorry,' Yi said quietly.

The car was jolted in the slipstream of a speeding lorry.

'Don't be,' he said. 'You were right to do it. Do you think we learned anything more?'

'We learned that it is definitely personal. As he said, he wants you to join him. He seems to know you very well. But what I think you need to explain to your Captain and your partner is *why* he knows so much about you.'

They drove to Yuen Long, a township at the far reaches of Hong Kong near the Chinese border, one of the places that manufacturing left behind when it moved north in the 1990s, giving its residents a foretaste of the bitterness many would experience a decade or so later after the financial crash. Alex pulled into an industrial estate and went through the heavy security checks before the compound of the storage facility. The gate opened after a minute or two and he parked in front of a heavy rusted metal door. The building had no windows, just solid brick walls.

His phone buzzed. He switched off the stereo and, turning towards Yi, put his fingers to his lips again before clicking on the phone.

'Hello?'

'Hello.' It was Jun. 'Where are you?'

'In Yuen Long.'

'Okay.' She paused briefly then launched quickly into her request. 'Will you be coming for Tash's birthday dinner and engagement celebration tonight? I'd just like to plan.'

Alex stammered briefly, suddenly uncomfortable in front of Yi. He instinctively looked up at her, and in response she indicated that perhaps she should get out of the car, but he waved away her suggestion.

'Are you okay? Is someone there with you?' Jun was asking.

'No. I mean, yes. I have a consultant with me.'

'The mystery woman?' Jun drew in her breath then announced: 'Well, nice to meet you, I'm Jun.'

'Mystery woman?'

'He'll explain,' Jun joked.

'Well, nice to meet you too,' Yi replied cheerily. 'I'm Professor Yi.'

'Ah, a professor. Well, please look after my husband. He's not too bright. He became a policeman, for a start.'

Professor Yi laughed. 'I will.'

'Alex, are you coming for dinner or not?' Jun asked him.

'I'll try.'

'Okay, do your best, please. Take care of yourself.' She was just about to break the connection.

'Hey, before you go,' he said, 'please can you switch back to caller ID when ringing me?'

'Why?'

'I've been getting some strange calls.'

'Other women? Professors?' Jun laughed playfully.

Yi laughed also.

'No. Just some nut.'

'Okay.'

His wife hung up.

'She seems a great girl,' Yi commented.

He avoided responding, taking the phone from the saddle and getting out of the car. As Yi closed her door, he leaned over the roof, feeling compelled to speak.

'She is great. Sometimes it's wonderful, and at others we just don't seem to get each other.'

They stood before the security unit in the wall and he pressed the entry button.

'Oh, I think she gets you,' murmured Yi.

They entered and were met by a large man in his late fifties, bald on top, with long hair straggling from the sides and back of his skull, sagging trousers pulled up high around a broad stomach. He guided them slowly to the crates containing Reverend Lu's belongings. Yi peered around nervously in the enormous space, which on the outer perimeter, and some way into the interior, contained metal shelving rising to a height of about eight or nine metres, stacked with various wooden and metal containers. The manager led them down several corridors between the shelves and Yi started to notice larger containers stacked at central nodes where shelves intersected. The manager stopped and referred to his clipboard, pointing to an open crate.

'This is the one Mrs Lu referred to. I hope you will find what you need.'

'Please can you wait here?' Alex asked him. 'I'd like someone to verify what I'm doing. This lady will stand with you.'

Yi and the manager stood back from the packing crates and observed Alex preparing to look through them. Once he was properly gloved, he sifted through the various boxes until he found three labelled with the word *Work*. The first contained nothing but ring binders holding accounts and the couple's personal information. It was in the second that he found a package, roughly twice the size of those in which expensive shirts are sold, wrapped in brown paper and red twine. Twisted into the twine Alex could see slips of red paper. He put the parcel back in the packing box.

'Sir, I think we're going to take this entire box,' he said. 'As it's not too big, I'm going to put it in my car.'

'Okay, but you'll have to sign for it.'

Alex completed the various forms, then carried the box out to the car and loaded it on the back seat. But before he could even turn the ignition, his phone rang. It was De Suza.

'Hey, Pike has pieced together the red paper that Lo chewed on. It's shredded but some of the characters are still legible. I suggest you get back here as soon as you can.'

'We're on our way now. I have the parcel Mrs Lu mentioned, but I brought the entire packing box it was contained in, as there could be other evidence.'

'Okay, fine.' De Suza paused for a moment. 'But it would have been better, and it would have been the correct protocol, if you had left the box there for Forensics to collect.' He sounded exasperated. 'We've had a few discussions about this and it's getting tiresome.'

'I know, but I was on the way back,' Alex said blithely, attempting to play down his mistake.

'Anyway, I'll let them know it's coming,' his partner sighed.

'I'll park in my usual spot and leave it in my car for them to fetch, it's in the back seat,' Alex replied flatly.

De Suza continued: 'Good. Also they have examined the envelope you received and there's nothing other than a high fungal spore count on the outside surface, though it's low on the inside. They identified the spores and they're from food. Not much help really. Well, at least it rules you out. Your kitchen has never seen any cooking and contains no food.'

The mood between the two men lightened a little.

'Very funny. Probably from Mrs Chan's across the landing.'

'Yeah, that's what I reckoned. Get back here as soon as you can.' De Suza hung up with a chuckle.

'You two get on very well even when you're annoyed with each other. It must be tough?'

'We have our moments, but yes, he made me welcome, and

made working here enjoyable. I've been lucky to find a good friend.'

She nodded quietly.

'What are you hoping for from the package?' Yi broke the silence.

'It's rope, so it may well have some DNA on it from the skin of the sender. That might give us a suspect, or at the very least some further information about the purpose of these killings and what made Lo decide to kill himself.'

As they approached the station, they could see the lighting of the camera crews and other media camped outside, now occupying the opposite side of the street and filling the side of the road with various vans and trailers. As the pack saw Alex's Mustang approach they turned around and photographed it entering.

In the station car park, various work units were assembling and team leaders issuing instructions for the evening's work and tomorrow's postings around the monetary talks. Alex locked the car, leaving the packing box on the back seat, and they walked to the elevator.

While they waited to travel up to the office, Alex turned to Yi. 'I just wanted to say that you made this afternoon easier for me.'

She smiled.

'My pleasure.'

He smiled back, a little uncomfortably, and they stepped into the elevator.

The months after Alice's death were most enjoyable. His colleagues sympathized and left him alone and the boy behaved himself generally, though sometimes a little force was necessary. He started to use the service lift by his office more often and stayed away from everyone else; he was called to speak to clients on occasion and certain clients would call him, but his value to the firm lay in his research and thoroughness, in the advice he gave, not in the business relationships he made.

Then one day the call finally came.

'Hello, this is Tung. We met a while ago in Jardine House at Chi Lam's office.'

He spoke confidently, seeming to know in advance the course the conversation would take.

'Yes? How can I help, Mr Tung?'

'I wanted to say that I was sorry to hear about your wife.'

In the beginning he had not known how to react to people's condolences and had simply looked awkward. So he had practised in front of the mirror at home, trying out a few phrases, and had decided one simple phrase was most convincing.

'Thank you, that is very kind.'

'You said you remembered me.'

'Yes, you picked me up from the ground on the day my father died.'

'And you remember what I said then?'

'Yes. But it didn't matter. The community there never forgave us until the day it was demolished for the public housing developments.'

Tung cleared his throat. 'Many of them were fools and knew no better.'

'Diamond Hill was a poor place filled with many uneducated people. They reacted to what they thought they saw – an attempt to prevent them exerting their will. In many ways they cannot be blamed for that. They were constantly confused and betrayed,' he replied.

'That's very fair of you. I liked what you said at that meeting six months ago, and your attention to detail on our project since then has been very impressive. Lam and Chun are sorry, as they have told you themselves.'

'Thank you. It doesn't matter.'

It had in fact been gratifying to watch them apologize.

'Maybe you can help me with something else. It isn't legal work, but your talent at research and record-keeping would be most useful. Would you like to hear more?'

'What's it about?'

'Supporting a cause. Work to restore China to its rightful place. We would be fulfilling a destiny that will wipe away the hundreds of years of humiliation we have suffered.' Tung was firm and direct in his response.

'And what would you like me to do?'

'I would like you to be our guide. Researching and identifying those who have contributed, our allies, those who may contribute in the future and those who hurt the cause and betrayed us. It extends over thousands of years, so there is much to do. There is previous work to conserve and record. And you can play a greater role in time.'

'You would like me to identify the traitors.'

'Yes, you could see it that way.'

He looked at the mirror on the back of his door and saw his own reflection.

'Are there others with us?'

'Yes, yes, there are many others. In time you'll meet them, but first there is a lot of work for you to do.'

'Yes, I'll join you.'

He felt he might have been too eager, but also that this was a question he had always been waiting to be asked.

'You don't want time to consider?'

'No, it seems a natural decision.'

'Good, we'll talk soon.'

Tung ended the call. He returned to his work.

Alex and Yi met De Suza on the second floor.

'We should go to Forensics to look at the envelope and red tags,' he said. 'The elevators are really slow today because of all the preparations for tomorrow, let's take the stairs.'

Two floors up, they sat down in a clean white room with scrubbed vinyl tiles and a central wooden workbench surrounded by more modern metal benches. In front of them was a large flat screen, and at the head of the bench nearest this a camera system. Pike came in to join them. On the screen they could see seven shreds of red paper, each in reality no bigger than a fingernail, the black ink from the calligraphy faded by Lo's saliva and chewing, though the lines of some of the strokes were still visible.

'We got what we could from Lo's mouth.' He walked to the camera system and with a pair of tweezers flipped over the paper to reveal certain Chinese characters. 'They are a bit broken, but even I can make out that the calligraphy is classical in nature and style.'

The Captain entered and sat next to Yi at the other end of the bench.

'Good evening, I recognize those. That is Qing writing. Professor Yi, what do you think?'

'Well, they aren't exactly correct. Obviously someone has taken care to write them, but there are a few radicals and strokes that have been abbreviated incorrectly because the person is used to simplified Chinese writing. What I think is most relevant is the meaning, which is the same as on the envelope addressed to Inspector Soong. Please can we see the tag from the sniper at the ICAC?'

Pike moved the camera to focus on the next item. 'Yes, here again it's the same characters, same mistakes and the same attempt at Qing script with the same phrase. "When they are wiped out, rain will fall and visitations will disappear." Once again it's the same Boxer chant. If you also include the red lanterns or balloons, which were used as a friendly warning to allies . . . Inspector Soong had one in his envelope . . . all this points to the same narrative.'

The Captain turned to Yi. 'Professor, please can you take us through the narrative, as you just called it. What were the Boxers doing? And, most importantly, what did they hope to gain?'

'Okay, gentlemen, back to your Chinese history.'

The Captain laughed. 'De Suza, Pike and I were educated locally before Nineteen Ninety-Seven, so we know more European than Chinese history. The two of us could probably list the English monarchs better than Chinese emperors, and Soong was educated in China, so his knowledge of China is what he was *told* was history. You'd better start from scratch and assume nothing.'

She sat up straight and immediately adopted the air of a lecturer; her raised tone and air of confidence held their attention at once.

'Beijing had been horribly exposed as a feeble government after the White Lotus Rebellion at the end of the eighteenth century and the Taiping Rebellion from Eighteen Fifty to Eighteen Sixty-Four. Both cost millions of lives and showed the dreadful failings of the Chinese military to the foreigners. Huge compensation was paid and land conceded, Hong Kong being the most significant, and then there was humiliation twice more against the British in the Second and Third Opium Wars.'

She broke off briefly, seeing Pike shift tiredly from foot to foot. 'Doctor, would you like to sit down? I'll come and stand at the head of the bench, and you can sit here.'

They changed places and Yi continued. 'China had little manufacturing, whereas the foreigners brought in railways, steam power and military materiel such as repeating rifles. Today much of this is edited out, diluted or aggrandized for effect, but the abiding sentiment is that Chinese people have found themselves humiliated repeatedly over the last one hundred and fifty years.'

She looked around the room.

'After five thousand years, are we proud of who we were or are we embarrassed? Perhaps the more facts we learn about this time, the more humiliated we feel.' She paused and smiled to herself. 'A Western woman called Eva Jane Price, visiting China in the late nineteenth century, wrote: "They think our eyes are different so that we have the power to see long distances and even into the earth itself." The British, wondering why the Imperial Army always shot high and wide, found that the Chinese soldiers believed that the more they raised the gun sights, the more powerful and quicker the bullets would be fired. And the Boxers believed in martial arts . . . that the magical powers of unarmed combat would make them impervious to bullets . . . and that coming into battle they should play trumpets and perform ritual acts, which would of course actually slow their progress, making them an easy target.'

She cleared her throat and caught Alex smiling at her encouragingly.

'However, looked at another way, the bravery of the Boxers was admirable, because they had nothing but still they presented a powerful threat. To paraphrase a Chinese scholar in the Nineteen Seventies, the Boxers were the pride and glory of the Chinese people. They gave the invaders, the foreigners, a taste of the people's heavy fist. During the Cultural Revolution the Red Guards were known as the New Boxers. Some of the original Boxers were found and wheeled out to reinforce this new role.'

She walked to within a few steps of the Captain, whose face remained expressionless.

'The starting point of the Boxer Rebellion is generally considered to be the kidnapping and murder of two missionaries, Reverends Norman and Robinson, on June first Nineteen Hundred, though actually, over the New Year of Eighteen Ninety-Nine, another minister had been murdered, though this attracted little attention at the time. Attacks on Christians, initially Chinese converts, started over the summer of Eighteen Ninety-Nine and became regularly reported events by the fall of that year.'

She took three steps back and said in a firm, declaratory voice:

'No rains come from Heaven
The Earth is parched and dry.
And all because the churches
Have bottled up the sky.

'This was one of the slogans used by the Boxers. It was about lack of government, the drought, their belief in the supernatural, but most of all their fear of a world that was fast changing beyond their control, with no one to explain it or to help them. Twenty days after the two ministers were tortured and killed, Baron Clemens August Freiherr von Ketteler of Münster was murdered by the rebels. That precipitated a full-scale attack on the German legation, and so the Western political powers entered into what became an international war, with the most highly developed nations of the time on one side and China on the other.'

She finished speaking and looked around the room.

Alex asked. 'You said the Baron was from Münster.'

'Yes.'

'One of the males in the container was a German from Münster. Oliver Derm. Mean anything?'

'The name means nothing. But Münster obviously fits the narrative and continues the Christian theme.'

'And you mentioned that the Christians were tortured. What was done to them?' the Captain asked immediately.

'There's no record of the acts performed on these two individuals, but the Boxers did do much violence to the bodies of their victims. As I mentioned to Alex . . . sorry, Detective Soong . . . in the car, they would stab and slash a victim many times, cut out eyes, remove ears, hands, fingers. It was done mostly to Chinese Christians.'

'Okay, get Ying up here,' the Captain instructed De Suza before turning back to Yi. 'We want to show you a photo of something that we discovered last night.' He passed Pike a USB stick. 'Pike, please can you put that up?' The Captain turned back to Yi. 'It is horrific, so please brace yourself.'

On the screen appeared the interior of the container, Lok's body in the foreground, his neck gaping, and the bodies of the four other individuals, starved and mutilated. The flash of the photographer's camera caught the pale skin, the creamy red of their eyes and the ivory of their bare teeth, the lips bitten or pecked away. Professor Yi recoiled a step from the screen.

'Professor, I believe this is far closer to history than you have ever been before,' he observed.

She said nothing but brought one hand up to her mouth. She stared at the lost expression on Lok's face; the dark glistening feathers shed by the ravens, their beaks protruding from the floor like spikes embedded in a barbaric trap.

'Yes, these are the things you would expect to see in a Boxer scenario,' she said, her confidence deserting her.

'But where does it end?' the Captain demanded.

'Historically, as I've said, it ended with war.'

In the silence that followed Yi's final words, Ying appeared.

'Inspector Ying,' the Captain greeted him, 'it would seem the two cases and Lo's suicide are connected. I'm turning the whole thing over to Inspector Soong. Please work with him.'

The newcomer narrowed his eyes and stared at Alex. 'Fine. But first I want an assurance that he's not part of it,' he said insolently.

'Soong, have you received any further calls?' the Captain demanded.

'Yes. I received another in the car today, which Professor Yi heard.'

'Soong, yet again, why didn't you mention this?' asked the Captain.

'Again?' Ying raised his voice in disbelief.

'He received an envelope at home and believed he heard someone calling to him from outside his apartment,' De Suza clarified.

'What?'

'What did the voice say?' the Captain shot back.

'It was the same as before. Asking me to join them, saying he knew me . . . nothing further.'

Alex looked at Professor Yi.

'Don't look at her!' the Captain addressed him sharply. 'On the basis that you seem to be making headway with this, you take the lead . . . but you work from here, where I can watch you. Ying or De Suza go out, you stay here. Understood?'

'Fine,' Alex answered reluctantly.

'Ying and De Suza, you tell me if there are any problems.'

The two men nodded in agreement.

'What do you want us to do, boss?' Ying asked Alex with a little sneer.

'We need to let Forensics get at that package I brought back from the storage depot. Maybe there is some trace evidence on it to help with an ID for the letter writer.'

Pike cut in. 'They're pretty backed up at the moment, so it'll probably take a couple of hours.'

'Ding and I will get the box and leave it with them,' De Suza suggested.

'Good, thank you.' Alex tossed him his car keys. 'Inspector Ying, I would be grateful if you would work on establishing whether there are any organized societies or gangs who might be interested in pursuing this kind of activity.'

'You've not included me in the previous discussion. What activities?' Ying said testily.

'Professor Yi has showed us that many elements of the recent crimes resemble the behaviour and background beliefs of the Boxers.'

'Those from Shandong who fought the foreigners a hundred years ago? You can't be serious.'

'Yes.'

The Captain stepped in. 'Professor Yi will explain the resemblances to you. We need you to find out who nowadays would feel so strongly as to want to attack foreigners and maybe even try to start a war.'

'People everywhere are poor. The country has all that useless European investment which those useless fuckers lied about. *Everyone* is angry. *Everyone* is sick of being played for a fool. Aren't you?' Ying stood in silence and stared at each of them in turn, waiting for an answer that did not come.

Eventually he sighed and gave in. 'Professor Yi, let's go back to the canteen, and please tell me what you have.' He looked at Alex. 'I'll find out what I can. There are countless angry people in China, but few who are organized enough and with the resources to do all this. But someone must have, right?'

The Captain and Alex were left alone.

'Soong, to what extent are you involved in this?' his superior barked.

'I'm not.'

The Captain breathed in, nostrils flaring, fixing him with a glare. 'I don't want to undermine you in front of your fellow officers, but someone has been in direct contact with you about this. Perhaps more often than you have told us. Perhaps not. Either way, as they have been in contact with you, then you need to take the initiative and get in contact with them. Find this person or people. This is no troubled serial killer.'

'Okay.' Alex hesitated. 'Understood.'

'A problem?'

'Well, this assumes I have any control over the conversations.'

'You don't?'

'No.'

'Well, then, you need to take control.'

'Was there anything else?' Alex enquired.

'We can't keep ignoring that fact you've been repeatedly contacted by a suspected killer. By rights you should have been suspended immediately. We must draw the line somewhere, understand? I'm giving you another twelve hours to come up with something, then Ying will take over. Meanwhile, don't leave here, for any reason, without asking me first. Clear?'

'Sir.'

The Captain left him alone. Alex sat down and stared at the grisly tableau on the screen. He felt an urge to speak to his long-dead parents and grandfather, to ask them what lay in his past that might connect him to this unknown man who was intent on recruiting him to join some cause to change the future. His grandparents and parents had always been politically engaged. They had been, for better and for worse, thinkers and doers, activists who had linked grassroots to the political elite. He was a policeman . . . a simple policeman, as Jun had said. He pulled out the USB stick and switched channels on the screen.

CNN was showing the growing media encampment outside the police station. He flicked through a few more news channels. One had an old photo of Lo, looking much younger, with the running titles suggesting he had killed the two ministers. Another channel was discussing the forthcoming meeting in Hong Kong with the defaulting G8 members, the piece finishing by showing demonstrators outside various embassies in Beijing, carrying placards bearing the images of devils spewing out foreign currency.

Alex phoned the Captain. 'See channel twelve now.' He heard the Captain change channel and the volume increase so that he could hear the reporter speaking.

'So, it's started.'

'Yeah, but it's still pretty small stuff.'

'Sir, can you get the cybercrimes team to check activity on the web and see how it's escalating?'

'Go down yourself and take a look. If they query you, tell them you have my full authority. And, Soong, keep me in the loop.'

The cybercrimes division was located on the lowest floor of the building, basement level 4, a team of geek technologists and white-collar crime specialists, sifting through thousands of terabytes of data, seeking patterns and pathways through both the public and the dark web. With rising concern about deepening social unrest, the team had added a new area of operations: the monitoring, tracking and analysis of social media networks. At its simplest level it followed groups, trends, forums and chatter – such as had grown from 4chan.org into the loose and powerful activist group Anonymous – but also the course that any significant new idea or story took to embed itself in the public consciousness. It was work that superficially merely required access to powerful computer systems, to search the web and crunch large volumes of data to show the movement and acceleration in traffic trends. But greater penetration into the denser layers of the web was required, to identify new nodes of interaction and exchange, to predict where points of incitement might arise and where strong new voices attracting eager listeners would be found. It also required access to more personal data, which rubbed up hard against data privacy laws and personal privacy rights.

The man responsible for this sensitive work wasn't even twenty-five years old, which sometimes made him inexperienced and careless, but also resilient and fearless enough not to worry about crossing any political line. Alex liked the kid's insouciant attitude, partly because it broke the monotony of the mostly conservative atmosphere of police work, but also because the kid saw the world from above rather than on the ground, the opposite of grassroots police work. He saw movements of people's thoughts and preferences like a weather satellite following storm fronts.

Alex took the elevator down to the basement level 4 and then used his security card to gain access to a room that was dimly lit by dozens of screens bracketed to the walls and locked on to desks. Sai Wong, 'Small' Wong in name only, sat in a confined space at the back, surrounded by eight plasma screens, each subdivided into various windows.

'Hey, Inspector Soong, what brings you to this level of hell?' he called out. Alex stepped up behind him and placed his hands on the big man's shoulders.

'I've come for the latest on the condition of the human race.'

'Well, you've come to the right place.'

Alex assumed a more serious tone to let Sai Wong know this was work.

'Have you been following the feed on the killings yesterday?'

'There's been little else on my screens.' He flipped round in his chair to look up into Alex's face. 'And you, my friend, are one of the stars of the show.'

Alex looked across at the micro-windows in the screens. In some, there were scrolls of text continually providing updates to forums, live newsfeed and blogs. Other windows showed trending patterns and histograms of web meta-activity such as the subjects with the largest numbers of hits and email traffic using key words. They showed movements through the web in search of various topics such as the recent Hong Kong murders.

'Have any photos of the warehouse killings surfaced?' asked Alex.

'Nothing yet. What's that all about?' Sai Wong said, feigning ignorance very poorly.

'Have you seen the pictures?'

Sai Wong coughed to clear his throat, tacitly admitting that he had.

'Great,' Alex moaned. 'Who showed you?'

'You know . . . someone.'

Alex let it go. 'It's been two days now. What do you expect by tomorrow and the day after?'

Sai Wong pointed one fat finger at the histograms and trending graphs.

'Look, it's already increasing exponentially in interest. It's cooking, man. It's in the high hundreds of thousands . . . early millions. Once it spreads deeper into the mainland, it'll be tens of millions. As you know, the most popular Chinese tweeters and bloggers have been attracting hundreds of millions of readers since Two Thousand and Nine. If one of them gets a good angle on this, then it's a global story.'

'What are the main theories about the murders being discussed online at the moment?'

'There's a lot of end-of-the-world-type stuff . . . serial killers, corrupt officials covering their tracks, new terrorist groups. Most people are stuck with speculating what it's all about. When someone takes responsibility then . . . vooom!' He rocketed his flat palm above his head and stood up, dwarfing Alex. 'But the serious money on blogs and Twitter is on the *lying* Europeans and the disrespect they've shown us. People are saying it's a conspiracy against China and this was always intended. They're calling for blood, like against Japan and their purchase of the Diaoyu Islands in Twenty Twelve . . . but this time many, many more people are involved.'

'I always forget how tall you are,' Alex murmured, momentarily distracted.

'Don't let it get to you, man,' Sai Wong shot back, and patted him on the head.

Alex laughed. 'How do you get away with this disrespectful attitude?'

'I don't. That's why I'm down here. No one likes a one hundred and ninety-three-centimetre, two hundred and thirty-pound American-Chinese technogeek. With arms like jack-hammers.' He flexed his biceps in a comedic routine then slid one arm round Alex's shoulders and turned him towards the exit. 'Don't worry, I'll let you know how it goes. But if you want to stop it from going global, I suggest solving this shit before it reaches the mainland good and proper. And best do it before tomorrow. You know what I'm saying?' The big man watched Alex head for the elevator. 'I'll let you know if anything significant happens.'

Alex raised a hand in acknowledgement as he walked on.

Out of the elevator, Alex's phone started to vibrate.

'Hey, where is that package? You said it was in the box in your car,' De Suza said aggressively.

'Easy,' Alex snapped back. 'It was, and it should still be there.'

'I've just been through the whole box with Forensics and Ding, and we've found nothing. What's going on?'

'I've no idea. It was there in the box. Then in my car. It couldn't have been out of my sight except for a minute or two when I signed the release form with the depot manager.'

'I told you to have Forensics collect it.' De Suza swung it back on him. 'Who could have taken it while you did that?'

'Only Yi really.'

'The Professor?' De Suza said incredulously. 'Seems unlikely. Are you *sure* you saw that evidence in the warehouse?'

'Yes. Of course. What do you mean by that?'

'Just that. Did you actually *see* it?' De Suza said bluntly.

'Look, I'll come down and talk to you about it. I'm just picking up the Professor from Ying now.' With that Alex hung up.

Alex continued walking down the main corridor towards the canteen. As he did so he thought through his actions at the depot. The package had definitely been there. It had been in the packing box. He had put the box down while he signed the form. After that he'd carried it to the car, where it had stayed on the back seat. There would have been a brief window of opportunity during the signing of the form, and perhaps another also while he was driving.

He turned into the canteen and from the entrance looked at Yi, sitting back in her chair with an empty bowl of congee in front of her, chopsticks laid across the right side of the bowl and spoon tucked in next to them. Ying sat opposite her, still pushing rice into his mouth. He nodded as he brought his rice bowl up to his mouth and levered the food in with the tips of the chopsticks.

She was looking straight at him, talking directly and listening intently, no phones, emails or messages to distract her. She was always so calm and self-assured, putting people at ease so quickly. He stood and watched her, his phone still held in his right hand. She turned and saw him, holding up her hand to wave. Ying glanced over and nodded, the bowl still covering his mouth and nose, and Alex walked towards them.

'Professor Yi, I'm going to take you down to Forensics. I hope we have learned something further, and if so you might be of great help.'

Ying put his bowl down. 'You sound a little hurried, Soong. Everything all right? Why don't you sit down?' He gestured at the empty chair by the table.

'I think I'll stand.'

'Okay, suit yourself.' Ying smiled and picked up his bowl, shovelled in the last mouthful and then wiped his mouth and resumed his grinning. 'Would you like anything further, Professor?' he asked, a toothpick back between his lips.

She smiled at him, very politely and sweetly. 'No, thank you. One bowl was enough for me. Thank you, Senior Inspector Ying.'

'Soong, the Captain asked me to drop the Professor at her

hotel. I assume I can leave that to you now. Call me when you need me.'

Alex nodded and Ying walked on. Alex took his seat.

'You look a bit on edge. What's the matter?' Yi brought her knees up to her chest, easily squeezing her entire frame on to the chair. She wrapped her arms round her knees and pulled them in.

Alex slouched back in his seat. 'Did you take the package from the bigger box we brought back?' he asked.

'No, I wouldn't touch a thing. Why?'

'Do you remember if I took it out when we were at the storage facility?'

'No, you didn't, you just held it up over the box then put it straight back.'

'And no one took it out after that?'

He could not help thinking how attracted to her he was. Her playful expression balanced against those penetrating eyes, wide and deep brown, made her appear flatteringly attentive rather than confrontational. He almost couldn't bring himself to look at her.

'Not that I saw,' she was saying.

'Okay, let's get to Forensics.'

'What's going on?'

'De Suza says he and Ding can't find the parcel.'

'That's impossible . . . it was in there,' she insisted.

At the laboratory they found De Suza sitting in a chair watching the Forensics officers busying themselves in their slow careful manner.

'What do you have?' Alex took control.

De Suza frowned at them both. The senior technician approached Alex, hands in the pockets of his lab coat. 'There's not much to work with,' he said, frustrated. 'Just one letter with the minister's DNA and that of an unknown female. Can we get a sample from his wife for comparison?'

Alex nodded in reply.

'So where's this parcel?'

Alex turned to De Suza.

'Where indeed?'

'We went through the entire box you brought back. Everything is laid out on the table in the next room. Are you sure you brought that package?'

Yi interjected swiftly: 'Yes, we both saw it, and it was definitely there.'

De Suza did not reply, but slowly turned to Alex. He remained in a seated position, jaw visibly clenched, pushing the corners of his mouth down. His eyes had narrowed, making the Eurasian looks seem more Chinese today.

'We? Professor, surely you weren't involved in the search?' De Suza kept looking at Alex.

'Mike, you know what she means,' he cut in.

'Yeah, I think I do,' De Suza said dryly.

Yi stood back, almost against the door of the laboratory. 'I'm sorry. I think I should go wait outside.'

It was De Suza's turn to cut in. 'No, Professor, I think it is Inspector Soong and I who need to speak outside.'

The two men departed for the corridor. Alex followed De Suza to the men's toilets. There was no lock so De Suza stood with his back against the door. Alex walked towards the basin and began to wash his hands.

'What's this about?' He looked up into the mirror at his partner, barring the doorway with his shoulders.

'Don't you ever hang up on me again!' De Suza snarled.

'What?'

'Earlier you hung up because you were so keen to see the Professor.'

'Seriously? You're angry because I cut you off?' Alex let the water run over his hands. It was cold and refreshing and he felt like bending down to splash it over his face. But if De Suza was intent on attacking him, then Alex having his eyes closed would provide a free hit. It would be better not to give the big man a free one. He let the water continue to run over his hands.

'Alex, stop jerking me around! You didn't tell me about the further contact you'd had with this guy, and now I feel I can't trust you. We both said this morning we would keep each other informed. Only you were lying at the time.'

Alex pumped some soap from the dispenser. 'I'm sorry. I did do that. I made a poor decision.'

'Come on, that's all you have to say?'

'I won't do it again.'

'It's going to take more that that. You need to concentrate on the case and nothing else. No more trading looks with pretty little professors. You're married, remember? Get it done and over with, if you must, or put it behind you . . . but clear your head.'

'Hey!' Alex shook the water off his hands and dried them on a paper towel from the machine hanging next to De Suza. 'That's not what's going on. She's been very useful to us, you know that.' He lobbed the paper towel into the bin and took a step nearer the door. 'Are we done?' he asked bluntly.

De Suza stood up straight but rested his foot firmly against the door. 'For now.' He looked down at Alex, his expression revealing little of the easy friendship it normally showed. 'Come and check the box for yourself.'

*

Alex returned to the lab a few steps behind De Suza. They passed Yi, sitting quietly on a stool watching the Forensics officers continue to work on other cases, and walked straight into the next room to look at the contents of the box, laid out on an examination table. Seeing the unyielding expression on both men's faces Yi got up warily, taking only a step towards the door to follow them before De Suza closed it in her face.

She sat back down again and one of the Forensics officers, an older lady completing a pile of paperwork at a desk to her left, turned to her and smiled.

'Best to leave them once they start looking serious, especially the young ones. You have history, we have science and the lawyers have the law, but the cops . . . they run this crazy path between wild instinct and strict procedure, two powerful but opposing forces.' She returned to her work, warning: 'Never fall for a cop.'

'Not me. I don't even live here.' Yi blushed a little.

'Those two are bright, particularly the short one, Soong . . . he's our rising star. Not that it should matter, but he's got the right family history as well. He should be in politics but for some reason he loves this job.'

She smiled. Yi smiled back.

'What's his family like?'

'Well, they're all dead now, but they were pillars of the Party, red-blooded technocrats. Grandfather was on the Long March, father just managed to keep out of trouble in the Cultural Revolution and served the country well, and mother was civil engineer on some big projects, such as the Three Gorges. Right kind of lineage for Beijing. He's young and gutsy and concentrates on fighting corruption. The other one's married with three kids, a regular Mr Normal.'

In the next room Alex bent over the examination table and,

starting at one end, methodically looked through the items set out before him. He combed through the contents of the box. A pack of postcards received from the minister's parents while they were in Austria. A small cardboard box, perhaps once for business cards but now holding loose keys. Some polythene bags of vacuum-packed clothes, four ring binders of bank statements dating from 2002 to 2006, a box of pens, stacks of leaflets dating over several years relating to how to deal with divorce, caring for elderly parents and a range of other family issues. The package he'd found earlier wasn't there.

'You'll have to trust me on this, it was there.'

'I do. But, as you know, in this job there is a line. And you are crossing it.'

'I know, and I'm dragging you with me towards it.'

'So what do we tell the Captain? You aren't supposed to leave here, remember?' De Suza needled him.

'I'll tell him what's happened, then ask permission to retrace my footsteps and look for the package.'

'What about the Professor? Did she have the chance to take it?'

'I thought we agreed she didn't?'

'No, we didn't rule it out. Not yet.'

Alex looked at the random detritus of part of a human life spread out in front of him. He replayed the whole sequence of events in the warehouse. The only time the box had not been directly in his line of vision was when he had rested it on the floor and taken two steps forward to sign the release document. In the car he'd kept the mirror angled so he could see it, he remembered, and Yi had not turned round at any time.

'All I can think is that when I stepped forward to sign the document, or when we were walking out of the warehouse, it fell out,' he said finally.

De Suza tutted and sucked on his teeth. '*Fell out*? Jesus, she's got you messed up, hasn't she? I knew it when I saw you last night.'

Alex ignored him. He remembered that he had been looking at Yi as he'd lifted the box and carried it to the car.

'I'll track back after I drop off Professor Yi at the hotel . . . with the Captain's permission.'

'Let's do that then,' De Suza said dryly.

'You stay here with Forensics.'

'Seriously, you're pulling rank on me after *you* screwed up?' De Suza was looking outraged again.

'No, of course not, but it's a waste of time us both going there.'

The two men didn't look at each other but stood with heads bowed over the table.

'Alex, this isn't good,' his friend said finally. 'The Captain asked me to report to him if there were any further conflicts of interest, and so I must tell him this. Mak from Internal Affairs will have to know too.'

Alex stood up straight and walked over to the door. De Suza called out: 'Look, take the Professor to her hotel. The Marriott at Pacific Place, under the name Bernadine Fu. I'll ring you if there's anything to report here. And make sure you get clearance to go.'

'You're ordering me now?' Alex said uneasily.

'No, just advising.'

De Suza cut ahead of him at the door, waving to Yi with a smile. Alex went to join her.

'I'm going to take you to your hotel then go and look for the package,' he said.

'It's not good that it's missing, is it?'

'Not good at all. It's no longer there, and there's no evidence it ever was.'

'It *was* there though. We both saw it.'

'I know.'

Yi watched Alex fidget silently in the lift, his index finger tapping out an unheard rhythm.

In front of him was a dark red leather-covered door, with a bolt across the top and bottom and a small red light set into the frame by the handle. There was a keyhole into which he placed a large four-sided cruciform key. He turned it twice and opened the door. Three naked bulbs hung over a surgeon's operating table fixed to the floor in the centre. The room was clean with a dark yellow vinyl-tiled floor and white walls. The bed had a pillow and a turned-down blanket on it.

He sat on the bed and placed his hands palm-down on the blanket. It felt a little damp and he took the remote control from the table next to the bed and switched on the air conditioning. He took his shoes off, distracted briefly by the scuff mark on the heel of the left one, and lay down on the table. He stared up at the bright yellow ceiling and extended his right arm, letting it fall on to an extended platform attached to the operating table, with straps to hold the arm in place. Sitting up, he replaced his shoes and opened the drawer under the table. Inside were plastic hand ties, a bottle of ketamine and loaded syringes. He took out two syringes and four plastic ties.

'You're here.'

He turned round to see the two he had summoned.

He stood up from the bed and walked towards them.

'You still intend to go through with this?'

'We must. Don't you understand? All circles must complete.' He sucked on his teeth. 'Or perhaps you're too soft, like your mother. It may be beyond your limited understanding at present.'

'Yes. Perhaps it always has been.'

The older man ignored him, as perhaps he always had done. He held out the two syringes, one to each of them.

The second man, young and skinny, took the syringe readily.

'I'd like to come and help later?' he offered.

'Just bring me the two women for now.' He looked at the first, taller and broader, man while he spoke. 'You get the Professor and he'll get the wife.'

'Leave the wife, she's done nothing. In fact, how does any of this help?'

'Just do as I say,' came the implacable voice.

He pushed his way between the men and through the doorway. They followed him outside and he closed the door.

Four of eight.

Five of eight.

A second leather-covered door stood in front of him. He unlocked it with the same key and pulled back the bolts. The others stayed outside while he entered. Inside the room stood a single heavy wooden chair. It was of simple construction, solid and immovable. The rest of the room consisted of blank white walls with the same dark yellow vinyl tiles and bright ceiling lights. He walked to the chair and round behind it. Inserted into the uprights were leather straps and buckles. He sat down and, with his right hand, awkwardly pulled one of the straps round his left arm. He tied it in place and then wrestled with the strapping, which easily withstood his considerable strength. Removing his arm from it, he stood up and switched off the light before closing the door.

'The Professor will be placed in the chair.'

The first man looked at him closely, eyes steady, but watching him carefully, waiting for his hand to be raised, a sudden smack across the face, a cut lip or cheek. He had felt the force of that right hand as long as he could remember. He flinched and stepped back.

The other standing next to him was content to observe his surroundings, sneaking the occasional look into the vast maze of corridors and shelving behind, with its meticulous records and sacred histories.

The older man looked up.

'There must be blood for the ritual. Something must be given, sacrificed to our ancestors. It is not just for me. You do understand?'

The thin one nodded respectfully and the other simply remained still.

'By the way, where is the message I sent to Minister Lu?' asked the older man.

'I have it,' the thin one turned back to reply.

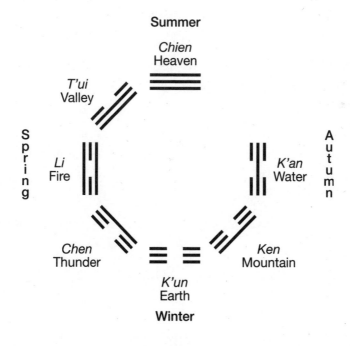

COMPLETION

Many of the roads around the Central District had been closed down in readiness for the following day's G8 meeting. Police officers were busily erecting Diversion signs and forcing four lanes of traffic to wait to be filtered into one. Alex sighed and drummed his fingers against the steering wheel.

'We're stuck here for a while, so is there anything else you can tell me about the Boxers?' he asked Yi, sitting beside him in the Mustang.

She betrayed no annoyance at the delay but pursed her lips in thought. Her easy self-possession and uncomplicated nature were some of her most appealing features, he decided.

'It's generally agreed that the Boxers were formed from various superstitious peasant sects, which believed and relied on heavy ritualism. An edict in Sixteen Seventy-Three mentioned nine different sects, which combined beliefs taken from Buddhism, Taoism and local rural superstition. Symmetry was an important element of the Boxers' ritual and belief system. The eight Taoist trigrams surrounding the yinyang, for instance, were considered pretty powerful magic by them. One of the posters that the Boxers created . . .'

'Posters?' Alex interrupted. 'They were quite advanced in their approach then? They understood the power of propaganda?'

'Yes. And they often used chain letters, exactly like those you see on email today, to swell their ranks. One, for example, read: *If you don't pass on this message from Buddha, you will not be able to escape an unnatural death. If, on the other hand, you copy this once and give it to another man, your family will be safe. If you copy it ten times and hand the copies to others, then your whole village will be safe.*'

It started to rain, and Alex watched the police officers disembarking from the fifteen or so vans ahead start to put on their jackets.

'Incredible,' he said.

'They would instruct people to wear the red cloth on their heads – foreign observers referred to these as red turbans – and to worship the Herd Boy and Weaver Girl, star gods, on the seventh day of the seventh month. They believed that on that night, no one should sleep or cook, or else the gods would refuse to intervene and save their lives in combat. Then, for a period of two weeks from the first day of the eighth month, everyone must abstain from eating meat and drinking wine.'

'That seems very harsh.' Alex continued to look ahead but smiled and joked: 'No meat for fifteen days? Not so good for northern Chinese.'

'Remember, many people then hardly ate meat, maybe a few times a year if they were lucky, so this wasn't too difficult for them. Abstaining from wine was probably harder. And . . .' Yi resumed, '. . . they should worship the gods three times a day. The Boxers believed this would prevent them from being harmed by gunfire.

'This belief dates back to the first century BCE. The Way of Hsien, or in English *immortality*, had one goal: achieving everlasting life. Adherents strove to be physically deathless and ageless by taking herbal concoctions, using breathing techniques, and practising virtue, which included Confucian filial piety and benevolence, or *jen*. It was understood that one bad action could wipe out the power gained from a thousand good actions. A Boxer believed that through a ritual called *lien-ch'uan* or boxing, hence the name, they could become temporarily possessed with the spirit of Hsien, and so become invulnerable.

'They were seeking immortality and invulnerability. It was not necessarily about fighting, though that came with the skills afforded by possession. A few days before the ritual, a recruit would be taught a manifestation spell, and on the appointed day he would go to a specific plot of ground to recite it. He would recite this three times and then his breathing would become short and difficult and he would start frothing at the mouth. Of course, such trance-like states are very common in many rituals. At the first sign of the frothing a witness would shout "God descends", and the recruit would then be deemed to possess the skills of a Boxer, fighting techniques but primarily invulnerability.'

A police officer rapped at Alex's window and they both jumped a little. Water dripped from the officer's jacket hood on to the window.

'You're going to be here for another fifteen minutes,' he announced.

Alex held up his badge against the window. 'That's fine,' he shouted back. The officer nodded respectfully to him then passed down the line of traffic to speak to the next driver.

'As I said,' Yi continued, 'the Boxers believed their actions could cause the weather to change and the crops to be fruitful, and to accomplish that they drew on traditional magic and related beliefs systems. The ancient Zhou classic the I Ching, for instance, is considered to be a collection of omen texts, derived from the ideas of the venerable Duke of Zhou, father of us all three thousand years ago, and collected and preserved by peasants. The eight trigrams are set round a central ninth, the centre of the compass. Here, you see . . .' She drew a rough diagram to remind Alex on the back of a flyer she took from her bag.

'This is the Boxer sect in diagram form. Each of the nine trigrams corresponded to one of the nine kungs or mansions, the name given to a group or clan of Boxers. Calling upon this ancient ritualism and magic to help them avenge and alleviate their suffering from the drought, they unknowingly created a singular cause with great political significance.

'*We support the Qing regime and aim to wipe out the foreigners; let us do our utmost to defend our country and safeguard the interests of our peasants. Protect our country, drive out foreigners and kill Christians,*' she finished.

'Yes, the message is pretty clear and simple,' Alex said quietly. He frowned as he thought about what she'd said. 'Earlier you mentioned that the rebellion proper started in Nineteen Hundred with the deaths of two preachers. At what stage did it escalate?' he asked, switching on the windscreen wipers to watch for the signal to proceed from the uniformed officers on the road.

'It was the death of the German diplomat Baron von Ketteler and his aide, followed by that of the Japanese consul, that caused international hostilities to break out. Officially the Germans took the lead. It was at that point that Kaiser Wilhelm II told his soldiers to "behave like the Huns and *take no prisoners*", which was how they gained their nickname. They and several other foreign powers with interests in China formed an alliance against China: Britain, the US, Japan, France, Russia and Italy.'

'All the players who are gathered here again tomorrow, but this time China has the upper hand,' he observed thoughtfully.

'You know the eventual outcome, but the war wasn't won easily by the foreigners, as they had presumed it would be. But one victory was complete. The Allied forces divided up Beijing and exacted a very heavy compensation. China paid between six and seven hundred million US dollars in silver and other precious commodities. The so-called Boxer Protocol was signed in September Nineteen Hundred and One, putting China at the mercy of the allied powers. For the Boxers, the rains finally came in early autumn that year, and the Boxers, thinking their actions had defeated the foreign religion, simply reverted to their peasant livelihoods and drifted back into the plains and mountains of Shandong. From a geopolitical perspective all this was further humiliation for the Chinese, but from the peasants' it was simply that the drought ended and they had won.'

'Had the peasants just been used?'

'The element of history that remains unknown to us is that of the original sect, the first Boxers from whom the peasant uprising derived its name. It is assumed by some scholars that the sect still manifests itself in the triads we have now.'

'Ying's pals,' Alex observed wryly.

'There is virtually no documentary evidence of ancient Boxer strategy, but if you consider the rituals and activities we've discussed, and the surviving chants and propaganda, then the original sect was clearly a highly organized movement. It seems as though a nucleus of hardline believers sowed the seeds, the very idea of rebellion, in the minds of hundreds of thousands of peasants at the end of the nineteenth century, and then just unleashed them.'

The police officer started waving at Alex and he put the car in gear and pulled out into Gloucester Road.

He drove past Admiralty, the site of the old naval dockyard immediately adjacent to Central, and its multiple bus lanes, and then made a left to curl up the flyover to the Marriott hotel. He parked a little before the busy entrance and quickly got out to speak to the valet and explain what he was doing, then returned to help Yi gather her belongings. They went to reception together to get the key.

At the lift, she stopped him. 'Look, you need to find that package. I can manage from here.'

Alex looked around. The hotel was very busy, with journalists of all nationalities gathering to cover tomorrow's meeting and the usual groups of mainland tourists loitering in the reception area. They were just two people among hundreds passing through the hotel lobby.

'Call me if you need anything. I'll check in with you later.'

'Will do.'

'I should take you up to your room,' he insisted. He touched her arm to turn her towards the lift doors, which had just opened. Yi walked in, pulling her mobile travel bag behind her. Standing close together they watched the doors close. Their twin images appeared in the reflection from the polished steel.

'There's really no need to accompany me to my room,' she protested. 'I am Bernadine Fu while I'm here, and no one is looking for Ms Fu.'

He stood half-turned towards her, closely observing the swoop of her hair across her forehead and down to one ear. She watched him look and saw his hand twitch slightly, as if about to reach out to hers, resting on the handle of her bag.

He looked away from her to his own reflection and stepped back against the wall of the elevator. They arrived at her floor and Alex held the lift open.

'Let me just walk you to your room.'

She said nothing in reply but took hold of the handle of her suitcase and pulled it out of the lift, turning left down the corridor. He followed three steps behind but neither of them said anything further. He studied her slender waist, her left arm brushing her thigh and trailing gracefully behind to pull the handle of her case. She stopped before a door and slotted in the key card. Inside the room the light came on. She left the door open and went to stand by the window against the backdrop of the Hong Kong city night. Alex remained standing in the doorway. He watched her take her earrings out and place them on the desk.

'Inspector Soong, are you coming in or leaving?' she said.

He couldn't answer.

She came back to the door and stood directly in front of him.

'Inspector, I'm a straightforward girl. I like excitement more than most. Even as a history professor one can travel to some pretty strange places, meet some dangerous and odd people in the name of research. You've given this girl an exciting twenty-four hours and we've made a connection. But what is too dangerous for me is the fact that you are a married man, with a nice girl of your own at home.'

He remained standing just outside the doorway. She took two steps back into the room.

'Come in, just for a moment.'

He stepped in and shut the door behind.

She stepped closer and took his right hand in hers.

'You're a good man. You don't really want to try and take this any further, and neither do I. Though I admit, in another time and place, it would have been very nice indeed.' She cocked her head to one side and looked up at him expectantly, prompting him to say the right thing.

He looked down at her, at the lips that had just talked such sense and the eyes appealing to him to do the right thing. There was so much more he wanted to say and do. How she, a woman he had known for only a day, already listened to him more than his wife did. But what she had just said made perfect sense.

'Yes, I should go,' he replied, the words leaving his mouth without conviction.

'Now, let go of my hand,' Yi instructed.

He looked at her a moment longer then let her hand drop from his and walked quickly away.

She watched him walk along the corridor and then closed the door. She went over to the window and sat down on the sill to look out into the cloudy Hong Kong night. The ambient light coloured the dense cloud dark purple and she could just make out the streets below, complex as a laboratory maze. Her room hung thirty-five floors up, somewhere between heaven and earth. Many roads had been closed for the meetings tomorrow, and she could see the place where they had sat chatting in Alex's car, waiting for the police to erect the barriers in advance of the anticipated protests and demonstrations.

The doorbell rang.

'Hi, who is it?' she called.

'Room service, ma'am. We've been instructed to take your order.'

Presuming that Alex had prearranged this, she went to the door, slid back the chain and began to open it. Simultaneously the person outside pushed the door hard, nearly knocking her down. She felt a hand go around her neck, a sharp pinch, then nothing.

Alex stood immediately outside the hotel on the red carpet, unable to bring himself to get back into the car. He thought of the possibilities that Yi represented for him, of being with someone whom he felt he could talk to and would want to listen to as well; someone who understood the meaning of commitment, to work, to another . . . He touched his wedding ring with his little finger as his hand hung by his side.

A valet approached him. 'Sir, do you need any help?'

'No, thank you. Just leaving.'

He got in the Mustang and headed back into the diverted traffic bound for Kowloon via the Western Tunnel. It bumped along until they were out the other side below the ICC tower, and then he sped along the highway back to the depot. He gripped the steering wheel tightly and allowed himself to scream at the road ahead. He screamed for ten, maybe twenty, seconds, then turned the volume of the music down and found his phone. He dialled Jun. Her phone rang out and eventually went to voicemail. He listened to her recorded message, voice sounding light and cheerful, free from any trace of worry.

'Hi, I wanted to come to dinner and still might, but I have to go to the storage facility in Yuen Long again.' He paused at the point where he would normally end a message. 'Look . . . I'm sorry I'm not there.'

He hung up then decided he wanted to hear her voice again, wanted to speak to her, even if just to hear her groan at him for letting her down. He phoned her girlfriend Tasha.

'*Wei?*'

'Tasha, it's Alex. Happy birthday, and congratulations! Great news.'

'Why, thank you. You out investigating those murders?'

'Yes, can I speak to Jun?'

'She's not here. We're still waiting for her. Do you think she's all right? She's not normally this late . . .'

'I don't know. Let me phone her at home.'

'We did that already, but no reply.'

'Okay. I need to get someone round there. Phone me if you hear anything in the meantime.'

He hung up and dialled De Suza, who answered at once.

'Hey, I can't find Jun and I'm getting worried.'

'Where are you?'

'Just going over the first bridge to Yuen Long.'

'Only there? What have you been doing all this time? Seriously, you didn't . . .'

'Don't start that shit again. No, I got stuck in the deployment and road closures in preparation for tomorrow.'

'They just asked me to help with that.'

'Great. Shows what their priorities are, doesn't it? Look, can you please do me a quick favour and get over to my apartment? Jun hasn't shown up at dinner with her friends and she's not picking up her mobile.'

'Did you speak to the Captain before you left the station?'

Silence.

'For God's sake!' De Suza exclaimed. 'Okay, I'll go now. But get to the depot and find that package fast. Maybe he thinks you're still in the building. Hurry up and get back here!'

Alex hung up and accelerated, weaving dangerously through the traffic. Within fifteen minutes he pulled up outside the depot and ran to the security panel. He pressed the buzzer urgently. It was dark in the security compound. He could not help but look around him and pat his hand against his sidearm.

'Hello? Hello?' It was the voice he remembered from earlier.

'It's Inspector Soong again. I need to check we didn't drop anything.'

'I don't think you . . .'

'Let me in. I need to check personally.'

The security panel went silent and Alex waited. He turned to look out into the car park. Just one other vehicle parked close to the steps leading up to the door, and his own directly at the foot of them. He heard the locks turn and the door open.

'Hi, officer, please come in.'

Alex pushed the door open, and nearly knocked the depot manager to the floor. He looked startled and Alex reached out to stop him from falling.

'Sorry, I'm in a rush.'

'Okay, but after you took that box away with you, I didn't find anything.'

'I have to check. Retrace my steps.'

'Sure. But I can show you the security-camera footage.'

'Let's do the retrace first and then the footage.'

They walked back to the crates and boxes containing the minister's belongings, but there was nothing there that Alex recognized. He grew more agitated with each minute that passed, and the manager suggested they head straight for the CCTV room so he could replay the footage.

'Just sit here.' He slapped the back of a worn swivel chair set in front of two small screens. 'It'll take five minutes to upload from the drive.'

Alex's phone rang.

'I've got to your apartment,' said De Suza. 'The door was open but there's no one inside. There's no obvious sign of a struggle.'

'What's in the living room?'

'Nothing unusual except for a wrapped present.'

'Shit! If she didn't take Tash's present, what happened to her? You need to bring in Forensics and the kidnap team.'

'Surely you're being a little paranoid. Jun's just going to be having a massage or something.'

'She was supposed to be at a birthday party an hour ago. She's the one who organized it.'

'Okay, don't worry, I'll get on it. Did you find the package?'

'I don't think it's here but I'm waiting to review the security tapes. Let me know as soon as you hear anything.'

Alex put his phone down on the desk and looked at its screen. It was 7.39 p.m. After another two minutes the footage was ready. They fast-forwarded through to his finding the package and holding it up. Yi and the depot manager acknowledged his find. They watched Alex pick up the box it had been in, place it on the floor, sign the manager's records then pick up the box again and walk to the door. They switched to the camera outside and watched a replay of him putting the box in the back seat and them driving off. The footage came to an end as the car went out of shot. Alex thanked the manager and ran out of the depot.

He started the car in a hurry, wheel spinning in reverse, and then pulled up sharply before the entrance to the compound, waiting for the electric gates. Once through them he drove fast. No music, just the lights and the road. The package had not fallen out. Which meant it had been deliberately removed. He called De Suza.

'Is she back yet?'

'No, no sign of Jun, but the team is here. Your lines are being tapped and they're waiting for any messages. We've started looking through the flat but, as I said earlier, there's nothing visible.'

'Okay, I'm already on my way. I watched the security footage and the parcel did not fall out. Nor did Yi touch it. I sat with the depot manager and watched it right up until it was in the car. Tell me, was Ding left alone with the box before you got it into the examination room?'

'Yes, for about a minute while I went to the toilet. He's now out on the street with the others, preparing for tomorrow.'

'You ring him.'

'Sure. Get back here . . . but make sure you tell the Captain what's going on.'

'I'm outside with his wife,' the caller reported hesitantly.

'Is she heavy?'

'No, not at all. Barely a hundred and twenty pounds.'

'Fine.'

He was carrying the wife, her long legs and arms hanging limp in his. He had a little time and wanted to watch the teacher, a great *sifu* at work, so he could learn the rituals.

'How is she?'

'Heavily sedated.'

'Good. Thank you.'

The man inside the building worked his way through the labyrinth of passages towards the entrance. He turned a key and opened first the metal security door, then immediately another door acting as merely the façade to the building.

The young man stepped out from the darkness. The master moved back.

'I thought you had to go straight back. Won't you be missed?'

'Maybe I could help you here? There's so much going on in the streets, they won't miss me.'

The older man frowned; he did not welcome opposition to his wishes. But he could use some help, he acknowledged.

'Fine, but do as I say and only as I say. Bring her this way.'

He turned to go back into the building, then looked over his shoulder.

'Is my son coming back?'

'He decided not to.' The skinny young man cleared his throat nervously. 'I don't think he agrees with this.'

The other man grunted and walked on.

Drugged on ketamine, Jun, like Yi, had lost consciousness within seconds of feeling the puncturing of her skin. The young sinewy man carried her through the passageways and to the room prepared for the ritual. He placed her on the surgeon's table at the centre. Her right arm was extended and properly restrained and then he stood back and waited. The old man entered but stood before her, studying her carefully, before sitting down at her side. He dosed her again with ketamine to ensure she would remain unconscious throughout the work. Then he positioned himself in front of her hand, as if at a dinner table. The scalpels, saw and sutures were to his right, the dish to his left.

'I have decided that I would like to be alone. This may take longer than anticipated. I've changed my mind, please leave.'

'They're not expecting me back . . . so I can stay.'

'Please do as I say.'

The young man frowned but did as he was told.

Yi was in the holding room. She had been brought to him twenty minutes earlier, and placed gently on the floor in front of the chair at the centre. Her kidnapper had checked the straps to restrain waist, wrists, ankles and neck, shortening them in readiness, then he knelt down and placed his hands underneath her shoulders to lift her up again. She slept on, hanging like a doll from his powerful hands. The chair was too big for her slight build, but with the straps adjusted she would be secured. The kidnapper had been reluctant to strap her neck back, but in the end had followed all the instructions he'd been given, leaving the slight frame immobilized before threading his way out of the maze.

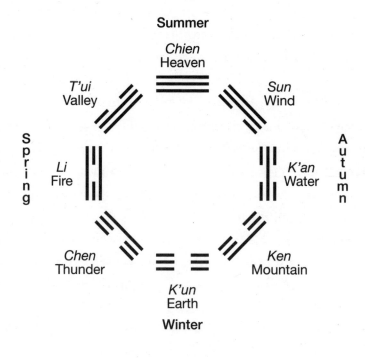

PENETRATION

Alex drove fast along the highway back to Hong Kong. Far to his right, he saw the lights of Hong Kong Island shimmering brightly through the rain. Most of the big neon signs for Western brands had been replaced by Chinese ones, massive characters stuck atop the buildings, in bright red and yellow neon, the final manifestation of Chinese success needed to wash away the last faded impressions of colonial days. He passed the foot of the giant ICC building and down into the Western Tunnel and up into Hong Kong Island.

He went straight up to the university and across Mid-Levels to Kennedy Road, as he had done in the van with Ding the day before, putting his siren on to help him through the traffic, and got to his own block to find five police vehicles and De Suza's car in the street outside. He parked and raced up the stairs, through the patchy lighting, to the apartment. Before going in, he knocked hard at Mrs Chan's door.

'Yes, yes, what is it?' he heard her call out.

'Mrs Chan, it's Alex. From next door. I need to talk to you urgently.'

She opened the door, keeping the latch in place.

'Did you see my wife leave?' he asked.

'Yes, I did. She answered the door, and then she fell ill and he helped her down the stairs. Is she all right? It was one of your fellow police officers who called on her, about two hours ago.'

Alex thought of himself sitting next to Yi in the car, stuck in the rain on the way to her hotel, while someone had been preparing to take Jun. He had allowed this to happen.

'Did you see what he looked like?'

The old lady looked panicked by his blunt question. He stepped back a little from the doorway.

'Sorry to rush you, Mrs Chan, but it's very urgent.'

'Yes, I see, just let me think. No, it was just a policeman. I saw his peaked cap pulled down very low over his eyes, like on TV. I'm sorry, I didn't get a good look at him. That's all I saw. He was holding your wife's arm. Is she okay?'

Alex listened carefully to the old lady but stared down at the scarred wooden floor inside her flat. Lines scored the surface from the front door all the way down the hall. It looked as though she regularly dragged furniture from the back room to barricade her door. The depth of the lines indicated that she had possibly done it every night for years. Such caution seemed suddenly admirable.

'A cap, you say? That's very useful. Now you go back in and lock the door,' he told his neighbour.

The old lady looked up at him, sensing his turmoil. 'You're looking pale. Would you like to come in and sit down?'

'No, I need to go, but thank you. You lock the door properly . . . do exactly what you do every night.'

She closed and secured the door and he entered his own flat. The hostage negotiation team had set up their equipment on the dining table and De Suza sat on the sofa where Jun had been curled up twenty-four hours before.

'I need to talk to you alone,' Alex said, and led him away from the other officers and into the study.

'Where's Ding?' Alex asked. 'Did you get hold of him?'

'No, they can't find him down on the street. They'll call me when they do.'

'He's new, isn't he? What do you know about him?'

'Graduated well. Enthusiastic, bright, very willing . . .'

'I think it's him.'

'What?' De Suza frowned. 'Doing what?'

'He took the package from the box when you had your back turned, then came here and snatched Jun. I spoke with the old lady in the flat opposite. She saw an officer in a peaked cap take Jun out of here.'

'A uniformed officer? That doesn't necessarily mean it's Ding. It doesn't mean anything.'

Alex sat down on the sofa.

'No, but he's the only other person to have had access to the package, so he's in this somewhere. We're going to leave here and find him on the street if he's there. If not, we'll go to his home.'

'Okay,' said De Suza as he followed Alex out, 'but if we think other officers are involved then we should tell the Captain.'

'So we shall . . . but let's find Ding first. I'll just speak to these guys here.'

De Suza waited while Alex spoke to the head of the negotiation team to ensure that his mobile was also connected to their channels, then they headed down to his car.

They drove in silence for about ten minutes on their way to look for Ding at the command office that was running the arrangements for the next day's meeting. Alex stared straight ahead while De Suza leaned his elbow on the window and looked out.

'Sorry for coming down on you hard . . .' His apology stalled for a moment and he swung round in the seat to face Alex. 'I'm still not happy about the way you didn't tell me you'd been contacted. But you wouldn't kidnap Jun yourself, so I'm sorry about earlier.'

'That's fine . . . I still can't explain why I've been singled out. I think there's a group of Boxer-inspired psychopaths out there, seeking to use the resentment and frustration that's been building up for years to unite people at a national level.' Alex took his eyes off the road and turned to face his partner for a moment. 'I visited Sai Wong to review the internet traffic on these cases, and we're close to tipping point.' He turned back to the road. 'Do you remember the bombing of the Chinese Embassy in Belgrade in Nineteen Ninety-Nine and the protests against the US or rioting in Twenty Twelve about the Diaoyu Islands? Look how quickly people came together then, and the violence and hatred they showed. You said it yourself this morning . . . there's a lot of tension and anger out there, and these guys are drawing on generations' worth of it, using historical precedents and powerful imagery. This is not just one event, it's a whole story woven around the debt owed by Europe.'

'To what end though? A popular uprising?'

'Why not? There have been constant revolutions in our history. This time people will be goaded into demanding that the government . . . the so-called People's Government . . . act according to their will, and European debt is the match that could be used to fire it. A collective call by hundreds of millions of Chinese for our country to assert its supremacy.'

Alex guided the car through the traffic of Happy Valley, past the racetrack and up on to the flyover, to the main road running parallel to the harbour. Two streets inland was a marshalling point for police officers manning the road closures and anti-demonstration barriers.

'Shit, I suppose I'm partly being guided by my own personal

feelings here,' Alex continued. 'That Western stance of natural superiority ... their constant assumption that *we'll tell you what to do*. Loud, pompous, dogmatic bastards! We're well past the days of being the white man's burden, when governing unruly Asians was a rite of passage in which young Europeans and Americans proved their manhood – but they don't seem to realize it yet. That assumption of superiority used to make people here feel inferior. Now it's just fucking condescending and hypocritical, and if someone is seeking to play on those feelings they could be about to drop a match into a barrel of napalm.'

He pulled up to the mobile coordination unit at the roadside and faced his partner.

'I mean, you should know all this yourself, half-caste *gweilo*. You half-Chinese child, half-devil!'

'Fuck you, you Chink!' De Suza said laughing. 'I know what you mean, though.'

'When I was at university in New York people would ask me if Chinese people *still* lived in houses on stilts. That was in Two Thousand and Two! Seriously, they would say it in all sincerity and with just a touch of pity. They obviously felt we were condemned to be for ever less fortunate than they were. It's why only a few thoughtful Westerners weren't shocked when the Emerging Markets became so advanced. Now they simply feel threatened by us.' He rested one hand on the door to get out while he told De Suza: 'If you take into account the grievances Chinese people have long held, fuelled by all those annoying, patronizing slights so many of us have suffered, then I'm sure there's enough anger and fury out there to fuel an uprising.'

'I think you're right,' De Suza concluded with a sigh.

They got out and stepped up into the bright interior of the mobile unit. It was a very simple set-up with drop-down tables fixed to each of the longer walls, computers and communications equipment arranged on them, and a secure firearms locker beneath.

'Sergeant, have you seen Officer Ding?' Alex asked urgently.

A female officer working at a laptop tapped away while shaking her head. 'He's not here. Not on duty,' she said dismissively.

Alex looked distraught and De Suza stepped in. 'Thanks. We'll take his home address, please.'

'Do you want us to ring him?'

'No, we'd prefer it if you didn't. We can do that on the way.'

They returned to the car with the address, and were starting up the engine when Alex's phone rang. He looked at the caller ID and saw his wife's name.

'Jun?'

'No.'

A familiar voice.

He slotted the phone into the hands-free saddle so it would be broadcast on speakerphone.

'Where's my wife?' he shouted. 'Tell me where she is?'

'She's here,' came the implacable reply. 'I have had her for over an hour. I also have the Professor.'

Alex glanced wildly around as if he might see the caller standing right by him. He needed a second to take in what had just been said.

'Yi? How . . .'

'Are you alone? Please turn off the speakerphone.'

With a nod to De Suza, Alex grabbed the phone and held it to his ear.

'Release my wife. Release them both,' he ordered.

At the same time he took out his pen and scribbled on an envelope that De Suza should ring Yi at the hotel. He got out of the car and Alex watched him make the call from far enough away not to be overheard. In a moment he was frowning and shaking his head. Alex held up his phone momentarily and tapped one finger against it: a signal for De Suza to have a trace put on the mystery caller.

'Senior Inspector, please listen,' the voice requested. 'This is the last time I will extend this invitation to you. I want you to recognize the justice of our cause and join us.'

'Join you in what? In war?'

'No!' the voice screamed back in anger. 'We don't want to destroy. We want to create. Raise the anger of the Chinese people against a world that has demeaned and humiliated them for too long.'

'This is crazy! You can't make that happen. It isn't possible.'

Alex frowned out of the window at his partner, willing him to succeed in tracing the call.

'Of course it's possible! On so many occasions before, the Chinese people have risen up and marched in rebellion, shaping the future of their country. We don't even need to fight this time. We have weapons at our disposal now, powerful weapons, but we also have trade, science, brilliant thinkers and a workforce of hundreds of millions. Now is our time to be dominant again, as we were for thousands of years in the past. We need to play by our own rules, no one else's, the way the West has done in Asia for the last four hundred years.'

'And me? Where do I fit into this crazy plan?' Alex intervened.

'I believe, along with many others, that you would make a natural leader. People would gather behind you.'

'I'm going to arrest you, or kill you.'

'So that is it? Your final answer? Your lovely wife and the cute Professor will be the ones to suffer for your refusal.'

'No!' Alex shouted down the phone when he had found his voice.

'To create a new world we must either have you on our side or break you. I'm not going to kill them. This time.'

'Leave them both alone!' Alex checked his watch furiously. The trace needed just a little longer. 'You want to reopen the scars of past humiliation . . . personal to you . . . only to create further damaging divisions in an already fractured world. Sounds to me like you're from the older generation. Meanwhile my generation and those who came after us are busy integrating into one global community, little by little, day by day. In fact, perhaps the best thing for the world would be for your angry, violent and selfish generation just to disappear.'

Alex tried to keep the dialogue going and, mercifully, the reply came calmly: 'The facts don't bear that out. It is *your* generation that holds worthless paper from the Europeans. They sell you harmful drugs again, pretending they are candy. Debt instead of opium,' the voice sneered.

De Suza lightly tapped on the window to indicate he had a general direction for the call. Alex, who had not yet closed his door, got out and went round to sit in the passenger seat while his partner took over the driving. They pulled away and raced towards the Eastern tunnel and Kowloon. The flashing blue light on top of the car warned other traffic to keep out of the way.

'You delude yourself,' the voice persisted. 'It is we Chinese who have been fooled once again, but our response this time will be very different. We will not pay in shame and humiliation the way we did before.'

Alex kept arguing, to obtain the trace to pinpoint the caller's location and because he felt he must beat this man. 'In America, they once published a book called *Becoming China's Bitch*,' he announced. 'It was a best-seller. They think we've already won. Your generation's just afraid of change. You cringe under the constraints of old ways of thinking, still indoctrinating the younger generation in that tired old "us against them" continuum. Your generation acts like the men in Plato's cave – shouting at the shadows. You're weak and you're scared!'

'We *were* weak, but no longer. We have five thousand years of history behind us to strengthen our cause. America is nothing. Europe is populated by arrogant children.'

'Yet by your own admission they best us repeatedly!'

'No longer.' The voice was rapidly rising in volume and pitch, in response to Alex's provocation.

'Why is it your responsibility to take on the world?' he asked, hoping to calm the caller at the same time as encouraging him to continue.

'Because I stood on the greatest of the five. Let me tell you, boy, I stood where the gods stood, on those huge rocks. Alone. Before the foreigners held it in such high regard and desecrated it. And it was then I realized it was time . . .'

'I don't know what you are talking about. You're fucking deluded! Hand over my wife and the Professor – now. Before we find you and kill you.'

'Don't be absurd.' The voice sounded almost avuncular, though weary now. 'This was not a negotiation, as I said, it was a final offer.' There was a sigh then. 'But perhaps you're not the man I thought you to be. You will get them back. Next time they won't be so fortunate.'

The line went dead.

'I'm better than you. And I'm going to find you!' Alex growled as he slammed the phone back into the rest. 'What a crazy fuck!' he continued to rage. 'Did we get the address? An area? Anything at all?'

De Suza was still connected to the negotiation team on their channels.

'Yes, just outside Choi Hung.'

'A couple of miles from the warehouse development,' said Alex thoughtfully. 'Where's Ding's apartment again?'

'Hung Hom. On the way.'

'No one's going to be at Choi Hung by the time we get there. He'll be long gone. But there may be something there to help us . . .' The road ahead was washed with heavy rain; the red glow of endless tail lights stretched in front of them.

Alex clenched his fists as he thought back over the conversation and remembered Sai Wong's warning from this morning. The chatrooms were already reflecting people's rage with what they saw as Europe's economic conspiracy against China. This man's work and words would go viral if he chose to let them. The re-emergence of the Boxers was a story no Chinese would ignore, particularly with the images of those violent deaths leaked the previous day. It just took one more push . . .

'Let's look at this from the social networking angle,' he said, pursuing his thoughts aloud. 'In Twenty Eleven, a man in Tunisia burned himself alive and it started the Arab Spring. Rioters and student demonstrators in London used BlackBerries to incite and coordinate action against the authorities there. In China, we currently have bloggers generating a massive amount of traffic, hundreds of millions of people looking solely to the web for information and encouragement. At what point does it turn from chatter to action? What exactly is required for China to create a real social movement from social network traffic?'

De Suza shrugged. 'Don't we have bigger things to worry about now? Like finding Jun and the Professor?'

Alex slammed his fist against the dashboard. 'Do you really

think I need reminding of that? I'll go to Choi Hung district. You go after Ding.'

His partner said nothing more.

They took the eastern tunnel down under the harbour into Kowloon side then turned left to Hung Hom.

'You're sure you should go alone?' De Suza questioned again.

'There'll be no one there,' Alex insisted. 'He'll know we put a trace on him. But maybe he got careless and left something. In the meantime, find Ding.'

De Suza pulled up to the kerb and they got out. Alex came round to the driver's side and the two men faced each other.

De Suza fixed Alex with his earnest gaze. 'Jun'll be fine. We'll get her back. The Chinese border police are looking for her. Airports and shipping are looking for her. Everybody is out there looking. It's only a matter of time.'

Alex nodded. 'I know. It's just . . .' His breath caught. He glanced down and said: 'At times I've failed her . . . particularly after William died and I turned in on myself. She wanted one life while I pursued another. I don't give her what she wants.'

'It'll be okay,' De Suza soothed him. 'Do you have your sidearm?'

Alex patted his jacket pocket. 'Yes.'

'Take it out.'

He did as his friend asked and they looked down at the hard grey metal. De Suza stepped in closer.

'*This* is who you are at this moment. *This* is your life. Use it to find her and kill that fucker! Afterwards you two can figure things out. Now get going. I'll see you later.' De Suza spoke firmly, but almost in a whisper.

Alex got in the car and left De Suza on the side of the street to find Ding. He turned on to Kwun Tong Road, then into the tenement blocks, where he parked and got out. There was a low wall to his right, on the other side of it nothing but concrete yards cynically painted grass green, a basketball hoop in the distance and the dim lighting at the base of the residential towers from the security offices, whose job was really to tackle and report to the management company any damage done to the buildings.

Another fifty metres and he saw a bench placed against the back fence of a playground a couple of hundred metres from the nearest tower, the blue light of a mobile phone glinting from the seat. It had been left for him, obvious and easy to find. There would be no fingerprints, he already knew. He drew his gun. A stray dog sidled out in front of him and sniffed the air. It bent down and followed a brief trail before trotting off towards another block of apartments. The playground behind the bench was lit up, revealing a tall playhouse with a slide made from red plastic, monkey bars and three hard plastic horses on springs. Alex reached the bench and holstered his gun. He looked back towards his car. There was no one visible.

He should have worn gloves, called in a team, a number of other procedures needed to be followed. But Jun was missing. None of that mattered now. He picked up the phone and recognized it immediately. It was his wife's. A text message had been typed on the screen.

You will get her back in 40 minutes. Keep this. Tell no one.

De Suza found Ding's place easily, located in the fourth of eight fairly modern tower blocks overlooking the strange shopping mall built by a billionaire tycoon in the shape of a giant octopus. The interior of the tower was strictly functional: a booth for a security guard, and then three elevators to serve twenty-six floors with ten apartments each. He got to Ding's and banged on the door. After a minute he called the landline and could hear the phone ring inside. He phoned Alex.

'Ding's not here. Do you want me to wait?'

'Yes.'

'Find anything at the location?'

'Nothing. I'm going to speak to a few of the security guards in the buildings around here. Call me in an hour.'

De Suza frowned and hung up. He glanced at Ding's front door and then down the end of the corridor to a glazed fire-escape door leading to the stairs. The corridor was long, with limited fluorescent light, and he could just make out a chair to the left of the escape door below a fire extinguisher. He walked to the chair and moved it a little further to the left, into a recess that housed a fire hose fixed to the wall. He would sit and wait, his location largely obscured, while he'd still be able to see Ding return.

He took out a switchblade from his jacket, released the blade slowly and held it up in front of him. The clean blade reflected his Eurasian eyes, large nose and full lips. He turned the blade slightly to study different aspects of his face. As a young man in his twenties he had often stood in front of the mirror in the bathroom, staring in dismay at what he saw there: a mixture of finer Asian bone structure and heavy Western features. In the distortion of the blade these became exaggerated, nose and lips bulging mask-like as he turned the blade this way and that to reflect his whole face.

He looked up and saw Ding at the far end, pulling his front-door key from his pocket.

She was still sleeping.

He pressed the blade under Yi's cheek and traced it across her lips and up over her temple but did not break the skin. Then he brought the knife down towards her waist.

'What have you done?'

The voice came from behind him. He turned to see the younger man standing directly behind him. A strong hand reached out and grabbed his wrist, pulling it up and away from Yi's body.

'What the fuck have you done to his wife?'

They stood together for a moment, the knife still held upright in the restrained hand.

'I told you that a circle must complete. He now has the phone and is waiting.'

'No more! Leave this woman. I'm taking her out of here.'

'I haven't finished.' The older man tried to wrench his hand away, but it was held fast. He looked up at the hard angry face, eyes that hated him. 'Who are you to stop me? I have been mandated to do this.'

'You have been mandated to bring us together as a nation, to follow a narrative . . . but not this.'

The older man still had plenty of strength. He pulled free and took a swipe towards the younger man's face, who instinctively swayed back from the passing blade and countered with a body strike that knocked his opponent down and away from the chair.

'Enough of this!' the young man shouted down at him.

'You don't decide what's right or wrong,' the other growled. 'That was laid down in the texts, centuries ago.' He quickly recovered his feet and stood two paces back with the knife extended. 'Stupid boy! This woman is Soong's sister.'

'What?' the younger man shouted in surprise.

'He was given a choice – join or be broken. He chose, and now we must make good on our word. We need to teach him. It was our good fortune that she appeared when she did. As soon as I heard her name I remembered it. Soong's father died trying to find her. Poor fool didn't know where to look, and got himself killed.' He nodded in the direction of the maze of passages. 'All these thousands of records are not for nothing, you know. They have been handed down from one archivist to another, for centuries. A story like that wasn't going to go unrecorded or get lost.'

'Then where's the other sister? How long have you known this?' the younger man demanded.

'She's lost,' the older man growled. 'And it's none of your business.'

The younger man looked at Yi, who was sleeping deeply, her head drooping awkwardly on her chest.

'Christ! Leave her alone.' He looked back at the knife and the man who wielded it, intent on gutting her. 'Give me that!'

With a fast stride forward he put a wrist lock on the older man's hand, took hold of the knife and disarmed him. They stood apart, the knife now raised in the opposite direction.

The older man smiled and stepped forward. He grabbed the blade with his right hand and clenched it tightly. He looked into his son's face.

'Take her if you must.' He smiled and drew his fist down the blade.

Blood dripped fast on to the floor but the older man ignored it. Without looking at the gash in his open palm, he turned his back and vanished into the darkness, leaving the younger man standing beside Yi with the bloodied knife in his hand. He used it to cut the straps, and Yi was hoisted safely into a pair of powerful arms.

Lights filled the twenty or thirty floors above Alex, but the area was empty at street level. He walked towards the security office of the nearest residential tower.

Six minutes had already elapsed.

He moved quickly, wanting to be in his car well before the forty minutes were up. Perhaps another four minutes to cover the few hundred metres.

He tapped on the window of the security office, disturbing a retiree who was sucking down some noodles in front of a small television. The old man flinched at the unexpected interruption. Alex placed his badge hard up against the wire-framed window and shouted through the glass in loud Cantonese: 'Are there cameras here?'

'No.'

The security guy turned back to the television. Alex banged on the window again. 'Hey!' He felt his temper running high along with his anxiety.

The old man looked round and was about to shout back when Alex cut him off: 'Sorry . . . Sorry. I just need your help.'

The chopsticks were rested on top of the bowl.

'What is it then?'

'Are there any security cameras in this area, under the

tower blocks or by the entrance? Anything at all?' he finished desperately.

'Yes, there's one over the basketball court and another over the playground.'

'Which way does the one in the playground look?'

'Through to the road.'

'So it catches the bench at the back?'

'Maybe. What's this about?'

'Who knows about the camera in the playground?'

The old man stood up and opened the window.

'No one. They were only put in last week, for insurance purposes. Waste of money . . . everyone knows the kids hereabouts don't use the playground.'

'Can I get a copy of the film?'

The old man looked suspicious. 'What's this about?'

'A murder.'

'What murder?' The old man watched Alex swallow hard and the colour fade from his cheeks.

'The one that may be committed in thirty minutes' time.'

The old guy knew not to ask any more questions. 'It'll take me twenty minutes to locate. You want me to do it?'

Alex looked behind him to the road in the distance and then towards his parked car. 'I'll come back later to collect it.'

'Up to you. I'll have it ready anyway.'

Alex turned and headed for his car, walking quickly without looking around. He reached into his jacket pocket and pulled out Jun's phone again. The screensaver was a photo of him at a restaurant taken a few weeks before, slurping down a bowl of burnt miso ramen. He flipped through the other photos before he realized it wasn't a good idea. He couldn't bear to look at the photos of them together. There were no new messages.

Seventeen or eighteen minutes left by the time he reached his car.

He jumped the low wall and started to run along the pavement. He wanted to get the shotgun and torch from the trunk then wait in the driver's seat, key ready in the ignition. He did not intend to allow communications with the station or even De Suza to interfere with his plan. Back in the car, he put the phone on the dashboard above the steering wheel, staring at it.

In the dark street nothing moved. Fifteen minutes.

His own phone vibrated. De Suza.

'Ding says he doesn't know anything . . . Alex?'

'Yes?'

He stared blindly into the empty road.

'I'll go back to the station to follow up with Forensics and Ying. I need to report to the Captain as well. Where are you? You okay?'

'I'm okay, very close, just stuck in traffic.' De Suza's reply was barely audible. 'But watch out for Jun and Yi.'

He hung up.

Alex checked the phone on the dashboard and then the gun leaning in the footwell at the passenger side, its barrel propped against the seat. As he felt for his pistol and knife he found himself thinking back to the video from the depot. The package had definitely remained in that box all the time. Ding and De Suza had gone to his car to fetch it. Which meant that Ding or *De Suza* . . . No. Not possible. He needed to clear his mind.

The Captain called. 'Where are you?' he demanded.

'Just waiting, sir.'

His superior did not ask for further details. 'I'll send what support I can, but we're stretched very thin this evening. Keep me updated. And, Soong, be careful. If you think there is going to be blood spilled, you should call for paramedic backup now so they can stay close.'

He hung up.

The dashboard vibrated and the phone lit up. The message was simple.

Tsz Wan Shan Central Playground, Wai Wah Street.

He called the paramedics and requested they meet him at the location. He accelerated fast then drove left up to Po Kong Road, a journey that would take him fifteen minutes longer than to cut across on foot to the grim playground, which was just another local playground painted green. But he might need his car, he reckoned. Fortunately there was little traffic on the way and he shifted up the gears, running every light. The area was now largely forgotten. Cheap efficient tenement blocks – modern versions of the old *tong lau*, but put up with no real thought for design quality or the benefit of the community – lined the streets. Between them stood even more basic accommodation, providing just a roof and some enclosed space to store goods against the elements. So much for economic progress.

He pulled into a school car park and grabbed the torch and shotgun from the car. He ran through a broad passageway between two blocks of buildings and could see the expansive green-painted playing surface beyond. One piece of concrete was marked out as a football pitch, the other a basketball court. Midway between the two he could see a figure huddled on the ground. He had come not knowing if he'd find Jun or Yi. Registering his own guilt, he hoped it would be Jun.

He shone the torch at the figure from fifty metres away and drew his firearm. Was the body alive? He could not tell. He lit up the ground beyond. Empty. In the distance there were trees and more school buildings. These could be concealing someone, but he would take his chances.

It was Yi, he saw. His only thought then – Jun.

He knelt beside Yi and looked at her still pale face. Three hours ago he had wanted to kiss her. Now he only wanted to see his wife lying in front of him.

'Yi?'

No response.

Again he shone the torch around the area. Still no one. He sat next to Yi with his fingers pressed lightly to her neck, checking her pulse, looking at her delicate face. This was all his responsibility. He had stopped her getting on that plane.

The situation had changed completely, he understood. What had been a clear focus of interest on him had now become an outright attack on everything that mattered in his life. He phoned De Suza.

'Hey, I'm with Yi.'

'Is she okay? Where are you?'

'I'm in Diamond Hill. She seems fine but heavily sedated. Medics are on their way so I'll just stay here.'

'I'll stay on this side and watch out for Jun.' De Suza took a breath, and in the silence Alex looked around again. 'Why didn't you tell me where you were?'

'I needed to find Jun. And if necessary do what was needed and not drag you into it.'

'For fuck's sake, Alex. I can decide for myself. We agreed you'd keep me in the loop, remember?'

Sirens nearby.

'Okay, now's not the time. I get it!'

'I hope so, man,' De Suza finished shortly. 'I'm trying to help you here.'

Paramedics with flashlights came running towards Alex and Yi.

'Senior Inspector Soong, can you step away, please?'

'Where are you going to take her?'

'Everything is messed up so we'll have to take her to the Ruttonjee.'

'That's on Hong Kong side.' The suggestion alarmed him.

'I know,' the medic told him, grinning wryly, 'but everywhere else is locked down and the Emergency departments and staff have been heavily cut. So that's it, I'm afraid. Don't take the eastern tunnel, it's too far away. Just use your sirens and bully your way through the tunnel leading into Happy Valley.'

Alex rushed along with them and watched them set off. He switched on his sirens and lights and followed the ambulance, which could make progress only by forcing the Kowloon traffic on to the pavement, and sometimes by nudging it into other lanes. They pushed their way through the tunnel traffic and then sped up past the racecourse and to the hospital driveway. He spun round the central barrier and parked in the unloading space in front of the Emergency department. The ambulance had drawn up outside. Its doors stood open and he saw a trolley being wheeled through the double doors ahead.

He was shocked to find De Suza waiting at the desk. Alex walked rapidly towards his partner then saw him glance down at a bed lying parallel to the wall. He could see the top of a woman's head. The crown of her hair, split high on the left, was immediately familiar.

Alex stumbled as his foot caught a chair to his right and sent him lurching towards the bed. He kicked the chair away and it slid towards De Suza, who stopped it. Alex stood beside the bed and looked down at the familiar head and body, and she turned to him and looked up and then at De Suza.

'Where were you?' moaned Jun.

Alex turned to his partner.

'How did she get here?'

'The hospital were contacted about ten minutes ago, asking for someone to go outside. They found her there sitting in a wheelchair. It took them a few minutes to identify her, then I got the call.'

Alex reached out his left hand to touch Jun's forehead, but as he tried she shook her head violently to push him away.

'Where were you?' She was crying uncontrollably and her voice emerged in jagged breaths between the sobs.

'I was searching for you.'

'Where?'

'I had a text on your phone telling me that someone was waiting for me. I thought it would be you. I wanted it to be you.'

He tried to stroke her hair.

She cried harder and shook her head more violently still.

'No, don't touch me! Not now.' She sobbed harder. Her eyes were red and swollen, rendered grotesque by the two lines of black characters taken from the Boxer trigrams inked down both her temples and across her face. 'Why didn't you find me? Why not *me*?' she screamed.

'I've been looking and looking for you,' Alex whispered, close to her cheek.

'Why didn't you call me straight away to say she was here, you fuck?' he screamed at De Suza. 'You're always going on about me calling you . . .'

'Because it only happened a few minutes ago. Why didn't you tell me where you were rather than go it alone?' De Suza asked angrily.

'I thought *you* were part of this!' Alex hurled back at him.

'What?'

Alex went up to him. 'That evidence was safely in the packing box while it was in my car. Yi didn't touch it . . . why would she? It must have been you or Ding. Or maybe both of you.'

'Fuck you!'

Alex took a step back and went to punch De Suza in the face with his right, who in turn tried to block it. Alex pushed away the block and sent his left and right through the gap to smack De Suza's eye. He followed through with his left again, landing a solid hit on his partner's nose. The big man was rocked back on his feet.

'What are you doing?' he protested.

Alex launched a hard full right hook into his left kidney, which doubled him over. De Suza saw his partner take a step or two away. Pulling himself up on a chairback, he lashed out with a powerful front kick that sent Alex reeling against the wall near Jun's stretcher.

'Stop!' she shouted, and started to sob.

From beneath the covers she raised her right arm to reveal a stump at the wrist, which she held in the air above her head. The end of her arm was bandaged and bloodstained.

Alex stared at it, unable to comprehend.

'Jun?' he whispered. He fell back against the wall and slid to the floor. De Suza, one hand clutching his side, picked him up under the armpits and pushed him on to a chair. Alex was conscious of nothing but the bandage wrapped over his wife's severed hand. It looked neat but amateurish, with blood forming a deep red lacquer over the five or six safety pins.

A doctor approached him. 'Senior Inspector Soong, your wife needs immediate corrective surgery.'

Two orderlies, standing behind the doctor and attendant

nurse, positioned themselves at either end of the bed and started to wheel it away through the double doors.

'Alex?' came an anguished call.

'Yes! I'm behind you ... Will you see to Yi?' he asked De Suza, forgetting their animosity of moments before.

'Yes, I'll take care of that. And the Captain will be here soon. I should warn you, he's going to relieve you of command and appoint Ying. After this, though, does it matter? Go to Jun.'

Alex looked up into his partner's rugged face. De Suza stared back at him for a moment and it was clear that he too was upset.

'She's your wife,' he said plaintively. 'Get out of here.'

Alex took a few steps more and then turned back.

'Thank you.' He paused. 'Is there any security footage on the man who dropped her here?'

'I've already asked them to review the footage and I checked with Jun when she came in. She remembers nothing, just a knock at the door and then a hand jabbed her with a syringe. Now, go.'

Alex was just about to leave when the Captain slid silently between the doors. He cleared his throat and they turned to find him only a step away.

'Soong, we need to speak outside for a moment, then you can go wait outside the theatre for the surgeon and your wife.'

'Sir.'

Outside the Captain leaned against the side of Alex's car. 'Your shotgun was in the passenger seat and your keys in the ignition. I've locked it in the trunk ... and here.' He tossed Alex the car keys. 'It's a very nice car. I've always liked your commitment to it, which is why I've allowed you to go on driving it.' He stood up and looked into the hospital entrance through the glass doors, and at De Suza sitting adjacent to the nurse's duty desk.

'The reason I wanted you in Hong Kong is because you always

reach the right decision in the end. You seem to be able to understand that the truth is often greater than the sum of its parts. Most people, even when they see all the parts, just work to slot them together – but you anticipate the difficulties in advance. Seem to know where it will all end, and why. This time I think you're too personally involved. I'm going to have to take you off the case and put Ying in charge. This has damaged your family and it's going to consume you unless you take a step back. So you're on suspension for now.'

'That's fine,' Alex conceded, immediately and readily, reaching into his pocket to hand the Captain his badge and his sidearm. 'I want to spend my time with Jun now. And I'm not getting anywhere on the enquiry. I've failed you on this.'

He turned and stood shoulder to shoulder with the Captain, following his line of sight to De Suza, still in reception.

'And what about him?'

'Up to Ying, but the teams guarding the impromptu meeting of the G8 and O5 finance ministers tomorrow have requested De Suza to assist them, if he's available, so I'll confirm that he is.'

'The O5?'

'The Outreach Five. Brazil, India, Mexico, South Africa and us.'

'All right, sir. I am going back to see my wife. Let me know if I can help.' Alex started towards the entrance.

'Soong, did you get anything further from your line on rebellion and the Boxers?' the Captain called after him.

'I had another background talk with the Professor before . . . We both think this person or these people are mirroring historical events. The death of two preachers started the Boxer Rebellion, which was a conflict characterized by peasants using magic and ritual as well as regular weapons. The eight trigrams were very important to them. I've just seen the characters drawn on my wife's face . . . We now have the Boxer chronology – the dead preachers, the murder of Chinese Christians and a German from Münster. Six plus Chan Lok Shing, the realtor, there must be two more to make the nine. Remember, eight trigrams with the ninth at the centre.

'That ninth component is probably our unknown subject. The mutilations he's performed are part of some insane fucking ritual consistent with Boxer belief. Apart from the sickening violence, his aim seems to be to stir up public feeling against the West and to encourage China's unheard millions to find their voice in a crusade against foreigners. The only real lead on him we had were the contents of that package from Reverend Lu's possessions.'

'Which is still lost?'

'Maybe.' Reluctantly, Alex remembered his earlier suspicions of his partner. He struggled with himself but chose not to speak.

'I'll follow it up, thank you,' said the Captain. 'In the meantime, look after your wife. Now get going.'

Outside the theatre the duty nurse informed Alex that Jun's amputation would need correcting by cutting the bone down further to provide enough skin to close the end properly. Alex sat in a visitor's chair and stared up at the plastic light fittings on the ceiling.

He awoke to the noise of porters wheeling Jun's bed back into the corridor. He followed it into a side ward. She was still sedated, her arms by her sides, a drip attached to the left and the other ending in clean bandage. He stroked her hair and looked at the eight trigrams drawn round her face, left intact by the medical staff for evidence purposes. There was bruising on her upper arms, particularly on her right where she had been tied down. Alex was afraid of how much she would remember of it. He hoped it would be nothing – no faces, location, directions – and that she could not be a witness. Nothing useful. He tried to ignore what the characters meant, wanting to forget the case and just concentrate on his wife, but it was impossible. His eyes kept returning to her right wrist, its incompleteness, the absence of a hand, one that he had held and kissed and entwined his fingers with.

He forced himself to stare at Jun's face. He had loved it since he first saw her through the blazing sunlight, standing over him on the grass at Beijing University. A vicious madman had turned it into a sacrificial altar. He wanted to remove the harsh black drawings and characters from her skin. He recorded them with his phone camera then took a damp towel and a little soap and gently started to wipe them away.

A nurse came in. 'How's she doing?'

'Still sleeping.'

'What happened to her?' the nurse enquired.

He swallowed. 'Someone made a terrible mistake. They were careless and thoughtless and let this happen.'

She checked Jun's vital signs and the IV drip. 'Well, I hope that person is punished.' She smiled to reassure him. 'Your wife's doing okay. I'll leave you both in peace. Do you want a camp bed so you can sleep here?'

'Yes, that would be great. Thank you.'

She left and he returned to gently cleaning his wife's face.

The Captain had stood back and watched Alex rush into the hospital, to wait outside the Emergency operating theatre. He ran straight past his partner, who remained in the reception area and made no attempt to follow. The Captain joined De Suza.

'Inspector, what do you know about this missing evidence?' he queried.

'Very little. Senior Inspector Soong looked for it at the storage depot and later viewed security tapes showing that it was in the box he placed in his car. Officer Ding and myself did not find it in the box when we took it to the Forensics department.'

'What is your view of this evidence? Inspector Soong seems to believe it's of key importance.'

De Suza glanced around, taking in the people coming and going through the Emergency department.

'I believe we should move the location of this conversation, sir.'

'Very well, let's take a walk along this corridor towards the theatre to see how Jun Soong is doing.' The two men walked together slowly and De Suza went on speaking in a low voice.

'The evidence is allegedly a replica hangman's noose that was sent as a threat to Minister Lu several years ago, together with a note referring to him as Judas. This morning, when we learned of its existence from Mrs Lu, it certainly seemed to hold the potential for a possible DNA trace on the rope. Discovering the identity of the sender could give us our first link to the individual or individuals responsible. Without it, we have very little to go on apart from the Professor's theories.'

'Ah, yes, the Professor. I'm sorry she has become mixed up in this. Very forthright and attractive.'

'Alex seems to think so too.'

The Captain frowned. 'Inspector De Suza, he's your partner and friend, let's not engage in such speculation. Tell me, in your opinion, could she have taken the package?'

'Well, there were four people with the opportunity. Alex, myself, Ding and the Professor . . . don't forget, the history behind this case is her passion, her life's work. Maybe she has loyalties and allegiances we know nothing about.'

'Have you looked into her background?'

'We just did the preliminary consultant due diligence background check. It showed nothing, but that's hardly conclusive.'

'Well, when she wakes up, please question her further. And the conduct of Senior Inspector Soong?' The Captain was expecting De Suza's usual ringing endorsement of his partner. He was surprised by the answer he received.

'He has not disclosed information vital to the investigation . . . first the letter on his apartment door, then the phone call he received this evening.'

'Would you have done things differently in his position? Someone has worked hard to isolate him, make him feel weak and compromised. I have been there too.' The Captain looked thoughtfully at De Suza, who stopped walking and stared back.

'Sir, don't defend his actions. He lied to us all.'

'I'm not excusing him. What I'm demonstrating to you is that the strong personal element in this case is not necessarily Soong's fault, even though we must view the situation objectively and professionally. You're angry with him, I get that, but try and look beyond it.'

'Yes, I'm fucking pissed off!' De Suza breathed out deeply. 'But, sir, I'll try to look beyond it.'

The Captain smiled sympathetically.

'Senior Inspector Ying will take over the enquiry. You will question Professor Yi when she comes round, and then write up a detailed summary of where we are to date and hand it to Ying later this evening. Once you've taken the Professor's statement, send the audio file tape to Mae, then go and report to the command and control team working on the economic forum. They've requested you specially.'

Minutes later the Captain knocked on the door to Jun's room.

'May I come in?'

'Sir, please do,' Alex answered.

He stood just inside the doorway, staring at the still figure in the bed and Alex sitting by her head.

'The Duty Nurse mentioned there were markings on Jun's face?' the Captain said, observing that they had been removed.

'Yes, I had to wipe them off. Couldn't let her wake up to such a reminder. I've taken photos of all the markings and a sample of the ink. I'll email you the photos. Here's the ink.'

Alex passed over a medical sample bottle containing a small patch of Jun's ink-covered skin for evidence. He also produced a plastic evidence bag with her phone in it.

'Sir, it will have my prints and Jun's on it. I don't suppose there are anyone else's.'

'We'll take a look. Tomorrow morning you need to make a

statement. Two other officers from different departments will come here. Okay?'

'Understood. Thank you, sir.'

'Within what is right we look after our own, and as Chinese we look after our families. Goodnight, Soong.'

His superior left. Alex went on holding Jun's hand until the camp bed was brought in, after which he positioned it at the foot of her bed and lay down. He closed his eyes but his mind filled at once with images of Chow's face, his smug smile and the cheap gun he'd held to the little girl's cheek. There was an explosion, and the money-launderer's eyes imploded, his bones fracturing and pushed through his skull by the force of the bullet. Alex sat bolt upright, his own eyes wide and staring. He looked through the window into the corridor and watched an orderly pushing a bed past. Jun was still sleeping soundly. He got up and went out to the nurses' station.

'How long will my wife be out for?'

'Until mid-morning most likely.'

'I'm just going out to my car.'

He went out and slumped down in the driver's seat. The dashboard clock ticked. Everywhere else was silent. He placed his hands on the steering wheel and dropped his head between them. His chest tightened and his eyes filled with tears. He clenched his jaw tightly, refusing to make a sound while they fell.

It was nearly 4 a.m. and the drive back to Choi Hung was quick. Alex parked outside the tenement block and walked quickly to the security office. The old man was sleeping, his head cradled on his arms over a crumpled newspaper. Alex knocked harder on the door.

'Sir, have you got the video footage?' he called.

'Hey, you're back late. I got it for you. I had a look and there's definitely someone on it . . . big fellow, sitting on the bench.'

'That's good, but do me a favour. Never tell anyone you watched it. Just say you gave it to the police. Okay?'

'All right, young man. I'll do that. Did you stop whoever it was from being killed?'

Alex swallowed. 'No one died.' He looked past the security guard and saw a toolbox underneath a bookshelf. 'Do you have a measuring tape in that box?'

'No idea. Wait a minute.' The man bent down and fished around in it. 'You're in luck.'

'Thank you, I'll bring this back with the memory card.'

Alex walked quickly back to the bench. After taking some measurements he sat down and stared straight ahead. There was the well-lit road; the tenement blocks opposite, filled with potential if unlikely witnesses. The tall man had not known of the playground camera. But what remained most curious was the choice of this location. The warehouse, this bench, the place where Yi was left, Ding's home – they were all on the eastern side of Kowloon.

Alex stood and surveyed the area for several minutes before driving quickly back to the hospital. When he arrived the nurse was checking Jun. She was still sleeping but the nurse assured him that his wife was comfortable.

'What can be done with her hand?'

'Oh there's all sorts of things these days. Before it was very limited. The rehabilitation doctor will come speak to her after the psychologist has seen her.'

He thanked her, and surprised her with his next request. 'Sorry, but do you have a map of Hong Kong?'

'I think there's one in the day room, I'll have a look for you.'

Alex stood and stroked Jun's cheek. He swallowed hard, gripping the bars at the top of her bed with his right hand. Tomorrow he would have to tell her parents the news, and who knew how her father might respond?

He started to look through the street maps the nurse brought in. The detailed map of Po Kong Village showed nothing of interest, but when he flicked to the smaller-scale map of the main roads it gave him a bird's-eye view of the area, and the symbolism of shapes and arrangements made by the roads became glaringly obvious: Hammer Hill Road formed the east and south-east sides, with Choi Hung Road leading up south and south-west and then Po Kong Village Road looping up and round from west to north-west, reaching the most northerly point of an octagon and then south again to join the two ends. In the centre lay Diamond Hill. To the south of the octagon was the site of the original Po Kong Village, to the north Tsz Wan Shan Estate Service

Reservoir Playground, where he had found Yi, and to the north-east was the warehouse development. Alex lay on his camp bed and traced the outline of the eight-sided shape the roads formed together, the old factories and warehouses at its centre, in the Fung Tak Estate.

He knew a little of the history of this area from his lonely neighbour Mrs Chan. Po Kong had been the epicentre of the vicious 1967 workers' and leftist riots against the British administration and local tycoons. It was where Mrs Chan's husband had died. He stared at the map, at the village – and, at the centre of the circular road, forming an octagonal shape, the Fung Tak Estate. Finally he closed his eyes.

Tomorrow, he thought before he fell back to sleep, listening to the quiet sound of Jun's breathing.

Saturday
19 August 2017

When Alex opened his eyes he saw Jun's truncated right arm waving slowly in the air above her bed. It was nearly ten and she had woken an hour before. He watched it make slow circular motions then bend at the elbow and straighten and cautiously raise itself from the bed. He stood up and she turned her head to see him.

She smiled at him weakly, eyes strained and tired. After a moment, the smile lost its shape and dipped into the painful crescent before tears.

'I'm sorry,' he said, and bent his head towards hers. He pressed his cheek hard against Jun's and she brought her arms around his neck. He could feel one hand and the absence of the other.

'I'm so sorry,' he repeated softly into her ear. 'I looked for you and waited, but it wasn't you. I didn't know what to do but just wait.'

They cried together. After some minutes he continued: 'I'm going to find this man . . . I will find him.'

Jun said nothing, her eyes still filled with tears. He took a tissue and wiped them away but they would not stop. Her arms lifted towards his face. Her left hand cupped his cheek but she was not yet fully aware of the loss of the other. Her bandaged wrist landed heavily against his neck. As her eyes widened in shock she gave a scream.

'It's okay, sweetheart. It's okay,' he soothed her.

Jun shook her head from side to side, her mouth falling into a deep O of distress. He stroked her hair back from her wet face. There was a knock at the door and Alex turned to see a Western woman in a white doctor's coat.

'Hi, I'm Dr Norrington, I've come to speak to Jun. I'm the psychologist here. Maybe you could let us have a chat?'

'She's very tired and upset.'

'Yes, she's in shock.' She spoke quietly. 'Please will you give us a little time together? I'd like to speak to her. It's important we talk a little. Just quickly, do you have other family? Children?'

'No, not yet.' He paused. 'Her parents are in Beijing and she is my family.'

Alex turned back to Jun and stroked her cheeks and patted her left hand.

'I'm going to leave you with the doctor, she says you and she must speak.'

Jun looked up searchingly into Alex's face. Her eyes locked on to his, then ranged slowly across his face, returning repeatedly to his eyes. She said nothing. He squeezed her hand a little then kissed her and left the room, to stand outside and watch through the window as the doctor began speaking.

Yi suddenly appeared next to him, wrapped in a hospital dressing gown, her face pale and tired.

'How is your wife?' she said.

'In great difficulty. Let's sit over here,' he suggested, pointing to a row of chairs a few metres down the corridor.

They sat down together.

'How are you?' he asked. 'I'm sorry I haven't been to see you. The nurse told me you were unharmed but sedated.'

'Fine, I guess. I was unharmed, but I'm very scared.' She brought her knees up to her chest and hugged them close. 'I got a message telling me that Inspector De Suza will be coming to interview me. You're not going to do it yourself then? I don't remember anything at all apart from a knock on the door ... I went to open it and ...' Yi's usual certainty and calm had deserted her. Her elfin face looked sharp-angled and drawn after the events of the night.

'Take it easy,' he said. 'You may remember something later. God, I'm so sorry I brought you into this. I need to tell you, I've been suspended. That is why it's Mike who will interview you and not me. So this is off the record. Is that okay?'

'Why? What have you done wrong?'

'Nothing wrong. I'll be able to continue.'

'Well, like I say, I saw nothing. The doorbell rang, I couldn't see through the spyhole, so I answered it. I'd barely got the latch up when the door was thrown open so hard it knocked me backwards. I didn't see who did it. I felt a pinch, which was a needle going in, and I was out. I think I was carried in a suitcase or trunk after that, because when I woke this morning my muscles ached and were cramped as if I'd been bending for long periods. I remember nothing about it.'

Alex grabbed Yi's hand and squeezed it.

'I need your help. I want this person.'

'I'll do what I can. What do you need?'

'I picked you up because he called me. We tracked the call and I found a phone, Jun's phone, with a message telling me to wait. I did, then I was told where to go next and I found you. I went back this morning to check a hunch and I think I found something. I'd like your advice on it, is that okay?'

He touched her hand hesitantly and Yi gripped his in return.

'Sure. I'm very sorry about Jun.'

'Thank you. I'll meet you in your room in fifteen minutes.'

She nodded.

Alex stood outside in the corridor, staring through the window and watching Dr Norrington standing over Jun's bed. The doctor was talking. It didn't appear that Jun was replying. Norrington was a warm sunny blonde in her late forties. She was wearing a simple white blouse under her white coat, and a pencil skirt with heels. Alex looked at her face, which had engaging freckles. She had earrings that looked to be of Indian origin. She stood there smiling, one hand on the bars close to Jun's head.

Alex tapped on the window and pointed to the map on the camp bed. The doctor picked it up and came over to the door. She opened it and held the map out for Alex to take.

'How is she?' he asked.

'Not very good. She's withdrawn and silent. Obviously losing a hand presents multiple problems . . . loss of function, damage to body image, loss of sensation . . . but in Jun's case there's also the nature of the way she lost it. The violence and fear have pushed her deep into herself. There may be resentment and deep self-doubt. Jun is a strong woman and I believe highly educated, but she is also beautiful, and a loss like this could make her feel very insecure. A quick question for you?'

'Anything. Please just tell me what you need.'

'Would you say she is a person who is very image-conscious?'

'Yes. She was an arts student and a dancer, very intelligent and with a sense of perspective . . . well, sometimes anyway.' He smiled. 'You're right, she's strong. She is very image-conscious at the moment, but it was not always so pronounced. Just since arriving in Hong Kong really.'

The doctor followed Alex's changing expressions and listened carefully.

'Thank you, that's very helpful. Will you be remaining in the hospital?'

'Yes. I'll leave my mobile number at the duty desk. Should I talk to her?'

'Yes, but not about recent events. She needs a lot of time to work through them by herself. Just talk and don't push for any replies. Basically, don't increase her anxiety level.'

Alex picked out an English accent similar to Lucy's. 'You're from London?' he asked.

'Well, west of there, Bristol. But I studied in London before coming here with my husband, who is a local obs. and gynae. up at the Mathilda. How did you know?'

'My wife has a friend who has the same way of speaking as you do.' Alex swallowed nervously. 'Should I ask her friends to come and see her? They'll soon start asking me where she is, as she didn't show up for dinner with them last night and they'll want to know why.'

'I think you should leave it for a few days. Just tell them she had an accident but is recovering and that they can see her soon.'

Alex looked at Jun. While they had been speaking, she had raised the head of the bed and was now sitting up a little. She turned her face to the window and held up her right hand, observing the stump silhouetted against the light. As before, she moved it about slowly, turning it round above her, swaying a little, almost floating in the air. He watched her gaze at this new unknown and unwelcome form.

'How long do you need with her?' he asked.

The doctor had continued to study Alex even though his focus was on Jun.

'Maybe another thirty minutes. Why don't you come back at around eleven a.m.?'

'Okay, I'll be back then.'

But Alex stayed a little longer. The doctor watched him blinking hard to quell tears. 'It's good you'll be here for her,' she said.

He turned sharply to face her. 'Yes, but I'm the reason this happened.' He checked himself. 'Sorry. Thank you so much, doctor.'

He walked off to the duty desk, where he left a note with his mobile number then walked down the corridor to Yi's room.

Alex found Yi lying on the bed watching the television fixed to the opposite wall. CNN was following the preparations for the arrival of the various members of the Group of Eight and Outreach Five at the Hong Kong Convention Centre, only a mile from the hospital, at the harbour's edge. There were long, deep pens full of demonstrators confined to an area about a hundred metres away from the entrance to the Centre. People were already sweltering under the harsh mid-August sun, pressing forward with their banners and placards.

'Police estimate that today's event has attracted more demonstrators than last year's First of July Pro-Democracy rally, which totalled 400,000 people.' The reporter went on to read out some of the messages on the placards, which stressed the fate of a wasted generation of youth, highly educated yet without employment, and the plight of the poor and the elderly, lives threatened by welfare cuts and fallen asset values.

The camera panned along the front row of screaming protesters to show a mass of people dressed in traditional costume, the men in dark red-collared long black flowing *maquas* reaching almost to the floor, black Western-style trousers and black slippers; the women in black cheongsams with deep red collars, and wearing high heels. They were all very elegant and none of them looked older than their early thirties. Many were recording events on their tablets and mobiles, and three held up a banner calling for the rejection of any European compromise on repayment.

The anchorwoman went up to one of the demonstrators. 'Sir, can you tell us what brings you here today?' She stuck the microphone in the face of a tall tanned young man, with a clean-cut open face and an engaging smile. He cocked his head back slightly and replied, slowly and clearly.

'We're here to make it plain that it is high time China reasserted itself. To help Europe, we purchased massive amounts of bonds and they agreed to financial objectives and guidelines, which they have failed to observe and meet.' His speech started to quicken. 'They suggested these terms, and they defaulted. The worst of it is, they don't even abide by their own rules. They overspent again, but not with their money this time. We're here to request that our government stands up for the people whose money they used to buy these bonds, and demand that the Europeans break into their prized assets. We wield no power in the IMF or the World Bank. It's time for us to seize control.'

He finished speaking and the camera swung back to the reporter.

'No longer weak and feeble . . . That is what one man thinks, and others believe it too, with rioting and demonstrating in support of these views breaking out in most Chinese cities yesterday and today.'

'Do you think that's the Boxer red they're wearing?' Alex asked over the commentary.

'It might be . . . but it's quite understated,' Yi replied.

'What else can you tell me about the importance of the trigrams in the Boxer sects?' He recalled his wife's face with a shudder.

'They are vitally important, adding substance to the Boxers' belief system. Without that reinforcement the Boxers are just groups of robbers and murderers with a peasant following. These rituals and symbols are crucial to the Boxer narrative, lending it legitimacy and purpose.'

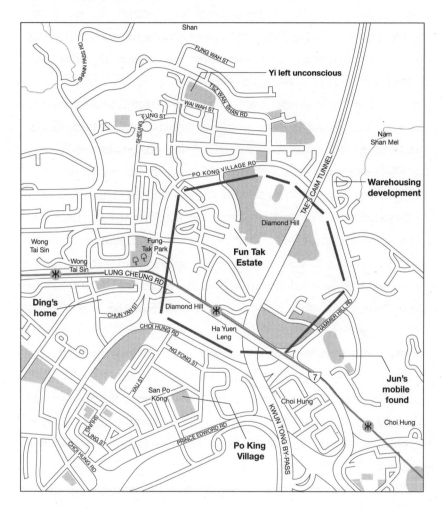

Alex produced the map on which he had outlined Po Kong Village Road, Hammer Hill Road and Choi Hung Road. 'I wanted to get your comment on this.' He pointed. 'Here, you can see these three roads form a circle. If you link the sites along them as I've indicated, you can easily see that they create an eight-sided shape. San Po Kong, the village, was where the workers' and anti-colonialist riots started in 1967. It is in the south, or yin position. It represents the *earth*, the feminine side, a place of birth, the beginning of the journey. Look . . .

'I found you to the north-west of the eight sides of the road, which corresponds to the trigram – *the valley*. I found Jun's phone to the south-east, or as it is described in the Taoist I Ching Octagram – *the mountain*. The warehouse where the container was found is to the north-east – *wind*. Now one of the people possibly connected with this is a police officer who lives to the south-west . . . that is the position of the *thunder* trigram.

'I believe there will be significant references at all the points. You mentioned the ninth trigram, which is at the centre, or *the compass*. There must be something significant at the centre of the circular road, most likely in the old Fung Tak Estate.'

Even lying flat in a hospital bed, Yi seemed captivated by the possibilities implied by the map. 'There's never been any research into the use of topography in the ritual of these sects because Chinese cities were originally planned by the Imperial elite. The sects never had that kind of power as far as we know. If you're right, this would be unprecedented evidence of their continued existence and power.'

Alex picked up his phone and punched in a number from memory. 'Sai Wong?'

'Alex, I was expecting you to call. Can I just ring you back?'

The phone went dead and he waited. The room phone rang and Yi answered it. She listened and then passed it to him. 'It's Mr Wong.'

'This is a safer line,' Sai Wong's voice announced. 'The Captain mentioned you might call. I know you're officially suspended but he thought you might need some help.'

'I do. I need you to go to Bernadine Fu's room at the Marriott and collect her bags. You know where we are.'

'Okay . . . Anything else?'

'I need to view some security footage from a memory card. Can you bring a laptop?'

'Okay, see you in about forty-five minutes.'

Alex replaced the receiver and looked down at Yi, now propped against the pillows of her bed watching the coverage of the protests.

'Just a single spark, that's all it's going to take,' she murmured.

'I agree. Think about all the small uprisings over the last seven years . . . The European debt is of even wider concern. I believe it will be the flashpoint – I just don't know how.'

The demonstrators on screen pushed against the barriers, shouting and waving their banners, cautiously, almost politely, knowing though that in Asia attendance in itself is a powerful statement.

'Think of the hundreds of millions of voices using the internet,' said Yi. 'They cannot be shut off now. Ever. There are simply too many of them.'

'Would you join them if you could?' Alex asked.

'Ten years ago, absolutely. But my job offers me a good future, and I love my home in the US.'

'Maybe the foreigners want China in chaos, and have achieved their aim either way? We've been fooled again . . . and our man is the biggest fool of them all, giving them exactly what they want.'

'I don't think so. These people, they are going to provide him with the flame, and the internet the fuel. I think chaos is part of his ritual. His ultimate goal is the rebirth that comes afterwards. The Chinese ascendancy.'

A reporter came on screen and recounted the arrival of the diplomatic forward teams from the various countries. It was expected that the Chinese would arrive last as a gesture of protest. Suddenly individuals with megaphones were hoisted up on shoulders and held above the crowds. The cameras swung round to capture them. They waited until they were on screen then started chanting in unison. What had seemed to be a scattered and disorganized mob of five hundred thousand people was looking increasingly well choreographed and structured. Soon every voice was raised to proclaim the foreign devils to be liars and thieves.

A hard knock on Yi's hospital room door announced Sai Wong's arrival.

'I got your bags but it's hell out there, man.' He propped them against the wall. 'I brought you a computer and mine too. Tell me what you want me to do.'

Alex threw him the ScanDisk memory card the security guard had given him and Yi crouched over her now open bags, pulling out clean clothes.

'We're going to use the hospital as our base so that I can remain here as much as possible,' Alex explained. 'Can you look through this video footage? There's a shot there of a man on a bench. He gets up and leaves a phone. I need everything you can get on him.

'Yi, I nearly forgot, there was a question too. Last night our unknown man boasted that he had stood where the gods stood, on the greatest of the five until the foreigners desecrated it. Is there any chance this is a lead?'

She smiled widely at him. 'That's an easy one. He was on the Immortal Bridge at Mount Tai in Shandong province . . . back to the Boxers again.'

'The Immortal Bridge? I like the sound of that. Where's it at?' Sai Wong interrupted, speaking from behind his laptop screen.

'You spend all day on the internet and you don't even know where the gods stood?' Yi quipped. 'Look it up.'

Sai Wong thumped at his computer and relayed what he had discovered.

'It's four massive rocks that lock together to cross a great chasm. Pretty spectacular. Mount Tai is a place of many temples, the centre of much that is Chinese Taoism and Confucianism, and the most revered of the five sacred mountains. An old saying goes: *If Mount Tai is at peace, so is the entire country.*'

'Your man's words suggest he believes that Mount Tai has not been at peace since the foreigners came,' Yi put in. 'Give me some time to consider what he meant.'

Alex nodded to her and then looked at Sai Wong.

'Thank you, both of you.'

Back in the corridor, he walked slowly to Jun's room. Earlier he had watched her examining her arm and its hard dead end. The blankness in her eyes, the still coldness in her expression, had scared him. They were things he didn't recognize in her, aspects of a woman no longer familiar. He stood outside and looked at her through the window. She was sleeping again. A nurse was checking her pulse as he entered.

'We have sedated your wife as she suddenly became very anxious,' the nurse explained.

'Did she speak?'

'No, I'm afraid she didn't, but it is very early yet. She's still in shock, needs a lot more time.' The nurse spoke matter-of-factly, and as she did she continued to tidy Jun's bed and clean her face. 'I'll leave you two together,' she said finally.

When she'd gone Alex took his wife's left hand, felt the familiar soft skin under his fingers. He looked at her other arm, and looked away. She slept deeply, her peaceful face more recognizable than it had been this morning. He knelt down and put his cheek against hers again, then closed his eyes and tried to forget everything except Jun. He remembered her demand two days before that he should not tell her anything about his world. She had said she could not live with such ugliness; now there was no escaping it.

Alex cried, clenching his jaw hard to suppress the noise inside him. His hands gripped the bars of her bed and shook with terrible sadness. He wiped his eyes. She was still sleeping. He wished she could wake to find it all just a gruesome dream. Eventually he left her room and headed back to Yi's.

As he approached he saw them both looking up at the TV screen. The presenter said that the Germans had already arrived and were now installed in the Centre. It was expected that the French and British ministers would arrive shortly. Initially it had been agreed that all the ministers would arrive together, to provide a show of unity, but this faltered as soon as the Chinese declared they would not enter the room until everyone else was already round the table. The presenter explained that the rumour was the Chinese finance minister had no intention of arriving for at least twenty minutes after the others, of whom the Russians were expected to be the last. The process of arrival might continue for another two or three more hours of politicking and gamesmanship.

This delay allowed even greater numbers of people to gather outside, and there now seemed to be a concerted plan to push policing to its limit. People generally remained behind the barriers but there were constant surges into the no-go zone. Onlookers had also gathered in their thousands on rooftops and in hotels nearby.

'It's looking pretty hairy out there,' Sai Wong commented. 'And you need to see the activity on the internet and the bandwidth traffic. It's intense. There seems to be a general sense of anticipation that something is going down. People are speculating there is going to be an attack by Anonymous, or else religious or nationalist terrorists. Some people are actually hoping that there'll be a bomb, to rid the world of corrupt politicians. There's also a lot of activity in the big mainland cities where riots are beginning.

'I know it sounds off the wall,' the kid said hesitantly, 'but there's something at work here – something very deep. Everyone is pushing each other along.'

Alex grunted, reluctant to confirm what he had intuited.

'What have you got for me?'

'Okay, video first. The man sitting on the bench was a big guy. I've enhanced and cleaned the noise off the footage, and if we know the height of the bench we can calculate his height.'

'The bench is forty-eight centimetres high.'

Sai Wong looked back at his computer. He spoke while he worked.

'Very good . . . then the guy's height is about one hundred and ninety-two to ninety-three centimetres. I mapped his shape from the back and I reckon he probably weighs two hundred pounds . . . so, as I say, quite a big guy, but not real big.

'And about your theory of Po Kong Village Road and Hammer Hill Road being some sort of eight-sided ritual space, like the Taoist trigrams . . . I peeked into some satellite footage for you and can tell you that there are a few old factories at the centre, but imagery shows only one with a lot of activity during the last few years. Repairs to the front exterior, people coming and going every month or so. If the Boxer Rebellion's eight-sided symbol has any relevance here then this old warehouse at the compass point has to be worth checking out.

'I also ran the data on overseas Chinese travel, but the Chinese government didn't keep computer records in the late Seventies. So I looked into people leaving from Hong Kong, and that database is quite extensive. Then I looked into boarding houses, friendship hotels, and later, in the Nineteen Eighties, international hotels, near Mount Tai, which gives us the names of some visitors even if the records are incomplete.' Sai Wong flipped his laptop round on his knees. 'You say your man was very interested in Mount Tai, so he may have stayed for a while, which was rare back then unless you were an academic. So . . .'

The screen showed a long list of names. Alex picked up the laptop and started to scroll down the list. 'How many?' he asked.

'Just under eight thousand men are recorded as visiting Mount Tai between Nineteen Seventy-Nine and Nineteen Eighty-Six.'

'How did you decide on the dates?'

'Nineteen Seventy-Eight/Nine was the beginning of the Open Door Policy, when China first declared foreigners, which included overseas Chinese, welcome to visit. Nineteen Eighty-Seven was when UNESCO declared Mount Tai a World Heritage Site, which I believe is the time this man believes the place was contaminated by foreigners. It's unlikely he means literally, because there have been foreigners passing through there for centuries.'

'That makes good sense,' Alex nodded. 'So we need to narrow this down further. We know what he wants: revolution and a new nationalism, to put China on top. Let's focus on the possible visit to Mount Tai. Like virtually everyone else he is unlikely to have been able to visit without innumerable State approvals until Nineteen Eighty-Four or Eighty-Five, two or three years before the UNESCO Declaration. Unless he worked for UNESCO himself, which is hard to believe. At the very least he'd have to be eighteen or nineteen to get the visa to travel alone, so if he travelled at the youngest age of eighteen in Nineteen Eighty-Four he'd now be forty-nine or fifty. To do what he's done today he's unlikely to be older than seventy now, so in Nineteen Eighty-Four he'd be thirty-nine or forty at the oldest. I reckon he wouldn't have been as young as eighteen in Nineteen Eighty-Four. He's educated, probably a university graduate, so he most likely went after university, which means he's more likely in his fifties now, or early sixties. So we're looking for someone who was between twenty-five and his early thirties back in the mid- to late Eighties. I think he was at the lunch I attended two days ago, and if so, then he's a big guy, tall and broad.

'We also know this man is trying to incite rage and anger. He's capable of sick and disturbing acts. And he's not just pissed off at the system, he has followed the narrative of the Boxers, identifying strongly with their cause and methods. He wants to bring Chinese people together against the rest of the world. He has waited for this moment a long time. But there's an underlying rage and fury that stems from more than just politics and was possibly even more overt and uncontrolled in his youth. It's possible he demonstrated and protested, stood at gates and shouted and waved banners.'

'Your point being?' asked Sai Wong.

'There were many housing protests in Hong Kong between Nineteen Eighty-One and Nineteen Ninety. These were led both by community activists, the new young and educated Hong Kong Chinese looking to participate in the decision-making process, and the Housing Movement activists, who rallied against the unequal distribution of housing resources. This was one of the big issues of the day. Our man had to have been there . . . younger, yes, but still a big man amongst shorter people. And he would have been at the front because that is his nature.'

'All this assumes he's native to Hong Kong. What if he's a mainlander or American Born Chinese, or from anywhere in the world?' Sai Wong queried.

Alex smiled.

'In the Eighties travel around the country for a mainlander was pretty difficult. One couldn't just go where one liked, if he'd been a Chinese national it's unlikely he would have got there. It would have been easier as a foreigner. If we're right about the roads around Po Kong Village, Choi Hung and so on then he's local. It's all about that area of Hong Kong.'

He looked at the two earnest faces.

'I'll go check out this old factory. You get over to the Radio and Television Hong Kong offices, and ask for whatever footage RTHK may still have of those demonstrations.'

'Will do.' Sai Wong poked around in his postal bag. 'Oh, I found this on my desk earlier. No note, just your name on it.' He tossed Alex a Glock G4 34 with xenon light and laser sighting. Alex caught it and turned it over in his hand.

'Competition gun. Who left you this?'

'No idea.' Sai Wong moved on quickly. 'Here,' he flipped the laptop around, 'take a look at a detailed satellite image of the warehouse on Fung Tak Estate.' One outsize finger pointed to the screen. 'These are the entrances: one large front double door, probably locked, and two small side doors, to left and right sides. I reckon the best way in is to rip out one of the extractor fans at the rear. The building is sixty years old. That metalwork will be rusted to nothing. One quick shake and it should just pull out.'

Alex nodded and left Sai Wong to pack up. The duty nurse pushed her head round the door.

'Professor Yi, how are you feeling?'

'I am fine, thank you, Sister.'

'I see you are all working in here,' she said in a disapproving tone. 'Well, I'll leave you to it so long as you promise not to overdo it. I'll look in on you again at three-thirty.'

'We'll see you back here,' Yi said softly.

Alex left and headed quickly towards Jun's room to look in on her. She was still sedated. He kissed her and lightly touched the bridge of her nose. He tried not to look at her handless right arm, then pulled himself up and went directly to his car.

Fung Tak Estate had once been one of the poorest areas of Hong Kong, the slum housing of Diamond Hill nearby creating a haven for drug-dealers and illegal gambling dens. With an endless supply of cheap labour, it became a good location to build a factory, but during the last thirty years most had been demolished to create public housing, though a patchwork of deserted warehouses, broken office spaces and old factories remained scattered across the area.

Alex parked in an archway underneath some industrial piping and walked quickly down an alleyway between two high walls to the rear of the disused property Sai Wong had shown him. There were signs of repair around the windows, which had been painted black to keep out prying eyes. Along the rear wall he found the area Sai Wong had highlighted. The rusted fans were three metres from the ground, just below the eaves. Alex would need to climb the nearby building and leap on to the roof of the warehouse to remove the fan-installation unit from above. The climb and leap were easy but the fan was stubborn. He sat on the edge of the roof and pushed the top of the unit hard with his feet. After a few seconds it gave way a little and he was able to reach down and pull it out. He laid it beside him, then sat still for a few moments to listen for any movement inside, but nothing stirred. He lay flat on the roof and dropped his head slowly into the hole to peer down the ducting.

Blackness.

His eyes adjusted and he saw a dim light at the end of the wide rectangular void. Grabbing the top edge of the hole, he swung himself inside and eased downwards, hoping that whatever was holding it in place could take the added strain of his weight. The dim light ahead resolved itself into a broader blue-grey hue coming from the main factory space visible through the metal filter at the end of the shaft. Once he had crawled to the face of the filter, he could see through its slats to a large dark space below about the size of half a football pitch. It seemed to be unoccupied at present. In the centre stood a table and eight chairs.

He pushed the filter a little and felt it give beneath the pressure. Another push produced a gap that allowed him to see that the retaining screws had rusted significantly. Using his knife, he worked at the body of each screw until he had cut and stabbed through the fragile rusted metal and the filter felt loose. He took off his watch and fed the strap between the slats of the filter, looping it round his finger. When he pushed the slats harder it dislodged, but was prevented from falling by the leather watchstrap. He peered out on to the factory floor, worried there might be guard dogs.

Nothing.

On the walls he could see the vague outline of faces. Aside from the table, chairs and images, there was nothing else. He refastened his watch and lowered himself into the factory space, dropping down around three metres.

The floor was covered in dark red lines, previously invisible from above. He turned towards the desk at the centre. Inscribed upon it was the character '*jen*' with eight others at equidistant points along the circumference of the table: the eight trigrams. It had a dark-wood trim, perhaps mahogany, with blood-red marble for the main surface.

He looked up and shone his torch against one wall. The picture it revealed was enormous. Swinging the beam across, he saw that it was repeated over and over again: the grainy image of a Chinese woman and man, perhaps from the beginning of the twentieth century. He wore a loose-fronted jacket and a broad diagonal red sash, staring heroically into the camera lens with fierce eyes. She stood proudly at his shoulder, barely a step behind. Her hair was pulled up and back, covered with a red turban, head held high and resolute. Most of the reproductions of the image focused on a specific element of their faces: her eyes, lips and fingers and the man's eyes and fists.

Alex's torch travelled slowly across the images, some reaching four or five metres high. On top of them someone had painted characters and added huge volumes of text – copied and enlarged and then pasted on. His phone began to vibrate. It was Ying.

'Soong, I thought I'd let you sleep in.'

'How can I help?'

'I've taken the case in a different direction. Lo was so scared he committed suicide in front of us. Whoever he was afraid of must be even more powerful and more committed than he was.'

'Yes, I would agree with that.'

'So I'm going back to Lo's organization to find out more. Just wanted you to know. I didn't believe your line of thinking was yielding anything useful.'

Alex looked around the factory walls and smiled.

'Okay, I understand. Good luck.'

'I'll let De Suza keep you updated. Enjoy your suspension.'

'Thanks.' He almost hung up before he asked: 'Oh, where is Mike?'

'He's about to go help with the conference.'

'Okay, thank you.'

Alex swept round the walls with the torch until he found one of the two single doors. He also saw a light switch. Fully illuminated, the scope and breadth of the images on the walls left him almost in awe at the obsession and commitment they revealed. The photo was repeated perhaps three or four hundred times, from floor to roof. At nearly five metres high, the largest of these were vague and grainy, and someone had applied black paint to the outlines of the woman's lips, eyes and hair to increase the resolution. Red lines were painted round the outline of the man's fists and arms; in some places his head was outlined in red as well, with bold characters painted across his waist.

'Insane. Completely insane,' Alex whispered to himself.

His phone vibrated.

'Alex, it's Sai Wong. We're at RTHK but they won't lend me the footage of the housing protests without written authority.'

'Okay, we can't use that method. What are the options?'

'I can access their digital stores. When they license any footage they upload it to the buyer. I can hack into the system the next time they upload something.'

'Fine, just do it.'

'Okay, I'll go back to the hospital to work. What have you found?'

'I've not found anyone living, but I have found this man's or group's headquarters or altar, the guiding compass. It's a shrine, nothing else. Now I just need to get out.'

'Are the doors alarmed?'

'Yup,' Alex sighed.

'Climb up back into the ventilation shaft if you can . . .'

'It starts three metres above me so that's out.'

Alex stood and looked around him at the huge images and then focused on the best place to start a fire. 'Okay, please get that footage as quickly as you can.'

'Will do.'

'And I'll be sending you some photos of this place. Please can you show them to Yi?'

He took as many shots as he could, and sent them to Sai Wong. Then he stared at the madness on the walls, all around him the obsession that had caused harm to Jun. Alex thought of the stump and shouted into the air above. He looked at the table of heretical Chinese symbols and eyes plastered over the walls staring at him. It should all be destroyed.

Above him were eight floodlights, each centred on one of the chairs. Alex followed the wires to the electrical mains box and pulled off the cover to reveal a standard industrial junction box. He groped on the floor by the walls and eventually found a nail. After switching off the mains, he extracted the fuse for the circuit to the floodlights and inserted the nail. He went back into the main area and pulled out one of the wall lighting fixtures, stripped out the wires and reconnected them loosely, but this time wrapped with paper stripped from one of the photos off the wall. At the junction box he switched the mains back on. The loose connection buzzed loudly. Alex stood under the light and watched it short and heat up. He looked round once more and walked over to the marble table. Placing the barrel of his gun at the centre of the character *jen*, he fired a shot into the red marble to erase the blasphemy of the ancient Confucian symbol.

He smelled smoke behind him; the paper was alight and the electrical connection continued to feed it. Flames ran from the paper round the wires to the walls. Soon the whole surface was ablaze and spreading towards the adjacent walls at both ends. The images stayed visible in parts, surrounded by curling yellow and bright orange. The door alarm went off as soon as Alex shot through the lock and kicked it open. He ran back to the car, called the fire department then Sai Wong.

'Anything?'

'Yes, got in while I was in the taxi back. I'm halfway through the download.'

'Okay, see you in twenty minutes.'

Alex pulled away in a hurry, reversing out fast from under the cover of the huge piping and down the narrow alley between the warehouses. In the rear-view mirror he could see smoke coming from the burning shrine. He drove through Hung Hom towards Kowloon tunnel.

As his car circled towards the tunnel entrance Sai Wong called him back on the speakerphone. 'The guy's a freak.'

'Look, we've got something interesting for you,' said Yi's voice. 'Turn around.'

Alex was in a single lane, so he quickly mounted the kerb to make room to manoeuvre. He swung a hard left U-turn across the road, causing traffic around him to screech to a halt, and put his police siren on to move cars to one side.

'Done.'

She continued. 'That image you sent is of a Boxer woman, a red lantern. There's no special historical significance to her, though she certainly looks a formidable personality. Powerful and striking. We didn't need to look through the footage for long to find a tall man, one hundred and ninety centimetres or more, attending rallies and protests at the specified time. Sai Wong ran the photos through the immigration system and there was nothing, but there was a hit from the Hong Kong Law Society, which identified this man as Seng Pok, a local real estate attorney with a practice in Wan Chai. I'll hand you back to Sai Wong now.'

'Hey! The guy owns an old godown that's sited just south of the warehouse development where the container was located, in the due east position of the octagram, *K'an* – water. Seng Pok appears at the front of every rally and protest in the Eighties and early Nineties that we have viewed. He's one angry guy. There are also letters to local newspapers from him, protesting against Chinese exploiting each other.'

'Does he have any family?'

Sai Wong paused. 'I found a newspaper article from Nineteen Eighty-Two. It says his father was murdered, stabbed by some of his fellow workers when he tried to stop them from joining the riots in Nineteen Sixty-Seven. They trapped his hand in a press and then stabbed him repeatedly and left him there to die. A Mr Chan came to free him and he was badly beaten as well, died on the spot. Seng's father was taken to hospital and died some days later. He was generally branded a traitor to the workers by the local community, loyal only to the *gweilo* owners. The factory was on the site of the building you just visited. There's nothing else about him. Or, if there was, then it's been deleted.'

The car raced through Hung Hom and up towards Choi Hung again.

'Okay, keep looking. Where exactly am I going?'

Alex passed through the monotonous blocks and tenements of Choi Hung and into the industrial wasteland he had entered two nights before.

'Turn right so the industrial warehouse development is on your left. Run the perimeter of the development for a few minutes and there should be six old godowns ahead. It's the last on your right.'

'Thanks. Can you update me on the situation at the talks?'

As he talked Alex rounded a final bend on to an expanse of tall wild grass growing over the rubble from demolished buildings. A hundred metres ahead he saw the familiar arches and curved roofs of traditional nineteenth-century storehouses, the location of the first commerce between Chinese people and the white devils.

'It's getting a bit rough there,' Sai Wong reported. 'It's been nearly two hours since the Germans arrived and it's understood the Russians are now on their way. The news reports say that the Chinese will arrive in an hour, so the other envoys will have been waiting for at least three. Some violent demonstrations are breaking out in mainland cities.'

'What about the internet traffic on this?'

'Increased about eight- or ninefold, which is now a few hundred million. Lots of anger at Western laziness and arrogance. Lots of speculation linking the recent murders to a Western conspiracy. It's seriously moved on since yesterday, almost a frenzy now.'

Compared with the massive modern industrial warehousing development to the north, the godowns were simple and tidy, long vaulted halls decorated with touches of elegance. Each had three whitewashed walls and faded coloured signage at the front. The first two Alex passed on his right had once sold textiles; two on his left sold rice and another salt. The last one on the right was unmarked, but although the door looked to be as old as the others it also appeared to be securely locked and the security grilles on the windows to either side were well maintained.

He drove past for another fifty metres then parked in the long grass for cover. He inspected the Glock 34 and checked its seventeen rounds; these were all he had, which meant he'd need to improvise when possible to save ammunition.

He crouched low in the grass and looked towards the building Sai Wong had identified. As with many godowns, the long walls were windowless, but as Alex skirted the building he could see air-conditioning units at the back, partly concealed by a screen wall set close to the rear of the building, which also concealed a parked car, an old Ford Escape. It was likely that Seng and whoever else knew of the destruction of their 'compass' in Fung Tak would be making preparations to leave, so Alex decided to disable the car first then use the same method of entry as he had at the factory. He also needed a decoy, and a couple of small fire bombs would distract Seng and whoever else was inside, giving him time to enter.

He kept wide of the building until he was parallel to the rear wall then ran in fast and low to the car, drew his knife and swiftly punctured the tyres. No cameras above him; they would have been too obvious a sign of use, Alex thought. At the base of the wall lay some empty plastic water bottles. He cut the top off one and placed it under the gas tank. He worked the hard tip of the ColdSteel blade through the gas tank and the fuel started to drain out. Petrol streamed into the container and then steadily on to the dusty ground below. Using his jacket to muffle the sound, he smashed the driver's seat window and cut and ripped the seating upholstery into strips.

He inspected the air-conditioning units. These were standard, three in a row, simply pushed into metal-framed cavities resting on platforms fixed to the wall. When he pulled a little at the first, it gave way easily. He manoeuvred all three units out of their metal framing to the point where they were very loose and could be pulled out in quick succession. Finding two empty glass soda bottles among the discards, he poured the petrol into them and created small Molotov cocktails with nice long tails from the strips of upholstery. He lit them then carefully set them down, and slipped the three units from their fittings.

He fired shots through the first and second holes as light poured into the building. Through the third he threw the Molotov cocktails, as far as he could into the space inside, and then jumped through the same hole, hoping to avoid flames and any gunfire.

As he fell through he saw that the bottle had hit the tops of some metal shelving three or four metres high and assembled in a labyrinthine structure. Books and filing boxes on it already burned brightly, revealing further shelving beyond that filled the building. He landed hard and a gunshot struck the wall close by. He looked to left and right but could see only the many branching rows of shelves with multiple passageways between them.

A familiar voice spoke.

'Senior Inspector Soong, you're in the wrong place. You're wasting your time.'

'Why keep hiding from me, Seng?'

The voice had come from somewhere in the interior of the maze, but he could not tell from where.

'I'm here, just keep coming,' it commanded.

Alex continued a stealthy but rapid movement down the passageways that seemed to lead in the general direction of the centre. These were dimly lit and barely wide enough for one person to use.

'Why did you do that to my wife?' he called.

'I didn't.' Silence for a few moments. 'I did it to you,' the voice finished.

'I'm going to kill you.'

'Yes, I know.'

Alex looked up for cameras and noticed several, but there could be a hundred. With only seventeen rounds, shooting them out was impossible. There was no need in any case. He understood now that this man was not intending to run away. Like the others caught up in his *mise-en-scène* he had fulfilled a predestined purpose. Now he was intending to die by Alex's hand. Whatever his role had been – creator, leader, or mere obsessive archivist – he had power and commitment. The man would stay. Alex tested the shelves; some could be moved but others were too heavy. Seng spoke again.

'We have been planning a long time, and when we learned you were coming to Hong Kong we thought it an interesting situation. You could have been either an asset or a liability to us.'

Behind Alex the fire was spreading. Smoke curled against the ceiling. The distraction caused by the petrol bomb had allowed him to enter unharmed but had blocked any chance of escape by the same route.

'*You* thought I would be an asset?'

'Leaders are needed and so we followed your development, enjoying your contempt for the system. But I wanted to see you face to face before we began, to be sure you would understand, and when I saw you that morning at the university I realized you might not join us unless you were broken and then rebuilt. I tried to reach out and break you down, but you'll never see, you can't be changed. You come here out of anger.'

'No, I'm here because of love.'

'Well, anger, love . . . up to you. Because of that you're in the wrong place. But you know that already. This is a dead end.'

'What do you mean?'

'Soon. You'll figure it out soon.'

The words were delivered as calmly as they had been in the pitch darkness of the warehouse two nights before.

'Changing everything? A very ambitious plan,' Alex commented, still edging his way forward.

'No more ambitious than your grandfather on the Long March or your father with the Open Door Policy. They both followed grand ideas that sought to lead the people and change the country. Except now these ideas are simmering inside the minds of hundreds of millions . . . all connected by the speed of twenty-first-century technology . . . all tired of being told what to do by people who have done no better.'

He switched on the audio to what sounded like multiple television broadcasts and flicked through the channels. The shouting and cheering of protesters and demonstrators filled the cavernous space.

'There's no longer any need to march around the country, to visit and preach to each person like your grandfather did. They can easily discuss the ideas among themselves. They just need a reason, an event, to compel them towards the same conclusion. With each conversation, blog, news report, they unify China and propel it towards its rightful place. The Europeans have made fools of us again. We helped save them from their own greed, buying their stinking debt, and they treat us with the same contempt they showed us a hundred and fifty years ago. But as a nation we now are strong. We have people, money and military might. The true self-strengthening movement was never defeated. This is the legacy of the Boxers.'

'So it is our turn to humiliate the West, bring them to their knees?' Alex stepped forward cautiously, realizing he was approaching open space. 'Is that really going to help? Don't we need to show that we are better than them?'

'We already have. They took our money, like they took our

silver, silk and land before, and when they couldn't pay then they sold us opium or made us pay "compensation". They default again because this is who they are. In them individuality is rampant, every little ego needing to be satisfied. They've broken their own laws and moral code many times before in history, and they'll break them again today. In the new world of global connection, they will show themselves for the spineless greedy cowards that they are.'

'Then why harm the two ministers, Jun and those poor people in the container?' Alex asked, inching forward.

'I am bound to my story, but once you rejected us I needed to hurt you as well. You became my enemy. Some people have desk jobs, suit and tie. We have this. Now,' Seng said with finality, 'you will shoot me in return for what was done to your wife. You must still play your role even though you rejected us. You waste time here on a personal matter when you should be elsewhere. I had hoped for better from you.

'We talked to your friend William too, you know, spent months on him. He was in so deep with the bribery and corruption in Chongqing that we thought we could persuade him to join us. But like you he went a different way, though his was more tragic. He told us a lot first though,' Seng said, with irony and satisfaction.

Ahead, through a gap in the shelving, Alex saw a central open space. Above it were television screens and at the epicentre a desk with an old chair behind it. Standing between the desk and the chair was a tall broad man in his mid-fifties. Alex recognized him from the lunch at the university two days ago. On the desk lay a severed human hand, the fingers embellished with nail polish that Alex knew well.

The man held a Type 77 Chinese pistol, but his grip looked loose and inexperienced. Alex recognized someone not used to firing a gun. This whole area was dedicated to superstition and information-gathering, not to weapons. About ten metres separated them: plenty of opportunity for Seng to miss if there was an exchange of fire.

'You're out of time,' Alex called to him.

'I know,' he replied calmly. 'But the job is done. If I can kill you it would offer a little extra for the gods.'

Despite his size and age, Seng had a handsome boyish face, with high cheekbones and a strong brow above penetrating eyes. His lips were full and he still had a thick head of black hair, cropped short.

His right hand was bandaged and hung by his side. He fired wildly twice with the other hand. When the shots went wide he sat down in the old chair and put the pistol on the edge of the desk.

'That was worth a try, but I was never much good with my left,' he said calmly, looking at his hand, then he smiled and returned to Alex. 'As you said, I'm out of time. But so are you.'

There was silence between them for a second. Alex kept the Glock pointed steadily at his target.

'Is that my wife's hand?'

'Yes.'

He kept his distance, watching the other man for any sign of movement.

'This place will burn down soon. What happens next?' he demanded.

'Soon you'll kill me so the next narrative can begin.'

'You're really crazy!'

Alex noticed the big man's rapid sideways gaze towards a clock hanging among the TV screens.

Alex looked at the laptop computer on the desk, and all the files surrounding it. Seng rested his elbows on top of the computer. Alex noticed that he leaned hard on it, perhaps protectively.

'Won't you beg for your life?' Alex challenged him.

'You don't have that power over me. When this body ends, I'll continue. Immortality is already mine. For me, the ritual is now complete.'

'So you're your own sacrifice? You know I burned down the altar to your ancestors.'

'Yes, I know. But you're wrong about the sacrifice. I made my sacrifice many years ago, a young woman.' He lost himself in thought for a moment, staring sightlessly past Alex for a few moments and then focusing intently on him.

'Who were the other seats for?'

Seng leaned back in his chair without answering. He raised his eyebrows and rubbed his chin with the palm of one hand.

'Belief is power, young man. The Chinese people are lending these events power because they believe they hold meaning. They just need one last little push . . .'

'What are you going to do?' Alex demanded.

Seng looked down at Jun's hand and lightly placed the tip of his right index finger on the varnished nail of her middle finger. Alex grimaced. Seng looked up to watch him instinctively recoil in sadness and anger.

'What's going to happen next? Tell me.' Alex lowered the gun slightly.

Seng smiled, in command of the situation.

'You already know.'

He put his index finger to the tip of the middle finger of Jun's severed hand and lifted it up and down slowly and repeatedly, as if the lifeless digit were tapping on the desk, waiting.

Alex shook his head to clear it. He raised his gun again and shot Seng in the forehead. The man was pushed back hard in the chair for a moment, then his body sagged forward over the desk. His head hit the closed laptop. Alex pulled it out and found a notebook underneath, which he collected too. He took a last look at Jun's hand, now covered in Seng's blood. The man's eyes were open, a smile fixed on his face. Alex turned away from it and called Sai Wong.

'I have a computer, can you hack into it?'

'You need to give me the IP address.'

The flames were advancing fast, devouring the dry paper and cardboard stored on the shelves.

'What else do you have?' Sai Wong urged him.

'Nothing. I have nothing solid except that there is another

event planned.' Alex looked back at the fire. 'There isn't time for the computer now . . . see you at the hospital!'

Clutching the computer and notebook under one arm he looked towards the other end of the godown, seeing more shelves and countless passageways to work his way through. He looked down at Seng's head again, wanting to put another bullet through it. But he knew that the rage he still felt would not be sated even by emptying the clip.

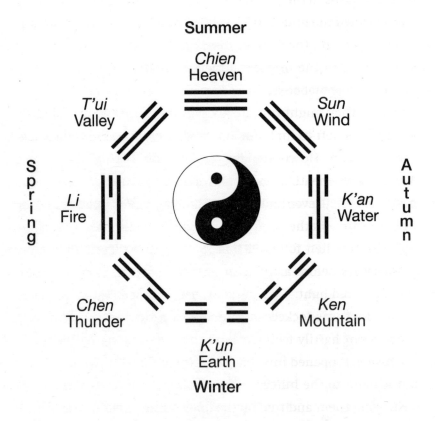

Alex ran across to the passageway to the left of the desk, hopefully aiming down the middle of the godown towards the front door. As before, he found the passage dividing again and again, but tried to stay true to the original direction. He passed shelves full of hundreds of notebooks, boxes, tapes, and piles of miscellaneous material. They might contain everything and nothing, but there was no time left to find out. Smoke was spilling into the passage ahead of him. He covered his mouth and nose and crouched down to get beneath it. Twisting and turning through the narrow passageways, he eventually emerged against the main supporting wall, unsure whether to follow it to left or right. He chose right, hit a corner then followed that, passing the entrances to more passageways before arriving at the front door. Above him there was a dim red light.

The door was locked and his first instinct was to try to kick it open, but hastily feeling round the edges, he found hinges on the inside. It opened inwards. Kicking would be futile. Instead he put his gun to the hinges and unloaded three rounds into each, destroying them and freeing the door. Using his knife, he levered the door a little out of its frame and used his fingers to prise it open. The false door behind it was merely wood, the shopfront of the old godown. He kicked it open and rushed outside, gasping and coughing. He stood in the road for a few moments, looking at the smoke rising from the burning building, then raced towards his car parked in the long grass.

On the way back to the hospital his phone vibrated.

'What?'

'It's Ying.'

'Yeah, what is it?'

'I just wanted to tell you that we found Officer Ding dead.'

'Sorry?'

'He hadn't showed up and wasn't answering his phone, so someone went to his place to look for him and found him dead. We're here now.'

'How long since he died?'

'Coroner says last night sometime. His neck was broken. Someone was looking for something in a hurry, no idea what. We've turned the place upside down and found that package from the storage depot in his locker and some rambling diaries that contain some diagrams and say his name was Tung. Ding was his mother's name. Mean anything to you?'

'No.'

'Probably nothing.'

'That package doesn't matter any more, but keep hold of it. Where's De Suza?'

'Down at the Convention Centre. Why?'

Alex hung up. He turned on his siren and raced back through Choi Hung towards the tunnel to Hong Kong Island. Time to call the Captain.

'It's Soong.'

'You're suspended.'

'I know. But I need to get into the Convention Centre.'

'Why?'

'I found the guy behind all this and he's dead. I don't know what it is, but De Suza is a part of it, I think he murdered Ding, and he's going to do something there too.'

'You need to give me more than that.'

'I don't know any more! Trust me on this . . .'

'Okay, but you'll have to get through the crowd on your own. I have your badge, remember. Approach Officer Martin Choy.'

'Sir, you'd better send people out to a burning godown outside Choi Hung, just south of the vacant warehouse development from two nights ago. There are masses of documents that might be worth saving.'

Alex hung up and dialled Yi.

'I found him and now he's dead.'

'What was he like?'

'Obsessed and yet very lucid. He began years ago, but quite possibly the whole thing started way before him. There were thousands of documents there . . . you'd have loved it. I'm going to the Convention Centre. There's a mobile command unit, you and Sai Wong should head over there.'

'So next is the G8, heh? The two ministers were the first act, then the Christians, the German, and finally some sort of action against the Eight. We'll head to the unit now.'

Their call ended, Alex sped through Hong Hum and towards the tunnel. It was relatively empty. As so many of the roads were closed to traffic and there were warnings of demonstrations, the people not already marching or protesting had stayed at home, abandoning any thought of going to the Island.

Once out of the tunnel he travelled up Gloucester Road as far as possible and had to park about two kilometres from the Convention Centre. The crowds here were vast. It would take him at least fifteen minutes to make his way through to the Centre. With the computer and notebook clasped under his left arm, his right hand pushing people out of the way, he strove to make haste, but the crowd held him back.

After twenty minutes, he reached a uniformed police office manning a barrier.

'I need to find Officer Martin Choy,' he panted.

The officer pointed to the Command Centre Alex had parked outside last night. He pushed his way through to it. 'Commanding Officer Choy?' he called.

'Yes.' An elderly officer stood up at the back of the mobile unit. His face was tough and uncompromising, with a long scar visible underneath his chin. 'Are you Soong?' he asked.

'Yes.'

'Go to that nearest part of the barrier there and they'll let you through. But first, two questions for you.'

'Sir?'

'I assume you are not carrying your *issue* firearm?'

'No. The Captain retained it and my shotgun and badge last night.'

'And do you want to leave your things with me?' Choi was pointing to the computer and notebook.

'Yes, but I need to pass them to my friends,' Alex said cautiously.

'I'll make sure they get them. You can trust me, Soong.'

Alex still felt unsure, but standing in the Command Centre surrounded by police officers there was little option but to agree.

'Sir.' He handed them to Choy, who took them and placed them on the table in front of him.

Alex started pushing his way over to the barrier again. To his left he heard glass being smashed, perhaps a shop window being broken. Tension in the crowd was running high. People shouted and pushed at each other, hostility mounting. He reached the barrier and two young officers instantly made way for him, separating the metal booms for him to pass.

Fifty metres' walk up Harbour Road, at the entrance to the Convention Centre, he looked back to see thousands of people pressing against the barriers, shouting and waving banners. Chinese brothers and sisters were finally making their feelings known to their government and the rest of the world.

Alex ran into the Convention Centre. The entrance for the ministers and their teams was in the new wing and he had to cover another four hundred metres up the escalators and mezzanine floors to reach the atrium. The meeting and breakout session would take place on the first floor in the largest of the halls.

When he arrived he found that the Chinese delegation had just entered the main hall for the introductory speeches; the Russians were ready to begin their opening statement. As Alex entered the hall he glanced around for De Suza and saw him standing next to the Chinese finance minister from Beijing, who, with his peers, was seated in a row on the stage. The Russian delegate was explaining his country's concern about the European commitment to solving the systemic financial problems of the West, which had never lived up to its own promises and ideals, repeatedly betraying them throughout history while forcing others to pay the price. That time was now at an end, he warned.

His statement finished, the Russian delegate nodded to the audience and stepped from the stage on to the floor. De Suza walked off-stage towards an exit at the back, and as he did so was replaced by another officer. Alex hurried round the perimeter of the hall towards the double doors that led backstage. Ahead of him he saw De Suza ascending a flight of metal stairs to the huge web of walkways and trussing for the lighting rigs. Alex followed.

On a high gantry directly above the stage, De Suza had begun to assemble a rifle. 'So you got here.' He concentrated on the construction of the weapon, merely glancing up quickly to show he was watching Alex's movements at the other end of the metal walkway. 'And you killed my father, I suppose? It's okay, I understand. I hoped that you would.' He locked the barrel into place as he spoke.

'Mike, what did he do to you? He was insane,' Alex said, as loudly as he dared, wanting to kill De Suza where he stood. 'And Jun was innocent!'

De Suza looked down at the weapon and stopped mid-action.

'Alex, I know. I didn't want him to do that, believe me.' There was a firm and purposeful expression on his face. 'I killed Ding for what was done to Jun. He was there and could have stopped my father.'

'Mike, what the hell are you talking about? *You* took her. It was you, it had to be. You knew what your father intended. You could have stopped it!' Alex wiped tears from his eyes. 'I should kill you . . . right here.'

De Suza continued speaking as if he had not heard the accusation. 'No, I tried to stop him. Ding took her. Look, you're going to have to kill me if you want to stop me.' Now he was inserting the bolt and reaching for the ammunition. He loaded one into the breach and clipped in a short magazine, then stood up and looked at Alex squarely.

'I'm sorry, I could never prevent him from doing anything he chose to. He killed my own mother in front of me when I was three years old. And the bastard beat me . . .' He swallowed and looked down at the rifle in his hands. 'He beat me as hard and as often as he could. Brought me up to act like a dog . . . But I believe in the work we are doing, and it is my job to finish what we started,' he said with resignation.

Alex stepped forward. Anger swelled dangerously inside him. His hand clenched around the grip of the pistol, but he kept it lowered. He did not want to use it.

'Mike, you don't need to do this. He's gone.'

'We all have our role to play. And we must play it, as you have, whether we recognize it or not.'

'What about Mary and your children?' Alex pleaded. 'Just put the rifle down and come with me.'

'They'll be fine,' De Suza replied, his face calm and remote-looking. Alex almost didn't recognize him. This was his friend, the man who'd done so much to help him in his move to Hong Kong after William's death . . . William, he realized with a twist of bitterness. Another best friend, another traitor.

'Was one of the eight seats yours?' he asked.

'It is. Not was. Is. Always. I was raised to sit in that seat.'

De Suza looked up at Alex, making full eye contact. His smile was a plea for understanding that Alex would never be able to give. He took another two steps forward and noticed a body lying behind De Suza.

'Who's that?' The big man ahead of him nearly filled the gangway, making it hard for Alex to see past him.

'The shooter.'

'What the fuck are you doing?' Alex raised the Glock that Sai Wong had given him.

'Where'd you get that from?' De Suza asked flatly. 'Probably from the Captain. Doesn't matter anyway. You can't fire it up here. You'd be in jail as soon as you got to the ground. You're suspended from active duty and a possible suspect. I could shoot you, though.'

He finished assembling the rifle as he spoke. Craning his neck, Alex saw that the body on the walkway was that of a white man in his late twenties or early thirties, blonde and muscular. De Suza watched him stare.

'It's the final stage of this battle. I'm going to shoot the Chinese finance minister, and then this man and I are going over the top.

The German kid's prints are on the rifle. It'll look like I tried to stop him, killing us both in the process.'

'Where did you get this person? We'll be able to research him and find that he's innocent . . .'

'Really? I think you'll find otherwise. He has some suspicious-looking connections with the German Militarischer Abschirmdienst, the military counter-intelligence service. What did Kaiser Wilhelm II say? "Take no prisoners, just like the Huns." Well, as my father would often remind me, it was the Chinese who beat the Huns and forced them back to Europe.'

'I'm not going to let you do this. Who do the other six seats belong to? Tell me! For Jun.'

'I don't know their names, they come and go. People were recruited, like my father, in protests, meetings, rallies, friendly gatherings we attended with like-minded people. There have been many different *eights* around that table before this plan was finally made.'

De Suza kneeled down but could not take the shot and keep an eye on Alex. He closed in and De Suza swung the rifle round on him.

'Enough, Alex! Put your gun down and handcuff yourself to the railing,' he ordered.

'I'm suspended, remember? No handcuffs on me.'

De Suza's left hand reached behind him for a set of handcuffs. Alex moved forward quickly to grab the barrel of the rifle and push it up in an arc, thrusting the stock back into his partner's face at the same time. He swiftly followed this up with a jab to De Suza's kidneys. It was hard to penetrate his heavy musculature but it made him double up and Alex jammed his knee into the large Eurasian nose and whipped the rifle out of his hand, kicking him hard in the stomach at the same time.

De Suza stumbled back a couple of steps but straightened up quickly and cleaned the blood from above his mouth. They stood off from each other, both instinctively looking down to the ground twenty metres below to see if anyone had registered the fight. Alex did not raise the rifle he had snatched from De Suza. Beneath them, the delegates sat motionless, staring out into the audience and press, waiting their turn as one speech followed the next.

'Why are we doing this?' he asked quietly.

'Because you don't understand that it's time for the humiliation to end. For China to step forward, for power to begin anew.'

'That time is over. It's ended already. Your father belonged to another era. People are unhappy, yes, but they're not going to call for war.'

'Don't be stupid . . . this is not about war. This is about respect and control.'

Alex knew he couldn't argue any further. He weighed the rifle in his hands.

'Please stop this, Mike. I don't want to kill you.'

'Ever the optimist! You have no choice. I still have two handguns.' He cocked his head, nodding at the sound of the speech below. 'Listen to the US delegate demanding democracy for China. Fairness in currency exchange. A list of reasons why it's *our* fault. The hypocrisy looms large, like a big neon sign reading *Liars*. So many free Americans with absolutely nothing. The successful ones saying failure is inexcusable, it's just down to laziness. Is that true, do you suppose? No, it's not. Do we want that attitude spreading among our brothers and sisters? They can keep it.'

De Suza pulled out his sidearm. 'Our finance minister is going to be shot any second by this man.' He kicked the body now lying between them. Alex looked at the nameless Western body. 'His bank accounts and personal documentation have been fabricated to indicate a possible terrorist or paid assassin. You and I will die in the process of killing him. Or maybe you and he will be accomplices ... Then China will challenge the West on its own terms and we will demand respect.'

Alex raised the rifle and aimed it at his partner's head. 'With that pistol you might hurt me badly, but I'll drop you with this.' He breathed in to steady himself. 'People in China have changed. New generations have started to see past the prejudices and insecurities your father had. The anger you see in them is not about how the West treats us, it's about how we treat each other. It has always been like that, for five thousand years. People need to be encouraged to move forward, not hurled back hundreds of years. Your father was obsessed with the past. You needn't be. Look ahead. Stop this now. For Mary and your kids if nothing else.'

De Suza cocked his pistol and pointed it at him. 'No. No. It's impossible. I love them but this is about our history and future. A few more lives added to the tens of millions dead during the last hundred and fifty years is nothing, and yet it will make all the difference.' He looked drained by exhaustion, his light brown eyes red and inflamed. 'I'd hoped you would join us. Instead you behave like all the rest. I wanted to believe you would come through for me. Like I've come through for you so many times, my friend.' Alex could see that he was struggling to concentrate. He seemed briefly to have forgotten the people below and his main objective.

'Then stop this, Mike. I'm here for you now. Put the gun down, please.' Alex was nearly crying, pleading with him desperately. 'Mike, come on, man!'

The big man looked suddenly crumpled and bereft. 'There's no going back for me. All the pain has to be for something. It can't just be wished away, can it?' He looked down to see the Chinese finance minister stand up and walk to the lectern. 'So, Alex, that's enough.' He raised the barrel of the pistol.

Alex had no choice. He shifted his aim, squeezed the trigger, and the round left the rifle barrel. De Suza had no time to aim and fire his weapon. Alex was so close to his friend that the round immediately knocked the pistol out of De Suza's grip and the rifle's muzzle flash enveloped his friend's firing hand, burning it. De Suza pulled his hand back towards himself and sank to the floor. A commotion immediately broke out below. Alex pointed the rifle directly at the fallen man.

'Give up now, Mike. I don't want to kill you. You need help. Whatever your part in this is, I don't believe you've killed any innocents.'

'You don't know that.' He clenched his fist and looked up at his friend below. 'And if you kill me, Alex, you'll never know where your sister is.'

De Suza stared at Alex, who seemed surprised but not distracted.

'Where is she, Mike?' he demanded and cocked his gun again.

De Suza reached round his back and drew his second gun.

'You don't even know which sister I mean, do you? Put your gun away, let me take the shot and I'll tell you.' He raised the pistol and readied his aim at the man below.

'You fucker, that's enough. You say she's here then I'll find her whether you're alive or not.'

De Suza sensed Alex's move and began to spin round. Alex fired as he did so, and the shot took De Suza in the stomach and sent him sprawling further along the gantry. Alex felt an intense flare of pain and knew that his friend and partner had managed to get one off too. He crumpled to the metal floor and held on to the railings before sliding on to his back to lie looking up at the lighting rigged above, while below him there were screams and the stampede of hundreds of people leaving the hall.

EPILOGUE

She had started to sit next to his bed on his second day of recovery. Though Jun still hadn't spoken to anyone, the medical staff were pleased to see her respond and engage again. Her parents had moved her to another private room so that they could set themselves up in the one next door, to oversee her progress. Alex slept, hooked up to an intravenous drip and sedated. A portion of his liver and spleen had been removed. Jun had started to eat again, learning how to feed herself with her left hand, and had begun the slow process of strengthening her weaker side to compensate for the missing right hand.

She sat in the chair by Alex's bed, Seng's notebook open in her lap. She had read through it already, tracing the lines of detailed notes, the clippings about her and her husband, observations on their marriage and the future of Alex's career.

There was also Seng's personal history: his father's death, the birth of Mike and the murder of Alice, which Jun had reread. She had been only twenty-three and Seng twenty-nine. Michael De Suza, who had taken his mother's maiden name, was barely an infant when she was murdered by her husband, pushed to the bottom of the steep stairs outside the apartment Seng had bought for his new family in Sheung Fung Street, half a mile away from the Po Kong Village circular road, a place originally intended to be their little haven. After that he'd cared for the boy alone, always treating him as an inferior and disciplining him for the slightest mistake. Jun cried as she read the descriptions of the daily beatings he'd given Mike in an attempt to make him whole and strong. Instead it had broken him in two.

Jun looked at her right wrist, raising her arm to the light, and felt fury towards Seng boil within her. She could think only in words of hatred and sadness, and so she would not speak at all until those feelings had passed. Looking at Alex, she knew she was angry with him too, but it was mixed with guilt. She had intentionally shut him out once they'd reached Hong Kong, but in time she knew her love for him would return.

The Captain knocked at the open door. Jun held up her right arm to beckon the caller in, but looking up she instantly withdrew it and hugged it to herself.

'Jun, it's all right. I just want to see you and Alex for a moment.'

The frown left her face, but sadness and fury still clouded her thoughts and memories of the woman she remembered being. She looked up at the Captain and he could read her feelings in her eyes. He reached out momentarily to touch her shoulder, but pulled his hand back and looked at her sleeping husband instead.

'He looks okay,' he said, as he stood over Alex, then turned back to Jun and saw the notebook in her lap. 'May I sit with you?'

She looked at the chair.

He sat, then leaned over and took the book out of her lap.

'It's dreadful reading, young lady. Professor Yi was left speechless.' He flipped the notebook over in his hands. 'And he did succeed in starting something. Not the violent reprisal he planned, but people are definitely showing their anger. There are calls for China to stand up to Europe and the USA, calls for protectionism, not just for China but together with other Asian powers, Russia and even Africa. They did not take us back, as they planned, but pushed us forward instead.'

His voice faltered as his gaze fell on her right arm.

'I'm so sorry about this. I do not know what else to say. Such evil . . .' He looked down and then up at her face and fierce burning eyes. 'It's no consolation, I know, but you both prevented this from becoming something much, much worse.' He settled back in his chair, encouraged that she did not instantly reject his words. 'There have been protests, demonstrations and riots, calling for the government to negotiate hard and dirty, demanding back not just the recent loans but also all the historical compensation wrongfully extracted by the Europeans. Europe will remain in our debt for generations. But there are already voices raised in dissent, saying we should find a third way . . . a more harmonious one.'

He stood up restlessly, propped the notebook against the windowsill and flicked through the pages. Jun's face remained expressionless.

'I also wanted to tell you that Mike De Suza survived.' He saw her blink with surprise and immediately place her good hand over her empty wrist. 'Your husband did not kill him, though De Suza will very likely be confined to a hospital for the remainder of his life. He told me that he's sorry for what happened to you, that he tried to stop it. He seemed genuine but he's a deeply troubled man.'

She looked up at him and wrestled briefly with the placing of her arm.

He pointed to the cover of the book and tapped it with his index finger.

'I should probably take this now, to return it to Evidence.' He paused and patted his jacket pocket. 'Professor Yi left Alex this letter. She returned to the US yesterday after a further medical and psychological check-up.'

Jun nodded and opened the letter, and as she did a photo fell to the floor. She reached to pick it up in her left hand. Then she read the letter and sat back at once in surprise.

'Jun, are you okay?'

She nodded and held up the photo. The Captain saw it showed a young boy with two little girls, identical twins.

Then Jun whispered with a smile: 'Yi is Alex's family. Hospital tests during our treatment showed they are siblings.'

'Yi is Alex's sister? Does she know where their other sister is?'

Jun looked up sadly and then turned to look at Alex. She shook her head.

The Captain turned the photo over and saw an inscription that read 'Together. Jan. 1984'.

He turned back to Jun, who was still looking at her husband.

'If there's anything you need, just call. There are many of us who will be glad to help you both.' He pulled an envelope from an inside pocket. 'Here is a list of telephone numbers.' Jun looked up at him, her face empty. She forced a smile, closed her eyes and cocked her head in appreciation.

The Captain nodded respectfully to Alex, still sedated and oblivious to the revelation that awaited him, and closed the door behind him.